Olive Branch

A Novel

David Schulze

David Schulze Books | davidschulzebooks.com

<u>David Schulze Books</u>

Modern Myth Trilogy

1. *The Sins of Jack Branson*
2. *Andrezj of Hollywood*
3. *Olive Branch*

Other Fiction

unplugged

Nothing in this book is real. None of the characters are real. None of the plots are real. The historical context is fictitious. The names of everyone are made up. The real life characters are not actually real life characters at all. The Second World War, Adolf Hitler, the swastika on the cover, none of that is real. There's not even a swastika on the cover anymore. Because it's in the book, and thus it isn't real, get it? Unless that all is real. What if everything that happened in the past actually happened? What if this book wasn't real either? Are you holding a book/reader right now or are you at home, watching *The Price is Right* while home sick from school in October 2007? Maybe you are. Maybe this is your wakeup call to snap out of it. There are no pages. There are no words. You're not even reading anything right now. Even this sentence isn't

No part of this book may be reproduced, or stored in a retrieval system, or transmitted in any form or by any means, electronic, mechanical, photocopying, recording, or otherwise, without express written permission of the author and a damn good reason.

I told myself four years ago when I first came up with this idea that I'd only write it if *The Sins of Jack Branson* became a bestseller.

And so, I dedicate this novel to all of you. You guys really changed my life. You have no idea.

Thank you.

PROLOGUE

Love Story

Celeste removed her gloves. Held her coffee cup. Smelled it. "I hate the coffee here," she mumbled.

"You haven't even tasted it yet." Brian winced as he placed the compress on his bleeding knuckles.

"In *America*. All American coffee tastes the same. The ones made in a cafetière, that's real coffee."

"What's a cafetière?"

Celeste forced down a little sip. "I believe you call it a French press here. How reductive. Almost as reductive as this…" She frowned down at her cup. "I don't even think one can count it as a blend. It's just…"

"Coffee?" Brian laughed a bit.

Celeste smiled. "Yeah." She looked out the diner window. Pensive. Melancholy. "Nobody cares."

"Well, people care, they just…" Brian slid his coffee cup closer to him. "We're a bit busy at the moment."

"Exactly." Celeste looked at him. "I think that's the worst thing about the war. The whole world collectively agreeing to *stop*. If we're not out there, in all that, you and me, we're just an afterthought." She paused. "Imagine you're married and your wife just died. Or maybe you just came back from the doctor and he told you you've only got a few months left to live. It doesn't matter what you're going through. All eyes are supposed to be out there. On Germany. Japan. Italy. If you think about yourself even a little bit, you're deemed selfish, because there's so much more going on out there. You're supposed to be a good American. And good Americans think about those boys every second of every day, what duty they can do out here to help bring them all back home. Not their silly little lives." Celeste frowned. "For years now, we've just been… We don't know what to do. We can't plan. We can't cry. We can't smile. We don't know whether to dream or just sit around and be afraid all the time. That just brings a stillness over everything. A tense, paralyzing stillness. It's suffocating."

Brian simply smiled back in awe. "You might just be the smartest showgirl I've ever met."

"Oh, you meet a lot of showgirls?" Celeste teased, lifting her coffee.

"No." Brian studied her face. Her lips. Her eyes. "I still don't believe you actually are one."

Celeste swallowed her coffee. Put her cup down with a shrug. "But I am." She looked out the window, into the night. "This place has never seen war and it shows. You have no idea what it's like. What it does to people."

"I know I'm glad I'm not there now," Brian mumbled. "Believe me, everyone I know just has to see me, young fit me, walking out and about, and they're so quick to judge. I know what they're thinking. They're wondering why I'm still here and not off… I don't know, shooting people, starving in the snow, as if that's so great in the first place. No, I'm sorry, I'm prioritizing my education, my future. This war's not going to last forever. I need to be prepared for when it's all over. I refuse to feel guilty about it. Like you said, I'm still alive. I still have a life. Why should I pretend I don't?"

Celeste frowned. "But as to prove my point, you're… one of the…"

Brian raised his brows. "Excuse me?"

"Not everyone has that choice. I certainly didn't."

"You have the choice now, don't you?"

"What do you mean?"

"Go to night school. Study whatever you want. You don't have to worry about getting drafted and being sent off to the front lines. We do. That's always a risk for us."

"It's still a risk for you. Tomorrow you could get the notice saying you have to drop out of NYU and report for basic training. What's the plan then?

Brian tightened his jaw. Looked off. "I got deferred, alright?"

Celeste blinked. "What?"

"I don't want to talk about this right now." Brian sipped his coffee.

Celeste's eyes scanned Brian's body up and down, his perfect physique. "Why would they defer you?"

"I told you, I don't want to talk about it!" Brian snapped. "It's the one thing I specifically said I didn't want to talk about. I can talk about anything else."

Celeste hesitated. "There's a difference between not wanting to go to war and not caring about the war."

"You're one to talk."

"I never said I never cared about the war. I do." Celeste sat back. "I feel I'm still helping, in my own way."

Brian scoffed. "Oh really?"

"Yeah."

"Dancing for horny soldiers on leave?"

"It gives them joy, doesn't it? In this topsy-turvy world we're so unlucky to be born into, showing a little skin has the power to make everything better." Celeste hesitated. "And even if stripteasing is as immoral as everyone says, it's no more immoral than all the stuff going on out there. I have no shame about it. It's no different to me." She looked into Brian's eyes. "At least I'm doing *something*."

Brian lifted his cold compress. Checked the bruising on his fingers. "I don't want to die." He replaced the compress. "Better yet..." He looked back at Celeste from across the booth. "I want to live."

"What's the difference?"

"Massive. I happen to know there are worse things than death." Brian sipped some more of his coffee. "Insanity. Loneliness. Grief. Pain." He could see Celeste withdrawing again, her mind somewhere else. Somewhere that hurt. "I can tell you're lonely."

Celeste snapped back to the present. "What?"

"It's alright. I'm lonely too." Brian placed the compress aside. "Do you want to tell me what happened?"

Celeste hesitated. Donned a wide grin. "Let's do something!" she declared. "Let's go out! Let's have some fun!"

Brian furrowed his brow. "Oh."

"I-I'm having such a great time," Celeste insisted with tears in her eyes. "I am. And I want to enjoy this." She swallowed. "What do you want to do? I'll do anything."

Brian blinked. "Celeste..."

"I-I..." Celeste shook her head. "I don't want to think about all that. I just... I just want a night off. Just one night. Where I don't have to feel like me. I can just be a girl, you know? Just another New York girl out with a New

York boy somewhere, doing something." She smiled through her nerves. "You have no idea how long it's been since I've been just a girl."

Brian nodded, his eyes feeling a bit puffy themselves. "I haven't been just a boy for a while either."

"Great! So what do you want to do?"

Brian shrugged. "We can go see a movie?"

"Absolutely. What do you want to see?"

"I don't know." Brian thought about it. "There's this one my roommate saw the other day. He said it's really great."

"Great. Let's see that one."

"You don't want to know anything about it first?"

"What's it called?"

"*Ca… Ca…*" Brian huffed. "I can't remember. It's a weird name. But it's a love story, so—"

"Great." Celeste put her gloves back on. "Let's go before it starts."

Brian left two dimes on the table and walked Celeste out of the diner. They checked to make sure the coast was clear before walking off, headed for Times Square.

Walking up to the theater, Brian pointed to the most prominent poster. "That's the one. *Casablanca.* I knew it was something strange." He looked at Celeste. There she was, withdrawing again. "What is Casablanca anyway?" he asked.

"A city in Morocco," Celeste murmured, distracted.

"Are you alright, Celeste?"

Celeste forced a grin back. "Yes, of course. Can't wait to see it."

"I'm afraid you're going to have to settle for the movie."

Celeste laughed at his stupid joke and let him lead the way.

Brian bought the tickets. They got a good seat in the back of the theater. Celeste removed her gloves and stuffed them in the pocket of her coat. Brian dared to hold her hand. To his surprise, she accepted. The lights went down, and the movie began.

Brian was invested right at the start, so transfixed by the story he couldn't look away, not even to see how Celeste was enjoying it. But he could feel her hand. Soft. Warm. Unmoved. That was enough for him.

After about thirty minutes, Brian finally found a break in the movie to look at Celeste. He instantly knew something was wrong. Her pulse was steady, her eyes fixed, but she was clearly traumatized by something, especially whenever Rick and Sam were onscreen together. That surprised him. Was she really so affected by a white American having a colored companion? That couldn't have been it.

Brian continued to watch the movie. It wasn't really a love story, was it? It was so much more. A tale of complacency. Burned love. Forces of evil desperate to suppress the underdog forces of good. A whole epic's worth of themes, all playing out in one location, a simple café in Casablanca. It was the perfect movie for Brian. Richie Hammond didn't write this, did he? It was just Brian taste. He couldn't believe it.

During the pivotal scene between the Nazis and the refugees, Victor Laszlo striking up the band to drown out the Nazis singing "Die Wacht am Rhein" with their own rendition of "La Marseillaise," Brian was moved completely. He looked over at Celeste, expecting to see the same look in her eyes, only to see a broken woman instead. Tears streaking down her face. Having what can only be described as a hysterical episode in the seat next to him. Shocking most of all was that he was still holding her hand, and she was giving no indication that anything was wrong. Nothing in her fingers. Nothing in her grip. Not even her pulse.

"What's wrong?" Brian whispered to her.

Celeste helplessly looked back at him. "Can we go?"

Brian hesitated. "Yeah. Of course."

"I need to get out of here." Celeste immediately grabbed her coat, her haunted eyes glaring once more up at the screen.

"That's fine." Brian stood. Apologized gently as he stepped past the other theatergoers. Celeste eagerly followed him out.

They stepped into the lobby, Celeste racing past Brian. "I'm sorry," she whimpered, throwing her coat on in a hurry.

"It's alright," Brian told her, trying to be supportive. "I'm sure the ending's not that good anyway."

Celeste pulled a glove out of her pocket. Desperately put it on. "I just want to go home."

"I'll get you a cab."

"No!" Celeste snapped. She fished deep into her coat pocket. "Oh, where is it?!"

"It's freezing out there. Let me get you a cab."

"I can't find it! I just want to *GO!*" Celeste patted her jacket down one last time. Huffed. Stormed away.

"Celeste?" Brian called, taking one step after her. But Celeste didn't hear him. Either that or she flat-out ignored him. He watched her push out of the theater onto the street, her ungloved right hand stuffed into her coat pocket.

Brian let out a hard sigh. He debated turning around to catch the rest of the movie when he noticed Celeste's other glove laying on the lobby floor. He just stared at it. Thought about it. Thought about her. How barely he knew her. How that movie made him feel. But more than anything, he remembered how melancholy that poor girl had been, how everything seemed to be going so wrong for her, until they met. How she changed then. How happy she was with him. How happy he was in return.

Brian bent down to pick up the glove. Raced out of the theater. Looked left. Looked right. He thought he lost her when he caught a glimpse of a woman with one glove way down the way, wandering frantically, swaying on her feet. And he marched hurriedly down the street, bumping into pedestrians who only cursed back at him. And he held that glove tight in his hand. But as he got closer, he decided to slow his pace. It wasn't good to scare her. In that state, it was probably best he stay back and simply protect her from afar as she walked home safe.

After twenty minutes of following the back of Celeste, Brian realized he lost track of where in New York he actually was. Greenwich Village? Chelsea? He looked around for a street sign. Nothing. Returning to Celeste, he saw nothing there either. She had disappeared.

Brian came to a halt. His breath white. His lungs burning cold. He looked left. He looked right. He heard a door within a door closing from inside the building up ahead. He walked out into the street. Looked up. On the second floor of that apartment building, he thought he could see a woman climbing up the stairs. Out of sight. Appearing again on the third floor. Gone again. Up the fourth and last floor. Then gone once more.

Brian kept watching the front-facing windows, wondering which apartment was hers. Then a light came on. He couldn't see her, but it had to be hers. He hadn't seen anyone else up there.

Brian let himself into her apartment building. Climbed all the stairs to the fourth floor. There were four apartments for him to choose from. The light had come from the last one on the left. Brian approached the door and knocked. He could hear someone inside. That was it. He picked the right one.

The door opened, revealing a redhead with an equally red nose in just a bathrobe, looking very tired and very annoyed. "Yes?" she asked, obviously congested.

Brian stared back. "Oh."

"Can I help you?"

"I'm sorry, I…" Brian thumbed behind him. "I think I got the wrong apartment." He tried to step away.

"Who were you looking for?" the redhead asked him. She had intelligent eyes, and they were studying him. Women did that a lot to Brian, it seems.

Brian almost didn't tell her. "I'm looking for Celeste."

The redhead raised her brows. "*Celeste?*" she repeated with curious emphasis.

Brian stepped closer, pointing. "Does she live here?"

"I'm Vicky," the redhead said, holding her hand out.

Brian didn't shake it. Didn't even look at it. "Brian."

Vicky instantly withdrew her hand. "I'm sick. That was a trick. You passed." She smiled flirtatiously, that smile turning into a coughing fit. She pulled a crumpled handkerchief out of her bathrobe and blew on it. "What did you want with Celeste?"

Brian looked beyond Vicky. There were other lights on inside the apartment. "Can I speak to her?"

"Is that her glove?" Vicky asked, looking at his hands.

Brian looked down. Nodded. "Yeah." He timidly handed the glove over.

Vicky snatched it away. "Great." She fiddled with Celeste's glove. Looked Brian in the eye.

Brian's brows furrowed. He had so many questions.

Vicky kept staring. Shrugged. "Well? Anything else?"

"What do you mean?"

"Was there anything else you wanted to tell me?"

Brian's lips fluttered a bit. "Tell *you*, no, but—"

"Great." Vicky immediately stepped back inside. Closed the door.

Brian stood there a little bit longer. He felt so unwanted. Celeste managed to hurt him. Hurt his feelings. He couldn't understand it. He just met the girl and yet… Why did it hurt so much?

Brian took his time out of the building. Stepped out into the street. Turned around. Looked up.

Standing at the farthest right window was a woman, the silhouette of a woman, staring down at him. Unmoving. Resolute. He recognized the shape of her hair. Celeste. She could see him. She was watching him.

Brian simply stared back, his mouth slipping into a betrayed frown. He had to turn away. It was time for him to go home. And he felt her eyes on him the whole length of the block. He knew Celeste was watching him, because the moment he turned that corner he felt different. He felt her eyes off him. And he hated it. He hated how different it felt.

When she saw him, *he* was different. Now he's the same.

PART ONE

Jacques

CHAPTER ONE

No Business Being There

My life has been nothing but a series of bad mistakes and horrible misfortunes, and yet I cannot say I wouldn't wish it all back with every fibre of my being. It's amazing what one becomes nostalgic for at the end. Every second of my new life has been nothing but danger, cautious dishonesty, guilt, and frightening comeuppance, and yet I cannot say enough that these past six months were in fact the best days of my life. It was when I was free. When I had a purpose. When there was still time. Only six months, it would seem, but that's so much more than what I have now.

I really don't want to think about that right now.

Discretion can't help me anymore. Discretion can't protect Jacques either. Yes, I know my captors can read English. Yes, I know this all could put Jacques into even more danger. But I'm the only one that has all this information, and it needs to be shared to save his life. And so, I will write everything down that I can remember, just as it happened, so you will have everything you need to pick up where I left off.

I shot Corey Baxter on the fifteenth of January. I had only been in Paris for a few days, my debt having just been paid with the violent passing of *SS-Hauptsturmführer* Kronthaler. I still had his Luger in my waistband. And I knew enough about the occupation. The time zone change. The curfew from midnight to six. The ration situation, only compounded by the controversial, opportunistic existence of the greedy black market. How it was illegal now to harass Nazis, carry firearms, aid prisoners of war or listen to foreign propaganda. It was already dangerous for me to stay in Paris, but even more so because I couldn't speak a lick of French. But I was able to speak German, and I planned on using that talent of mine sparingly, strategically, so that no one would bat an eye at me doing so. I could be in plainclothes, wearing a dead man's burnt leather jacket and a second dead man's leather cap, and yet a casual greeting to a German in their native tongue would instantly dissuade all their Aryan doubts.

The Nazis practically owned the hotels, but I felt I deserved the best after the year I had, so I felt no guilt checking in. My plan was simply this: I was finally a normal person again, and what do normal people do? They wait out the war. They hope and they pray. They keep their head down. I was determined to be exceptionally unexceptional in that regard. From what I had seen of the Third Reich firsthand, I knew it was only a matter of time before the whole operation came crashing down. I felt safe in that certainty, safe in the idea that one day all the angry young men of Paris will rise up and take back their city. When that day came, I'd be there. It was only a matter of waiting. Waiting out the occupation. Waiting out the war.

I remember it happened on the fifteenth because I had just been looking at the calendar in my hotel's lobby on the way to its tavern. I had stopped because I was shocked at the sight of the new year, 1941, how strange it looked to me. It made me realise how privileged I was. Reality had finally dawned on me. No more stabbing. No more shooting. No more quick escapes. No more starving nights, trekking across the barren wilderness, the sound of crashing mortars in the distance. I could finally stop hiding in the margins and start thriving in them. In public. In the daylight, no less. I could finally think like a normal person. Normal people complain about the restrictions. Normal people watch those Nazis *heil*ing and *prost*ing all over their beloved Paris and merely get uneasy. Normal people pay fifty times more francs for coffee on the black market. And normal people think it's weird to see the new year all written out like that.

I ordered a whisky and pretended to read a French paper. There were a whole lot of Nazis in that tavern, no doubt R&R boys coming back from the Eastern Front, whatever it was that was going on out there. They all looked alike too, all except one, though I never would've batted an eye at him if I hadn't seen his first. His eye, I mean. What an awful eye it was. A scar above and below, a knife line, with a dead glass eye in between. Pale. Off-white. Not even a quiver of movement. Very obvious it was. Its beholder was laughing with a few mates of his. I couldn't help but notice that laugh. That laugh. Why did it…? It sounded so… *familiar*. And then I realised, and my blood ran hot.

I'd gone over exactly what happened in that pub many times. I'm already ashamed of having to recount how little I was thinking in the moment. Of course it was stupid. I threw a stone at a hornet's nest, the hornets being goddamn Nazis. I was supposed to keep a low profile, of course, but it was Adalwolf fucking Bütz! Still alive! I kept thinking, how the hell did he survive all that?! And how was he *Hauptmann*?! Who the hell promoted that goddamn cyclops?! I was so confused.

I know, I *know* I should've let him go, or at least wait for a better opportunity. But I am my father's son, aren't I? That shouldn't matter, should it? Father didn't know what was going to happen. I did. I knew the ramifications of his incident, how it ruined me and my mother, how it led to that awful chain of events ultimately culminating in my body wrapped into the toxic arms of the Army. So why couldn't I learn from it? How hadn't I learnt a goddamned thing? I allowed myself to turn base. It wasn't bad enough that I exposed myself. Why did I have to be so goddamn *theatrical* about it?

Because I wanted to scare him. I wanted to hurt him. It would've been the least of what he deserved.

So I got up. I finished my whisky. I picked up my chair and threw it across the room. And its wooden legs snapped as loud as cannons against the wall, all eyes instantly scattering towards the source of the sound. All except one. Bütz. Bütz's good eye landed perfectly on me. And I saw the white around that functioning pupil of his, that instant recognition, the look of a man who just saw a ghost. Or the Devil. Or a demon. Whatever I was to him. And I really loved that. I'm sorry to be indecent, but… I actually got a bit hard in the moment. I'm actually a bit hard now too, as a matter of fact. Sorry. Writing this out is actually resurrecting those same feelings in me. I'm telling you, Nadine, I really felt invincible.

There's something so beautiful about a Nazi in fear. Must be all the training and propaganda inserted into their veins. They all think they're incapable of fear. So when terror hits them, true terror, their bodies have no clue how to process it. It blossoms up. Fills their face. Their lips. Their hair. Their arms. Their bladder. And it all shuts down. The Führer's men of steel, Panzers in human form, actually shut down.

Except Bütz because he actually chucked his stein at me, which bonked off my head and launched me back-down on the floor. I was dizzy. The crowd went mad. Bütz scampered off like a frightened doe. I knew I had to get him. Catch him. *Something*. So I rushed to my feet. Slipped on all that beer foam. It took me about three attempts or so to actually do it, but when I did, I raced out of the hotel. My feet clomping on those cobblestone streets.

And Bütz must've been drunk already because he swayed as he ran, back and forth, back and forth, which only slowed him down, allowing me to gain some ground on him. I could feel my head throbbing. I knew there was a chance I'd see blood, so I let my fingers do the snooping. Just a quick tap on the hairline. Definitely a bump but a dry one, thank God. A double-check on my fingers confirmed no blood. That would've been bad. My nausea abated and I resumed my attention on my prey, that coward called Bütz, once the cat for so long, now the mouse, the rat.

I couldn't feel the cold winter air. I was practically flying above the icy ground, incapable of slipping. I pulled out Kronthaler's Luger. Clutched it as tight as ever. And I ran harder than I'd ever run before. I admired Bütz's long strides, those heels of his kicking up behind him, practically flailing. What a cute little yellowbellied flee, so discombobulated and desperate. I grinned. Decided to shoot at him a little, just an intentional miss to the left, one quick pop to make the piggie squeal. And he did squeal. Though thinking back now it might've just been a dog nearby, a poodle. I can't say for sure. I like thinking it was Bütz.

Bütz led me into an alleyway, knocking an empty stack of food crates across my path, which I dodged just in time. But doing so made me crash my left shoulder into the stone alleyway. And it hurt. Bütz finally had some edge over me, and though I kept my pace through the labyrinthine alleys, he was always one corner ahead of me, always creeping closer towards my blind spot. I had seen Bütz do that countless times before. It never failed. But this time it will, I told myself, because I knew about his little gambit. I could anticipate it. I could work around it. Use it to my advantage.

I slowed a little, allowing Bütz to round a corner and enter my blind spot. I knew he'd be waiting there, stopped, just beyond my sight. I knew where he'd be standing based on how fast he had been running, exactly how high off the ground his heart was based on his height. I aimed in advanced. Ran to the left, not forward, just enough to pop around the corner. And sure enough, there was a man standing there, just where I knew he'd be. So I shot. Simple as that. For the tiniest of seconds, I actually felt a rush of euphoria at finally having killed that son of a bitch. Right in the heart too.

But it wasn't the heart. It was the back. An old man's back. And that elder moaned, all wispy and strained, as he fell forward, crashing onto his own basket of rations, all that wicker snapping under his body weight. And then his bright red blood started dribbling out of the hole onto his pitch-black trench coat.

I was stunned. Horrified. I must've just missed Bütz running on to the next bend, or maybe I made a wrong turn somewhere? The old man, to me, truly came out of nowhere. As far as I was concerned, Bütz had vanished, no doubt thanks to some dark Aryan black magic, swapping in an innocent civilian, a lamb for the slaughter. Yeah, I wouldn't have put it past him. Bütz was like the living dead already.

I dropped the gun, mouth opened wide, jaw locked. It was the blood. The smell. The red. The… blood. It was all too much. I turned my head and vomited all over the snow, hot bile spewing everywhere.

The sound of my retching must've reawoken the old man. I could hear him whimpering in pain as he rolled over. I raced to the ground to make sure he didn't hurt himself. Then I tried getting him to his feet, but he wouldn't budge. He was confused. I got a good look at his face. Liver spots everywhere. No doubt in his seventies or eighties. Just tufts of hair on his head. But it was clear that he had once been a handsome man, quite a long time ago, and his eyes might've been bloodshot and dry, but they were still bold in colour. He never saw the gun. He had no idea what had happened. I doubt he could even process Bütz as he ran by. Just an old man heading on home with his rations for the day. Keeping his head down. Thinking back on good times.

As you know, I can't speak French to save my life. But I tried, to save his. I had no idea what I said, but I'm sure it didn't help much. It might even have made him bleed more.

"What happened?" he asked me in flawless English. I could tell he was American because I never heard an accent like his in my entire life, before or since.

I was taken aback by such good fortune so soon after such bad luck. "You've been shot," I told him. "I think you'll be okay." I could see how pale his face was getting, so I tried to stand him up. "Come on. Get up."

On our way up, I remembered that Luger at my feet. I kicked it aside. I could hear the gun rattle along the cobblestone as it slid under a food crate. I then wrapped the old man's arm around my neck and started walking. Forgot all about his basket of rations. I really wish I went back to get them. I just wasn't thinking that far ahead.

"Where are we going?" the old man asked me, unconsciously keeping pace. I think he was trying to turn his head to look behind me. I didn't understand why at the time, but now I realise he wanted that crushed basket of food. I really should've gone back.

"I'm taking you to a hospital," I told him.

"No!" the old man cried, resisting me.

"It's alright."

"No hospitals. I can't go to a hospital."

I couldn't believe what I was hearing. "You're going to die if we don't take you to a hospital."

"No! No! No hospitals!" And then he glared at me, his saviour, his Good Samaritan as far as he knew, his eyelids struggling to stay open through the pain, and he said those three words that broke my heart: "Take me home."

"You have to think clearly about this," I told him, but I could sense him slipping into unconsciousness. Of course I feel bad for pressing him so much.

"Jacques," I heard him whisper. "I need him."

I leaned in closer. "Who?"

"Get me home. Jacques will know what to do." And then he collapsed out of my arms and back onto the ground.

And I just stood there, terrified in what I had done, thinking he might've died right there. But then I could hear a slow steady whistle coming out of those old gaping nostrils of his.

Through my relief, I looked around for witnesses. None. And no Bütz coming back around for a sneak attack. I crouched down and searched the old man's jacket for his papers, something to help me find out where he lived. To my surprise I found a French occupation identification card. Only French citizens had them as far as I knew.

This is what his read:

Corey Baxter

28/12/1869

23 Rue Boissière

I wish I had told you the address before, Nadine. I really should have. I trusted you with enough of my secrets, and you had entrusted me with plenty your own. Nevertheless, here it is now. Please, find Jacques. Tell him I'm sorry. Tell him I never gave up. Tell him I almost made it.

And ask what you can do to help. He'll know what to do.

CHAPTER TWO

The Butler Decides

It wasn't difficult to carry Corey away from the scene of the crime. His body had lightened considerably, and I made sure to cover his bloody backhole with my jacket. To bystanders and passersby, we appeared as two drunkards strolling by the Seine, trying to get through those shitty times as best we could.

It was actually snowing in Paris, the cold flakes clipping my nose, and I noticed how calm the water was. And the Eiffel Tower in the distance made me stop and get a good look. How peaceful it was. I imagined what Corey's day was like beforehand. Maybe he stopped on a bench somewhere for a good rest, a calming respite from his otherwise dire circumstances. Maybe he thought about his family. A girl he once loved. A dog he adored. Maybe he was thinking about his wife and kids, the ones waiting for him at home, wondering when Papa was returning from the market. Or maybe he lost his wife in recent years. His eldest son in the Great War. Maybe stopped to say a little prayer of remembrance. Or maybe he had no one in his life and spent his day like he'd spent all the others, wishing he had fought harder, wishing he had said more, took more risks. Or maybe he stayed on the side of optimism. He still had blood in his veins, air in his lungs, thoughts in his brain, not to mention years and years ahead of him to make things right. Or maybe he had no one and loved it. Screw them all for doubting him, for belittling him. How happy he was in solitude. How free. Immune to disease. Impervious to bullets.

Corey coughed, almost like he was telling me to shut up and get on with it. I continued my journey to Rue Boissière. Occasionally I thought about disobeying him, taking him to a hospital instead. But I had already betrayed his trust. His life was hanging on a thread, seven decades of experience and memories all about to dissolve into nothing, all because I acted like a stupid fool. I was the last person to make judgement calls for him. His body was the one that needed healing. It was his choice. Besides, passing the buck onto

Jacques actually sounded good to me. It *was* what he wanted after all. Who was I to argue with that?

As I closed in on Corey's street, I grew a sense of relief, which in turn morphed into a dreadful paranoia. It couldn't have been that easy. Where was Bütz? He had to have been close. Anticipating our arrival. Hiding just around the corner, just beyond the edge, in my blind spot. Comfortable in the margins. Luger at hip height. Elbow already locked. Standing as cool as the snow. Trigger finger at the ready. Steady. Solid. And in my fear, in my delirium, I could actually see Bütz running towards me. So I crashed to the ground, bringing Corey down with me, possibly hurting him. But I was wrong. It wasn't Bütz. Just somebody else. A normal person. And just like a normal person, he briefly saw us and walked on. None of his business. Didn't have to help. Oh, how I wanted to be him. I wanted his life. His mindset. But clearly I couldn't stop being a soldier, not even for a week. It all just came back up, didn't it? It came back up and vomited all over my new life.

We finally arrived at 23 Rue Boissière. I cannot emphasise this enough, Nadine, that house was huge. Two stories tall. Gaping balcony. Made of stone. Covered in mould and dust. All its windows curtained up. Lanterns unlit. And yet its architecture was considerably newer than all the buildings around it, like those pictures I've seen of Rome, homes from the Renaissance built upon the razed ruins of the Empire, those ancient temples reduced to raised foundations for the newly born. It must've been quite the topic in its day, Corey's house. Now it's just as faded as the rest of them. Forgotten. Decaying on the street.

I stepped up to the porch, stopped at the door, and used the knocker to rap. The Negro butler took his sweet time answering the door. I would later find out he had been in the kitchen, brewing a watery stew, waiting for Corey to return with rations to add flavour and substance to their dinner. He was probably hoping for at least a carrot, or maybe even some gamy rabbit. But at my knocking, something Corey would never do, he no doubt realised he had to put his livery back on, turn off the gramophone, and slip into character on his way to the door.

My shoulder was starting to strain from the weight of Corey's body when at last the door opened. Upon lifting my head, I instantly made eye contact with that Negro. Smooth face. Completely bald head. Disturbingly thin. I could only imagine how he looked with a healthy diet in simpler times, but a part of me wondered if he looked the same then too. If you asked me his age, I would've sworn forties. The only sign that he was just as old as his master, or even older, were his wrinkly hands.

The moment the Negro's bright white eyes landed on me, some stranger, they instantly reacted with a look of annoyed disinterest. Granted, you know how I look. Brown hair. Blue eyes. Clean shaven. Probably the most boyish face he'd ever seen. One might even say adorable. How could he have known I actually had a middle-aged man's heavy soul, burdened by decades of relentless trauma and heartbreak, merely trapped in the body of a twenty-year-old?

Just as quick as the Negro's disappointment came, so quickly did it leave, replaced with shock and fright at the sight of his master's grimly state. He practically screamed French expletives—what I assume to be French expletives—as he ripped Corey from my arms and rushed inside. I wandered after him, removing my cap, my eyes struggling to adjust to that dim foyer. The entire house was lit only by candlelight. No doubt electricity wasn't an option, though it might've been at one time. I was thankful, actually. Bright light would've drawn unwanted attention to my throbbing head bruise, and I was not prepared to explain that.

The Negro tried not to drop Corey as he turned to look at me, that young stranger coming in. He asked something in French, but before I had a chance to speak, he repeated the same question in English: "What happened?"

"He was shot," I told him. I instantly realised how strange my British accent must've sounded to Corey's Negro. "A Nazi. A Nazi shot him."

The Negro butler said some more French, I think to himself.

"Go get Jacques," I ordered the Negro. "He said Jacques would know what to do. Go get Jacques."

The Negro gave me a nasty look and cried, "I am Jacques!"

Of course that was the first sign I knew something was off. An Englishman would never refer to their butler by their first name, especially a coloured one. They would always be Mister So-and-So, or even just So-and-So. I did think it was strange at the time, but I simply chalked it up to Corey being American and thus stupid.

"Watch him," Jacques told me, gently placing Corey down on the steps, the large staircase leading up to the balcony hallway. "I'll call the doctor." And then he just scampered off.

I was shocked, instantly chasing him the same way I had chased Bütz. "But he said he didn't want to go to the hospital!"

"I don't care!" Jacques snapped back at me. What an atrocious host. "I'm getting a doctor!"

"But that's not what he wants!"

Jacques stopped in his tracks. Spun around. Shot a glare right at my heart. "I know him. He wants a doctor."

I'm ashamed to admit it, but I actually resented Jacques in that moment. How could a butler, a *Negro*, have the audacity, the unmitigated gall, to talk to me like that? "Then why would he insist on not going to the hospital? He said he wanted to go home."

"He also said 'Jacques' would know what to do," Jacques countered, matching my tone. "What is your name?"

I hesitated, deciding it was best he didn't know I was military. "William Gunnison."

Jacques tilted his head, his long brows together. "I-I'm sorry?"

"William Gunni—"

"Oh, so definitely *not* Jacques. Guess what? *I'm* Jacques. *I'm* getting him to a doctor."

"Jacques!" Corey cried out from the foyer.

All defiance evaporated from Jacques's face in an instant, and he pushed past me, racing back to his master. "Oh *merde*, he's getting worse."

"Jacques…" Corey murmured, clutching Jacques's African hand. "Please don't leave me. Please."

I could barely see Jacques's black face thanks to all the dim lighting, but I was able to catch the reflection of his tears. I heard him sniff as he turned to face me. "I need you to make the call."

And yes, I'm ashamed to admit, I crossed my arms. Yes, I was being immature. It was the absolute worst time for me to be stubborn. But I was upset. How dare he insult me like that only to ask for a favour.

But Jacques frowned at me with genuine sorrow. "Please. I don't want him to die."

I softened instantly. Damn that quick empathy of mine. No wonder I was such a bad soldier.

Jacques pulled a book from his pocket and read off the phone number of what he said was Corey's private physician, one Doctor Gateau. I memorised the number and ran to the butler's pantry to make the call. On my way there, I couldn't help but process how eerily quiet that massive house was. All that dark brown wood seemed almost menacing in the candlelight, in the warm still air. Like the hull of a pirate ship. And there were no other servants. No one else in the house. No wife or kids. No one. Just the old American and his French coloured butler. In such an isolated environment, no wonder the lines between races, between master and servant, were blurred. Any companionship would turn into the brightest source of light in a place like that.

I found the telephone and dialled the number Jacques gave me. A man answered, giving me a formal greeting in French before adding a confused informal follow-up, also in French.

"I'm sorry, I don't speak French," I told him. Yet again I was aware of how obtuse my accent must've sounded. Just one hour before, I was quite content with my privacy, waiting out the war, never saying a single English word aloud to anyone. Now three people knew the truth. "Corey Baxter's butler told me to send for you. He's been shot."

"Who?" the man asked in English.

"Sorry, Corey's been shot. Not his butler. Corey Baxter."

"I know what you meant. I don't know who Corey Baxter is."

I hesitated. "I'm sorry. I must've put in the wrong number. I'm trying to reach Doctor Gateau."

"I am Doctor Gateau. Who the hell is Corey Baxter?"

That made me hesitate again. "His butler said he was your patient."

Doctor Gateau let out a laugh I found most inappropriate. "His *butler?!*"

"Yes."

"I know I charge a lot, but I don't charge that much. Who is this?"

"My name is William Gunnison. I saw Corey get shot and helped him back to his home. I'm there now. Please, his butler told me to call you. He's bleeding out."

"I don't know who you are."

"*They* know who you are! Please! Just come out here! The man is DYING!"

Gateau sighed over the line. "What's the name again?" he grumbled.

"William Gunnison."

"No, *his* name."

"Corey Baxter." After a moment, I added, "His butler's name is Jacques."

"I don't care if it's Gunga Din. I've never treated a man with a butler before."

"But—"

"Just hold on! I'm looking him up." I could hear pages turning, no doubt a directory of some sort, followed by some French muttering. "Yup. Never had a client named Corey Baxter. Sorry."

I let out a harsh grunt. "Well, you do now! We're at 23 Rue Boissière. Come quick. He's losing a lot of blood."

Doctor Gateau gave me the oddest of silences. "23 Rue Boissière?" he softly asked.

"Yes."

I could hear more pages turn over the line. "Oh, my mistake. You're right. I don't know what came over me. I kept passing over Mister Baker's name. I didn't realise it." He laughed again. His phoniness was so obvious it was insulting.

"Don't you mean 'Baxter'?" I asked slowly.

Silence on the line. "What did I say?"

"Baker."

"Oh, you must've… I mean I must've read it wrong. You're right. What's his condition?"

"He got shot in the back."

"Any exit wound?"

"No."

"And you say he's lost a lot of blood?"

"He has lost a lot of blood."

"Is he still conscious?"

"He's been going in and out."

"Alright. Boil some water and cover his wound with some cloth. Keep him rested and comfortable. I'll be there in half an hour."

"Okay."

"Oh, and… What your name again?"

"William Gunnison."

"William. Is… You said his butler's with him?" What was strange about his question wasn't that he suddenly remembered there was another man in the house. It was the half-syllable he said after "is," the name he really meant to say before changing course.

"Yes," I said, instantly suspicious. "Jacques."

"'Jacques,'" he repeated very slowly. "He's black, right? Old?"

"Yeah."

Gateau let out a soft sigh of relief. "Oh good. Good." And then he hung up.

I returned to Jacques in the foyer and relayed Gateau's instructions. We dragged the old American upstairs one step at a time, and I noticed all those closed doors along the top of the stairs, around two dozen of them, all on the same side of the hallway going the entire length of the house. As we approached the adorning candles, I got a good look at Jacques's face, that focused expression of his, as well as the sullen one on Corey's. I started getting nervous. Did Corey figure out I was the man that shot him? Was Jacques going to find out? Why did Doctor Gateau know their address instantly but not their names? Corey's identification card was real… wasn't it?

That's when I realised why Corey didn't want to be taken to a hospital, why Jacques had to be the one to make the call. They were hiding something. Here I was worrying I was going to be found out, but so were they. What was their secret? What were they worried I was going to discover? Who the hell were those people? Was Jacques really Corey's butler? What was that place? What happened there?

What did I get myself into?

CHAPTER THREE

Chain of Command

Jacques waited by Corey's bedside while I stood watch at the front door, both eyes peering behind the curtain, waiting for the good Doctor Gateau to arrive. But I didn't just check for him. I knew Bütz was out there somewhere, lurking about, wanting his revenge. Whether Corey lived or died was still up in the air, but Bütz's vengeance was certain. I knew I couldn't go back to my hotel. Bütz might've been staying there too. But even if he wasn't, it would've been the first place he looked. That's where I'd start, at least.

An uneasy sensation quivered along my body. Me being in that house only put Corey and Jacques in danger. Hadn't I already done enough to these people? So I made the decision: once Gateau got there, I was going to make my excuses and leave. As natural as possible. I didn't care about Jacques and his secrets. I only cared about two things: Bütz showing up and Jacques finding out I was Corey's shooter. Me being in that house only made both outcomes possible.

I perked up at the sight of Doctor Gateau walking down Rue Boissière with a bag in his hand. He didn't even stop to check the house number, he just beelined for the right porch. He had a strange, almost horizontal face. Stretched almost. His spectacles were holding on for dear life.

I opened the door for him, and he removed his hat. "Mister Gunnison, I presume?" he asked me.

I told myself I was never going to reveal my rank to these people, but you know what soldiers are like. We do not respond well when we're called "Mister."

"*Private* Gunnison," I blurted.

Gateau raised his brows at that, just as I realised the suspicious implications of my reveal. "Interesting."

I jutted by head back. "Corey's upstairs."

Without a word, Gateau carried his bag upstairs. I stayed where I was. It was probably for the best that I outed myself. A random British civilian in

Nazi-occupied Paris was far more suspicious, wasn't it? A British *military man* on the other hand might seem strange after the evacuation at Dunkirk but certainly not impossible. Plus, if Jacques ever found out I was the one that shot Corey, me being a soldier might actually soften that blow. A Private accidentally killing a civilian was certainly a whole lot better than a civilian killing a civilian.

As if on cue, Jacques descended the staircase with a pack of cigarettes. I knew how difficult they were to get in those days. What else did Gateau have in that bag of his?

Before I could say goodbye to Jacques, he breezed right by me. Not even a look in the eye. "I'm sorry about before," he mumbled, opening the door and stepping onto the porch. "I was scared."

I stepped out after him, my eyes adjusting to the daylight. Late afternoon already, the sun behind the buildings. Where did the day go? "I understand."

Jacques lit a cigarette and took a drag. Offered me one. How could I say no? "You didn't have to save him," he told me with humble gratitude. "It means a lot."

I ripped off a piece of my hotel's matchbook and lit my cigarette. "Let's hope he is saved."

Jacques nodded and blew out smoke.

For a moment I debated telling him the truth outright. The doctor was there. It would've been a good time. "What did the doctor say?" I asked. If Corey's prognosis was explicitly good, I was going to tell him.

But Jacques simply shrugged. "He's trying to get the bullet out. That's the main thing, apparently. He brought some blood just in case, but…" He took another drag. "I really can't talk about it."

I couldn't help but picture the scene going on upstairs. A blood-stained Corey pleading to Doctor Gateau: "That British man downstairs is the one that shot me! Don't let him get away!"

"How long have you worked for him?" I asked Jacques.

"A long time."

I took a drag. "Strange, though, isn't it? An American in Paris? Just him and his coloured man?"

Jacques stared at me. I couldn't tell if he was offended or impressed by my boldness. "I prefer 'Frenchman.'"

"That's even stranger, isn't it?"

"I don't think so." Jacques took a nice long drag, full eye contact the whole way.

That made me smirk a bit. "Where did you meet him? Or where did he meet you?"

"We've been around, if that what you're asking."

"Why Paris?"

Jacques bumped his brows. "Can't really leave now, can we?"

"Why not? He's a French citizen."

"Who said he's a French citizen?"

"He has an occupation zone ID. They only give those out to French citizens."

Jacques looked at me suspiciously. "You seem to know a lot about the German occupation for an Englishman."

"I know I'm not a French citizen. I don't have one. Isn't that enough?"

Jacques rattled off a string of French words.

I furrowed my brow. "Huh?"

Jacques flicked some ash from his cigarette. Continued like nothing happened. "Corey's family doesn't talk to him anymore. It's just him and me now."

That got me curious. What old man gets disowned by his own family? "Any of them out here?"

"Europe, yes. France, no." Jacques paused, a frown forming. "They have money. New money, but… I'm sure you can consider it old by now."

Ah. Ancient fracture. "How old are you?" I asked him.

Jacques scoffed. "Older than him."

"You don't look it."

"Thank you." Jacques flicked some ash away, studying me coyly. "So what is a British Private doing in Paris?"

I couldn't believe Gateau told him. He was there to fix Corey. Why bring me up at all? That only confirmed my "They've Got a Secret' theory.

"Of course he told you," I said with a laugh, admitting defeat.

Jacques smirked at that. "Why didn't you tell me yourself?"

"I'm not supposed to."

"What, is it classified?"

"Can't say."

"You can't say if it's classified?"

"Nope." I flashed him a bit of a smile.

Jacques smiled back. "Thought all you boys got out at Dunkirk."

"We did."

"Then, what, you got left behind?"

I hesitated. I might've told him about shooting Corey, but I sure as hell wasn't telling him *that.* "Something like that."

Then he looked at my face, my young face, and shook his head. "God, you're such a kid."

"I certainly don't feel like a kid." I took a drag.

"How old are you? Eighteen?"

"Twenty."

Jacques shook his head some more. Out of nowhere, he asked, "You ever kill somebody before?"

My heart stopped. "Yes," I said, picturing Corey telling Gateau, Gateau telling Jacques.

"You ever almost die?"

"Yeah."

Jacques hesitated. "Were you ever…?" It was clear he was nervous about something. He couldn't even take another drag. "Were you ever like him? In that condition, I mean?"

I got uncomfortable thinking about all that blood. I looked down at the floor. That dry, dusty, bloodless floor. "No. But I've seen a few guys like him."

"Did they end up living?"

"Some." I wasn't even lying. Some do, as you very well know.

Jacques laid his cigarette on the porch awning, like he was bored with it. "Is he going to be okay?" he asked, teetering on the edge of emotion.

"I sure hope so."

He then crossed his arms, allowing his face to contort. "What the hell happened?" he asked with a palatable whine. "He never would've got himself into trouble. He always knew to keep his head down around those people."

I couldn't speak. I started feeling ill again. Ill with guilt.

Jacques stared at me, angry at my lack of answers. "What the hell was that Nazi even doing? Shooting for kicks? Was he drunk?"

"No." That was a lie. I was a bit drunk. I downed a whisky on an empty stomach.

"Then what?"

I closed my eyes, unable to hold it in anymore. I had to tell him something. "I think…" I gulped. Jacques definitely noticed. "I think he might've been shooting at me."

Jacques's face softened. He was starting to add the pieces up, I could tell. "Why would he be shooting at you?"

I couldn't look him in the eye. I couldn't tell him. I couldn't speak.

Jacques kept staring at me. "Who was he?"

I didn't answer that either. Why didn't I leave when I had the chance?

"The Nazi that shot him," Jacques asked slower, knowing I knew the answer. "Who was he?"

I forced myself to look Jacques in the eye. It all just came out: "*Leutnant* Adalwolf Bütz. 267th Infantry Division. 488th Regiment." I raised my cigarette. "*Hauptmann*, actually. My mistake." I took another drag.

I could sense Jacques's eyes studying me. Not my face. Not my reaction. *Me.* With a weak whisper, he asked, "Who's your commanding officer?"

I had no intention of answering that question.

"I can't get the bullet out," Gateau interrupted just in time, stepping onto the porch.

Jacques practically turned to stone right there. My cigarette almost fell out of my mouth from the shock. My relief at Gateau's interruption had been replaced by the worst punch in the gut imaginable.

"What are you going to do then?" Jacques asked him.

Gateau's lips tightened as he gave Jacques gentle, chummy eyes. "There's nothing I can do. He's lost too much blood."

That was too much for me. I wanted to vomit right then and there. But I couldn't. It just stayed inside me, along with everything else.

Jacques closed his eyes to force back the tears. "How much longer, do you think?"

"An hour at most." Gateau put a hand on Jacques's shoulder. "I'm sorry."

Jacques's body hunched over. He had to rest a hand against the doorframe to keep from falling over. Lowered his head. Forced himself to accept it.

I felt like shit watching him. Whether or not he was really Corey's butler, it was clear to me how much he truly loved the man. I had experienced enough loss in my day. I know how bleak and helpless Jacques must've felt. He sure took it better than I did, that's for sure. He simply coughed a few times, erected his back, and gave the two of us a resolute look. "I'll just say my goodbyes then."

Gateau nodded, understanding completely. I, on the other hand, was a nervous wreck. I knew what was coming. Corey, after Jacques tells him he's only got an hour left to live, will reveal I was the man that shot him. I needed to get out of there.

Jacques gave me a thankful look as he reopened the door. But then he gave a queer look at Gateau, accompanied by a tiny head-jut. Gateau followed him inside, deliberately leaving the door ajar as the two talked in the foyer. Their four eyes watched me as they spoke French to each other in soft whispers.

A chill ran down my spine. I was right the first time. Corey had already told them.

Jacques turned and walked up the stairs as Gateau gave me the widest, friendliest, phoniest smile I had ever seen. He approached the open door and asked with pleasant, cordial confusion, "You're not *going* anywhere, are you?"

I swallowed. "Actually, I—"

"Quite the bump you got there," Gateau told me, his eyes fixed on my forehead. "Come inside. I'll take a look at it."

I casually smiled back, not letting my terror show. I willingly stepped back in and allowed Gateau to lock the front door.

Gateau made a cafetière of very weak coffee, the last of what Corey had left in the house (one of the many rations he was bringing back before I shot him). I sat in the dining room as he inspected the bump on my head. As he poked and prodded, asking me if it hurt, I was busy thinking about Jacques upstairs, sitting beside Corey's deathbed, no doubt sharing one last conversation. Did Jacques tell Corey he was dying? I sure hope so. Knowing you're about to die is the absolute worst thing to know… at first. Then you're left with a brilliant sense of closure.

I know there's no saving me, Nadine. I've accepted the inevitable. The last moments of my life will be me standing before a firing squad, a blindfold tied around my head, the smoke from my last cigarette still in my lungs, the last sounds I'll ever hear being the large crowd of people in front of me, then gunfire, then nothing. Corey's last moments were that of peace, conversation, warmth. I hope Jacques told him. Knowing how you'll go, with enough time to accept it, is one of life's greatest gifts. The second best is dying so fast you didn't even know you were going to die. Everything in between is hell.

But enough about that.

Gateau broke my concentration with a string of French words. No offence, Nadine, but I really do think French words sound genuinely ugly. I'm glad I didn't waste my time learning any.

"I keep telling you people," I grumbled, "I don't speak French."

Gateau smiled. "Now I know you don't. If you did, you would've punched me across the face just now."

I looked up at Gateau. "Why? What did you say?"

And Gateau laughed at me. He took the seat across from me. Sipped the last of his coffee. "I didn't mean it. It was just a test."

"A test?"

"Jacques knows you're hiding something." Gateau had the nerve to pause for effect. "For a bit there he thought you might've been a spy loyal to Vichy."

"I'm not French."

"Well you're certainly not British. Your English is flawless, of course, but you don't sound British. You don't act British."

I stared back at him. "Who are you to know what Englishmen sound or act like?"

"I never said I did. Jacques's the one."

"And what makes him such an expert?"

"He and Corey lived in England for a time."

I hated that metaphorical magnifying glass to my head. "Don't you mean 'Corey' lived in England?"

Gateau's expression changed. "What?"

"You said 'He and Corey.' It's just Corey. Jacques is Corey's butler. A Negro, no less. Why do you keep talking about Jacques like he's equal to his master. He's not... right?"

Gateau looked away. Said nothing else.

I wasn't satisfied with that. "Why didn't you know who I was talking about on the phone earlier?"

Gateau rolled his lips, but still nothing.

"It's not their real names, is it?" I asked.

"Neither is yours." Gateau looked directly back at me.

My body stiffened. I refused to blink. "That's a lie."

"Who are you really?"

"Private William Gunnison."

"Who's your commanding officer?"

"That's classified."

"Why would it be classified? You're just a Private."

"Who said anything about me being a Private?"

"You did."

I hesitated. "Perhaps."

"What are you doing in Paris?"

"That's classified."

"I don't believe you."

My lips fluttered. "Would you believe me more if I had a perfectly reasonable cover story?"

"Not necessarily."

"Alright then." I shrugged. "What else is there to say?"

"The truth."

I tightened my lip. I had to tell him something. As close to the truth as possible. "Fine. I'll tell you. But you cannot tell Jacques. It would compromise my mission."

Gateau sat up, eager to hear.

I rubbed my eyes. Let out a rough sigh. "I was airdropped into France only a few days ago. No one's supposed to know I'm here."

"For what purpose?"

I looked Gateau in the eye. "My orders are to assassinate *Leutnant* Adalwolf Bütz."

Gateau raised his brows. "I see."

"267th Infantry—"

"I know *Hauptmann* Bütz."

I blinked. He knew about the promotion. How did he know about the promotion? "You do?"

"Very well, actually."

I almost had a mental breakdown right there in the chair. Gateau knew Bütz? How? Was he going to tell him everything? He already knew the address by heart. Oh wait, I even told him my name over the phone. What if he tipped off Bütz before he got there? Was Bütz already on his way? Did he know where I was?! Jacques was going to get hurt too, wasn't he?! What was I supposed to do?! Why was I still there?! *I needed to get out of there!*

"Not personally, of course," Gateau added casually. "He's been to my clinic a few times. Venereal disease."

I'm pretty sure I let out a madman's laugh. "Why doesn't that surprise me? Hahahaha!" I cleared my throat and returned to my serious soldier face. "Of course, I know you won't give me away. Even if you did, I've been trained to deny it under all forms of interrogation."

Gateau nodded back. "Don't worry, I understand." He looked around for Jacques. Leaned over the table. "I know about the SOE," he whispered. He gracefully leaned back. "Only rumours of course, but…" He chuckled. "In these times, word of Churchill having a special assassination squad tends to get around!" He laughed some more.

I stared back at him. "Churchill's… got a special assassination squad?"

Gateau laughed heartily. "They really did train you well. I actually believed you there." He stood, collected our empty coffee cups, and carried them into the kitchen.

I noticed the hour was almost up, so I snuck upstairs to Corey's bedroom. His door was left ajar. Inside I could see the back of Jacques's head, the black butler sitting beside his dying master. Corey looked worse than ever, paler than his sheets. I couldn't hear what they were saying, but I could feel the loss from my place in the hall. The history between those two. All those years of companionship. The pleasant nights. Those crises they've endured. The food. The drink. The sunrises, sunsets. All over Europe, the Americas. It wasn't just one man dying. It was a bond between two people. Without Corey, Jacques had no one. He'd be alone. And I knew what that felt like. I've been there. That quiet and isolation. It wasn't just loneliness. It's despair without witnesses. Regret without release. Aimless thought without verbiage. Memories without colour. Food without texture, shape or flavour. Abyss. And I did that to Jacques. I put him into that pit. Not because of a noble sacrifice or some greater good, but because I was stupid. Because I hated Bütz so much that I lost all sight of reason. I stopped being a soldier, a strategist, the moment I decided to run around with a gun like a fool without a plan, the moment I decided to risk putting civilians in danger. It really didn't have to happen. There were other ways I could've taken out Bütz. Far less dramatic ways.

I watched Corey Baxter die. I watched Jacques hunch over that last time in grief. And I removed myself. Hid in a dark corner. Sobbed myself into oblivion. I thought I would stay there forever had Jacques not found me. He must've recognised the pain on my face as his own. So he invited me to at least stay for dinner, the humblest dinner he could provide under the circumstances. And I accepted, because doing so would give Jacques one last bit of companionship, just enough to keep him going.

CHAPTER FOUR

A Simple (Re)Quest

I returned to my seat in the dining room, lost in my own state of grief, replaying the incident that got Corey killed, counting all the different directions I could've moved, all the different zones I could've shot, somewhere that wouldn't have been so fatal. I knew I had to get out of that state, so I focused instead on those voices coming in from the kitchen, that French conversation between Jacques and Doctor Gateau, who evidentially was also staying for dinner. The hushed nature of their interaction meant it was obviously about me, and hearing the letters "SOE" spelled out by Gateau made it clear to me that not only did he buy my hogwash, he was also passing it along to Jacques's fragile mind as fact.

That stressed me out again, so I returned to my familiar realm, grief-stricken regret. I kept telling myself I had nothing to be ashamed about. I never intended to hurt Corey. My true intention was always to save his life. But every time I tried playing the optimist, I kept having a vision of Jacques alone in that house, that big mouldy house, after Gateau and I left for the night. No more ears around to hear him. How devastating his cry would be. What a monster he'd unleash.

Jacques served us all generous helpings of bland, watery soup. I barely ate, not only because it tasted like dogshit. Why couldn't I think long enough to bring the rations along with us? Corey really wasn't dragging me down. I could've done it. I could've carried both.

"Private Gunnison?" Jacques asked me.

I grabbed my spoon, realising I was being rude to my dead host's butler. "William's fine."

"William then." Jacques wiped his lips with a napkin. "I want to thank you for all you've done for Corey."

I forced some soup down, just punishment for my sins. "My pleasure."

Jacques put his hands together, avoiding all eye contact with Gateau. "I know you've already done so much for us, but if it's not too much trouble, I do have a favour to ask of you."

I put down my spoon, too tired to move much. "Name it."

Gateau noticed Jacques was avoiding his inquisitive gaze. "Jacques…"

"Corey has a brother living in New York City," Jacques told me.

"Jacques! What are you doing?"

"It's what he wanted," Jacques told Gateau. "We talked about it. It's happening."

Gateau frowned. Looked apologetically at me.

I looked across the table at Jacques. "What is?"

Jacques hesitated. "I just think…" He paused. And it was a strange pause too. "Victor needs to know what happened to him."

"What do you mean 'what happened to him'?" I asked a bit too harshly. I thought I didn't have to worry about that anymore.

Jacques was puzzled by my reaction. "That he passed."

I nodded, trying not to be even more obvious. "Of course."

"I know with this war going on, and the occupation, it will be rather difficult to get a letter out there, but… I'm sure someone in your position might be able to help. Maybe one of your superiors can make sure it gets there safely?"

"Jacques," Gateau spoke up. "I mean, really. I'm sure Private Gunnison is far too busy to—"

"No," I interrupted. "I'll do it."

Gateau was shocked by my response, how casual and eager I was. "But what about your—?"

"I don't know what you're talking about," I said with big angry eyes.

Gateau understood what I meant and said nothing else.

Jacques gave me a small, casual smile. "Thank you." He picked up his spoon. Returned to his sipping.

I gently moved my soup bowl away. Now that I agreed to help Jacques out, I didn't have to pretend to like it anymore. "Where in New York?"

"Greenwich Village, I think. It's in Manhattan, wherever it is. I'll look up the address and write it down for you." Jacques sipped some more soup. "Do you know someone you can trust to deliver it safely?"

"I'll do it myself." I smiled at Jacques. "I'll start tomorrow. Is it okay if I stay the night?"

Jacques smiled a bit. "Actually, I think I prefer it."

"Thank you."

Jacques finished his soup. Wiped his lips. "There is one thing I need to tell you about Victor."

"Oh?"

"It's nothing…" Jacques flapped a nonchalant hand. "It's just that he won't accept the letter unless you say the words 'Olive Branch.'"

I stared at Jacques for a long time. "'Olive Branch'?" I repeated, as if that wasn't the sketchiest thing he could've said.

"Yes. He's a bit of a shut-in, especially when it comes to friends of his brother."

I narrowed my eyes. "But I thought you said his family was all out here."

Gateau looked at Jacques.

Jacques forced a smile back at me. "No, I believe you asked if *any of them* were out here, to which I said, 'Europe, yes. France, no.'"

Gateau turned his head towards me.

"But you never said anything about New York," I responded. "Why not?"

Gateau turned his head back to Jacques.

Jacques kept staring at me. "You didn't ask."

Gateau turned his head back to me.

I maintained my stare. "Where else in America does his family live?"

Gateau turned his head to look at Jacques.

"Besides New York?" Jacques asked me. "Chicago. Boston. Newport. Philadelphia. Do you want everyone else's addresses or just Victor's?"

Gateau turned his head back to me.

"Victor's is fine." I looked off. Brought my brows together. "But why him specifically? Is he a favourite brother or something?"

Gateau turned his head towards Jacques.

"No," Jacques answered me. "Matter of fact, they hate each other. Haven't spoken in years. Hence the codeword."

Gateau turned his head back to me.

I tilted my head a bit. "But isn't a letter from his brother's *butler* enough? Why even have a codeword?"

Gateau turned his head back to Jacques.

Jacques flashed a glare at Gateau this time, silencing his immaturity. Then he returned his eyes to me. Stared silently. After a moment, he said slowly, conclusively, "Because he won't open the letter if he thinks it was written by a nigger."

Gateau's whole face cringed. He hissed in through his teeth.

I admitted defeat by saying nothing more. Slid the bowl closer to me. Finished my penance broth.

Jacques made my bed like a good butler while Gateau called for the ambulance to pick up Corey's body. I waited in the main room, nodding politely at Gateau and his men as they carryed Corey out. Before leaving himself, Gateau whispered some more French to Jacques. Whatever it was visibly reassured him.

The ambulance left with Gateau and the big house had only Jacques and I. He admitted he was tired and wanted to go to bed, and I agreed, so the two of us moved upstairs. On the walk up, I couldn't help but feel betrayed by Jacques's continued secrecy. Throughout our interrogative banter, our clever snipes bookended by knowing looks, I had actually developed quite a fondness for the man. I had assumed that fondness was mutual, but it seemed Jacques didn't respect me enough to tell me the truth about Victor. He certainly trusted me enough to deliver a letter all the way to New York. He certainly believed my SEO cover story, or SOE, whatever Gateau called it, Churchill's execution organization, if such an organization even existed. So why was he still lying to me? Why was he still pretending to be Corey's old butler? Why all the fake names? After all I did for him, didn't I deserve an answer to that at least?

I stripped to my undergarments and sat on the bed. Jacques knocked on the door. Gave me the letter. It was a fat one too. Heavy. Full of folded paper. It definitely wasn't a mere death notice, and Victor was no estranged brother of Corey's. No way. This was all Jacques's doing.

In regards to the address, I remember the street name itself was a number, a double-digit number, like ten or twenty. And there was a flat number too. I really hate that I can't remember it right now. I'd write it out a thousand times over if I could, but I simply can't remember one bit of it. I did have it memorised at one point. I know it'll come back to me. I think the more I write this out, the easier it'll come to me. I just got to keep going. Keep remembering.

"Thanks again," Jacques told me, and he closed the door, walked down the hall, and retired to his own room. I blew out my candle and waited an hour, just long enough to really guarantee his sleep.

I opened my eyes. No light. No sound. I tiptoed out of bed. Grabbed my book of matches. Turned the knob all the way, nice and slow. Pushed the door open, just slow enough for it not to creak. Made my way through the dark hallway. Opened the first door down. My eyes had adjusted very well by that point. I was practically a mole. Behind the first door was a simple, plain, unslept-in guest bedroom. That was when I realised I had no idea which of the two dozen hallway doors Jacques was sleeping in, so I made sure to always stop, put an ear to the wood, hear for breathing or snoring or anything, and *then* waltz right in.

Door number two. Nothing. Another bedroom. Door number three. Nothing. Another bedroom. Door number four, also a bedroom. I couldn't believe it. How many bedrooms could one place have? They couldn't all be bedrooms, right?

The fifth bedroom was different from the others. On the bed and covering every inch of the floor were boxes, nailed-shut wooden crates of varying proportions. Some large and vertical. Some square and compact. Some stacked all the way up to the ceiling. I took note of how weird it was and closed the door. Moved on to room number six. Listened for sounds. Nothing. Opened it to reveal another bedroom of boxes. The next three doors, all full of boxes. That's when I, the smart detective that I was, realised Jacques's secret might be *inside* the boxes. Five rooms it took me to get to that conclusion, Nadine. Five.

Quietly as I could, I approached the stack of crates inside the newest bedroom. I tenderly lifted the top lid, and as much as I wanted to explore, I could barely read the papers inside. I grabbed my book of matches and lit the candles hanging on the wall. It allowed me to see the first box was full of letters. Just letters. I heaved the crate off its column. Placed it on the ground. Opened the next box down. Full of sketches this time. Drawings. Some in colour, some not. Portraits for the most part. They were quite good too. Hardly a secret worth changing your name over.

I slid the crate over. Cracked open the bottommost box. Right on top, like a punch in the face, was a familiar name. I think I actually gasped. Austrian citizenship papers made out to one Corey Baxter. Same birth date as his

French identification card. I kept reading it over and over again. Corey definitely sounded American when he was alive. He had to have been American. But what if he wasn't? What if this identification, the one stuffed in a nailed-shut crate, buried in a spare bedroom, was the real one?

Could Corey have been Austrian, all along? Perhaps. Could he have been an impostor the whole time, a charlatan passing himself off as the real Corey Baxter with the real Corey Baxter's papers? Perhaps. Was Corey Baxter even real to begin with? That wasn't guaranteed anymore, was it? Where was the real one now? What did these people do to him? Who the hell did I kill?

CHAPTER FIVE

The Picture

"What are you doing?!"

I spun around, startled by Jacques's sudden appearance. He was standing in the hall, wrapped in a dressing gown, with a horrible look of betrayal on his face. He was breathing fast too. He didn't look it, but he was terrified of me.

I lifted the Austrian document. "Who are the hell are you people?"

Jacques's lips fluttered. "What are you talking about?"

"Your name's not Jacques, is it? Who was Corey Baxter?"

Jacques swallowed. "Can we talk about this tomorrow?"

"I want to know now." I couldn't help but shake my head. "Why all the secrecy? Why won't you just tell me?"

Jacques hesitated.

"Don't worry," I added, feeling I had to. "I'm still delivering the letter. I promised you that I would. But you're asking me to desert the Army, and they kind of need me right now. I'm not doing that unless I know why, so… Why?"

Jacques tightened his robe. "I didn't know…" He sat on one of the crates. "Why would you do that?"

"I have my reasons," I murmured.

Jacques didn't ask. But he didn't tell me either.

"I won't say anything to anyone," I insisted. "I promise."

"It's not that. I believe you. I know you wouldn't try to." Jacques paused. "I've been burnt in the past, that's all. Someone I knew I could trust with my life, someone I *knew* wouldn't say anything… said something. The Nazis have ways of getting information out of people, ways you couldn't possibly imagine. If *he* talked…" Jacques shook his head. "Believe me, it's better you don't know."

"I don't have to know everything. Just give something. Anything you can give me."

Jacques took a deep breath. "I'd rather you ask."

I looked down at the Austrian certificate in my hands. "Was Corey American or Austrian?"

"American."

"Was he really a French citizen?"

"Yes."

I hesitated. "Was Corey Baxter his real name?"

Jacques frowned off with disappointment. "No."

"Is Jacques your real name?"

"No."

"Were you really his butler?"

"*Yes,*" Jacques snapped back. "Yes, I was his butler. I served him faithfully for decades, before you were even born. I've been to London with that man. I've been to Rome. Saltzberg. Geneva. Marseilles. Barcelona. You have no idea the things I've done for that man. None at all." He threw in a grimace. "And you never will."

I placed the certificate back in the box. Sat across from Jacques. Crossed my arms. "Then why did Gateau swear over the phone that he never had a client with a butler… even after I told him your names… until *after* I told him the address?"

Jacques let out a soft sigh. He looked off. Shook his head. "Because he's not Corey's physician. He's just a friend. We haven't seen him in years."

I nodded. "What about Victor?"

"What about him?"

"He's not his brother, is he?"

Jacques shook his head. "He doesn't have a brother."

"Then who is he?"

Jacques kept staring off.

I closed my eyes impatiently. "Who—?"

Jacques abruptly stood up. Before I opened my eyes, he was already in the hallway.

"Hey!" I cried, standing up. "Wait!"

I heard Jacques open the next door down. He left it open. I waited where I was for him to come back, testing to see if I could trust him. I listened to him rummaging around different boxes. Then I heard the door close. Jacques reemerged with a large framed photograph, about one metre in length, half a metre in width. He stood close to the candlelight. Turned the picture around. Held it up with both hands for me to see.

I approached the picture, taking it all in. Eight men and two women were standing in what appeared to be a pub or some sort of nightclub, all posing for the camera, some with arms around shoulders, others shaking hands. Whoever they were, their camaraderie was apparent. And there were a few others in the background, stragglers caught in the flashing camera's cross-fire, some of their faces blurred by motion. But one bystander in particular stood out to me, standing on the far-left side of the photo with a strange look of rejection on his face, like he had just been told to get out of the shot. And yet there he stood, perfectly in focus, defiantly in the shot anyway. He had a brutish face I recognised instantly.

Jacques pointed to the only Negro in the picture. "That's me." He pointed to the man standing next to him. "That's Corey—The man you'll only know as Corey." He then pointed to the grinning man in the bottom righthand corner. "And that's Victor."

I briefly looked at Victor, just enough to acknowledge his face. I really wish I took more time to register his appearance, his features. I was too distracted by that brute standing on the lefthand side, the Brownshirt. "You never said you were in Berlin," I mumbled.

I could sense Jacques's blood curdling. "H-how did you know that?"

"What year was this taken?" I asked coldly. "'26? '27?"

Jacques stared at me. "'27."

"I thought so." I pointed to the brute. "That's the uniform he wore before he went to Bolivia in 1928. His insignia was different when he got back, so it had to have been before."

Jacques turned the photo around. Got a good look at the brute's face. "How do you know about him?"

"In my training…" I stopped to rephrase. "My bootcamp, as it were… we learnt a lot about the history of the Third Reich, especially when it came to its commanding leadership." I pointed at the picture. "You need to destroy that thing. It's pretty damn incriminating."

"He's been dead for years, hasn't he?"

"Doesn't matter. Goebbels made quite the stink about him. Every German who sees that photo will be able to recognise that man. Save yourself the trouble and get rid of it. I mean it."

Jacques looked at the people in the photo, his eyes softening. "I can't."

I felt for him. I really did. "You were his friend, weren't you?"

I know I said at the start of this, Nadine, that I would tell you everything, anything to help you locate Victor. But I cannot in good conscience reveal to you the Nazi in the photograph. I don't want you to use that information to justify not saving Jacques.

Jacques stared into the eyes of the dead Nazi in the photograph. "I wasn't really his friend." He placed the picture aside. "For obvious reasons."

I nodded, understanding his implication. "So where does Corey play in all this?" After a pause, I asked, "Was he his friend too?"

Jacques made odd eye contact with me. "His family's full of Nazi sympathisers. I was his butler. No one asked any questions. Gateau told me he'll do everything he can to keep his death a secret, but one day, someone might wonder why they haven't been seeing him around lately. If any of them figure out I've been squatting here by myself, they might get suspicious and call the Gestapo." Jacques paused. "You know what they do to men like me."

I nodded solemnly. "Unfortunately, I do."

"Without Corey around to protect me, they'll send me away to a concentration camp." Jacques frowned. "Who knows? Maybe they'll just kill me then and save themselves the paperwork."

"Why don't you run? Join the refugee trail. Get to America the long way."

"Because it's not just me that has to get out." Jacques looked around at all the boxes in the room. "All this is coming too."

I furrowed my brow at all the stacks. "All of it?"

"We spent years getting it together, Corey and I. Ever since the *Anschluss*. We had to stop because of the occupation, but now…" Jacques lowered his head. "If I'm found out, they'll destroy all of it. I can't allow that. I've lost too much already. Too many people have died."

I simply bowed my head, trying to process it all.

"But Victor can help me," Jacques whispered. "That letter is a series of instructions. Please don't lose it. It's best way he can get me and all this shit out of France as soon as possible. You're the only option I've got." He shrugged. "Maybe the best one I could've had, actually."

"I don't know about all that."

"You're not French. Frenchmen these days would sell their mother out for some Vichy leniency. Please, keep all of this to yourself. No one can know. About our names, where I am, that photo…" Jacques paused. "I know I can trust you, William. After what you did for Corey… What you tried to do, at least."

I stayed silent. Corey never told Jacques I was the one that shot him. It's possible he didn't know, but… if he did know, he might've kept it to himself for this very reason. Jacques protected the boxes, but Corey protected Jacques. And me too, I suppose. "Yes, you can," I told Jacques. "Of course you can."

Jacques took a deep breath. "Well? Are you satisfied? Can I go to bed now?"

I hesitated. I know he was tired, but… there was one more answer I needed. "That phrase you told me?"

"Olive Branch," Jacques said clearly.

"What does it mean? What am I telling him?"

Jacques opened his mouth. Closed it. Opened it again. "I don't think I can answer that tonight," he said slowly, his voice wavering. "Not after… It's still too…" He shook his head, fighting back tears. "Just ask Victor when you get there. He'll tell you all about it." With that, Jacques turned and left.

I restacked all the boxes I disturbed. Sealed them up as best I could. Blew out the candles. But instead of returning to my bedroom, I tenderly approached Jacques's. As I got closer, I could hear him crying into his pillow. My heart broke at the sound of it. I swiftly returned to my room. Took a moment to stare at that letter by my bedside. What a mystery in its own right. Part of me wanted to open it right then and there, an instant answer to all my lingering questions. But I heeded Jacques's warning. Knowing too much could get me killed—or worse, other people. Bütz was after me. That much was true. Maybe it was better I never opened it. I had already endangered that poor man enough.

I blew out the candle and slept like a baby.

CHAPTER SIX

Mine

I awoke the next morning to see that big old house full of sunlight. I stayed lying in bed, suddenly aware of the daunting task ahead of me. I had never been to the United States before. I'd never even left the Continent. How was I supposed to find my way across the Atlantic? How was I supposed to get out of Paris with Bütz on my tail?

But I took a deep breath. Glanced at the letter on my bedside, that New York address clear as day. I knew where I was going. I knew *exactly* where I was going. It was only a matter of going, right? How hard could it be?

I slipped on the same clothes I was wearing the day before. Dead man's jacket. Dead man's cap. I tried to slide the letter into my jacket pocket, but it was just a bit too thick. I had to crimple it on the sides, but even then it rested on an angle. Nevertheless, I headed downstairs to say goodbye to Jacques only to find a pot on the cooker. Could it be breakfast?

Jacques wandered into the room with a fresh cafetière of coffee. "Good morning," he greeted cheerily.

I stared in wonder at the bubbling pot on the cooker. "That's not the soup from last night, is it?"

"But it is." Jacques grabbed a ladle. Gave it a good stir. It actually smelled heavenly. "Repurposed as really runny oatmeal." He scooped me a hearty plateful. "Believe me, feeding myself won't be a problem. Three of the boxes upstairs are full wigs. Maybe if I'm bored, I'll go a week as a Zazou." He scooped his own plate. Led me into the dining room. "Just hurry up, alright? I can't avoid detection forever."

I smirked. "Alright."

As we ate our breakfast together, I stopped a bit to give Jacques a glance of profound gratitude. Jacques responded with a look I can only describe as sarcastic confusion, as if it was nothing more than a natural act of hospitality, but it wasn't. It was so much more than that to me. If he had any idea what

I had been living on the last year… A hot breakfast with a friend was more than anything I'd had in a long time.

Jacques finished his plate and pulled a roll of francs from his pocket. "For boat fare, or whatever." He tossed it at me.

I flipped through the stack. Counted it. It was a whole thousand. One thousand francs.

"Before you say anything, remember how worthless that is to me now that they're here. I won't be missing it, really." Jacques wiped his lips. "That being said, do try to stretch it."

I nodded. Pocketed the money. "I will." I finished my plate and stayed long enough to finish my coffee.

I walked onto the porch a half-hour later. Double-checked to make sure that letter for Victor was still on me, still intact. It was, but it wasn't staying in that pocket, not for long. I knew I needed to watch for that.

Jacques stepped out of the house to meet me. Looked around Rue Boissière, how quiet it was in the morning. "Well," he started, trying to think of something remotely dignified to follow that with, at least apropos to the Herculean task he was sending me on. "Good luck, I suppose."

I stared at him. "Victor's not his real name either, is it?"

Jacques cocked his head back, offended I even had to ask. "Of course not." He slipped on a smirk.

I smirked back. Took his hand. Shook it. He even pulled me in for a hug. And I hugged back. I made a vow to myself, right there to God Himself, that I would do anything to save Jacques's life. I would save Jacques's life or die trying.

I watched Jacques return to that big old house of his. I heard him lock the door behind him. And so I started my journey to New York City. My first stop was the scene of the crime, the alleyway where I shot Corey. I needed to retrieve my gun, the Luger I had pulled from *SS-Hauptsturmführer* Kronthaler just one week prior.

I deftly retraced my steps, reversing my course along the Seine. The way there was uneventful. No police mulling about. No Nazis goosestepping or sneaking around. It was all too easy.

I found the correct alleyway and tiptoed down. My eyes darted everywhere, just in case. I found the crate I had slid the gun under and reached down. Couldn't feel it. It wasn't there. I even got down on my hands and knees. Looked under the grate. Nothing. Just the other side of the crate. And a pair of footsteps creeping into view.

I rolled over just in time to literally dodge a bullet. I looked up. Not one. Not two. Three Nazis. I even recognised them. Bütz's buddies from the pub. No doubt sent by the coward himself. And they were armed, all of three of them. I dashed out of the alleyway. Bullets hit the walls left and right, just missing me as I weaved. I could feel Victor's letter already slipping out of my jacket pocket. Of course just as I tried to grab it, I bumped into it, making it dislodge. It fell to the ground. My shoes just missed it. I double-back-crouched to pick it up, almost faltering at the sight of Bütz's buddies racing towards me. I gripped the letter. Rolled left, just the way I did in bootcamp. I even used the ice to my advantage. Curved my trajectory *around* one of the men. And just before that unlucky Nazi knew what was happening, where I was, I had kicked his leg out from under him. Grabbed his gun mid-air. Shot him in the foot. A nice clean *painful* hit. And as the Nazi screamed, I crawled back over to use his body like an organic Nazi sandbag. Stabilised my shooting arm. Shot the other two men dead. One bullet each. Right between the eyes.

And I let out a sigh of relief. Adrenaline was rushing through my veins. Right where it belonged. I tuned out the Nazi's sissy screams. Stood back up. Tried my hardest not to look at that bloody toe of his. I had a great breakfast that morning, I was NOT throwing it up because of Bütz!

I looked down at the Nazi, that poor blond Aryan just following orders. "You know who I am?" I asked him in German.

The Nazi spat curses at me through his pain.

"I'm not asking you to talk," I told him. "Do you know who I am?"

The Nazi nodded.

"Adalwolf sent you, didn't he?"

The Nazi hesitated before nodding a little.

"I thought so." I crouched down. Cocked the gun in my hand. Pointed it at the Nazi's face. "I'm not going to kill you. I'm keeping you alive because I want you to tell him something. Do you want to know what I want you to tell him?"

The Nazi stared down the barrel of his own gun, scared shitless.

"Tell him he failed." I uncocked the Nazi's pistol, which evidently was now *my* pistol. "And if I ever see him again, I'm taking both eyes this time."

I stuffed my new Luger into my back waistband. Checked to make sure Victor's letter was still on me. It was.

I gave the Nazi a little a tip of my cap. Ran for the hills.

I didn't have to blast my way out of Paris, thankfully. I simply walked out. Greeted the checkpoint guards in German. My plainclothes didn't give me away at all.

I stopped in Nanterre after six miles of walking for a bite to eat. After lunch, I decided to stay at the inn for the night. I had a feeling Bütz didn't like my taunt. Instead of obeying my threat, he'd be coming after me. And though I might be stupid, I don't think Bütz thought me stupid enough to hide in the first commune outside Paris.

The next morning, I walked out of Nanterre and headed west, every hour getting deeper and deeper into the French countryside. My plan was to hit a main road or major town, somewhere out of the way where I could ask for directions to a friendly port. Ideally, I'd find a way to snag an auto. That would make things much easier.

10! Oh my God, Nadine, I remember part of the address! The street Victor's on in New York! It's 10th Street! Oh wow, I can't believe I actually got that back! I remember because I was reading the front of Victor's letter to pass the time as I crossed some boring, barren field, all scorched and scarred by some battle long ago, no doubt the *Westfeldzug*. And as I was reading Victor's address, I kept thinking how curious it was that the street didn't have a proper name. It was just '10th Street,' as in the tenth street. How quaint. But really, how would they know it was the tenth street? Cities aren't grids. Tenth from what? What was it relative to? Tenth from the west? Tenth counterclockwise? Were the streets layered like rings, like the ones in Dante's *Inferno*? Was it the tenth street built chronologically? That wouldn't make much sense. How would anyone know where to find it? Or what if there weren't any other numbered streets, no 1st through 9th? What if "10th Street" was the only one? But why would that be the case, unless the man that built it was named Tenth and the numbered version of the name was just the one that stuck?

Anyway, that's what I was thinking about when I stepped on that landmine. I'm sure you can imagine the rest. Loud explosion. Disorientated senses. Shrapnel ripping my right calf muscle open. Good thing I didn't see it. I couldn't even feel it. I had no idea what was going on. One moment I was standing on both feet, next thing I know I'm suddenly dizzy. Soaring through the air. Landing a couple metres away. Hitting the ground so hard I pass out instantly. And then all those little flakes of paper, what used to be Jacques's letter to Victor, the envelope and all its pages reduced to ashy shreds in a mere microsecond, they all just fell around my body, gracefully drifting through the air like warm paper snow.

PART TWO

Nadine

CHAPTER SEVEN

Mystery Man

You probably thought you knew me so well by the time I woke up. I can't imagine how intimate it must've been to sew up a man's calf muscle. No clue who he was. Where he was born. Where he was coming from. Where he was going to. We knew everything about each other by the end, didn't we? In the middle there were some rough revelations, but in those infant days of ours, so full of sweet curiosity, mystery, perpetually on the cusp of discovery, that might've been the easiest we've ever got along.

When they brought me to Crespières, you were the one that pulled off my jacket. You found the roll of francs in my pocket. You brushed away all the charred paper remains still clinging to my eyelashes, my cheeks. You removed my cap, my sweaty hair all bunched up. You slipped off my shirt and trousers. And you could see all my scars, all those raw regions of my skin. My armpits. Under my breast. The side of my abdomen. The tender part under my feet. You saw me on full display. Oh wow. Yeah. You saw me naked, didn't you? I only just figured that out. That's... Well, that makes it weird now, doesn't it?

You were told to wait for Doctor Garnier to arrive from Neuilly-sur-Seine, but you knew you couldn't wait. In those crucial first hours, you singlehandedly stopped the bleeding and prevented infection. You used anaesthesia on me and operated immediately. The only reason I can get out of bed now, the only reason I can walk down these halls, is because you went and disobeyed direct orders. Thank you.

I know how romantic it sounds, how novelistic, but in truth your face really was the first thing I saw after I woke. I can still see you the way you were that day. Dirty blonde hair. Sweet hazelnut eyes. A bit of dirt on your face. Not much of a smile, but you had a glow to you nonetheless. You were fully erect in that chair of yours, like a lady reciting for her governess, but of course you were speaking French, like a lady reciting for her governess. I had to be rude and cut you off with my coarse English. "I don't speak French."

You let out a surprised coo at the sound of my voice. "I'm sorry," you said to me in English, your accent still there but controlled. And you laughed a bit, not at me, more at the situation you were in, which is something you do quite a lot. I actually find it cute. "I had a whole speech prepared for what I was going to say when you woke up. So much for that."

I was disorientated by my surroundings. That cabin we were in, passing as a wartime hospital. The sounds of motors and farming equipment outside. All the voices of men mulling about. All those the strange things in that hospital. The patient lift system just above me, that series of pulleys connected by rope. The bed dividers to my left and right, their curtains drawn, revealing two other empty beds. My torn jacket, hat, and blood-stained trousers folded on a chair. On the opposite side of the room a solitary door without a lock, a wood burning furnace, and a couple of small windows with veneers, natural daylight coming in. All that empty space in between and yet you chose to sit by my bedside.

"What happened?" I asked you. Trying to sit up made me wince in pain. My right leg felt so tight. I could barely move it. And that burlap sack I was wearing scratched me ever so dearly.

"I was explaining that," you told me, and as if by magic, a strand of hair dislodged itself from your hat. As you gracefully moved it behind your ear, I noticed you had a rifle slung across your back. I had never been more confused sexually and territorially at the same time. "You're safe, don't worry. I got all the shrapnel out and stitched up your leg. It didn't hit any bone, thank God, but your muscle did get torn up quite a bit. It'll hurt when you walk, probably for the rest of your life, but you will be able to. *Running* on the other hand, well…" You shrugged. "One step at a time, I guess. Pardon the pun. You should be out of here in a week, two at the most. I suggest you stay in bed until then."

I dared to lift the sheets and look down at that awful stitching. Not awful because it was bad. You really did an amazing job. I'm not saying you didn't. But don't pretend for a single second it didn't look ugly as sin. I'm not trying to give you feedback, you're fine, but… I'm not a burlap sack. Couldn't you have made it more aesthetically pleasing, for my own psychological betterment if not for others'? "How long was I out?" I asked.

"Two days. I worked on you the first day then knocked you out all day yesterday while you recovered."

"Knocked me out?"

That's when you explained to me what anaesthesia was. I had never heard of it, so don't be shocked that I can't recount it all these months later. But at the time I knew I was safe, just from the way you explained how it worked. You were paraphrasing an expert, no doubt your teacher Doctor Garnier. I know you didn't invent the thing, but he absolutely would've been proud in how you sold it to me. "We only had three doses," you concluded. "I'm glad we were able to use one. They're very state-of-the-art. It would've been a shame for it all to go to waste."

I just kept looking at your eyes, those soft brown pearls. "Resistance?"

You nodded. "I'm Nadine." You held out your hand like a proper lady. I shook it, unprepared for the abundant field of calluses on it. "Nadine Sauvageot."

But I kept staring at your eyes. I knew as soon as I saw them they looked familiar to me. I couldn't quite place how. "William Gunnison." I had a feeling I was making you uncomfortable with the staring. The way you pulled away from me made me think so. "I'm sorry, have we met before?"

Your eyes shifted at my words, a self-consciousness taking over. "No," you said with confidence, shaking your head. "You did open your eyes once during surgery. That could've been it."

I believed that at the time. I had no idea how anaesthesia worked. Maybe it was possible. And yet I couldn't stop thinking in the back of my mind, always the soldier: how did I know those eyes?

You told me you were going to get me some food to help me regain my strength, but just like myself you were combining lies with as much truth as humanly possible. Yes, you were getting me food. Yes, it was to regain my strength. But in the process, you were also reporting to your commanding officer, Captain Roul Lesauvage, that Mystery Man finally woke up… and he's English? That's when you received your orders: lead me on with your feminine sex appeal, seduce me, lure the truth out of my penis or however you Frenchies describe things in that awful swill you call a native tongue. I know you hated receiving such degrading orders. Up to that point they never treated you like a woman, a girl. You had always been equal to the men, a bona fide member of the French Resistance, until the day they needed a woman on-hand to act like a seducing siren honeypot. You spoke nothing to your superiors about it. You accepted your orders without question. There was a war on after all. It was not about you. It was not about your feelings. It was about taking back your country. If I was a French spy sent by Vichy to infiltrate your operation, the Resistance needed to know. And if I really was a British soldier trying to desert the Allies, well… they needed to know that too.

While you were off being sneaky, I was taking stock of my own situation. Speaking of stock, the first thing I noticed was that you confiscated my gun. No doubt you would've found my Luger P08 absolutely suspicious, a firearm of Nazi German origin. I had to come up with an explanation for that. And the other missing piece of my arsenal, Victor's letter. I hadn't immediately remembered that I was holding it when the landmine exploded, you see. I was worried it might've fallen out of the jacket pocket in transit or something. It made me so anxious to the point of tears. But then the door opened, you returning with my sandwich, a nurse's smile and new marching orders, and I switched off my distress to give you a cordial grin of my own.

You were by my side the rest of the day. Checking my vitals. Keeping me company. You didn't ask me anything. I didn't ask anything of you. If I was in pain, you gave me morphine. If I wanted quiet, you sat in the corner and read in peace. Just before bedtime, I finally acknowledged the elephant in the room. "What happened to my gun?"

"Obviously it was a safety hazard. Don't worry. We've got it in a safe place." After a pause, you added, "Interesting choice of gun. Where did you find it?"

I combined the truth with fiction. "I was in a pub fight on the fifteenth. A Nazi officer threw his stein at me."

"I was wondering how you got that," you said, pointing at my head bruise. "You picked up his gun?"

"I think he's still after me." I laughed, implying it was a joke. It wasn't. "Thought I'd be safer with it."

"Well, there's no need to worry about it now. Get some rest." You stood up, ready to leave.

"What about my letter?" I asked. I wouldn't have been able to sleep without possessing the truth.

And you gave it to me, the sad, ugly truth. "We found you covered in bits of burned paper. There wasn't anything else on you, so… That must've been it. Destroyed by the blast."

It was like the landmine all over again. I shrugged it off in your presence, but after you left, I cried. I downright wept. How could I be so stupid? Two days out of Paris and I stepped on a goddamn landmine, destroying everything Jacques had entrusted me with. All its contents. Victor's address. And I couldn't return to Rue Boissière. Bütz was still after me. Jacques was in hiding. I couldn't risk luring him there. The only option I had was to keep going to New York and find Victor the old-fashioned way. I knew enough about the situation with Jacques. I knew what Victor looked like. (I didn't have a clear enough picture from memory, but if given the chance I might've been able to match the face on sight.) I knew he was in a Manhattan flat, in a village called Greenwich. And I knew the password, "Olive Branch." Maybe that would've been enough. Maybe Victor knew how to discreetly contact Jacques on his own, or at least knew of an alternative escape plan for Jacques and his menagerie of crated secrets.

Nevertheless, I needed time to mourn my loss. I didn't feel like talking to you the next day. You noticed. I refused to explain why at the time, but that was the reason. I needed to grieve.

CHAPTER EIGHT

Chain of Command, Part II

I woke up on my third day of consciousness and spent those lonely morning hours coming up with a gameplan. I was not safe at Crespières. The longer I stayed there, the more danger I'd be in. But I wasn't getting far on foot. Thankfully you guys had a couple autos on the premises. I knew you did. I could hear the start and stop of a motor not too far from my bed, your resident mechanic Coste in the garage repairing the spare. My plan was to persuade you, kind you, selfless you, into letting me stow away on one of your vehicles on one of its routine runs out of the camp, just as far as a friendly port. To get you to agree, I knew I had to explain part of my situation, something Jacques explicitly told me never to do. But his name wasn't really Jacques, and Corey's wasn't really Corey. Neither was Victor's. As long as you didn't know that, I wasn't really telling you anything, was I?

I planned on starting slow, first by mentioning Victor's letter, the one I had been holding, saying nothing more besides how important it was that I get out of there as soon as possible, that I was in the middle of an important mission. For a bit there I considered labelling it a military effort, but decided to steer away from that. The Resistance might've had the resources to disprove that alibi. Besides, staying as close to the truth as possible had always made things easier for me. If my mission's time sensitivity wasn't enough to evoke your sympathy, I'd go into detail about the victim of the story, Jacques the Frenchman, one of your own. Hopefully your patriotic altruism would outweigh any disappointment you had in me for deserting France in her hour of need.

I was quite sure of the strength of my strategy… until eight o'clock rolled around and you came into my room with a bucket of hot soapy water and a sponge and announced I was about to get a sponge bath. As you slipped my garments over my head, I realised this was not going to be easy. It was going to be very, *very* hard.

And it was hard. To concentrate, I mean. To keep control. You certainly knew what you were doing, following through with that covert mission of yours. I didn't suspect a thing, even though it's so obvious to me now.

"What are you doing in France?" you asked, lifting my arm, rolling the sponge all the way down to my pit.

My mouth was suddenly dry. "What do you mean?"

"You're a soldier, aren't you?"

"Of course. Why wouldn't I be? Not many English civilians roaming around."

"So?" You redunked your sponge, smiling ever so gently, your eyes off and on meeting mine. "What are you doing here?"

My heart started racing. I tried playing it off. "It's classified."

You rubbed the sponge across my chest. I could feel your warm breath against my skin. You were really close. "So what are you?" you asked, roaming your sponge down my abdomen.

"What?"

"Army? Navy?"

I nodded, my eyes unable to leave your face.

"Army or Navy?" you asked again.

"Oh, uh…" My ticklish skin was distracting me. "Army."

"Mmm." You resoaked the sponge. Restarted at my belly button and moved downward. "Corporal? Sergeant?" I could feel the sponge graze my…

"Private," I said, sharply moving away.

"Is the water too hot?"

"No, it's… I don't think I've ever had one of these before."

"It's alright. I've done this loads of times. You're in safe hands."

"Oh, I know." I smiled back. "It's just weird, is all. For me."

"Mmm." You redunked the sponge. Guided me on my back. Gently lifted my left leg. Sponged all the way down. "What did you say your mission was?"

"My mission?"

"The reason you're still in France."

I avoided eye contact with you. "I didn't."

"Why not?"

I fixated on the rafters above my bed. Your warm hands and wet sponge were roaming a bit too freely for my taste. "Because it's classified."

"That's right."

"Can we talk about something else? Let's talk about you."

"What's there to say? I'm just the nurse."

"No, I mean… I couldn't help but admire your handiwork down there. How'd you learn how to do that? Did you study medicine before the war?"

And you laughed. "No, I didn't study medicine. How old do you think I am?"

"Twenty-five at least."

"Twenty-one."

I lifted my head up. "Really?"

"Head back down please."

I obliged. "You didn't study medicine? That's impressive."

"There's nothing impressive about not studying medicine."

"No, I mean it's impressive considering."

You lowered my left leg. Tenderly lifted the right, making sure to sponge extra gently over my stitching. It didn't hurt so much that time. "There's a surgeon at the AHP loyal to the Resistance, Doctor Garnier. He taught me everything I know. He's a really sweet guy. Patient. That's important in a mentor."

"So you're not really a nurse?"

"Not from birth, no." You resoaked your sponge. Made another pass at my wound. "Are you a soldier from birth?"

"No." I was very comfortable laying like that, having you take care of me, asking me things. I stopped thinking. The words just flowed out of me. "Honestly, if it were up to me, I'd have spent my whole life away from war. Somewhere safe."

"I'm the same way."

"Really?"

"Mm-hm. My father was a dairy farmer, but…" You paused. I think the words were flowing a bit too freely out of you too. "My mother was a seamstress."

"I can see where you get it from."

"I have a steady hand, that's all."

"That's not nothing."

"I know." And you changed the subject. "What would you have been, had the war not come?"

I had never been asked that before. I had to think about it. "Maybe a librarian."

You stopped your sponging, as if I had said something too shocking for a lady's ears. "A librarian?"

"Or maybe a professor. Something involving a classroom. A place I could use my brain."

You paused too long so I lifted my head. The way you were looking off… it was like you were in another world. "My mother studied *haute couture* in London," you told me, lowering my leg, placing the sponge aside. "She kept all her patterns. They were the most beautiful dresses I had ever seen. And she made all our clothes, my brothers' and mine. Even my father's." You pointed to the burlap sack I was wearing before. "I made them myself."

"You made those?! Holy hell, Nadine!"

You smiled with great joy as you dried your hands. It was a real smile, unlike all those others. "I know how. I'm not that good, but… I did learn from the best." Your tone got warmer as you talked here. "I was going to go to university before the war came. Father wanted me to. He loved his wife being so intelligent. To him, a smart woman was a beautiful woman. I wanted to learn everything I could. Philosophy. History. Politics. If my mother could learn how to make such beautiful clothes for us, what could I do? What could I do for others? What company could I lead?"

"What would you be? A doctor?"

"No. I'd run a hospital before becoming a doctor."

I nodded at that. "You said your father was a dairy farmer?"

You nodded. "Raised poor. He only had dumb farmer's daughters to choose from growing up. To him, intelligence was a sign of wealth. And she loved him, my mother. Her family had problems with the pairing, but… She always said she never settled for a farmer. She brought him up to her level, in a way. And she still sewed, just leather instead of silk. The rest was history."

I sat up. "She studied in London?"

"Yes."

"Is that how you know such good English? Your mother?"

You nodded. "I was quick to pick it up too, apparently. They always told people I was bilingual by the time I was six."

I smiled. I had no qualms about sharing some more of myself to you. All the caution I had before seemed not to matter. "I'm bilingual as well."

Your face lit up at that. "Really?"

"I can speak German."

"Really?"

I nodded proudly. "My father taught me. He was a professor."

"In what field?!" you asked. You made me laugh with that gaping mouth of yours.

"He had a doctorate in Political Science."

"What are the chances of that? No wonder you wanted to be in academia."

I nodded. "I love universities."

"Oh, me too."

"There was a time when Mother…" I felt the cold sting of vulnerability. I was losing myself. Had to rein it back in. "She was away for a bit in my youth, so… I spent a lot of time with my father at his university. I'd lose myself for hours in that old library. I was addicted, literally addicted, to the smell of old books."

"I love old books too."

"And poetry. There's just something about Rilke that just warms my heart."

I could tell you loved seeing that side of me, that side I could never share with other boys my age out of fear of teasing, bullying. "My favourite's Apollinaire," you told me.

"Who?"

"Guillaume Apollinaire."

"I haven't had the pleasure. I'm assuming he's French?"

"Polish actually. He emigrated to France in his late teens and changed his name. He's a Surrealist. Quite imaginative."

"I bet."

"He never thought when it came to his poetry. To him, art was about imagination. Intuition. Getting as close as possible to life, nature, the environment, human beings. That's how he saw the world, so that's the only work he wanted to make. It's beautiful. Like a dream in real life… and yet, just as accurate as reality."

I simply stared at you. Never had I felt so warm. Real warmth. Nothing like that silly sponge bath you tried to put me through. "I've never wanted to be able to understand French more than I do right now."

You were actually blushing at that. "I'm sorry."

"No, I'm sorry for not trying for three. You're quite the salesman. Sales-*woman.*"

You scoffed at that. "'Salesman' is fine." You stood, ready to take the bucket with you. But then you sat back down. "See, I knew there was something about you I recognised. I couldn't quite place it."

"What?" I asked, hoping you had the answer to what's been nagging me about your eyes.

"Intelligence. I mean real intelligence. You notice things. I can see it. It's all there. How you talk. The way you move. I've spent the last seven months in the company of grain farmers and labourers. I doubt many of them even know how to read. You stand out. You really do."

I nodded at that. "Maybe that's all it is."

"All what is?"

I waved it off. As I watched you collect your things, I really wanted you to stay. "So what happened?" I blurted out.

You gave me a curious look. I think you wanted to stay too. "What?"

"Your plans for university. Why didn't you go when you were eighteen?"

"Father didn't have the money yet." The joy in your voice wilted a bit. "'Next year,' he said." And then your face went cold, the way mine did at my mention of Mother. And I realised I reached too far. You were ready to leave. And I couldn't say anything. I had to let you walk out.

I redressed, realising how much better my leg felt. A sharp pain, yes, but I was able to stand out of bed. Using the furniture in that room, I hobbled over to the window to get another look at you.

I found you out there, walking about the camp, thriving in your natural state. And I finally got a good look at exactly where I was. What used to be a provincial farm town in simpler times had been converted to a bustling Resistance hub. The farmhouse was a mess hall and administrative office. The chicken coop was now a barracks. The barn was still a barn but also a make-shift printing press, your underground newspaper. That garage you built for your two autos. Mulling about were civilian farmers and studious men dressed like you, fellow Resistance fighters, and I saw how they all greeted you as you passed. I'd eventually learn all their names. Blaise and Émile, practically joined at the hip, always smoking together. Durant. Scragg. Coste. And that quite tall fellow, no doubt taller than six foot, your CO Roul. But none of it really seemed like a military operation, at least compared to the ones I've seen. Yours came off far more friendly, brotherly. And you were one of the brothers. More than that, actually. You were a star. Their faces brightened at the sight of you. I saw it myself. Their enthusiastic handshakes. Their smiles. Those laughs coming out from your jokes. And it's no wonder. You have that in you, Nadine. You really do.

After resting for the remainder of daylight, I returned to the window to see Crespières at night. There was a light inside the farmhouse, a family dinner in progress, all those rowdy Frenchmen no doubt making bawdy soldier talk. I could hear the laughter all the way out there. Deep cackles. Inconsiderate in volume. And then I saw you, wonderful you, stepping out onto the stoop for a smoke. Roul came out and joined you a few minutes later. You two simply sat there, staring off, talking softly to each other, intimately. I realised the line between CO and Resistance fighter had been blurred when it came to you two. There was a paternal nature to him, I could tell. The shoulder bumps you gave each other. The way he kissed your temple before he returned inside. You must've shared something with him then, something vulnerable. Was it our conversation earlier? Did it stir unpleasant memories? Memories you knew he could help you handle? If that's the case, I love that for you. I love that you had that relationship with your brothers-in-arms. I love that you had a father figure on-hand to guide you, to help you. I love that you had pride in your country, in what you were fighting for. You had everything I never had. And I love that you did.

I first suspected there was a dishonest nature to your frequent visits when you arrived the next morning with Roul and Émile. You stayed in the room to translate—They weren't bilinguists the way we were—and hearing their inquisitive, sceptical questions coming out of your mouth felt strange to me. It aided my realisation that something was amiss about the whole thing. Was it Roul's idea to pull rank on me or your own? Was that delightful conversation we had about poetry and Surrealism real or simply an extension of the same duplicitous charade? It really hurt me thinking that way about you.

"Captain Roul Lesauvage," you translated for your CO. I shook his hand. Émile shook my hand next. "Baudouin Émile."

"We're the ones that found you," you translated for Roul. "I do hope our Nadine has been taking care of you."

"Of course," I responded in English. "I thank you all for your generous hospitality." I maintained my smile as you translated it all back to him.

"I'm sorry we couldn't have visited you sooner," Roul told me. "We've been very busy here, as you can imagine."

"Busy with what exactly?"

Roul chuckled a bit. "Nice try." He crossed his arms. "I'm sorry for being so formal, uh… I'm not sure what to call you other than Gunnison."

I opened my mouth uneasily. "I'm not sure how much Nadine's told you, but—"

Roul interrupted with a string French, but you didn't translate it. I looked to you, confused.

I could sense your discomfort. "I didn't tell them everything," you told me in English. That was you talking.

I narrowed my eyes. Looked up at Roul. No reaction from him. He didn't understand English. You knew that. Interesting. Why would you sneak by him like that? Why didn't you tell him everything? And define "everything."

"I'm just a Private," I told Roul. "William's fine."

"Nonsense. This is a Resistance camp. We respect rank here," Roul told me in French, if your translation was to be believed. "And you may call me Captain."

"Captain. I apologise."

Roul looked to Émile. Back at me. "Private Gunnison, why are you still in France?"

I hated that question. "It's classified."

"Who's your commanding officer?"

"Winston Churchill. Who's yours?" You didn't want to translate that one, I could tell.

"Please don't disrespect me," Roul spat in French. "We did save your life. The only reason you're able to walk is because of us. Or to be precise, because of me. Now please, if you're truly grateful for our hospitality, I'm afraid I must insist on an answer."

I licked my lips. "And I must insist on knowing why—"

"I am a Captain addressing a Private. For the last time, Private Gunnison, why are you still in France?"

"Just tell him," you whispered to me in English. Roul gave you a startled look. You humbly translated what you said to him. You must've broken protocol before. It was an ongoing concern between you two, wasn't it?

I had no choice. I had to tell you all something. Something believable that wasn't the truth. Luckily, I had recently come into possession of three little letters that were bound to convince you of my allegiance. "If you must know, I'm a part of SOE."

Roul instantly furrowed his brow. "SOE?"

"Yes. SOE."

Roul looked helplessly at Émile. "You're SOE?" he asked me again.

I started getting nervous. I thought that would instantly win you all over, the way it did for Gateau. Did I just make things worse? How screwed was I? "Yes."

"What does SOE stand for, Private?"

I had to think fast. "Special Operations… Executive?"

"Yeah, you pulled that out of your arse." Roul thought for a moment. "What section of SOE?"

"What section?"

"What letter, Private? Answer me."

My heart was racing. I had no idea what to say, so I just blurted out, "F… for 'France.'"

Roul's face went blank. "Of course you understand, Private, that in these times we're in, all precautions must be taken."

Did I just get that right? Oh wow. Churchill really needs to get his shit together. His secret ministries have way too simple names. "I understand completely, Captain."

"Where are your dog tags?"

I admit, that one threw me off. "I'm sorry to say it, but I've lost them."

"Where?"

"I don't know, I *lost* them." That was a lie. I left them behind at my hotel in Paris. No doubt they were in Bütz's possession by that point.

Roul shrugged. "Don't you understand how difficult it is from our perspective to verify your identity considering how little you've actually given us? How am I supposed to verify you're SOE if no one is willing to admit SOE even exists yet?"

"I have my identification number memorised. Would that help?"

Roul hesitated. "It's a start."

"775924."

You rattled off the French version of those numbers and Roul nodded. He looked at Émile and spoke some French. Then he looked at you and gave you some French orders as well. I hated not having a translator loyal to me. I hated all that suspicion. I hated having to prove I wasn't a Vichy spy, *again*. So I snapped. I'm sorry I did, but I just couldn't take it anymore. That interrogation had to end before the truth came out.

"CAN YOU PLEASE, FOR THE LOVE OF GOD, STOP SPEAKING FRENCH IN FRONT OF ME?!" Only after I screamed all that did I realise you, Nadine, were the only one who could actually understand me. "It's bloody rude, you fucking Francos!"

You all just stared back at me. You didn't even translate. You were too stunned to.

"Three times now!" I rambled on anyway. "Three times now I've been spoken French at this week as some sort of test! Yeah, I don't speak French! Believe me, it's very inconvenient! 'Join the war,' they said. 'You're gonna fight Germans in Germany,' they said. Well no one bloody told me I'd still be here in bloody FRANCE, alright?! Believe me, I WISH I had learnt French, just so I'd know how to talk to the bloody locals and read fucking Apollinaire in its original language, but I DIDN'T, did I?! No, I went and learnt fucking GERMAN instead! *HOW DARE I?!* What am I, STUPID?!" I put both of my palms together. "And yes, believe me, I'm flattered that everyone seems to think I look like I know how to speak French, but really, if this conversation's over, if you're just gonna spend the rest of our time speaking French in front of me, do me a favour, please, take it outside. I'm done. I don't want to hear another goddamn French word ever again for the rest of my fucking life! I'm actually starting to HATE the French! No wonder you all collapsed like a house of cards after one month of fighting! It's the 20th century, people! Learn how to fight like bloody Englishmen! And while you're at it, TALK LIKE ONE!" I crossed my arms.

You, Roul and Émile didn't know how to react to that. You meekly started to translate in French.

"OUT!" I hollered, pointing at the door. "I said OUT!" You finally all left and I could finally breathe again.

You returned at dinnertime. I pretended to be ashamed by my outburst, but you made me feel better about it. Roul secretly loved my monologue, apparently. You translated the whole thing to him in his office afterward and he laughed. He respected my balls, first off, and it helped prove I wasn't a Vichy spy. If I really did speak French, I certainly wouldn't have forced you all out of the room just as you were hissing secret French orders to each other.

After my meal you checked on my leg, determining whether or not I was ready to start walking again. I faked some pain, just so I'd be able to stay the full two weeks of recovery. I know it wasn't wise for me to linger too long there, especially after I was forced to give up my identification number. It was only a matter of a time before you found out the truth about me, and that would make everything so much worse. But I loved being there. I loved being in the room with you. I liked thinking we were actually getting along, that you weren't just pretending.

Of course I know now that, no matter how much I winced, you could tell my leg was ready to move around again. But you let me go on. You pretended it to be true. Told me to stay around a bit more. Did you not want me to leave either? I think so. We were kindred spirits. Bookish souls forced into a violent world of war and procedure who managed to find each other. A new friend to talk poetry with, and philosophy, and history, and politics. It was nice to forget, wasn't it? Nice to forget our sad new lives. Memories of who we were before. They were still in us, those people. Not gone. Not blasted out of us. Not corroded. Only sleeping. Hibernating. Just as strong as they were the last time we saw them.

Before you left for the night, you revealed a nice little surprise: your own personal copy of Apollinaire poems. You read some to me, translating them on the fly as best you could. And I reciprocated by reciting a few Rilke back to you. We did it all again the next night and the four after that. That really was a magical time for me, Nadine. I will always hold those nights with you in my heart.

CHAPTER NINE

Just Following Orders

You fed me breakfast the next morning and I dared to ask if my suspicions were true, if you were initially assigned to pump me for information.

You confirmed everything with reluctant embarrassment. "Of course you understand we have our reasons. Vichy would do almost anything to bust our newspaper. We had to be sure."

"So am I finally free from suspicion?"

You poured two cups of coffee from an old cafetière. "I'm sure you're fine. You're on our side at least." You handed me a cup, smiling through and through. "I hope you don't take this with anything. We really don't have much on hand."

"Black's fine." I took a sip. "Believe me, I'm thrilled you have coffee at all."

"Only because a bag ripped. It's good too. It's from the south." You raised a toast.

I clinked my cup. "Cheers."

"Cheers." You took a tiny sip.

I licked my lips. "That is good." I held the cup in both hands, warming them up. "What else do you guys get?"

"Everything really. Fruit, meat, cheese, milk, vegetables."

"And you relay it to Paris for it to be rationed?"

"Yes. We use the ration supply run to cover our paper distribution to the citizens of Paris. And the rest of France too. There's a man up there who takes a shipment to the east, another one to the south, and they spread them around the country from there."

"Sounds really nice. The whole country banding together, helping each other out in times of crisis."

You nodded sadly. "France means a lot to us. She's our mother. Our home. She brings a lot of passion out of us. And she's worth it too." You put your cup down on a bedside table. "I just hope it'll actual happen."

I took a deep breath, realising I needed to switch the subject. "So, uh… all that sponge bath stuff…"

You covered your face with a bashful chuckle. "I'm so sorry about that. I guess I got a bit carried away with the assignment."

"Hey, I'm not complaining."

"No, I know I'm smarter than that," you said, reassuring yourself. "I'm better than that." You reached back for your coffee. "Honestly, I wish I didn't have to do it at all." You took a nice, slow sip. "I should've said something this time. Roul would've listened."

"Is that why you didn't tell him what my rank was? Because of what he made you do in order to get it?"

You put your coffee down. Folded your hands. Hunched over. Your voice got raspy too. "Last summer, they found me in a plough shed. I was scared by the sight of them. I didn't know what side they were on. But Roul… he encouraged me. All of them did. Émile. Scragg. Blaise. Coste. Durant, all of them. And I needed that. I needed their help to get here. I wouldn't have lasted a day if not for them."

"They're like your family."

You nodded. "I had three brothers growing up, so… It's very similar. I knew how to handle them. That's why they like me so much. And I'm the daughter Roul never had. At least…" You stopped yourself. "Yeah, I'm practically his daughter."

"What were you going to say?" I asked tenderly.

Part of you wanted not to say anything. But military logic didn't exist in that room, not when it was just we two. "He told me once he… He and his wife had a daughter once. She was just a newborn when she got Spanish Flu."

I frowned. "I'm sorry to hear that."

"It's alright. It's just… It's not a secret I can tell everyone. It's not really mine to tell. The other guys don't even know about it."

"Why would you tell me then?"

You hesitated. "I don't know. I just felt like I could."

I nodded. "So you two… you're not strictly based on rank."

You shook your head. "No. We're way beyond that. That's not to say he treats me like an equal. He doesn't. He wouldn't ask Scragg to do this. He wouldn't ask Durant. I'm the woman. He told me the only reason men would tell me anything is because deep down—or not so deep down—they all want to fuck me. Sorry."

"It's alright," I said, a bit uncomfortable hearing you talk like that.

"I hate it. More and more it just reminds me that they really see me as something I'm not. I'm not a nurse. I'm not a spy. I'm a strategist. I should be alongside them, not under them. I should be planning operations, not running ration drops and flirting with the suspicious intakes. This is beneath me. It's not what I signed up for."

"There's nothing to be ashamed about being a nurse. You're saving lives."

"I know that. I'm glad I'm doing this. I'm using my skills. I'm learning new things. And I'll be honest, I was okay with waiting until they saw I was ready, but…" You looked at me. Drank some more coffee. "It's not just France I'm fighting for. It's the woman I was supposed to be. The woman prepared to go to another country, wherever they let women study philosophy or history or poetry. It's what my parents wanted for me. I was meant for better things, bigger things. Someone who didn't belong to anyone. A woman that belonged to herself."

I put my cup down. "I love that your parents wanted that for you."

"I just think Roul will always see me as that little girl in the plough shed. The little girl who could shoot better than most men. The girl that didn't need to be told a Latin medical term twice. The girl who could sew a leg back together like it was a pair of trousers." You paused. "But that's not me. That's the girl they found. The girl they made. The girl *they* needed me to be." You looked into my eyes. "The way the Army turned you into the man they needed."

I felt so validated by you saying that. I had truly felt alone in that regard.

You shrugged. "So if I have to bend the rules a little bit to feel like myself again, so be it. I know I'm right. I've got good sense," You sipped some more coffee. Put the cup back down. "What about your father? The professor? Was he hard on you, or… more like mine?"

I didn't answer at first. It's always been so painful for me to talk about, but I made a special exception for you. "I'm not really sure."

"What do you mean?"

I could tell my face was forlorn. "He died when I was twelve."

Your face hardened with sympathy. "I'm sorry."

My frown actually started to hurt. "It's fine. You didn't know."

You sat on the bed, close and tender. You took my hand. "How… If you don't mind me asking, how did he die?"

I rolled my teeth over my chapped lower lip. "Weirdly enough, he also got into a pub fight with a Nazi."

"A Nazi?"

"We were visiting Berlin. Back when Germany was a republic, you know, before…."

You nodded.

"We stopped in for some food." I went quiet, bile bubbling up just below my throat. "There were a few Brownshirts at the counter talking rubbish about… democracy, I guess. I don't really remember." I sighed uneasily. "And he just saw red. So much… red." I hacked a little bit.

"What's the matter?"

"Water. I need water."

You got up. Poured me some water into a steel cup. Rushed it back to me.

I drank it slowly. "Thank you." I tried some calming breaths. "I'm sorry. I'm not very good about…" I squashed down some more bile. "Every time I see blood or even think about blood, I get ill. It's very embarrassing."

"Oh." You refilled my water cup.

"Because when I saw his face," I hesitated, checking to make sure my throat could take it. "The way it was… I can't, I couldn't…"

"It's okay." You watched me drink my new cup of water. "So when you were in that pub fight in Paris…?"

I laughed. "You remember all that?"

"I remember everything everyone says. I surprise myself sometimes." You hesitated. "Was that why you started something there? You saw red too?"

I nodded imperceptibly. "Of course I realised the irony afterwards."

"So he didn't do anything to you first? You didn't know him?"

"No, I knew him." I paused, realising I shouldn't have said that. "I mean, I know him now. His name's Bütz. Adalwolf Bütz. He's a Lieutenant, I believe… No." I shook my head, remembering. "No, he's a Captain now. Of course. How could I forget?"

"I don't blame you of course. More people need to stand up to them."

"I almost got hurt. People could've got killed because of me. Because I started all that." I sighed. "I know there were better ways. Civilised ways. I shouldn't have made a scene, I should've… I shouldn't have made a scene."

You took a deep breath, gathering strength. "Nazis killed my father too."

I looked at you and my heart just broke. I had already assumed that was the case, but I was too afraid to ask outright.

You met my eyes and added, "My mother too, as it happened."

That I didn't realise. Overshared and emotionally spent, we both changed the subject. Neither of us talked seriously for the rest of the day.

You determined I was ready to try walking the next day. We started out small, limiting ourselves to the inside of that cabin. At that point I realised I hadn't even mentioned Victor's letter yet, anything regarding Jacques or my mission to New York. Part of me was afraid you'd reveal too much of it to Roul, but after our conversation the previous day, I felt I could trust you with it.

"You remember that letter I was holding when I stepped on the landmine?" I asked as you held my hand, helping me walk.

"The one that was destroyed?"

"Yes." I rerouted back to the bed, needing to sit down for a bit. "I've been meaning to tell you this. It wasn't my letter. I was in the process of delivering it."

"To Paris?"

"I was coming from Paris."

You tried not to laugh. "I'm sorry, you…?"

"Yes," I said with slight annoyance. "Yes, I only got two days out before it got destroyed. I'm very sad about it."

"You can go back and get a new one, right?"

"I can't."

"Why not?"

"I'm not supposed to. It's a time-essential message. I… I really should just go on and tell Victor."

"Victor?"

"The man I was supposed to deliver it too. His name's Victor."

"Victor," you repeated. "Is that his first name or his last name?"

"I don't know." I shouldn't have told you that.

"Where does Victor live?"

The big question. "New York City.

You raised your brows. "You were on your way to New York City?"

"I still am. I need to get there, Nadine. Really. I could really use your help, actually. I—"

"Who wrote the letter?"

I hesitated. It was all too fast. I didn't like it. "His name's Jacques. Obviously he's French."

"Obviously. Who was he?"

"Corey Baxter's butler."

"Who the hell's Corey Baxter?"

"I don't know. An American, apparently. Rich enough to have a butler. A Negro butler, no less. What's more American than that?"

You smirked a tad. "Where do they live?"

"I don't think I should be telling you that."

"Why not? We're on the same side."

This was not going my way. I was trapped. "They really don't trust other Frenchmen right now. I think they've been burned by collaborators in the past. It's made them a bit paranoid."

You nodded. "But you understand, I have to take your word that Corey and Jacques are real."

"Believe me, they're real."

"You're not trying to desert?"

My face hardened a bit. "Of course not. Why would you think that?"

"Do you know Jacques personally?"

"No. Not really."

"Then why would you agree to hand-deliver his letter to New York City?"

I didn't want to answer that. I couldn't reveal Corey's death. That was one of the things Jacques explicitly told me to keep quiet about. What Gateau was full-on covering up. "It's private business. Jacques's private business. He doesn't want me telling anyone. Only Victor. That's what he said." I pointed to my jacket. "I had a roll of francs in my pocket. Jacques gave me that. For the boat fare." I hesitated. "I could really use a drive to a friendly port. I'm not going to be able to run in this condition."

You sat beside me on the bed. Stared off. Processed everything. "It's hard for me to think about the troubles of one man when there's a whole country to save."

"But he's a Frenchman."

"Freeing France is more important. It's always been more important."

You hesitated. "You don't have a letter to deliver anymore, so… Why don't you stay here? We could really use you. You're really smart, William. And it would help both of us, to… you know… keep ourselves grounded." You shrugged. "So to speak."

I really wanted to say yes, Nadine. Never had I ever been so tempted. But I had to refuse, as gently as I could. And we resumed our exercise, and just we did the day before, we refused to talk seriously for the rest of the day.

The next day was unseasonably warm. You helped me get dressed and led me on an outdoor walk, my first foray outside that cabin in nine days. You even gave me a cane. Watched me navigate myself. Every so often you helped me out, and we paced ourselves with the occasional break. I was making tremendous progress. You really did such a great job helping me. You were patient, just like Garnier had been with you. And you were kind, encouraging, strong, just like Roul and the others were with you. You absorbed the best qualities of your mentors. I know they all would've been so proud of you.

We ate lunch under the trees. Fresh air flowing through my hair again. I was comfortable trying again with my escape plan, this time using a card I could never play anywhere else. "My mother had a dream once. More than once, actually. It started right after I was born." I finished my sandwich. Licked my fingers. "Eventually, it made her lose her mind. My father had to put her in a sanatorium. She didn't get out until I was seven."

You looked at me with fearful eyes. "What was her dream?"

"I was all grown up, apparently, and there was another war on, and…" I looked at you, the way the wind moved your hair around, and I laughed. "I don't know why I'm telling you this."

"Tell me."

I hesitated. "She told the doctors she knew how I was going to die. She kept seeing me die, over and over." I wiped my fingers on my trousers. "Of course it's all ridiculous."

"How did you die?"

"She really couldn't talk about it to me, which made me think it couldn't have been that bad." I paused, bad memories slipping in. "But my father told me once."

"What is it?"

"It's really stupid."

Your eyes started to glare. "You have to tell me now."

I nodded. "Fine." I paused. "I was shot by my own men."

"Shot by your own men?"

"That's what she told the doctors. That's what he said."

"'Same men' as in beneath you or on the same side as you?"

"I have no idea. Probably the second one, based on how she acted."

"How did she act?"

I frowned. If this was what I had to share to get an easy ride out of Crespières, so be it. "We had nothing to live on after Father was killed. Mother had no skills. It was horrible." I paused. Where was she, I wondered? How was she doing without me? I hadn't really thought of her since the war started. Honestly, I was better off. "I knew what it would mean for me to go to war. What it would mean for her. Financially. Emotionally. But I didn't want to enlist. I wanted to run after I got drafted, but..." I frowned. "She would've turned me in. I knew she would've. She's such a patriot. The shame alone..." I shook my head. "I really had no choice."

You listened intently, sensitively. "Considering how your father died, I don't blame her."

I looked off. No comment.

"You've actually killed people?" you asked. "Nazis, I mean. Not people."

I nodded.

"How many?"

"Nazis?" I stopped to count. "Seventeen. No, sorry, sixteen."

"Sixteen?"

"Sixteen Nazis."

You hesitated asking. "What was it like?"

I took a deep breath. "Quite satisfying." And with that, I ended our lunch break. We continued our walk and said nothing serious for the rest of the day.

The next day, after walking around the camp some more, we spent the night in the mess hall having dinner with the rest of the Resistance boys. You introduced me to all your brothers. I had been hearing their names every day for a week straight, and I was happy to finally see their faces. Scragg. Blaise. Durant. Coste. Roul and Émile were there too, though they said nothing to me but pleasantries.

I noticed Roul in particular studying me from across the room. I thought he was just being territorial, protecting his surrogate daughter. I did the maths. His little girl would've been your age had she survived the Flu. But I had never suspected he was still suspicious of me not being SOE. He wouldn't have heard back from the Brits so soon about my tag number. Of course I didn't realise he had direct contact with SOE and knew instantly I wasn't one of them. But he never let on. I truly thought I was in the clear in that regard.

At the end of the night, after you helped me into bed and read me some Apollinaire, I asked you to stay behind a bit. "I didn't want to say anything before," I whispered. "But the reason I need to deliver that letter…" I made awkward eye contact with you. "Remember that pub fight I was in?"

"With Captain Bütz? Of course."

I smiled. Oh, that brain of yours! I loved it. I still do. "Well, I went a little too far with it. I chased him out with his gun, and…" I hesitated. "I thought I was shooting at him, but I ended up hitting someone else."

"Another Nazi?"

"A civilian." I hesitated. "Remember Corey Baxter? That American I told you about?"

"Jacques's master?"

"Yeah."

You stared at me, adding all the pieces. "You killed him?"

"It was an accident. His physician tried to save him, but he lost too much blood."

"Wait… Where did he get shot? Where did you shoot him?"

"In the back."

"In the *back?* That would take hours to die from."

"I carried him home. I'm sure he lost some blood on the way. I wasn't looking. I couldn't. You know."

"Why didn't you just take him to the hospital?"

"I wanted to. He kept insisting not too." I couldn't believe I was telling you that. What was wrong with me? "He and his butler were hiding something, Nadine. Mostly his butler, but… Corey was protecting him. Now that he's gone, Jacques is in danger. That letter of his was a series of instructions for Victor to help him escape. I was supposed to hand-deliver it to him in New York and tell him the words 'Olive Branch.'"

You furrowed your brow at that one. "'Olive Branch'?"

"I can't understand it either. Jacques said Victor wouldn't accept it otherwise. Bit of a hermit, apparently." I looked at you. "Does that mean anything to you? Is it some Resistance codeword or something?"

You shook your head definitively. "But why would he ask *you* to do all that? You the one that shot his…" Your eyes widened slightly.

My eyes drooped. I felt seen. I felt judged.

"He didn't know, did he?" you asked, my reaction already confirming it. "You didn't tell him."

I shook my head. "How could I?"

"You were in his house for *hours* and you never told him you were the one that shot his master?"

"I wanted to. There just wasn't a good time."

You took a deep, uneasy breath. You were still sympathetic to me. You understood who I was. I wasn't a bad person. I wasn't self-serving. Our time together helped you realise that. "But what has Jacques done exactly? Why is he in danger?"

I had no intention of telling you that. Jacques never meant to reveal that to me when he showed me the photo. He didn't expect me to recognise that Nazi. But I had to tell you something. "I have a theory about that. He has all these boxes in his house. Crates he had shipped, everything mostly unopened. He showed me a few. One is nothing but letters. And he showed me a photo too. He had it taken in Berlin, before the war. It was him, Corey, Victor, a whole bunch of other people… and a Nazi."

You stared at me. "A Nazi? In a photo with a Negro?"

"Let's just say he was a very controversial Nazi."

"Aren't they all?"

"Hitler had him killed. That makes him especially controversial."

You licked your lips. "You're saying the Nazis would kill Jacques because he knew that other Nazi?"

"It's why I can't go back for another letter. It would draw too much attention on him. He's probably in hiding right now, waiting for Victor's instructions to come to pass."

You hesitated. "There's something you're not telling me about all this."

"There's a lot I'm not telling you. I promised to protect his privacy."

You frowned at that. "So why doesn't he just flee Paris himself? He's one man. He can do it."

"The boxes are coming too, apparently. There's a lot of them, too much for one man to take away safely."

You scoffed. "That's ridiculous. If he's in that much danger, he'd only take the essentials, or better yet leave them all behind."

"That picture was taken in "27. That's not nothing."

"So let me get this straight… You're really running away from this war to go to New York to help a man move his things?"

I sat up sternly. "That picture was from Weimar days, Nadine, *long* before the war. Nazis love destroying Weimar things. Jacques has to protect it. I bet most of those boxes aren't even his. He promised to protect them too." I paused. "Just like I promised to keep that letter safe. It's not just a man and his things, Nadine. It's the man I put in danger. And those "things' are the only things he's got left. It's proof that old world even existed. A simpler time. When those men and women were still alive, still together. The rest of those boxes probably have books, documents, diaries, photos, private possessions, things the Nazis would destroy it a heartbeat. Protecting them now is the only thing giving him hope. Hope that someday the world can go back to the way it was."

You frowned. Looked away. Realised your shame.

I scooted closer to you. "I really don't think I'm asking for much. Just a ride to a friendly port. That's all."

"I may not always obey Roul, but that doesn't mean I'd ever directly disobey the Resistance." You rubbed the back of your neck. "I-I want to. I do. I know how hard this war has been for you. What it's done to you. Of course I sympathise. But I can't drive you anywhere. I'm sorry."

I sighed. That was all I could do. It was all I had. It didn't work.

You tried a smile. "Roul put your tag number out on the wireless. He said he should be hearing back about it tomorrow."

I got chills down my spine. "Tomorrow?" I asked, trying to hide my fear.

You nodded, completely oblivious to the turmoil going on inside me. "As long as you are who you say you are, I don't see why I can't help you plan a route to New York. I happen to know a lot about the refugee network. I know all the shortcuts. I can help you with that, at least. For Jacques's sake."

I lowered my head. "Thanks."

"Of course." You tilted your head down, looking me in the eyes.

I saw you looking. I looked uneasily back at you.

You leaned in and kissed me on the cheek. And then you gave me a new smile, one I hadn't seen before. A flirty little girly one. "Good night." You got up and left to retire.

I couldn't sleep the whole night. I just laid in bed. Eyes wide open. Scared beyond my wits.

CHAPTER TEN

Do No Harm

You were late the next morning. I knew what that meant. Roul had learnt the truth behind the dog tag number I gave him. I had to anticipate your reaction. What you were going to say. What'd you expect me to say, downplay, *et cetera*. It was awful, that anticipation. Knowing a confrontation was approaching. But I thought it all through. I was prepared the moment you walked in with that piece of paper.

You stood at the foot of my bed, your fingers dragging along that crinkled paper, and just stared at me.

I tried to appear ignorant of what you had written down. Little did I know, I actually was. "What, no breakfast?" I quipped.

"What did it say?" you asked me coldly. What a loaded gun of a question.

"I don't know what you're talk—"

"Yes, you do." You gave me a hefty pause. "What did it say?"

I inhaled softly. "Does it say I'm dead? Or MIA?"

And you hesitated. You weren't expecting me to know, that's for sure. "MIA."

I nodded casually. "Good. Mother would've been so worried. She's already been through enough heartbreak."

You folded the paper. Hid it behind your back. Your eyes looked off. "What date?"

"June 4th, 1940." I crossed my arms. "The evacuation of Dunkirk."

You didn't nod. I thought at the time it was you feeling bad for doubting me. For daring to question my word. "So you were there."

"I was."

You wiped your brow. Gathered your thoughts. "When you first told Roul you were SOE, he didn't believe you."

"I figured."

"Because he's been talking to SOE. I didn't even know what that was when you told us. I wasn't allowed to know. But I do now. Roul just told me.

89

They're not due to drop into France until May. Once they're here, they'll organise the Resistance, gather intel on the ground, plan sabotage operations… which means they'll absolutely know how to speak French."

My heart raced a bit, but I shrugged it off. "I said what I said."

"I know. Roul believes you now."

I froze in my bed. "Good," I said, trying desperately to figure out why, how.

You unfolded the paper in your hands. "He did some snooping and found out something." You read the first name on the list. "Does the name '*Leutnant* Dietrich' mean anything to you?"

I deflated into a toxic cloud of anger. I'm sure my face gave me away.

You bumped your brows. "That's a yes." You read the next one down. "What about *Hauptmann* Ebersbacher? *Hauptmann* Beckenbauer? *Leutnant* Aben—?"

"How did you find out about them?" I interrupted, feeling the betrayal.

"Roul listens to Nazi wireless traffic. He has access to police reports. Of course he figured it out. He knows there's a side of SOE he's not supposed to know about, and that's killing Nazi officers off the books."

I tightened my lip. I couldn't even look at you. "That's not—"

"So what? Did you deliberately leave yourself behind at Dunkirk? Did you assume the identity of someone who did? That's Roul's theory." You stared me down with unblinking eyes. "So I'll ask you again. Were you or were you not at Dunkirk on June 4th, 1940?"

"I was!"

"Then how do you explain this?!" You showed me what you had written down on that sheet of paper. "Sixteen Nazi officers over the last five months killed under suspicious circumstances. Stabbed in their bedroom. Shot in their auto. In the whorehouse. Places that don't make sense. Look how far back it goes." You pointed to the name at the top. "*Leutnant* Dietrich. Killed on leave, only 35 kilometres from Dunkirk. THREE MONTHS after the evacuation. We cross-referenced all the locations using the map in Roul's office. It forms a trail, a one-man trail from start to finish. This was you, wasn't it? All of it?"

I clenched my jaw.

"Sixteen Nazis. That's how many you told me you killed. Sixteen. Actually, you said seventeen at first, then changed it to sixteen. That Nazi you were in that pub fight with in Paris, *Hauptmann* Bütz. Was that why you started it? Was he supposed to be number seventeen?"

I shook my head, furious at you, actually hating you at that moment. "He was supposed to have been number *one*." I finally looked at you, my glaring eyes meeting yours. "*SS-Hauptsturmführer* Kronthaler was number seventeen."

You looked at the bottom of the list. There he was.

"It was over," I grumbled. "I was done. But then I saw Bütz alive in Paris, all happy and *breathing* and I lost it, alright? You know the rest. He gave me the bruise. I chased him out of there. I rounded the corner and shot Corey Baxter in the back. I never LIED to you, Nadine! And the fact that you'd think I would is just…" I grimaced. Shook my head.

You softened a bit. "I always thought you were some Private nobody, scrubbing latrines and shooting birds in your spare time. You never told me you were a secret government assassin!"

"It's a lot more complicated than that!"

"Is it? You knew what you were doing in France this whole time, information you conveniently left out in your attempts to sway me into helping you run away—"

"I'm not running away!"

"Do you plan on coming back from New York?"

William hesitated. "I'm not thinking that far ahead."

"We're in the middle of a war! If you want to desert, desert on your own. I'm not helping you."

"I'm saving Jacques's life, Nadine! I put him in that shit! I need to get him out of it!"

"He's one man, William. What you're doing here is more important than that. The people you're killing have the blood of millions on their hands. Millions of Frenchmen. Millions of Englishmen. You're doing something no one else can do. Why would you run away from that?!"

"THAT'S NONE OF YOUR *FUCKING* BUSINESS!" I screamed. "*THAT'S* WHY!"

Tears built in your eyes. "None of my business?" you asked harshly. "Last summer, a group of Nazis raided my farm. We weren't a secret Jew-hiding house or some military aide. We were just dairy farmers. Our only crime was living in Nancy, a few hundred kilometres from the German border. They had nothing to gain from harassing us, but they did. You know what they did? They took my father, Claude Sauvageot, put him up against the wall and shot him in the head. Right there in front of his wife and sons." Your lip quivered. "And then they took my brother Pierres and… They shot them one by one. All of them. Paschal. Thierri. And they saved my mother for last, Monique. Monique Sauvageot." Your breath wavered. I remember how sickening it was seeing your throat bobbing like that.

I couldn't move. I remember my eyes drooping, a cold, dead feeling crawling along my skin. I really don't remember much after that. I do remember you curling up in the corner and crying for about an hour or two. Your face was crusted with dry tears by the end, your red eyes emotionally spent. I could feel you looking at me as I was staring out the window. You probably thought I was preoccupied with something, a tragedy of my own, something just as traumatic as yours. You probably thought you overstepped yourself. Was I replaying my father's murder? Was the state I was in all your fault?

You asked me if I still wanted breakfast, ever the nurse. I didn't answer. You left anyway. Made me breakfast. Returned with a new attitude. An apologetic one. You made sure to ask nonjudgemental questions, simple ones. What I was thinking. Why I wasn't eating. I didn't answer. I didn't say anything. I barely blinked, apparently. And you said I only said one thing. I barely remember doing that, but you said it felt like a stab in the gut. Not a punch. A stab.

"I want to be alone."

You offered to read some poetry in the corner. Even silently. Just to keep me company. But I refused to look at you. I just kept staring out the window. And so you left.

You made me lunch a few hours later. You peaked into the cabin and saw me still in that same state, still staring out the window. My body hollowed out. You knew I could hear you out there, so you felt no problem with leaving my lunch outside the door and walking away.

Night came. You were too upset to do anything around the camp. You were too ashamed to talk to me. You didn't know what to do. When you took your smoke break, you realised the lunch tray you had left for me was still out there. I never got out of bed to look for food. You started getting worried. The way I got all quiet all of a sudden. How cold I was to you. How it was so unlike me. Something had to be wrong. Was my father's death the reason I wanted to stop killing Nazis? Ambushing them in bars? Brothels? Bedrooms? You realised you should've listened to my reasoning instead of just assuming you knew the whole story. And even if I did lie about my work with the Army, did that really mean I was automatically lying about everything else? About Jacques? Corey? Victor? You loved the connection we had, that brutal honesty between us. You wanted me to be a good person. I couldn't have been a two-faced liar. I couldn't have been a charlatan. I was just like you, wasn't I? You saw the darkest side of humanity before your very eyes, and even then you refused to believe I was evil, only pretending to be good. It was simply a matter of getting to the truth. Unearthing the real man inside of me. Sticking him up. Making him better again.

You told me later about the carrot you planned on feeding me: an offer to initiate the conversation between me and Roul regarding Jacques, a way for the Resistance to protect Jacques and his things as long as I stayed in France and fought the good fight. You thought, as long as I didn't want to assassinate Nazis anymore, that I'd stay there for you if you asked.

I wish you did, Nadine. If you had the chance to pitch that compromise to me, I would've said yes.

You threw away your cigarette, readjusted the strap of your rifle, and tenderly approached the hospital. I remember hearing your footsteps up to the door. You said you noticed the candle was lit inside, proof I was still alive, but you didn't want to peek in. You just opened the door. And you were about to say something. You couldn't remember what it was you were going to say. Because the sight of me hanging by a rope tied to the rafters was too much. I had just gone up there, having spent too many hours trying to figure out how to slide the rope out of that pulley system. You said my body was still twitching when you found me.

"OH MY GOD!" you cried. In French? English? You couldn't recall. Then you ran across the room, grabbed my kicking legs, and tried desperately to lift my body up, just long enough to get the bed back under me.

I remember coming to at that point. I remember gasping. But even I knew your grip was failing. I remember looking down at you, both your arms around my knees, lifting as hard as you could, your left leg jutting out, trying to hook under the bed.

I tried to tell you no. You claim I also said, "Please," but I don't remember saying that.

"Stop it," you muttered, inching the bed a little bit closer. Almost losing your grip again, you put your foot back down to restabilise and lifted my body higher. "You're going to be okay. I'm just getting the bed over."

"I'm sorry."

"It's okay. I'm just getting the bed over."

"I'm so sorry."

"I said it's fine! Just hold on!" With a deep breath, you heaved me high. Lifted your leg. Hooked the underside of the bed. Moved it closer. Got my right foot on the bed. It was my bad leg.

Life was filling its way back inside me. And it hurt. All of it. Life. It really, really hurts.

As you tried to catch your breath, you told me, "Just hold on, William. I'm going to move the rest of the bed over and then I'll help you down."

"No."

"I won't let you die, William."

"That's not my name."

I remember you looking up at my eyes. No doubt they were bloodshot, wide open with fear, with pain. "What?" you breathed.

"I'm not William Gunnison," I whined, my throat hurting. "My name is Wilhelm Gunter." I could feel tears streaking down my cheeks. "I'm a Nazi."

You stared. Horrified. Shook your head.

"I knew I recognised you from somewhere. Today I finally remembered…" I had to gargle my throat. Tried readjusting my right foot. Ended up putting more weight on it. "I was there. In Nancy. My platoon was the one that killed your family."

As ill as you felt, you couldn't look away from my horrible eyes.

You said my face contorted as I rasped, "I'm so sorry, Nadine," and that I was about to say something else when my right foot slipped off the bed. The frame slid away. You told me I was choking violently. My legs kicking around. My fingers clawing at my noose, suddenly filled with an urge to live, to explain.

But you didn't want me to live. In that moment, watching me struggle like that, you said you felt a darkness inside you. You wanted me to die. You were going to let me die. You saw your father's face. Your mother's. Your brothers', Pierre, Paschal and Thierri's. All of them, just before they were shot. You felt an awful, twisted tingle in your body. Something you never felt before. You couldn't understand it. But you knew instantly it didn't belong. It wasn't you.

"Oh *fuck*," you groaned as you unstrapped your rifle. Locked a bullet into the chamber. Aligned your crosshairs with the line above my head. Pulled the trigger.

The rope split instantly. The bullet ricocheted off the wall as I fell to the ground. Landed on my good leg, thank God. I was on the ground, writhing, suddenly able to breathe again. Gasping hard for air. A series of short, loud hacks.

And you just watched me like that, a disappointed frown on your face, shaking your head a bit. You ejected the casing, put the rifle down, and helped me off the floor.

In our long recount of that night, neither one of us could agree how long we sat in silence before we started talking again. I thought it was only an hour. You swore it was more. Either way, we sat on opposite sides of the bed, me on the left, you on the right, facing away from each other, back-to-back, our bodies hunched over. I kept rubbing my sore neck. I broke the silence first. "Why did you save me?" It wasn't out of gratitude. It was an accusation.

You were holding the back of your neck too, staring off into space. "I don't know," you said slowly. "Probably because I'm weak and can't bear to let a man die when I have the opportunity to save them." I remember being hurt by your word choice there. "Or maybe I just wanted answers. One rarely gets the opportunity to… you know, actually get answers. Not to mention you owe me. A bit."

"I owe you?"

"If you died, who was going to save Jacques?"

I closed my eyes. I admit, I hadn't been thinking about him at all. "So you believe me about Jacques?"

"You just confessed to being one of the Nazis that shot my family. If that doesn't make you the most honest person in the world—"

"I never said I shot them," I corrected sternly. "All I said was that I was there."

You hesitated at that. "You didn't kill any of them?"

"No." But that didn't feel right to say. "Not directly at least."

You didn't know how to interpret that. "So who did?"

I took a deep breath. "*Schütze* Ebert Konstantin and *Gefreiter* Emil Landoberct, they're both dead now… and our commanding officer, *Leutnant* Adalwolf Bütz."

You turned your head around in shock. "Bütz was your commanding officer?"

I nodded. "He's an absolute monster. You have no idea."

"I have some idea."

"No. You do not." I refused to elaborate. I'd already done enough to you. "His father's an *SS-Gruppenführer*. That means he can get away with anything. And we knew what would happen if we didn't go along. So we said nothing. In Belgium, he got us not to judge. To encourage. Participate even. All throughout the madness, I told myself, 'I can do this. This is fine.' I bought the bullshit. I ate it up. I had to." I closed my eyes. I hated the pictures I saw. "Somewhere down the line, after we got into France, I stopped participating. Then I stopped encouraging. Then I started judging." I opened my eyes. Rolled my lips. "Then I stopped altogether."

I could hear you were still listening. Your breathing was nice and slow.

"I tried to make up for it," I continued. "One German officer for every civilian he forced me to shoot. Seventeen total. Any time an officer came to France for R&R—a *Hauptmann*, *Leutnant*, something more, whatever it'd be—I was there. Five months it took me to get to seventeen, but I made it, just after the new year. I was finally free. Free to wait out the rest of the war in Paris like a normal person. In plain sight no less." I pointed to my clothes, still folded on the chair. "Wearing Dietrich's jacket and Ebersbacher's cap."

You looked over at them too.

"I swore I would never hurt a civilian again," I said. "But I did. I saw Bütz and got Corey Baxter killed. Now his butler's in danger because of me, and…" I turned around to look at you. You instantly turned away. "And of all the people to save me, it was you. Whose future I took away. Whose family I couldn't save."

You closed your eyes when I said that.

"Nadine," I whimpered. "I've spent my whole life standing by and doing nothing. I've seen too many people get killed, *and worse*. I didn't do a thing to save them. Now I have a chance, a real chance, to go above and beyond to save someone. So above and so beyond. I need to take it. For once in my life, I actually have a chance to make things right for somebody."

You heartlessly rolled your lips together. "You've always had a chance. You've had so many chances."

"Nadine."

"I saved you for *Jacques's* sake." You finally looked at me. No sympathy in sight. "Of course I think it's noble you're willing to go all the way to New York to rectify what you did to him. I always have. But don't think for one second that that makes up for all the times you didn't."

I frowned, wounded by your words. "That's your opinion. I understand."

"Let me finish." You stood. "My family might not have been one of your precious seventeen, but they're all still dead because of you. Every person Bütz and Konstantin and Landoberct killed are still dead because of you. You never stopped them. You never stood up to them. Not once. *And you could have.* You had a gun. They never would've seen it coming. It would've worked."

I tried hard not to cry at that. "I know."

"So why didn't you? I saved your life. I certainly didn't have to. I certainly didn't *want* to." You didn't mean to tell me that. It wasn't true. You just wanted to hurt me. "But I did. It wasn't that hard."

"It's not that simple. They had guns too. You don't understand—"

"I'm not discussing this anymore. Not with you. Good night." You turned and left.

In the silence of that empty room, I let out a sombre whisper: "Good night, Nadine."

CHAPTER ELEVEN

Judgement Call

In-person breakfast and conversation had been replaced the next morning by a cold tray and three hard knocks on the door. By the time I got up there, you were already gone. I was hurt by you doing that. I felt the loss of your presence, your companionship. Believe me, I had no idea who you were before you told me about Nancy. I never misled you. I wasn't trying to flee this world out of guilt. I simply wanted an uncomplicated death. That way you'd never know the truth. That way you'd always remember me the way I really was, as William Gunnison. But now you know the horrible truth, the Wilhelm Gunter truth, the worst lie of my life. I don't blame you for hating me. I just wish I never lived to see what had happened to you after Nancy. What my cowardice, my inability to speak up, had done to you. How trapped you were in this new life you longed to escape from. How alone you were surrounded by soldiers.

In another life, I know we would've been the best of friends. Maybe even something more, I feel. But fate has brought us together twice now, once for destruction, and once more as a tease, what could've been, what had been, before revealing what had always been. Believe me, the realisation hurt me just as much as it hurt you.

After so many days depending on conversation, poetry, words fluttering freely without the use of a filter, the constant need to keep secrets, I was alone again. I was a soldier again. I stood by the window at lunchtime, hungry for just a passing glimpse of you. I did find you, thank God. You were sitting by the pond just beyond your makeshift mess hall. The sun shimmering off the water. I knew you were thinking about me, what you had just found out the night before. It must've been too much for you to process on your own. I so wanted to go over there and help you. Answer all those questions you had buzzing around your head. But part of me wanted you to forgive me on your own. I held onto faith that you would.

I saw Roul walk up to you. Sit beside you. I could sense it was a significant moment in both of your lives. How could it not have been? You'd tell me later that Roul started by apologising for putting you in such a situation, assigning you to interrogation honeypot duty instead of your usual tasks. You didn't join the Resistance to become a spy, muddling the line between nurse and soldier.

You loved hearing that, the way it was so unprompted. And you allowed yourself to open up to him, the way you had been allowing yourself to open up to me. You told him your fight to free France wasn't the same as the others'. Roul, Scragg, Durant, everyone, they all had wives, girlfriends, fiancées, children, futures, careers waiting for them when the war ended. But you had nothing. No family. No home. No future. You told Roul you needed something more to fight for, something concrete to actually win back.

And Roul opened up to you in that sensitive moment in a way he hadn't before, revealing he intended to try for another kid when the war's over, and if he were to be blessed with a girl, he'd want that girl to be just like you. And he went on, you said, listing all the good things you brought to the camp. Physically fixing many of them. All the civilian lives you saved from nearby skirmishes, earning your stripes on the fly like that. And your emotional impact as well. Making them all laugh. Reminding them all of the happier times. And he acknowledged how much smarter you were compared to the rest of them, how you brought them up to your level, the same way you said your mother had brought up your father. You fixed them, he said. And he insisted your "family," those Resistance men, really were your family. They'd never throw you aside when the war ended. Those relationships were forged for life.

I know that meant a lot for you to hear. It gave you the confidence you needed to forge the thorny troubles I had brought upon you. It gave you to courage to be in the same room with me again, back to the nurse you were at the start. But nothing else. No more casual conversation. No more vulnerable sharing. Just a nurse treating her patient. You had no interest in connecting with me anymore. That stung. It really did. But I didn't pry. I didn't stir. I allowed you to undo the bond we had built.

You checked my neck, pressed hard fingers along my noose-line. I swallowed. "I should probably be going soon," I said.

"I don't think so," you murmured. "You might've broken something."

"It really doesn't hurt—"

"I'm the nurse. I say you might've broken something." You gave me an impersonal glance. "I think you should stay another week, just to be sure."

I knew, looking at your eyes, that that was a lie. You told Roul. I could tell you did. And he ordered you to keep me there. "Really, I'm fine," I said with a cordial smile. "My leg's better. I really shouldn't be bothering you anymore."

"It's no bother."

"Even still—"

"It doesn't hurt to stay." You stood up. Re-strapped your rifle. "And I feel it's important to remind you that there's seven of us and only one of you. You're not likely to outrun us."

I forced a chuckle, but I understood the message. I was trapped.

The next day I thought I was in for the same treatment, the cold Resistance nurse downplaying the calvary already on its way, the trap already laid out for me. But to my surprise, I saw the same Nadine I had grown to admire watching me from across that room.

I tried not to say anything, but I couldn't resist. I made a joke about your threat the previous night.

You didn't comment on it. You simply spoke, and I remember every word you told me. I still replay it from time to time. "I don't really think about that day anymore," you started. "It used to be all I ever thought about. I simply can't anymore. Not because it's too painful to, it's… It's just been over-examined. That's all. Plus I'm happier when I don't." You paused. "Lately I've been thinking about it again. Not by choice, of course."

I nodded.

"Roul reminded me yesterday that, when he first found me, I was wracked with guilt of my own. I blamed myself for not doing more to save my family. I had the opportunity. They never saw me. I could've ambushed them if I wanted to. That might've saved one of them at least." You stepped closer to the bed. Thought twice before sitting on the mattress, right there by my feet. "But I would've been shot. Roul helped me accept that. And he rerouted my guilt into the Resistance itself. It was a way for me to avenge them safely, a way I never had at the time. And I'm stronger now because of that. I know I am." You nodded gently. "All this to say I'm sorry for what I told you that night. I shouldn't have been blaming you for not saving them. I couldn't even do it myself."

I smiled from your support. You actually understood what I meant to say. I didn't even have to force you there.

Then you looked me in the eye. "But then I remembered something else. Something I always blocked out." You hesitated telling me. "When Father first saw Nazis walking towards our farm, he told Mother and I to hide in the barn, quickly, before any of them could see us. I ran in to hide in the hay, but Mother refused to follow me. I think she realised what Father was doing, that doing so would run the risk of her never seeing him again. Doomed to a life without him. So she stayed behind to stand with her husband. At least that's what I assume. I don't know for sure. I just… I just did what I was told. From the barn, I could hear them rounding them all up, those men speaking that awful language. I was worried they would search the barn next. I had no real place to hide in there. I just stayed where I was and prayed. I prayed and I prayed that God would spare me somehow. And then the barn door opened and a Nazi was standing there with a gun in his hands. He saw me instantly. Pointed his gun at me. Stared me deep in my eyes. And I felt such a fear take over me. I couldn't move, I just… stayed there. It must've been an entire minute, that man standing there, that gun pointed at me. Until at last, he shouted some German to the men behind him and lowered his gun. Then he walked out. Left the barn door open. And there was this awful silence afterwards. I crawled out of that hay. Walked to the door. Poked my head out. The Nazi was right there, standing just outside the door. Waiting for me. I would've screamed if I wasn't so afraid he'd see me. But as I moved past him, I could've sworn he did see me. As if… as if he was pretending *not* to see me. That's how I was able to get away. None of the other soldiers knew I was in that barn. They weren't looking for me at all. It was too easy of an escape."

I said nothing. I just stared back. No expression.

Your eyes drooped a bit. "That was you, wasn't it?"

I looked away. "It doesn't matter."

"'It doesn't matter'?! Of course it matters! It makes all the difference in the world!"

"Which is why I didn't tell you." I frowned. "I don't deserve blanket absolution. Like you said, your family still died and I never even considered their deaths to be on my hands. There were hundreds more, Nadine. Hundreds I never shot but still let die. Hundreds of men and women with plans just like you. Who were just as smart as you. Full of ambition and hope and drive, just like you were. They loved and made sacrifices, just like you did. And your brothers. And your parents. All those men I killed, those seventeen Nazi officers, they all had sons. Those sons lost their father, just like I had. My father's death ruined my mother. It ruined me. It ruined both our lives. But what did I do? I went and did that to *other* people, for no other reason than to make up for what I did to *other* other people. None of them did anything to me personally. They didn't deserve that fate." I sighed. "Deep down, I guess a part of me is just using Olive Branch as an excuse to run away from all this. This life. Why I'm trying so hard to pretend to be someone I'm not. But what's the point? Guaranteeing Jacques's safety won't be enough to undo all the damage I've done to this world."

You took my hand, startling me with your kindness. "How many others did you save?"

I hesitated. "It doesn't matter."

"How many?"

"I never kept track."

"Give me a range."

I didn't respond at first. "At least thirty. I don't know."

You nodded at that. "I've saved at least a hundred and fifty lives in the last seven months. I am the only one in this area who knows how to do what I do. If you had let me die in Nancy, there wouldn't have been another around here to save them. That means you saved them too, by saving me. And I've healed people in other ways. Roul, Durant, Scragg, everyone. They've all been bettered by my being here, which never would've happened if not for you. One person is not nothing. And you saved thirty."

I looked up at you, trying not to cry.

You smiled back. "You're not a Nazi, William," you whispered. "You might've acted like a Nazi for a time, but you were never one in your heart. Nazis don't care about people. Nazis don't try to save civilian lives. Nazis don't kill Nazi officers. Nazis don't get shot at by Nazis. You stopped being a Nazi a long time ago."

My lips fluttered. "Do you really believe that?"

"If you're just a Nazi, then I'm just a nurse." You shrugged. "As much as we all like to think so, we can never know everything about a person. Just because they seem like they're one thing doesn't mean they are. No matter what you've done, no matter how long it's taken you to get to this point, you're still on our side, William. All those men I saved only got saved because of you. You saved so many lives and didn't even know it. And I know saving Jacques might seem like nothing to you now. With this war going on all around us, one person's life can look quite small and worthless. But one life saved is still an act of good. And acts of good can only bring about more good. That's what the world needs right now."

I smiled sweetly. "So you're helping me after all?"

Your expression turned suddenly. "Yeah, about that..." You scratched your nose. "Yesterday I told Roul you weren't SOE. That you were acting as courier for Corey Baxter and you were on your way to New York City when you stepped on that landmine."

My heart dropped. "You did?"

You nodded. "Also that you asked me to help you get there somehow."

My mouth went dry. "That's all you said?"

"That's all I said. Nothing about Jacques or Victor or the fact that Corey's dead. None of that."

"Alright."

"So now he no longer thinks you're SOE. Sorry." You let out a sigh. "But he thought 'Baxter' sounded familiar, so he looked it up. Turns out the Baxter family is one of the Nazi's top coal suppliers. This war has made them very wealthy."

I was so confused. I thought Corey Baxter was an alias. How could that be? "So Roul thinks I'm a Nazi courier?"

"Yes." You paused. "Of course it's possible you're telling the truth about Olive Branch *and* Corey was a prominent Nazi sympathiser, but I don't think he'd have a Negro butler if that was the case."

I shook my head. "No, he wouldn't."

"And it would explain how Corey having Jacques in his employ acted as a form of protection for him. Not to mention it proves Corey Baxter was real to begin with."

"He certainly was."

You went quiet again. "My orders are to keep you here and not tell you anything about the reinforcements we have coming to take you away to a POW camp."

I stared. "For Germans?"

"I never told him you were German. He'd kill you on the spot. That wasn't my job. My job was to save you." You paused. "But when you get there, it won't take them long to figure out what you really are. Mark my words, they will. And then they'll kill you."

I swallowed nervously. "When will they be here?"

"Tomorrow morning." You scratched the top of your head. "I can't let them take you."

I furrowed my brow. "Nadine."

"It might not be the right decision, but it's my decision to make and I'm making it. I cannot in good conscience allow them to hurt you for what you're doing for Jacques. And the rest of it. Every Nazi should be doing what you're doing. We need to encourage that, not punish them for it."

"But Roul, won't he—?"

"I think I've built enough credit in this place to actually spend it on something." You looked at me gently. Caressed the hair on the back of my head. "It's my duty as a human being to help you keep your promise to Jacques."

I had to hug you. I was so moved by you doing that for me. And you hugged me back, and I felt your warmth. I felt genuinely loved by you, just as I was.

CHAPTER TWELEVE

Refugee

We spent the rest of the day planning. We were going to take the second auto the next day, the one Coste had just finished repairing, and you were going to drive me all the way to Marseilles, where a great man by the name of Varian Fry would hide me in his safehouse, the Villa Air-Bel, until it was time for me to be smuggled out. He would then take me across the border to Spain, where another man, an associate of Fry's, would take me to the Unitarian Service Committee in Lisbon, Portugal. There, I'd wait in safety for an exit visa and whatever necessary papers I'd need to gain passage across the sea to New York City.

As airtight as that plan sounded, I asked you to draft an alternate route, just in case something went wrong. That was more than likely in those days. You insisted it would never happen, but I insisted harder, so you came up with a more roundabout path, one that veered outside Fry's influence.

The out-of-network backup plan was as follows: I would buy a standard ticket in Marseilles to sail across the Mediterranean to Oran. Once there, I'd take a train or auto (or worst-case just walk) 800 kilometres east to Casablanca in unoccupied French Morocco. There, I'd have to wait for an exit visa for who knows how long, but once I did, I'd catch a direct plane to Lisbon and go to the USC myself, dropping Fry's name to get the same paperwork as before.

The last thing we did together as nurse and patient involved my leg. You double-checking to make sure it was safe for me to be discharged. Which cane was the best for me. What I should take in case of pain or fatigue. And you read me one last Apollinaire, I recited one last Rilke, and you wished me goodnight. I slept well despite our escape being so soon. Our escape or my capture, whichever happened first.

I woke with a start at the sight of Scragg sitting beside my bed with a gun. He was smiling at me.

"Where's Nadine?" I asked in English, in a daze.

Scragg rattled off some French. And he rattled for a while, no doubt a clever monologue he thought I could partially comprehend. I would later find out the whole story. He had been originally assigned to join you on a newspaper delivery run to Orléans, one you had insisted on taking alone, and you had asked him to assume your role as my guard instead. Of course I couldn't comprehend if that was in fact what he was telling me. I simply watched him with an uneasy look. That seemed to have made Scragg more comfortable than if I had just stared at him blankly.

After about ten minutes of nonstop French chatter, Scragg noticed a full cafetière of coffee sitting by the sink. He asked me a question, what I had assumed to be in the lines of, "Did you make this?"

I simply shook my head.

Scragg nodded with satisfaction. Grabbed himself a cup. Poured himself some coffee. Took a nice big sip. Gave me a nasty smile. And then he slumped out of his chair, both eyes rolling back, landing face-first on the floor. Scalding hot coffee got everywhere, but he didn't react or anything. He was out.

I couldn't believe it. He blindly drank it, just like you said he would.

I double-checked for witnesses and sprang into action. I checked to make sure there was nothing you forgot to take with you. My jacket. My cap. My roll of francs. My new cane. All good. And then I fought through the pain as I waddled towards Scragg's anaesthetized body. Bent down. Removed his garments as fast as I could. Once he was naked, I slipped off my burlap sack bedgown and put it on Scragg. Dragged his body step by step over to the bed. Tucked him in. Positioned his face away from the door. Then I put on his clothes. It was just about my size, just like you said it would be. And with the donning of Scragg's cap, my disguise complete, I was ready to leave. I threw a salute to sleeping Scragg and left the cabin on my own volition.

I took my time walking to the garage, where I saw you were waiting for me. A few of your brothers-in-arms nodded at me, greeting me as if I were Scragg, and I did everything just as Scragg would've done, just like we rehearsed. Everyone knew you and Scragg were assigned to go to Orléans together, Durant assigned to be my guard. They didn't know you changed the plans just that morning, discreetly telling Roul that Scragg was flirting too much again, that he made you uncomfortable, that you'd very much prefer to go to Orléans alone. And Roul did exactly what you asked him to do:

he told Durant, and only Durant, that Scragg was going to watch the prisoner instead. Durant was free to join Roul on perimeter duty.

I hid in the back of auto with the newspapers as you drove us to the perimeter of the camp. You stopped at the gate and waved up at Roul and Durant. They saw you were driving alone, just as they had expected you to be, and they waved back at you. And so, you drove on. Only after a kilometre of road did you allow me to resurface. You pulled off to the side of the road and parked. I got out and changed back into my old clothes. You folded Scragg's in a neat pile. I checked my pockets. The roll of francs was still there, all one thousand. The only thing you couldn't grab was my Luger. I understand why. You never could've gotten it past Roul. It would've drawn too much on myself in Marseilles anyway. Firearms are illegal, remember.

I hopped into the passenger's seat and you drove on, avoiding Orléans entirely. If someone had already found Scragg in my bed instead of me, Orléans would've been the first to be notified, their orders to arrest us on arrival. If there was a world of chaos going on back at Crespières, we weren't aware. That made it easier for both of us to defect.

In those eight hours on the road to Marseilles, we talked about so many things. There really was nothing left to hide for the first time. No secrets. No shades. So we let it all out. We recapped those two weeks we shared but from our true points of view. Clarifying how much was real. How much was an act. To our mutual relief, the parts we wanted most to be real were real all along. You told me what Roul told you beside the lake. I told you what it was like to live in Germany during the rise of fascism, forced to go along with such moronic ideology under the threat of death. And we were full of smiles, you and I. We couldn't say why. We did not dare. But I knew. I wish I could've stayed there forever, just the two of us driving on for hours. No threat behind us. No threat ahead of us. Just us. It was so nice.

We didn't reach Marseilles until after dark. You had trouble locating the Villa Air-Bel from memory, but you had a good feeling it was nearby. You stopped the auto and helped me out. It started to rain as we stood there, saying our goodbyes. And I did the one thing I told myself I wasn't going to do, knowing I'd regret it if I hadn't: I asked you to join me on my mission. I think a part of you wanted to say yes. You had left such a mess behind you with that treasonous act of yours. How tempting it was to desert, to leave that awful world behind, the one constantly reminding you of your trauma, the men determined to keep you pigeonholed as the nurse, the woman, the experienced honeypot. But alas, you took the honourable route. You declined my offer, vying instead to accept the consequences of your disobedience. To face the music.

We hugged each other one last time. I turned to walk down that pitch black road, hoping to find a neighbour to direct me to Fry, when I heard you say something. I turned back and asked you to repeat it.

"I never got the chance to thank you, so…" You shrugged. "Thank you."

"For what?"

You smiled enigmatically. "Saving my life."

I smiled back. Nodded. Walked on.

I know you stayed standing there a few minutes more. I could see you from across the way. But you ultimately left. You got back in the stolen auto and drove yourself back to Orléans. To deliver those papers. To allow yourself to get caught. I hope Roul forgave you the way you forgave me.

And I hope you can forgive me for getting caught the very next day, even after everything you did, everything you sacrificed, to get me there.

PART THREE

Wilhelm/William

CHAPTER THIRTEEN

Better to Say Nothing

Call it a curse, call it fate, I was not allowed to leave Marseilles. Everything that could've gone wrong went wrong, one right after another, despite all my successful efforts to swerve the tide.

It took me about a half-hour to find someone that knew how I could get to the Villa Air-Bel, but I found it in the end. I knocked on the door of that dilapidated château and asked the man that answered to speak to Varian Fry. I mentioned your name, just the way you told me to, and the man himself emerged. His English wasn't great, not like yours, but he was clear enough to comprehend. "Unfortunately, we cannot leave at this time," he told me, standing at the door.

"What do you mean?" I asked him. "When can we leave?"

"Until it's safe."

I laughed at that. "There's a war on. France is a bit occupied right now."

"Under normal conditions, I can do. But the Nazis… they're cracking down. They're searching for a man, a… a-a trait-or. That is the word, yes? Trait-or?"

I nodded uneasily. "Yeah. Traitor."

"Killed many Nazis, apparently, this trait-or. A German too. You don't see many of them, no?"

I had a gross feeling in my gut. "No."

"No. See? So until they find this trait-or, I will not risk a ship. My operation stay going, yes? It need to stay going."

I took a deep breath. "How long will that be? If they don't find him, I mean. How long until they call off the search?"

Fry shrugged, stretching his mouth out, bobbing his head. "One month, maybe two. Big price on man's head, I hear. One million francs. Wouldn't be surprised if it goes until summer. Even then, you will have to wait your turn. I have at least three ships' worth of refugees in Marseilles before you."

I sighed harshly. "Is there a ticket counter still open somewhere?"

Fry personally drove me to a standard port in the main part of town, all those ships outside his aegis. The clerk Fry led me to was a rat-faced Frenchman half asleep in his own chair.

"One ticket to Oran, please," I told him, pulling out the roll of francs Jacques gave me.

"Everything's booked," the clerk said dryly. "Next available crossing won't be for three weeks."

Three weeks sure beats one to two months. "How much?"

"Four hundred francs." That price was gouged, either because of the occupation or that man's personal greed. Luckily for me, I had one thousand francs from Jacques. He must've anticipated a situation like this when he gave me so much for "boat fare."

I handed four hundred francs over to the clerk. The man noticed the rest of the roll in my hand, and suddenly he was quite alert and awake. "There *is* a boat leaving for Oran tomorrow morning," he said slyly. "It's fully booked, I'm afraid, but… for the rest of that roll, I can get you on."

I was appalled. How dare he take advantage of me like that. It still makes me sick to my stomach, but I had to weigh all the possible outcomes. The longer I stayed in Marseilles, the likelier I'd be caught by Bütz and sent back to Berlin. If I took the boat to Oran, I'd have to find some way to Casablanca and then another way out of Casablanca over to Lisbon, but at least I'd be in unoccupied territory. I'd have more options down there. "Alright," I told the clerk. "But I'm only giving you half now. You'll get the other half tomorrow morning."

The clerk didn't like that answer, but he begrudgingly accepted the terms. I handed over an additional three hundred francs and pocketed the rest. He wrote up a makeshift ticket and handed it over. He even made sure to circle the departure time: 7:00.

Fry drove me back to the Villa Air-Bel and let me stay the night. It was crowded in that château, and it reeked of body odour, but I was able to get some sleep.

I dreamt of you, if that matters.

The next morning, Fry drove me back to Vieux-Port. I thanked him profusely for his hospitality. I met that sleazy clerk at the dock, gave him the last of Jacques's roll as promised, and boarded the ship. He had an arrangement with the deckhands, apparently. The very expensive accommodations I had just booked was nothing more than a spot on the floor of the engine room, which was already filled with at least four dozen other dirty-faced, sullen refugees, the other victims of that clerk's greedy manipulations. There was a woman sitting close to me. She was young. Eighteen or nineteen. And she had long dishevelled brown hair. As I sat beside her, she gave me an uncomfortable glance. She looked like she hadn't eaten in weeks. I can't say what drew me to her. It might've been my lingering feelings for you. Your presence, I mean. Your company. Anyway, she reminded me of you. That's all. That's all I wanted to say.

The boat engine roared, making us all go deaf. We could feel the ship start moving ten minutes after 7. There were no windows in that room, so I couldn't see the sunrise, the view of France getting further and further away, that nice feeling of peace maritime travel is known to bring. Instead I looked at the faces of those pitiful refugees. Some of them were French. Some Eastern European. A few Poles. Czechoslovakians. Maybe a Russian or two. As I sat on the floor with both arms tight around my knees, I thought about my life going forward. I swore right there never to speak a word of German again, not even if it benefited me the way it did in Paris. Never again would I speak that awful language, even if it made me more suspicious. It was the least I could do. From that day on, William Gunnison no longer spoke German.

I looked over at that young woman sitting next to me. Her eyes were barely open. Her mind probably in some horrible place. Full of tragedy and misery. And I thought of you sitting by the pond with Roul, how sad you were until he sat next to you. And the way he inspired you, giving you confidence… and then you did the same for me. You inspired me. You gave me confidence. I couldn't help but feel the need to do my duty and pass that goodness along.

I leaned in. "Excuse me?" I asked her in English.

She looked up at me, her eyes wide and terrified.

"Oh, I'm sorry," I said with a chuckle. "Do you speak English?"

She nodded crooked. "Little. Hear better than speak."

"My name's William. What's yours?"

"My…?

"You name."

"My name? Elżbieta."

"What?"

"Elżbieta," she said slower. She put a hand to her chest. "Hungarian."

"It's alright. It's nice to meet you, Elżbieta."

"And you, William."

I smiled at her. Looked off. I could see her studying my face in my peripheral.

"Why you no scared?" she asked me.

I looked back at her. "Because I'm not." After a moment, I asked, "Guess that clerk stole your money too, huh?"

Elżbieta nodded sadly. "Bad man."

"Very." I looked to my left. To my right. Leaned in. "Listen," I whispered to Elżbieta. "Don't tell anyone this. Keep this to yourself, alright?"

Elżbieta nodded with a serious look on her face.

"You need to get to Lisbon. Doesn't matter how, just get there. And when you get there, look for the Unitarian Service Committee. USC. You understand?"

"USC," Elżbieta repeated.

"Good. When you get to the USC, tell them Varian Fry sent you. Alright? Varian Fry." I paused. "Will you remember all that?"

"Yes. Lisbon. USC. Varian F-fry."

"Yes, very good!" I said with a laugh. "Do all that, just like I told you, and they will give you a visa."

Elżbieta let out a warm sigh. "Thank you."

"Thank me when you get to America." I returned to my spot. Flashed her a knowing smirk. Closed my eyes. Let the engine rock me to sleep.

And of course the engines cut off right that very second. I opened my eyes. All the other squeeze-ins were confused too. Some spoke in anxious tones to each other. It all seemed so sudden. And nothing was smoking or fizzing. The ship had been deliberately stopped.

A crew member descended the stairs. Tenderly stepped his way through the crowd on the floor. I stood up. "What happened?" I asked. "Why did we stop?"

"A U-Boat ordered us to stop," the crew member said in a hurry. "They're boarding now. Excuse me." He made it to the opposite side the room. Opened the engine room door. Kept on walking.

I sat back down. Did they find out I was on the boat? How could they have? Was Bütz in Marseilles? Did someone recognise me? We couldn't have been that far into the Mediterranean.

Three pairs of boots descended the stairs. A few snickers preceded the faces of three Nazis, U-Boat crew members, each carrying large machine guns. "Oh, look," the first crew member teased in German, "refugees."

"Don't worry, little ones," the second one told us. "We're not on refugee duty right now. Else you'd be overboard."

"Let's just get the stuff and go," the third one scolded. No doubt their commanding officer. He seemed the type. He led the two others across the crowd, all of us flinching as they passed through.

I couldn't help but notice Elżbieta looking especially scared. I leaned in. "I don't think they're on refugee duty right now," I whispered in English, throwing in a humorous tone. "I'm sure they're just stripping the ship. We're not going overboard, don't worry."

Elżbieta nodded back, but she was giving me a strange look. It didn't mean anything to me at the time. Now it makes all the sense in the world.

The three Nazis left the room via the same exit as the ship's crew member. They returned fifteen minutes later, their guns strapped to their bodies, both arms full of technical equipment. Wires. Radios. Technical stuff. They marched upstairs, presumably handed everything to more men on the deck, and descended again for another round of stripping. The second Nazi stopped in his tracks as he passed me. I thought I was done for, until I realised he was staring at Elżbieta with a horrible blankness. A hungry blankness. I had seen that look far too many times before. I was terrified, but Elżbieta had no idea what was happening. The Nazi removed his gun. Nudged her back with it. When she turned to look, he flicked up a few times. Elżbieta was scared, too scared to refuse or even express a disapproving glance. Or maybe she was too smart to argue. Either way, she stood and let them lead her upstairs. I stayed where I was.

I knew what they had planned for her. What they were going to do to her. I tried hard not to picture it, but I had seen enough of it firsthand, how could I not. But I told myself to stay put. Think of Jacques, I told myself. There was no use acting all emotional again. There was no point. I would only get myself killed. But I couldn't bear it. I couldn't willingly do nothing again. I couldn't let another a civilian get hurt again. So I snuck upstairs. Poked my head up just above the threshold.

Just as I expected, they were ripping her clothes off. Elżbieta was resisting, of course she was, but that only made them happier. And just before the next part, that awful next part, Elżbieta did the stupidest thing she could've done. She slapped a Nazi. The one that led her up there to play with his friends. That awful brute. And he struck her back. She fell to the deck. And he grabbed his gun.

I ran up the last of the stairs, grabbed the pistol from the third Nazi's holster, and shot that rapist in the head. I couldn't even enjoy the visual, that awful blood spatter that would've made me puke on the spot, because I was forced to my knees by the other men, five of them, and one of them had a gun in my face. A machine gun. I knew I was dead.

"Wait!" Elżbieta cried to them in German. "Stop! He's German!"

I looked up at her in horror.

The Nazi holding the gun to my face lowered his weapon. Looked at her curiously. "Him? German?"

Elżbieta nodded. "He's the deserter you're all looking for."

I was too stunned from being so close to death to really understand what was happening. How close I was to getting shot. How fragrantly I had been betrayed. I couldn't understand why, after everything I did for her, that she'd turn me in like that. So swiftly. So instinctively. I had no concept, no prior precedent, of such a thing.

The Nazis spent a while debating amongst themselves. The U-Boat had orders to fulfil, a mission to continue. Then again, they knew the man putting up the bounty, specifically on the condition that the deserter be kept alive for the Third Reich to be made an example of, was the son of *SS-Gruppenführer* Lamprecht Bütz. One million francs was quite the motivation in its own right, but the connections that would come of it too? That was worth derailing *anything*.

And so they let Elżbieta return to the ship's engine room and forced me at gunpoint into their U-Boat. I was thrown into the brig, and I waited there for what felt like hours, just long enough to realise the tragic irony of my situation. Jacques was as good as dead now because I didn't allow a Hungarian refugee to get gang raped and/or killed. What awful luck. I kept replaying our interaction in the engine room. How did she figure it out? Why? Was it to keep my Fry network intel to herself? Was she really that two-faced?

"You have a visitor," a Nazi guard told me, walking into the room. Behind him was Elżbieta, Judas herself, with that same sullen look in her eye.

I glared back at her from behind those bars. The Nazi left the room. Closed the door behind him.

"I'm surprised they let me on," Elżbieta told me in German. "I can't believe I even dared to ask, but I needed to."

"Why would you do this to me?" I asked in English, defiant English.

Elżbieta swallowed. "Can we please speak in German?" she asked in German, defiant German.

"I'll be speaking English, thank you." I hesitated. "You don't have to. If you can explain yourself better…"

Elżbieta nodded thankfully. "That deserter they're looking for is worth so many francs. I could send this U-Boat to the bottom of the ocean and they'll let me, just as long as I keep you alive. Just in case you were, you know…" She bobbed her head. "*Him.*"

I furrowed my brow a bit.

"They're going to let us disembark soon," she continued. "I think they said something about bringing you back to Marseilles so they can take a photo of you. To identify you, I suppose. To make sure you're the one they're looking for." She gave me a gentle smile. "When they find out they have the wrong guy, they'll let you go, no?"

I donned a sympathetic smile. Nodded. "How did you know I could speak German?"

"When they came downstairs, you quoted what they were saying to me in English, word-for-word."

"But you said you were Hungarian."

"Hungary was once part of the Austrian Empire. Of course I speak German."

I smirked self-deprecatingly. "Here I was thinking I was so smart."

Elżbieta approached the bars. Took my hands. "You saved my life," she whispered. Never had I heard German being spoken so sweetly. It nearly brought me to tears. "You were going to die. I wanted you to live. I needed you to…" She stopped herself, frowning slightly. "I'm sorry if that was a—"

"No, thank you, I…" I grinned, my eyes getting misty. "I thought the worst of you there, but…" I swallowed. "Thank *you* for saving *my* life," I whispered in German, just for her.

Elżbieta was crying too. She petted my cheek. "I'll never forget what you've done for me."

I nodded over and over, practically sobbing. "I'll be alright," I lied, reverting back to English. "I'll see you in New York. We can go get coffee sometime."

Elżbieta laughed at that. "You'll be alright. I know you will."

"I know." I wiped my eyes one at a time. "They got the wrong guy."

"They got wrong guy," Elżbieta repeated in broken English.

"Yeah." I sniffed. "Go on. I'll be okay."

Elżbieta was escorted off the U-Boat. They allowed the ship to leave and the U-Boat returned to shore. As they escorted me off, chains around my wrists, I could still see Elżbieta's ship on the horizon. And I felt a strange calmness. Elżbieta saw William Gunnison in that cell, not Wilhelm Gunter. She only knew the real me.

I hope she made it to Lisbon. I hope she's alright.

CHAPTER FOURTEEN

Cautionary Tale

We stayed docked at Marseilles for about a week more, my greedy captors waiting for confirmation that I was in fact the infamous Nazi-killing deserter the son of *SS-Gruppenführer* Lamprecht Bütz made such a huge stink about. The rest was a blur, a stewing of sorts. I was a shell of a body. Very certainly a corpse. A dead man walking. I knew what was to come. Confirmation over the wireless. Those rapists that derailed their own mission for a million francs getting paid in full. Me getting loaded into a train, transferred across multiple lines all the way to Berlin. And then it all happened, just as I said it would.

I was sent to Sachsenhausen, now a concentration camp. My accommodations in the Gestapo prison on-site has been significantly better than I thought they would be. I haven't been beaten, tortured or lynched. I've not been starved or whipped or worked. I'm allowed a solicitor, even if it's just to show the world they gave me one, and I chose Steffen Schäfer, my father closest friend. They were students together at the *Universität Frankfurt am Main*. I saw him quite often before my father's death. He was a great comfort to me in a way my mother never was.

We aren't allowed to prepare for the trial, but I am allowed visitors here at Sachsenhausen. Steffen has provided me a pen and all the paper I could ask for. Writing this out has been my last act of resistance.

I can't believe it's been six months since I left Jacques in Paris. I know it's been quite a long time, since we saw each other last, but I do hope this extra time hasn't turned you away from the memory of me. I hope Roul and your de facto brothers haven't punished you too harshly for aiding my escape. I hope you still think fondly of me as well as my mission to find Victor. But should that not be the case, I hope this recollection of our time together sparks pleasant memories and reignites your sympathy towards me. I hope you forgive me for letting myself get caught so quickly and so stupidly. But more than anything, I hope you find Victor, whatever his real name is. I hope you save Jacques, whatever his real name is. And I hope you hold on to the memory that was William Gunnison. He really was the true me. I'm so glad you were able to meet him.

And thank you, Nadine, for everything you've done for me. When I die, I will die a happy man knowing you will resolve my unfinished work. I just wished this farewell could've been made in person.

God bless you.

With the humblest regards,
Pvt William Gunnison

* * *

Wilhelm Gunter put the pen down, his face and body bruised from months and months of beatings, humiliation and torture. For the first time in months, he had nothing more to write. And now he had no choice but to see, truly see, that awful hell he was living in. Mould everywhere. Dust on the floor. The sounds of the laborious prisoners outside. Whistles. Gunshots of the concentration camp. There was nothing more for him to do. Nothing more he could use as a distraction. Nothing more to motivate him. Nothing more to fight for. Just a couple more weeks of going through the motions and then… death.

A cold chill crept its way into his brain. His ghoulish imagination started going wild. It was awful, that sting. Those thoughts. The reality of those last moments just before one gets shot… He had to avert it somehow, those thoughts, just a little bit more. So he returned to the last page of that over-sized letter and added a postscript:

> *P.S. I thought writing this out would inspire the rest of Victor's address. Sadly, it has not. If I think of it before I send this to you, I will add it below:*

Wilhelm smiled at that inconclusive end note. Ingenious. Now he had something new to do. Something new to occupy his mind. Something mortal. Something small. Something selfless.

A hallway door opened. A guard escorted Steffen Schäfer to Wilhelm's cell. "Good morning, Wilhelm," Steffen greeted in English, respecting his client's wishes.

"I'm finished." Wilhelm folded the document. "Did you bring the envelope?"

Steffen sighed. "There really is no use."

"It's just an envelope."

Steffen gave a crooked frown. Reached into his jacket pocket and pulled out the perfect envelope, big enough to fit all those pages.

Wilhelm took the envelope and wrote on the front:

Nadine Sauvageot
Crespières

He then slid in the folded pages. Sealed the envelope. Smoothed out the front. Held it out for Steffen to take.

But Steffen stepped back, holding up both hands. "Stop. We talked about this."

"I've got no one else, Uncle Steffen." Wilhelm held the letter out more. "Please."

"They'll shoot me."

"The Führer wrote an entire novel at Landsberg! No one shot him then!"

"He had already been convicted."

"Yeah, for trying to overthrow the government!"

"Wilhelm," Steffen scolded.

Wilhelm shut his mouth. Such treasonous talk was still dangerous, even if his fate was certain. "You won't be in danger. It's just the ramblings of a prisoner. They can't possibly be threatened by a bunch of ramblings."

"It's still against the law."

"So is the *Volksgerichtshof*!" Wilhelm cried, reverting back to his radical impulses. "Don't pretend you approve, Uncle Steffen. I know Father didn't. Your profession, your entire field, has been reduced to a means of judicial murder!"

"I won't hear any more of this—"

"They've already decided I'm guilty! No presumption of innocence! No jury! No statements from the defence! Isn't that humiliating for you?!"

"Wilhelm!"

"How can you stand by and just watch them make a mockery of everything you love?!"

Steffen frowned. Lowered his head, his anger dissipating. "When you talk like that…" he whispered. "You really are just like Kiefer. In every way."

Wilhelm smiled sadly at that. "I keep imagining him cheering me on throughout all this. Getting back at them. All of them." His smile faded. "In between, however, he's screaming at me for making the same stupid mistakes he did."

Steffen nodded. "I'm not your father, Wilhelm. I never was."

"I was never an Englishman until I started acting like one."

"Pinching the dog tags off a Dunkirk casualty does not an Englishman make." Steffen paused. "And neither is pretending to be Kiefer Gunter. Even if I were to be the second coming, I'd be fated for death, killed by the same brash disobedience you want me to unleash."

"He made his choice. Fate had nothing to do with it." Wilhelm opened the envelope. Pulled out the letter. Stacked it on top of the envelope. Held it all out. "Use his sacrifice as a guide of what not to do. Don't let it go to waste."

"You're the one with nothing to lose if you…" Steffen stared at the opened letter in Wilhelm's hand. "What are you doing?"

"Read it."

Steffen laughed at the size of it. "The trial's tomorrow!"

"And what do you have to prepare? Statements? A case? Come on."

Steffen said nothing in response to that.

Wilhelm nodded with encouragement. "Just read it. If you're not convinced, give it back. I'll find some other way."

Steffen hesitated. He slowly took the letter. Put it under his arm. Turned and left the cell.

Wilhelm lay in bed the rest of the day. He thought about Steffen reading that thing he wrote. He thought of Nadine. He thought of Jacques. He thought of Victor. He even thought of Elżbieta. Their faces. Their voices. What they did for him. He felt a strange connection to all of them. All those chance encounters. The effect of his interaction on all of them. For a moment he started to understand the connection between all human beings. It seemed so obvious to him. Even if he were to die an infamous traitor, that very infamy would only help in the end. He'd be forever known as the man that stood up to Germany. The man who refused to speak German at his own trial. Maybe his execution would inspire others to do the same, his story, his sacrifice being used as a guide of what not to do. Maybe someone would even dare to take out the Führer. Maybe those camps would be overrun. Liberated. All those men and women freed. What if his death was the very thing that guaranteed Germany's demise?

In the same way, what if Jacques's collection of Weimar relics proved to be the last bits of evidence dating back to the Republic? What if future historians needed those things to start rebuilding Germany history books, to preserve the lives of all those destroyed by fascism? The good democracy thrown aside so emotionally, so blindly? What if knowing what had been there before, so easily taken from the world, was enough to prevent what happened to Germany from happening anywhere else ever again?

Wilhelm woke the next morning. Guards came in and gave him a cheap suit to wear. They let him keep his cane. And he bore what was to come as best he could. Never resisting. Once again a walking corpse. But on his way out of his cell, he saw Steffen waiting for him there at the end of the hall. He was wearing his best suit. So professional. A stoic expression. And he moved his right hand across his chest. Tapped the outside of his suit, just in line where the jacket pocket would be. It was just a quick double-tap, made with just the flats of his fingers, but it was everything to Wilhelm. He looked Uncle Steffen in the eyes. Recognised that look of resolution he received in return. It was the same one his father used to have. And as the two men walked to their car, they were filled with a great ease, a wonderful floating feeling inside them. Two rebels standing up for what they believed in. Two tricksters about to outsmart the Huns.

CHAPTER FIFTEEN

The Crimes of Wilhelm Gunter

Wilhelm Gunter's trial took place at the *Volksgerichtshof* on the 12th of June, 1941. The room was adorned with bright red swastikas and a painting of Hitler behind Otto Georg Thierack, president of the court. Sitting to Thierack's left was *General der Panzertruppe* Ernst Feßmann, commanding officer of the 267th Infantry Division. Sitting to Thierack's right was Maik Zimmer, chief public prosecutor of the so-called "People's Court."

Waiting across from them at the Defence's desk was Steffen Schäfer and an empty chair beside him.

The gallery was filled with reporters, some recording for wireless, some filming newsreels, and about a hundred or so hand-picked spectators.

The doors opened. An excited hush ran across the room as the accused, infamous *Soldat* Wilhelm Gunter himself, was led to his seat under armed police escort. Wilhelm sat in the chair beside Steffen and the trial officially began.

Thierack started the proceedings by reading off the charges made against *Soldat* Gunter. Twenty-one counts of treason. Twenty counts of murder. One count of attempted murder. One count of mayhem. One count of possession of a firearm in occupied territory. Four counts of harassment in occupied territory. One count of illegal evasion. Wilhelm was not given the opportunity to state a plea. He simply stood with a stoic expression until he was ordered to sit back down.

The first witness for the prosecution was *Hauptmann* Adalwolf Bütz, *Soldat* Gunter's commanding officer. The court reacted with shock at the sheer sight of the man. What a horrible scar over and under his right eye, the ball itself so conspicuously made of glass. Wilhelm revelled in how visibly uncomfortable Bütz was being seen like that, the walking monster he was.

"*Hauptmann* Bütz," Zimmer asked from his place beside Thierack. "When did you first meet *Soldat* Gunter?"

Bütz took a moment to look at Wilhelm. He was loving this. "It was the 26th of August, 1939. Five days before the Gleiwitz incident."

"And where was this?"

"Hanover."

"Under what context?"

"The 267th Division had just been formed. I was a *Leutnant* at the time, assigned with leading the 488th Infantry Regiment."

"*Soldat* Gunter was assigned to your platoon?"

"Yes."

"Who else was assigned to you?"

"*Schütze* Ebert Konstantin and *Gefreiter* Emil Landoberct."

"Where are they now?"

"Dead."

"How did they die?"

"Killed by *Soldat* Gunter."

"Were you in battle at the time?"

"No. We were relaxing. Drinking vodka. Manning our post along the English Channel."

"Did either *Schütze* Konstantin or *Gefreiter* Landoberct provoke *Soldat* Gunter into such violence?"

"No. It was entirely unprovoked."

Zimmer nodded, flipping the page of his notes. "And what did *Schütze* Konstantin, *Gefreiter* Landoberct and yourself think of *Soldat* Gunter when you first met him at Hanover?"

Steffen tightened his lips. How ready he was to object to Zimmer's leading question. It was simply hearsay. Bütz could never accurately report what Konstantin and Landoberct thought of Wilhelm. But Steffen wasn't allowed to speak. He wasn't allowed to object. He was merely a prop.

Bütz swallowed, thinking back. "It was clear to me when we were first introduced to *Soldat* Gunter that he was an absolutely disturbed individual. At first, I tried to get him transferred to another regiment, but I felt in part pressured to—"

"Oh my God!" Wilhelm groaned in English, rolling his eyes. The crowd reacted strongly to the frank outburst. Steffen whipped his head in horror at his client. Even Bütz was shocked, his one good eye flinching just at the sound of Wilhelm's voice.

Thierack slammed his gavel. "*Soldat* Gunter, you are not permitted to speak at this time!" he shouted in German.

Steffen leaned over to Wilhelm. "What are you doing?" he whispered in English.

"Give me the letter," Wilhelm whispered back, gesturing with one hand.

Steffen's face went cold. "What?"

"You want me to be quiet? Give me something to do." Wilhelm impatiently gestured again.

Steffen reluctantly withdrew the envelope from his breast pocket. Gave it to Wilhelm.

"And a pen," Wilhelm whispered.

"Herr Schäfer," Thierack grumbled in German.

"Just a moment, Herr Thierack," Steffen responded. He whispered at Wilhelm, "You can't spend the entire trial writing."

"What are they gonna do? Convict me *harder*?" Wilhelm did the gimme gesture again.

Steffen exhaled. He could feel all those eyes, all those cameras and microphones on him. "I apologise, Herr Thierack," he said in German as he discreetly handed a pen to Wilhelm. "Continue."

Zimmer cleared his throat. "*Hauptmann* Bütz," he resumed. "Describe in detail the first time you suspected *Soldat* Gunter was mentally unwell."

But Bütz didn't answer Zimmer's question. He was too distracted by Wilhelm, that large document he was writing so passionately on the back of.

Zimmer huffed. "*Hauptmann* Bütz."

Bütz snapped back to the present. "I-I'm sorry, can you repeat the question?" And Zimmer did, but Bütz never stopped looking at Wilhelm. What could be more important to him than the trial of his life?

✳ ✳ ✳

I cannot bear to hear such slander. They're painting me erroneously, insultingly so, which only makes me realise how crucial it is that I write the truth of my time as a German, my life as a Nazi, exactly as it truly happened.

I was born Wilhelm Gunter on 5 April 1920 to Kiefer and Iga Gunter. I grew up in a town called Bamberg in the Upper Franconia district of Bavaria.

It was there that my mother had her first nervous attack, brought on by that reoccurring dream I told you about, the one in which Germany was at war again and I was killed by my own team. My father's best friend Steffen, whom I always called Uncle Steffen, told me that my mother got drunk once and tried to drown me in the bathtub, an act my father interrupted just in time. It was that attempted infanticide that prompted my father and Uncle Steffen to send Mother to a prominent psychoanalyst based in Vienna, Doctor Sigmund Freud. He was quite renowned in academic circles for being a keen interpreter of dreams.

According to Doctor Freud, my mother was trying to prevent her dream from coming true by killing me herself, which presumably would also prevent Germany from returning to war. Doctor Freud claimed her extreme patriotism was what fuelled those dreams, exacerbated by the fits of childbirth. Not clairvoyant in the slightest. So he prescribed her cocaine and sent her to a sanatorium in Zürich. Father and I visited her there twice a year, though I was never allowed in the same room as her.

I was happiest in those days without Mother, to be honest. Father, Uncle Steffen and I often took trips, to Berlin, to Father's university in Frankfurt, all over Bavaria. Father taught me English, the history of Bavaria, and quite a lot about politics. Uncle Steffen taught me the importance of ethics, human rights and the law. I was so happy with my two fathers, dreading the inevitable return my mother. But when she returned to Bamberg in the summer of 1927, it seemed she had made a complete recovery. Everything was fine after all.

But the Germany she left back in '22 was not the same Germany she returned to. A fierce party of brutes were causing frequent street fights, making people uncomfortable with their anti-communist, antisemitic, ultranationalist rhetoric. We all called them Brownshirts back then, but they were the first Nazis. Nazis with no power. No one really saw them as a legitimate threat in those days. Germany had nothing to be upset about. Our economy had finally stabilised thanks to all loans we were receiving from the United States. But then the Wall Street Crash of '29 put a stop to that, and then the Great Depression came after. Unemployment hit 30%, the highest it had been in decades, and out-of-work Germans were desperate to find someone to blame.

One by one, the great minds of Father's university started to adhere to the philosophy Hitler wrote about in *Mein Kampf.* Father couldn't understand how so many men he admired were so easily corrupted by utter nonsense. He loved the German Republic. He thrived in those days. He never fought in the Great War, sure, but he'd heard stories. Based on what he told me, Germany was better off as a Republic. Though not everyone thought as strongly about it as he did.

One day in 1932, Father got into a fight with one of his superiors at the university and got himself sacked. He drank away his pain, often luring me to Berlin so we could have fun the way we used to with Uncle Steffen. On one such trip, he encountered a pack of Nazis talking nastily about the Republic. Blaming the Jews for the Treaty of Versailles. Getting all the facts wrong in the process. Father just couldn't take it anymore. He was still sore about his sacking. So he attempted a rematch against those hoodlums. I tried to stop him, but it was too late. They stomped his face in. I was catatonic. Unable to call for help, I just sat there. Frozen in fear. Sick to the point of paralysis. The bartender sent word to my mother, but she never came to get us. She slipped into another hysterical breakdown, apparently, her first since she had returned from Zürich, but this one was worse than ever. Her dream had come true, but I wasn't the one that died. It was the love of her life. Her Kiefer. If only it was me, she told me once.

Uncle Steffen was the only one comforting me in my grief. He's the one that brought me and Father home. But Mother forbade me from ever seeing him again. He reminded her too much of my father.

As Hitler rose to power, so did our troubles. Everyone in Bamberg knew the circumstances of my father's death. That he was an alcoholic. That he spoke so passionately against the Führer. Mother was ignored by local merchants, by all her friends. I couldn't get a job good enough to support her. We were snubbed by people on the street. A burglar broke into our house one time. Stole all her valuable jewels, gifts Father bought her. But my mother got no sympathy from the police. They said she must've done something to deserve it.

Every day was a war between me and Mother. Erratic mood swings. Paranoia. She kept saying over and over how important it was that I never speak out against the Führer, that I was doomed to be killed the same way Father had been. I was a lot like him. I never believed the Aryan master race theory, not even a little bit... but I was misinformed enough about fascism to be sympathetic of Hitler as our Chancellor. We really had no better way to improve our economic status. I truly believed Hitler was the best choice in a batch of bad options.

My opinion of the Third Reich changed the moment rumours of war reached our ears. I was always against war. Mother wouldn't hear of it. To her, me enlisting would revive our social status. The money it'd bring to the family would be enough for her to live on. But I tracked down Uncle Steffen, who was disillusioned himself by the creation of the *Volksgerichtshof*, the People's Court, and we came up with a plan together of what to do if I was ever conscripted, should the time arise. I managed to avoid it for a little bit, but the call finally came in August of 1939. Germany was about to manufacture an attack on themselves and blame Poland so they could justify an invasion, which no doubt would cause Britain and France to declare war on us. I was all packed and ready to flee the country… but I changed my mind at the last minute. I called Steffen and told him the plan was off. Mother would give us away, I knew she would, and I couldn't bear the thought of Uncle Steffen being punished for anything I've done.

I was shipped off to Hanover and inducted into the 267th Division of the *Heer*, the German Army. We called ourselves the Horse's Head Division because our emblem looked like two Knight chess pieces intercrossed. I was a *Soldat*, the lowest you could be, assigned to the 488th Regiment. I met my commanding officer, *Leutnant* Adalwolf Bütz, and the rest of his command: *Schütze* Ebert Konstantin (*Schütze* being a junior ranked rifleman) and *Gefreiter* Emil Landoberct (*Gefreiter* being a *Soldat* or *Schütze* that has passed primary recruit training). They didn't have time to properly train Konstantin and I before the scheduled invasion, but Adalwolf taught us everything we needed to know.

The Horse's Head Division never saw Poland. On 1 September, 1939, when the rest of the *Wehrmacht* were in the throes of battle, we were posted to the *Westwall*, what the rest of Europe calls the Siegfried Line. Adalwolf, Landoberct, Konstantin and I spent a lot of time there, just the four of us, waiting for our orders to invade Belgium and move into France. During those eight months of waiting, we developed quite the bond. Those boys were very interested in me. Curious by my intelligence. My idyllic life in Bamberg. All those trips through Bavaria.

Adalwolf in particular took quite the liking to me. He was a year younger than me, having earned a small platoon, the 488th Regiment, solely because of his prestigious Great War veteran of a father. I was envious that he had such a strong connection to his father, and he pitied me having lost mine so young. And he was no small help to me psychologically. He helped me acknowledge my mother's madness as abnormal behaviour, something that wasn't my fault, something that I shouldn't be expected to control or fix. I felt validated by Adalwolf. He really was a true friend to me. Thanks to my father's death, I was never able to make friends at school. I had always wanted a great friend of my own, the way my father had Uncle Steffen. Those two men when they were together… I'm telling you, Nadine, it was like magic. One time, when the three of us were in Berlin, I overheard my father crying in the next room, worried to death about Mother and her safety in Zürich, and Uncle Steffen was there holding him, hugging him, being there for him in that vulnerable moment. I always wanted someone like that for myself, and for a time I truly felt I had found one in Bütz. Adalwolf, I mean. Wilhelm and Adalwolf, they called us. Even Konstantin said we were inseparable. Because we were. We really were.

The orders finally came to invade Belgium in May 1940. I was expecting to spend the war entirely on battlefields, fighting over long stretches of land, bayonets and rifles firing from all sides, mortars and bombs dropping on us from above, but that didn't happen for us. Bütz never led us into battle. For our platoon, the Belgian invasion was a casual detour across the farmlands. And it is there that I saw the sadistic side of Adalwolf, the side he had successfully hid from me for nearly a year. I had already formed an attachment to him by that point, a social dependency. Having a bad opinion of him was tantamount to being a pariah. I had already been a pariah against my will. Was I really prepared to put myself in that position again, this time on my own? Well, as I soon discovered, I cared more about what my friends thought of me, those boys, my brothers in arms, who I had considered the greatest mates I could ever have in the whole world, than the safety of innocent human beings.

* * *

"The Court calls Iga Gunter!"

Wilhelm stopped writing. Looked up in shock. The doors opened and the newest witness for the prosecution walked in: his own mother. Every muscle in Wilhelm's body started contracting. His face tightened. And Iga looked back at him with brutal disapproval.

As Iga was sworn in, Wilhelm looked uncomfortably at Uncle Steffen. He was just as disturbed by her presence.

"Frau Gunter," Zimmer started, "when your son was just the boy, was he—?"

"May I address the court myself, Herr Zimmer?" Iga interrupted.

Zimmer looked uneasily at Thierack. Thierack nodded.

Iga glared down at her son. "No matter what he claims, Wilhelm Gunter is not English. And he certainly isn't German. Too much like his father, he is. He and *that one*—" She flicked a dismissive finger at Steffen. "—conspired to get him out of Bavaria when the draft came. They thought I didn't know, but I knew everything that was going on there. I know what he'd do. How low he'd go. Dragging my poor son down with him. Of course I wasn't surprised. Look what happened to his father. Delusional. Drunk. Angry about things, things he never believed. My Kiefer was a true German, but he lost himself. He needed me to reel him in. But I wasn't with him, was I? No. If only I was. He'd still be alive. I've always said it. Maybe he'd knock some sense into this one. He's not a man. Instead he sat there and watched my Kiefer get his face bashed in!"

Wilhelm's lip trembled.

Iga's face turned grotesque with hate. "You're a fucking coward! How could you do that to your friend Bütz? Don't you know who his father is? Don't you know how much better our life could've been if you just stayed his friend? You sick, monstrous troll! You evil little golem! I should've killed you when I had the chance! Everything would've been fine! We would've been safe! We would've been happy!" Iga started crying in her seat, her fat cheeks flushed bright pink, tears seeping down in waves, not drops. "Why do you hate me?!" she gargled at Wilhelm. "What have I ever done to you?! Why would you take him from me?! Why couldn't you let me keep him?! I'm nothing without him!" She sobbed herself into incoherence.

Steffen's breath shook. He looked at his client, expecting to see a horrified, traumatised little boy, but Wilhelm was stone faced the whole time. Indifferent to his mother's meltdown. He was used to it, those words. Those very words too, said just like that. The only difference was the time and place. But Wilhelm did feel the hurt, that new way his mother found to hurt him.

She killed him, Steffen realised. She's making her own dream come true. She's the one that turned on him.

Wilhelm felt nothing as he returned to the paper. He simply tuned out his mother's ramblings and resumed writing his addendum.

* * *

Adalwolf had a specific *modus operandi* that he repeated over and over wherever we went. He only wanted to go after civilians. We rarely ever saw combat with actual military personnel. I think Adalwolf was too afraid of getting shot, or perhaps he thought he'd have more fun terrorising unarmed, untrained farmers.

Whenever we got to a new farm, he'd pick out a woman, usually the eldest daughter, never the matriarch. Always someone young. Blonde more often than not. Then he'd kill every other member of the family in front of her. Her brothers. Her sisters. Her mother. Her father. One by one. Slowly. He'd always save the one he picked for last. Then, when she was at her most terrified, he'd rape her. Violently. And then when he was finished with her, still coming down from his orgasm, that shame creeping in so sharply, he'd call her a piece of shit and shoot her in the head. He followed that exactly procedure every day, sometimes more than once a day, with only small variations. Sometimes we'd take turns killing the family. Maybe he'd torture a brother a bit before shooting him, especially they resisted. And when it came to the raping, sometimes he'd invite Konstantin, Landoberct and I to join in after in.

I was too afraid to stop him. I admit, I joined in with the shooting. And one time... yes, I admit, I tried to force myself to... God, I can't even write it out. It was only once, and that was the last straw for me.

The last straw for Adalwolf happened in France, just after we crossed the Belgian border. We got a bit lazy. Rote. Unprepared for an ambush. We were on a farm in Maubeuge when one of our captives pulled out a secret pistol. He was about to shoot Adalwolf, so I raised my rifle to stop him. Shot him in the head at a strange angle. The man's face blew off. I got a horrible look at what was left. It reminded me so much of my father, lying on that pub floor in Berlin, his face stomped in so dastardly. I couldn't control myself. I vomited everywhere. Adalwolf was so disgusted by me, even after I tried to explain why. He was angry as well, since the smell of bile made it impossible for him to get it up for his grand finale. I tried to apologise, but Adalwolf unofficially demoted me to watchdog. From then on, I'd round up the captives and search for hiders, but no more was I allowed to participate.

Secretly, I was relieved. I hated the war. I hated what I had done. I had been hoping for break. Even better, I was hoping for an end. And Adalwolf, like the good friend he was, gave me that end. In my own twisted interpretation, I felt validated. Seen. He acknowledged a significant flaw in me as a soldier and adjusted accordingly, like a proper CO should. And so we went through France in June of 1940. I found the girls that Adalwolf and the others would rape. I subdued the men they'd kill one by one. Many times a hero would break out, and Adalwolf would allow himself to be chased, only to turn around after a corner and shoot them dead. It always worked. They fell for it every time.

There was nothing special about Nancy. It was just another dairy farm. I was just doing my job as always. Find the girls. Subdue the men. Stand by and do nothing else. Don't ruin the mood. Wait until it's over. But when I found the only daughter hiding in the barn amidst the hay, and I stared into those brown eyes of hers, I decided… no more. Adalwolf doesn't get this one. I'll simply pretend she wasn't there. Stand outside. Watch her flee. That's when I started my own special kind of resistance.

From that day on, I never found the girl. I let them all go. Claimed there wasn't a daughter to find. And Adalwolf, being a complete moron, never suspected a thing. I got away with it for months.

In September 1940, the Horse's Head Division was stationed at the English Channel. The four of us were sitting by the fire one night, talking about home. We had been away for an entire year. And Adalwolf was drinking, having swiped some vodka from a local farm. By that point, I really started to hate Adalwolf. If you asked him at that time what he thought of me, I'm sure he'd be more upset by my vomiting more than anything. I, on the other hand, genuinely hated him as a human being. What a pig. Spoiled. Lazy. A coward too. He never cared about Germany. To him, the war was just one big playground, a way for him to feel like a real man. I couldn't stand the way he laughed, the way he looked, the way he talked. And that night he decided to go off on the German Republic. And of course, he got everything about it wrong, passing errors and assumptions as fact. Yes, the fight that ultimately split us up was a matter of politics, not how he mistreated civilians. Nevertheless, it got heated.

In his drunken rage, Adalwolf revealed how little he actually thought of me. How I was nothing but a weakling, like my father. And I threatened him for that. But Adalwolf simply grinned that nasty grin, like he always did, and ordered Konstantin and Landoberct to kill me. Yes, actually kill me. And they were about to. Konstantin was reaching for his gun when I shot him in the head, and I was about to shoot Landoberct when he kicked my gun away. I grabbed his gun. He jumped on me. We fell to the ground. Wrestled over his rifle. Landoberct was about to shoot me up the chin, his finger just about to pull the trigger, when I kicked him in the balls, grabbed my ankle knife, and stabbed Landoberct in the heart. Over and over, I stabbed him. Blood got all over my fingers. And then, at last, he was dead.

Bütz, throughout all of this, remained sitting by the fire, horrified by the sight playing out before him. When he saw me turn towards him, that bloody knife in hand, he tried to scutter away. But I stomped on his bare foot with my boot. He fell to the ground, nursing his broken toes like a weakling. And I saw all that blood on my hands. The firelight flicking off of it. Nausea forming in my throat. No, I said, not here. Not now. But then I had an awful idea. A perfectly awful idea. Bütz deserved to die. He deserved to die for all those horrible war crimes he committed. All that terrorising he did to all those innocent people. I was able to avenge all of them in that moment. So why not do it the perfect way: exactly what he did to everyone else?

I started by straddling him, just like he straddled those girls. I tuned out Bütz's screams as I reached for his right hand, that bloody knife still in my left. He tried to fight me off, and in our struggle, I ended up slicing a line along his right eye, cutting into the ball ever so slightly. That was enough to subdue him. I then grabbed his right hand, held it down, and stabbed the knife as hard as I could. It broke through his hand and into the dirt, pinning him onto the ground. I then looked down at Bütz. Savoured the sight for a few seconds. I then pulled out my gun, cocked it, and shot him in the ear, just the very tippy top of it.

Bütz barely felt any pain. He laughed at me and shouted, "You missed!"

But I didn't. I shot him exactly where I wanted to shoot him. And all that blood gushing out of his ear, getting everywhere… it made me so sick.

I vomited all over Bütz. Every inch of him got covered, just like I planned. And he cried out, all humiliated, disgusted, just like every one of those women he had raped. And I admit, I was dizzy from all that vomiting, but I still had enough strength to say those magic words, the words he always said to them all: "You piece of shit." And I recocked my gun, aimed for the face, and shot him. Then Bütz went quiet. I took that for him being dead and I wandered off into the wilderness.

Of course I would later see him in Paris just four months later, sans an eye, promoted to *Hauptmann* to boot. I was so nauseous that night, and I suppose that vomit all over his face made it hard to discern where everything was in the dark. Either I shot him in a non-fatal part or I truly missed that second shot point-blank. What rotten luck.

* * *

Wilhelm had to stop writing again. It was time for the sentencing.

To the surprise of no one, *Soldat* Wilhelm Gunter was found guilty on all counts. Otto Georg Thierack sentenced him to death, ordering him to be transferred to Plötzensee Prison where he'd await his public execution by firing squad for crimes against the Führer and the Third Reich. Thierack banged the gavel and the session was adjourned.

"I can take that letter back now," Steffen whispered solemnly.

Wilhelm kept starting at that last page he wrote. That note he ended on. What he didn't have time to say.

Steffen could sense the guard approaching to take his client away. "Wilhelm."

"I'm not finished yet," Wilhelm said. He folded the letter back into its envelope.

"You're joking."

"Just one more night." Wilhelm nodded at Steffen with assurance. "I'll finish it tonight. You can pick it up at Plötzensee tomorrow."

Steffen sighed uneasily. "No more delays, Wilhelm. We've got to get it to Nadine."

"I know, believe me." Wilhelm stuck the letter in his trouser waistband. Pocketed Steffen's pen. "There's one last thing I have to tell her."

CHAPTER SIXTEEN

Dead Man's Gambit

For two weeks I wandered about Northern France. Starving. Mad with thirst. Horrified by my actions. I couldn't go home. They'd kill me for what I'd done. There were no witnesses to verify my killings of Konstantin and Landoberct were in self-defence. And Adalwolf... I was proud of myself at the time, but I was so sickened by it afterwards. How could I do that to him? How could I demean him so savagely? I was no better than Adalwolf demeaning those poor girls. Girls he hated for being impure. Girls he felt entirely justified in torturing, raping, killing. I was lost, cold and afraid. I felt like my father had he won that pub fight, but I still failed. I turned traitor to Germany. Lost in a foreign land. Ashamed before God. I wanted to die. And I wanted to do it facing the ocean. I always loved the ocean.

I found my way to the closest beach, which coincidentally happened to be Dunkirk. I stared out at the water, those waves crashing softly. I even had a pistol pressed to my temple. But just as I was about to end it all, I saw a decaying body floating on the water, wafting its way towards me. A young man around my age. A lost casualty of that evacuation three months earlier. Killed in action perhaps. Or maybe he merely fell off the boat, officially declared MIA, presumed dead. No matter. But looking at him just then, I realised I was about to make myself like him. Dead like him. My mind just as dead as his. My body. My arms. My ears. My mouth. My insides. No different from his. That was enough for me to see reason.

I felt that young man, so far from home, deserved a proper burial. And so I buried him, right there by the sea. I formed a cross out of sticks. I pulled off his dog tags. I looked at them, ready to carve his name onto that wooden headstone I made for him... when I realised his name was eerily similar to my own. William Gunnison. What were the chances of that? So many months later, and yet he just floated over to me, right that very second. It was fate. It had to be. It had to be a sign from God.

And so I decided to be that man. I donned his dog tags and continued living his life. The life of a hero. The life of a man on a mission. And that mission was to kill one Nazi officer for every civilian I had been forced to shoot. Adalwolf Bütz retroactively became my first kill. No longer was his death a cold act of revenge. It was chapter one of my redemption. And so I wandered about France, hiding in the shadows, waiting to find someone, a Nazi officer on R&R in a nearby town. When I did, I snuck over, killed him, and moved on. And I succeeded in getting my seventeen kills. Wilhelm Gunter's toll was paid and William Gunnison's life could truly begin. You know the rest from there.

I'm writing the end of this addendum having already been sentenced to death. This will be the last paragraph I'll ever write in my life. I just wanted the opportunity to tell you, Nadine, something I wish I had the chance to tell you in person. I'm so happy I saved you. That I was rewarded by you saving me physically. And I finally found that friend I had been searching so long for. It's because of you that I have hope in this world again. You are the one I strive now to be like. It's you that makes me want to be a better man. A man worthy of your respect. Worthy your love. That is, Nadine, what I wanted to say. I've killed Nazis, braved battles and frightening circumstances, from Bavaria to Belgium to France to Berlin, and yet I'm too scared to say four simple words: Nadine, I

＊　＊　＊

The hallway door opened and Wilhelm whipped the papers away. Fiercely folding them. Stuffing them back into his trousers. Threw his shirt back over them. He heard the door slam and lay back on his bed. Rested his arms underneath his head. Waited for the guards to pass by. He closed his eyes. Pretended to be asleep. Plötzensee Prison was far scarier than Sachsenhausen had ever been, his treatment being far worse now that he was convicted for treason and murder. But his execution wasn't scheduled for another two weeks. Steffen was coming by in the morning. Everything was going to be fine.

A pair of knuckles rapped on his bars. Wilhelm opened his eyes, pretending he just woke up. He looked up at his visitors and froze.

Adalwolf Bütz. Grinning back at him. The one-eyed devil he was. He raised a saucy hand. *"Heil."* A guard was standing next to him, both hands behind his back, his chin up, eyes facing forward.

"What are you doing here?" Wilhelm asked in English.

"Oh, that's right," Bütz answered in English. "You're really committed to the whole… thing. Fine by me. I'll play along." Bütz leaned against the bars. His body lit only from behind. All those shadows creeping in. "I really studied up on my English for you, Wilhelm."

"William."

"Don't push your luck." Bütz looked the man up and down. "Where is it?"

Wilhelm felt his stomach turn. "What?"

"I finally built up the courage to sit across from you after what you did to me and you ignore me? Where's that thing you were writing?"

Wilhelm looked at that stationary guard. Back to Bütz. "What, did you call your Daddy to allow a midnight visit to Plötzensee?"

Bütz laughed. "Close. I called Father to make me *Kommandant*."

Wilhelm's lungs evacuated.

Bütz nodded, thrilled to see it. "I wanted the best seat in the house to see that body of yours fall to the floor." He paused again. "So I'll ask once more. As *Kommandant* of Plötzensee Prison. Where is that thing you were writing?"

Wilhelm couldn't even breathe.

Bütz sighed with disappointment. "Open it, Diehl," he ordered in German. Diehl revealed a ring of keys in his hands. Slid the iron into the keyhole. Unlocked the door. Slid it open. Bütz wasted no time strolling inside.

Wilhelm tried to cower away, but Bütz quickly grabbed the side of Wilhelm's head and SLAMMED it against the wall. Wilhelm grunted in pain, struggling as hard as he could to resist. "Search him," Bütz ordered, smushing Wilhelm's cheek against the wall.

Diehl patted Wilhelm down. Stopped at the lump at the back of Wilhelm's trousers. Flipped up his shirt tail. Pulled the letter out.

Bütz let go of Wilhelm's head and stepped back. Wilhelm collapsed on the bed and watched in horror as Bütz flipped through the letter, stepping out into the hall to get closer to the candlelight. Diehl stood between them, blocking the open cell door. Both hands behind his back. Chin up. Eyes forward.

Bütz squinted as he struggled to read Wilhelm's scrawls. He looked at how long it was. Noticed the envelope at the end. He flipped it over. "Who's 'Nadine Sauvageot Crespières'?"

"Please!" Wilhelm desperately cried. "Please, please, please, please give that back! Please!"

"Oh, she's a girl. Of course she is."

Wilhelm dropped to his knees, his hands together, tears in his eyes. "Adalwolf, please!"

Bütz looked up, stunned by Wilhelm's uncharacteristically pathetic reaction. "Oh, it's 'Adalwolf' now?"

"Please, Adalwolf, please!" Wilhelm's lip trembled. "I'll do anything!" he begged in German. "Please let me have that back! Please!"

Bütz's eyes narrowed. "*Kommandant*," he snarled.

"Please, *Kommandant*, please, please, please! I'm sorry, I just… I'll do anything!"

Bütz bit his lip, studying the situation. "I'll tell you what… I'll have Diehl here get us a chess board. If you win, I'll give this back to you. It makes no difference to me what you wrote. Your fate's already been sealed. I win either way." He smoothed out the letter. Made sure it was nice and stacked in the proper order. "But if *I* win, I get to burn it in front of you."

Wilhelm could feel his whole body trembling. His knees hurt. His face stung.

Bütz held up both hands, a charming smile on his face. "What do you say?"

Wilhelm sniffed. Wiped his nose. "If I win, you'll burn it anyway. What's to stop you?"

Bütz raised both brows. "Do you really want to take that chance?"

To Wilhelm's surprise, Bütz wasn't joking about the chess game. As they waited for Diehl to return, Bütz sat just outside Wilhelm's locked cell and thumbed through the manuscript, his brow furrowing as he read.

Wilhelm watched him read, knowing he was on the addendum, the part where he got his revenge on him. But he said nothing. He let the words do all the talking.

Diehl returned ten minutes later with a box of chess pieces, a board, and a small table. Bütz unlocked the cell door, set up the table, and handed the letter to Diehl for safe keeping. Diehl stood tableside, propping the letter up like a bottle of wine. His chin up, eyes forward as usual.

Wilhelm and Bütz sorted out the pieces. Laid them on the board. Just like they used to back at the *Westwall.* "What colour do you want?" Bütz asked.

"You know white is statistically more likely to win, right?"

Bütz shrugged. "Then take white."

Wilhelm slowly rotated the chess board around until white was on his side, thinking it over. "Actually, I want you to take white." He quickly rotated the board back the way it was before.

Bütz shrugged. "Alright." He took a deep breath. Moved the King's Pawn to e4.

Wilhelm thought about his opening move. After a moment of tense silence, he moved his Queen's Pawn to d5.

Bütz captured Wilhelm's pawn. "Uh-uh."

Wilhelm instantly moved his Queen to d5, capturing Bütz's pawn. "You were saying?"

"Yeah, that's not good." Bütz stopped to think over his strategy. Glanced up at the letter in Diehl's hands. "So what is that anyway?" he asked gently.

"A letter."

Bütz moved his Queen's side Knight to c3. "Pretty long for a letter."

Wilhelm scoffed. "Letters seem to be so long these days." He slowly moved his Queen to a5, out of capturing distance of Bütz's Knight.

Bütz moved his Queen's side Pawn to d4. "Who's Nadine?"

Wilhelm stared at the board. Sighed. "After I fought off your goons in Paris, I stayed the night in Nanterre."

"No way! You were only in Nanterre?" Bütz gave an impressed smirk. "Damn. No wonder I couldn't find you."

"That was the idea."

"Go on."

Wilhelm moved the Queen's side Bishop's Pawn to c6. "The next day, I stepped on a landmine outside Crespières."

Bütz winced, his teeth hissing. "Oh my God. Are you alright?"

Wilhelm furrowed his brow. "Yeah. I'm fine."

"Oh. Good." Bütz folded his hands, questioning his next move.

"It happened not too far from a French Resistance camp. The nurse they had there sewed up my leg. Helped me walk again. That's who Nadine is."

Bütz moved his King's side Knight to f3. "How long were you in Crespières?"

"Two weeks."

Bütz hesitated. "Is she pretty?"

Wilhelm nodded slightly, his heart aching. "She's perfect."

"Ah, one of the perfect ones."

"The only perfect one." Wilhelm moved his Queen's side Bishop across the board to g4. Held his thumb there. Lifted. "You killed her parents, you know."

Bütz moved his Queen's side Bishop to f4. "I've killed a lot of people's parents." He did a double take at Wilhelm. "Wait, what do you mean? Where?"

"Nancy."

Bütz looked off. "Nancy…"

"Dairy farm. Mother. Father. Three sons." Wilhelm moved his King's side pawn to e6. "You saved the mother for last. Remember?"

"I thought there wasn't a daughter at Nancy."

"There *was* a daughter at Nancy. I just didn't tell you there was."

Bütz gaped. "You sneaky dog! You let her go, didn't you?!"

Wilhelm jutted his chin out. "Your turn."

"Sorry." Bütz moved his King's side Rook's pawn to h3. "Can't believe you actually got one past me."

"Wasn't that hard, believe me." Wilhelm captured Bütz's Knight at f3 using his Bishop.

"But what are the chances, huh? She being the one to fix your leg after you let her go?"

"I know."

"Good thing she never found out you let her family get killed. She'd throw that letter in the bin." Bütz moved his Queen to f3, capturing Wilhelm's Bishop.

"No, she knows."

Bütz looked up. "What do you mean she knows?"

Wilhelm shrugged. "She knows. I told her everything."

"She knows you're a Nazi? That you were there when…?"

Wilhelm nodded over and over.

Bütz shook his head a bit. "And she didn't turn you in or anything?"

"Nope." Wilhelm moved his King's side Bishop to b4. "Matter of fact, she helped me escape. Drove me all the way to Marseilles."

Bütz stared off into space. Sighed. Lowered his head.

Wilhelm stared at him from across the board. His humble expression intrigued him. And that disquieting silence…

Bütz brushed his fingers across his mouth. Soft breath in. Soft breath out. "You should've married her," he said solemnly.

Wilhelm's eyes drooped a little.

Bütz shrugged, trying to downplay his vulnerability. "She knew everything about you and still would do all that for you? God knows I'll never have that." He looked down at his pieces and sighed. "You arse. You really got me."

Wilhelm swallowed. He felt very exposed. "I just wish I could see her again," he said quietly.

Bütz bumped his brows. "That's why it's so many pages, huh? Love letter?" He cautiously moved his King's side Bishop to e2.

Wilhelm rubbed the back of his head. "I really felt like myself writing it." He looked up at the letter in Diehl's hands. "If you look at only what I've done, I've been a Nazi. I've killed people. But I'm not a murderer. And I was never a Nazi. I was a human being. And now… anyone who reads it will know the real me was William, not Wilhelm."

Bütz hesitated. "But I liked Wilhelm."

Wilhelm gave Bütz sceptical eyes.

Bütz held up both hands. "Hey, I never did anything to you. Ever. You're the one that keeps trying to kill me here."

"You ordered Emil and Ebert to kill me."

"As a *joke!* I didn't think they actually would!" Bütz crossed his arms. Looked off. Thought back. "I thought there was nothing wrong with Wilhelm. Everyone else thought there was. I never had a problem with you. Matter of fact, I felt bad you didn't have a dad. I felt bad he died that way. It caused you and your mother so much grief. Left you penniless and ostracised. You were stuck raising a lunatic of a mother instead of following your dream of becoming a professor like your father."

Wilhelm moved his Queen's side Knight to d7.

Bütz scratched the right side of his face with a single finger. "I even actually… I actually thought you were my friend."

Wilhelm didn't say anything. He just stared off. His mind in the same place as Bütz's.

Bütz shook his head. "I found another person that didn't believe in the war. Forced to participate, just like I was."

"Don't pretend you didn't enjoy hurting those people, because you did."

"I had to make the most of it," Bütz said with a defensive whine. "I told you about that time we had Oskar Dirlewanger over for dinner."

"Who?"

"Oskar Dirlewanger? My father's old friend from the Army? He runs the Dirlewanger Brigade now. Hell of a guy."

Wilhelm bumped his brows. "Emphasis on 'hell.'"

"Hey, *they* call him 'The Butcher.' It's a matter of opinion." Bütz crossed his legs. Leaned back. "Anyway, a few years ago, probably '34 or something, my father had him over for dinner. And Oskar told me all the awful shit he's seen men do to civilians during the Great War. Rape. Murder. Torture. Everything. Things we're not supposed to do, right? But no one gets punished for any of that after wartime. He's seen it. He told me specifically that if there was another war, so soon after that last one, he was going to take advantage of it this time. There's never a better time to be a man, he says."

Wilhelm leaned back in his chair. "I don't know about that."

"You know what happens if we lose this war? We're dead. Doesn't matter if we did something to deserve it or nothing at all. They'll shoot us just for this." Bütz pointed to the swastika on his arm. "Somebody out there will find a reason to shoot us for this. Just for having it on. But if we win, you know what's going to happen?"

Wilhelm didn't react.

"Desks," Bütz said with venom. "A lifetime pushing papers. Politics. Wages. Bills. Insurance. Raising kids. Providing for families. Bureaucratic hell. I've seen what happened to my father. How peacetime made him fat. No adventure in sight. No hope. Just atrophy. Banal atrophy. And that tears at the soul, it does. It destroys the fire of life." Bütz shrugged. "So I'm sorry. I wanted to have as much fun as I could before everyone's brains turned back on and the world reverted back to civilisation, because the way I see it, I'm dead either way. And I wanted you, you specifically, to have fun too. You didn't have those opportunities. I wanted to give that to you. And I don't know if you noticed, I was one of the few that actually made fun a priority. Most people have to dance around having fun. They have to pretend they're not having fun. Keep it all in the background. Because real war isn't supposed to be fun. It's work. But real war is death. I happened to be in the fortunate position to guarantee we wouldn't see a man blown to bits like my father did. You're lucky to have been spared those stories growing up. And let's be honest, it's not like they needed us. There were thousands of others marching over France and Belgium. And now the Horse Heads are about to invade the Soviets. The Soviets! Can you believe that? Thank God for this transfer. I would not want to be part of that!" Bütz laughed heartily. Looked down at the board. "Whose turn is it?"

"Yours."

"Alright, give me a second." Bütz licked the front of his teeth. "You fucker." He moved his Queen's side Rook's pawn to a3. Left a finger on. Lifted it off. "Of course everyone will be doing what I did to those people once the war's over. Either side. Whoever wins. Mark my words. When word gets out that Allies had won, they'll rape civilians for days. Torture POWs. Probably rape them too, if you ask me. Maybe five at a time. And you know what they're going to say? Roosevelt? Churchill? Stalin? What they're going to say when they find out what their boys are doing that to all those poor, defenceless human beings?"

Wilhelm castled his King. "What will they say?"

"'*Let them,*'" Bütz enunciated. "'They just won a war for us. Let the boys have their fun. They earned it.' They'll always deny they said that, of course, but don't expect anyone to actually stop it from happening. Don't expect them to be charged for all their war crimes, for breaking the Geneva Convention. It'll be just like Dirlewanger said: whatever happens during the war will stay in the war."

"What you did to those people?" Wilhelm looked up at Bütz, scrunching his face. "You know that was *treason*, right?"

"Apparently not."

"You went against orders taking us on all those hedonistic detours. We were supposed to be fighting at front with the rest of the Division. So why am I being sentenced to death and you're the one getting promoted?"

"It's all about who you know." Bütz furrowed his brow at Wilhelm's side of the board. "Did you just castle? Why would you do that?"

"I'm not telling you."

Bütz captured Wilhelm's Bishop at b4 using his Pawn. "Think about it. I wouldn't have had this promotion if not for my father."

"You're telling me."

"And you wouldn't have had that whole manhunt after you if you hadn't tried to kill me again in that hotel in Paris. If you had been nicer to me, maybe you'd be in Casablanca by now."

Wilhelm fixated his attention on Bütz's glass eye. "You realise now everyone will always know what I did to you the first time."

Bütz looked back at Wilhelm.

"You made such a big stink about capturing me," Wilhelm continued. "All the papers got word. And now that you testified, the whole world knows now what I did to you. It'll be all anyone thinks about when they look at you. They'll point at those scars, that fake eye of yours, and they'll say to each other, 'You know how he got that, right? His subordinate sliced his eye open with a knife before stabbing his hand down to the ground, shooting his ear and *vomiting* all over him.' Wilhelm smirked. "That's my legacy. Sure as hell beats yours."

"No, your legacy is being a hypocrite," Bütz retorted dispassionately. "You think you're such a good person, but you're not. You have a problem with me killing civilians? Raping girls? Getting you, Ebert and Emil to go along with it all? Why? Because they weren't soldiers? Because it didn't happen on the battlefield, so they all should've been off-limits? They weren't pieces in the game? They never swore an oath? They were just humans on the sidelines, trying to get by, waiting out the war in fear? Then what about those Nazis you killed while they were on R&R? Weren't they human? Were they on the battlefield, fair and square for you to take them out? No, they weren't. They were ambushed. Assassinated. Tortured. How were they different from all those civilians simply minding their own business, tending to their cows while the war raged on?"

Wilhelm's blood went cold at that.

Bütz leaned in with a devilish smirk. "You remember that one in Belgium? The blonde with the thin waist? She knew how to take it, didn't she?

Oh, and she could scream. Remember her scream? I know you do. I let you all have a piece of her. I even went twice. What a night, huh?"

Wilhelm frowned hard, trying his hardest not to remember.

"That was the real you," Bütz whispered. "Don't pretend… for a single second… you didn't enjoy it. Don't pretend you didn't love us cheering you on. You were a fucking god that night, Wilhelm. For the first time in your life, you were a real fucking man and you loved it. Any shame you felt later was you telling yourself you needed to feel ashamed, but I know what was real and what wasn't, and that, my friend, was real. *That* was the real you. So don't pretend you're better than me. Don't pretend. Because I know if the roles were reversed, you wouldn't have done the same exact things I did."

Wilhelm tried not to cry. "This is who I am now," he whispered, his red eyes frozen with fear. "William is who I want to be."

"I don't believe you. Wilhelm Gunter had Aryan blood. Wilhelm Gunter had a nation that loved him. Wilhelm Gunter had a mother that would do anything to protect him. Wilhelm Gunter had brothers in arms, if not by blood. Wilhelm killed. Wilhelm raped. Wilhelm *succeeded.* He was strong. He was passionate. He was fucking invincible. But not William. William was a fool. William was weak. William shot at Nazis and only hit civilians. William got himself caught sticking his neck out for some Hungarian bitch that thanked him by turning him in. William stepped on a landmine like an idiot. William slithered around the dark, killing poor exhausted men finally back to civilisation like a fucking coward, just as they were allowed a break from all the madness. And William went for the fucking eye, didn't he! Of all the things to go for, he went for the fucking *eye!*"

Wilhelm closed his eyes.

Bütz shook his head. "I don't understand. Why aren't you proud to have been born Wilhelm Gunter? Wilhelm Gunter was the best man you ever could've been. William Gunnison? What was he? At the end of the day, could you even say he was worth it? No. He wasn't. He was just an idealist's waste of time. An act of denial. Just you pretending your shit didn't stink."

Wilhelm opened his eyes. Stared resolutely back at Bütz. "That's where the faith comes in."

Bütz scoffed. "Faith? Why would you of all people have any faith in anything? You had the opportunity—*twice* you had the opportunity—to kill me, and you missed! Fate, it seems, keeps sparing me and punishing you. Why?

Why is God doing that? Is He telling you the William experiment ran its course? Face it. Everything you've done has only made everything worse for yourself. When has fortune *ever* been on your side? When has your faith amounted to anything other than you doing nothing and hoping for a miracle. Because I don't think you're aware of something. *I'm* the one the seems to be getting all the miracles."

Wilhelm looked down at the board. "I really pity you, Adalwolf." He moved his Queen to a1, capturing Bütz's Rook. "Check."

"I don't know why." Bütz instantly moved his King to d2.

"You have no idea how many lives you've ruined. No clue at all. Not one inkling. It's not just an intelligence thing. You simply don't care. I do. Because it's so obvious. If you only knew how simple it was, how every human interaction ripples across the world, across nations, across borders, you'd stop what you're doing in a heartbeat."

"Spare me. If your father was the *SS-Gruppenführer* and my father was the dead professor, you'd shoot me in a heartbeat. Because you could. Because you know you'd get away with it. You wouldn't give a damn about ripples getting back to you. It wouldn't even cross your mind."

Wilhelm moved his Queen to h1, taking Bütz's other Rook. "But my father is dead. And I'm telling you, the way I am now, if the roles were reversed, if I was the *Kommandant* and you were the one in this cell, I still wouldn't do it."

Bütz laughed out loud. "Bullshit! You're telling me if Diehl wasn't standing right there…"

"If Diehl wasn't there, and I had every opportunity to kill you with no collateral damage, I wouldn't do it."

"Even after everything?" Bütz moved his Queen to c6, capturing Wilhelm's Pawn. "Check."

"Even after everything." Wilhelm captured Bütz's Queen with a Queen's Side Bishop's Pawn. "I already learnt my lesson. Learnt it twice, as a matter of fact. If fate really does control everything, Adalwolf, then maybe you are being spared for a reason. Could that reason be that you're supposed to follow my lead? Renounce your Nazi uniform? Have the chance to redeem yourself? Use your power and influence to save lives? For good, not evil?"

Bütz stared at the board, fixated on all the pieces.

Wilhelm smirked. He was getting to him now. "I know this is all a front.

I know you wouldn't have been this passionate against me if you being brought so close to death meant nothing to you at all."

Bütz didn't react. He just kept staring.

Wilhelm tenderly looked at Bütz's fake eye. "Did you cry when you first realised it was gone? When you first saw it in the mirror? Scrubbing all that vomit out of your clothes? Were you scared when woke up that night? All cold and bleeding? Covered in fresh sick? Smelly from head to toe. All that dried grime caked on you? Did you feel the lowest you'd ever been? Did my betrayal make you realise the cost of your behaviour? What was that like, Adalwolf? How did it feel?"

Bütz closed his eyes, desperately tuning Wilhelm out.

"I know you too well, Adalwolf," Wilhelm said sympathetically. "I know this power play of yours is nothing but a cocky way of you deflecting. Just you covering up how deep down you know I'm right."

Bütz opened his eyes a bit, but he refused to look at Wilhelm.

Wilhelm simply frowned. "I think a part of you liked me so much because in your heart you wished you never had a father. You wanted my level of education. You wanted not to have to be forced to hurt people in your twenties to make up for an early demise or a lifetime of piggish bureaucracy." He paused. "Until you change, Adalwolf, as far as I'm concerned, you'll always be powerless."

"I actually thought this was going to be fun," Bütz said slowly. "One last chance for us to be the way we used to be. To be friends again. Just like we were at the start. Before everything went wrong." He looked up, finally making eye contact with Wilhelm.

Wilhelm stared back, his heart pounding.

Bütz looked off again, shaking his head, his tongue pressed to one side. "But this isn't fun at all, it's just..." He furrowed his brow. "*Sad.*" He looked Wilhelm in the eye again. "I was so afraid of you, all this time. And a part of me..." He scoffed. "A part of me actually respected you for doing it at all. You managed to get one over me. You actually had the balls to do it." He half-smirked. "But it makes me sad seeing someone like that..." He lifted his Bishop. "...be so wrong..." Floated it across the board. "...about himself." Placed it on a6. "Checkmate."

Wilhelm's blood went cold. He gaped. "No." He scanned the board over and over. "No. No, no, no, you're wrong."

"No, that's definitely checkmate." Bütz stood. Took the letter from Diehl. Walked out the cell.

"No, please, no!" Wilhelm cried in a panic. He couldn't believe it. His King was trapped. It really was checkmate. He lost. Wilhelm tried to stand up, but Diehl grabbed both of his shoulders and forced him down. Held him in his chair. "PLEASE!" Wilhelm screamed.

Bütz pulled out his lighter and lit the bottom edge of the letter. He held the paper by a corner as the flames crawled its way up, consuming everything. "Leave the board, Diehl." He dropped the burning letter, its flames crackling, bright orange light dancing about. "Let him stew on it."

Diehl let go of Wilhelm. Took big strides to the cell door. Stepped over the pyre on his way out.

Wilhelm at first couldn't move. He was frozen with shock. But at the last second, he jumped up and ran as fast as he could towards that burning letter, but Diehl slammed the cell door just before he could make it through. Locked it. Pocketed the keys.

Wilhelm tried to reach the burning letter through the bars, his armpit hurting as he strained. But it was too late. The fire was now full-blown flame. No matter how hard he tried, he couldn't get close enough. Wilhelm slumped down. Wailed into the dust, trembling as he cried.

Bütz stayed behind to watch Wilhelm's pathetic cell floor meltdown. How hurt he was. How devastated. The greatest thing he treasured most in this world was gone... and yet no one could say it wasn't entirely his fault. "*That's* what it felt like," Bütz whispered, too quiet for anyone to hear. "You piece of shit." He slowly turned. Followed Diehl out of the block. Slammed the door behind them.

CHAPTER SEVENTEEN

Blindfold

Steffen arrived in the morning, just as he promised, only to find a pile of ashes outside Wilhelm's cell and a distraught young man inside. Too tired to stay awake. Too hurt to sleep. Wilhelm had curled himself up in the corner, rocking himself with frozen, traumatised eyes.

Steffen and Wilhelm sat in the same chairs Wilhelm and Bütz sat in just the night before, the board untouched. Wilhelm couldn't even look at it. It was like Bütz was mocking him, but he didn't have the strength to knock it over.

Steffen frowned in his chair, having just heard the whole story. "Jesus."

Wilhelm removed Steffen's pen from his pocket. Handed it back. "Thanks anyway."

Steffen reluctantly took the pen back. Studied it in his hands. "I can get you some more paper. Surely you can pump out an abridged version."

Wilhelm shook his head. His eyes stung from all the dried tears. "It took five months last time. I'll be dead in a fortnight."

Steffen slowly pocketed his pen. "I can go find Jacques."

"Don't you dare."

"I can at least tell him what happened to you."

"You've already done enough for me," Wilhelm rasped. "It's about time I accepted my defeat. It's over. I lost. I've been beaten."

Steffen said nothing more. He simply stared down at his hands.

Wilhelm swallowed. "How long do you think it'll take for him to realise I failed?" He looked up at Steffen. "Getting to New York from Paris during wartime is no easy task. He knew that, I'm sure. Not to mention finding Victor. Coordinating whatever plans he had in that letter. That has to take a while, right? Because then we'd have to get back to Paris and get all those boxes out too. I couldn't have done all that in six months."

Steffen nodded. "I agree."

"So he probably still thinks I'm on task, right?" Wilhelm hesitated. "So how long, do you think? How long does it take for someone like that to give up on me? When will he realise help isn't coming? Nine months? A year?"

"What's the point, Wilhelm?"

"If he realises I failed, he won't have to wait for me. He can find someone else." Wilhelm paused. "Or will he die years from now, convinced I'm still coming back?"

Steffen shrugged. "I don't know."

"But he's not going to die years from now, is he?" Wilhelm mumbled. "He'll be on his way back from the Black Market when they grab him. And they'll send him to a concentration camp. And all those boxes, they'll burn them all, won't they? All that history they had. All that personal weight…" He looked at the pile of ashes just outside the cell door. "God, I hope he won't be there to see it."

Steffen stood. "Wilhelm, you can't think about that…"

"What else is there for me to think about, Uncle Steffen?!" Wilhelm snapped. "If I've done enough good to get into Heaven? What Hell's going to smell like? If there even is an afterlife and not just some void? What if it's just a void? It won't be like I'm asleep! Sleeping at least is something. Nothing is *nothing*. No movement. No thought. Nothing. Just nothing, forever and ever." Wilhelm's body started shaking. "I can't… I can't…"

Steffen crouched before Wilhelm. Held him tight.

Wilhelm squeezed back hard, his eyes closed even tighter. "I don't want to die!" he whined, his voice bouncing with rough sobs. "I don't want to die! I don't want to die!"

"I know." Steffen petted Wilhelm's back, trying not to cry himself.

"Oh God, I don't want to die! Please! I don't want to die!"

Steffen closed his eyes. Buried his head into Wilhelm's shoulder. "Just get some rest. You'll feel better."

"Don't leave me."

"I'm not." Steffen kissed Wilhelm's forehead. "I'll be back tomorrow, alright? Just sleep."

Wilhelm sniffed. "No…"

"You'll feel better, believe me." Steffen forced a smile. "I'll be back tomorrow. We can talk then."

Wilhelm wiped the tears from his eyes. "Tomorrow?"

"Tomorrow."

Wilhelm sniffed. Forced a smile. "Okay."

Steffen reluctantly left Wilhelm's cell. His soul was exhausted. He held back tears just long enough to make it out of the block. Finally out of Wilhelm's earshot, he let it all out.

Wilhelm lay on his side. Curled up on his bed. His mind finally calm. No letter again. He already tasted thoughts of death. That was enough for the rest of the day, wasn't it? And he already thought about Jacques. Wondered who Victor was. What plan was written out in the letter. What 'Olive Branch' meant…

Wilhelm jolted up with wide eyes. The address. The address on the envelope. He had it. He remembered. It just came to him, just like that. The moment he stopped looking for it, it came to him. Victor's address. He was reading it just before he stepped on that landmine. He could still see. It was right there in his mind's eye:

195 W 10th Street
Apartment 4B
New York, NY

"195 West 10th Street, Apartment 4B," Wilhelm said under his breath. He grinned. "195 West 10th Street, Apartment 4B! That's it! 195 West 10th Street, Apartment 4B! 195 WEST 10TH STREET, APARTMENT 4B!" Wilhelm laughed like a madman. He patted his pockets down, looking for Steffen's pen. It wasn't there. The pen. It wasn't there. Wilhelm looked up at the hallway door. "UNCLE STEFFEN!" he cried. "COME BACK! I NEED THAT PEN AFTER ALL! UNCLE STEFFEN! *STEFFFFEEENNNN!*"

But Steffen was too far away to hear him.

Wilhelm repeated that address for hours, unable to write it down, making sure he had memorised. 195 West 10th Street, Apartment 4B. 195 West 10th Street, Apartment 4B. Why didn't he just keep the pen? 195 West 10th Street, Apartment 4B. 195 West 10th Street, Apartment 4B. He'll tell Steffen tomorrow. 195 West 10th Street, Apartment 4B. 195 West 10th Street, Apartment 4B. He'll carve it into his hand if he had to. 195 West 10th Street, Apartment 4B. 195 West 10th Street, Apartment 4B.

Diehl knocked on his cell door.

Wilhelm flinched, not having seen the man approach. "What is it?"

"A message for you," Diehl reported in English, his voice deep and moronic. "Herr *Kommandant* wanted me to tell you personally that you're no longer allowed visitors." Without another word, Diehl turned and left.

Wilhelm gaped, too numb to process the reality of him never seeing Steffen again. Never being able to tell him Victor's address. Never being able to change his mind and give Steffen the address to go seek Jacques out after all. He really was all alone. But he couldn't think about that. He simply cleared his mind. Rolled back over. Went to sleep. Steffen said sleep would make him feel better.

When he woke, he didn't feel better.

He didn't feel better the next day either.

On the third day, Wilhelm felt a hand on his left shoulder. He was shaken awake. It was a woman in his cell. A woman in a Gestapo firing squad uniform. Black and red hat. Rifle in her gloved hands. In his half-asleep delirium, he actually thought it was Nadine.

"Wake up," she said in German. "Come with us."

Wilhelm sat up. Stared at Plötzensee's Gestapo commander and the three other firing squad members standing just outside his cell door. "What's going on?" he asked in English.

The firing squad woman and one of the men hoisted Wilhelm up. Dragged him out of his cell. His bare feet hung in the air. His toenails scraped the ground.

"No, wait, you got the wrong guy!" Wilhelm cried at them in German. "It's not supposed to be today! Where are you taking me?!"

"*Kommandant*'s orders," the Gestapo commander reported heartlessly, leading the squad outside.

"NO!" Wilhelm screamed, stepping on the ground. He tried to fight his captors. The Gestapo commander turned and hit Wilhelm in the gut with a nightstick. All the wind escaped him. He felt weak again. Slumped down. They continued dragging him out.

It was early, just before dawn. Wilhelm's eyes hurt. Cold grass tickling his bare feet. He could hear the sound of digging. He lifted his head and saw he was in the back courtyard of Plötzensee Prison, just before the thirty-foot-high perimeter surrounding the grounds. It was quiet out there. No prisoners. No guards. No crowd of spectators. Everyone must've been still asleep. Everyone, that is, except two gravediggers finishing up a plot, a warden, three guards (including Diehl) and *Kommandant* Adalwolf Bütz himself, giving Wilhelm a big toothy grin of recognition.

"What is this?" Wilhelm croaked in English, his eyes never leaving Bütz's. "I'm not supposed to die for another week and a half."

"Yes, you'd love to be a martyr, wouldn't you?" Bütz teased. "The world remembering you as the traitor instead of the Nazi you really are." He stepped up. Got real close to Wilhelm's face. "Well, I don't think that's very fair. I'll never be allowed that option. Why should you?"

"You know I think you do."

Bütz slapped Wilhelm across the face with one of his gloves. "Maybe you committed suicide. Maybe we shot you trying to escape. I'll think about that. Either way, your death will be just like your life, Wilhelm Gunter: completely immemorable.

Wilhelm glared up at Bütz.

Bütz giggled back. Signalled the firing squad commander. Stepped back. Took his place on the sidelines.

As the Gestapo commander tied Wilhelm's hands behind his back, he couldn't help but stare at that open grave. Unmarked. Under the lawn. All those prisoners walking over him. No way for anyone to locate his body. No way for Nadine to visit him when the war ended. They'll never even know he's down there. They'll never know who he was. Who he really was. Without a public traitor's execution, everyone will forget all about him.

The Gestapo commander covered Wilhelm's eyes with a long black blindfold. Tied it at the back. It was dark in there. And when those fingers tying the knot disappeared, that's when it really got scary. Wilhelm truly felt alone. He could hear the crunching of grass. A few whispers between Bütz and the warden. And he could feel his body shaking. This was it. This was finally it. The end of it all. He could feel all his pores tighten. The hair on his arms standing on end. He could feel the inside of his body open up. He could feel every drop of that morning dew. That awful breeze wafting through him.

"Ready!" the Gestapo commander shouted in German. Four rifles cocked themselves simultaneously.

Wilhelm could feel hot piss trickling down his leg. He began to cry on his feet. He had never been so scared.

"Aim!" The sound of four guns moving around a bit. Their barrels no doubt pointing right at his heart.

Wilhelm's wrists hurt. His head hurt. His brain was going nuts. All his senses heightened because of the blindfold. Everything was making him dizzy. But clearer than ever, he could see Nadine. Smiling at him by that hospital bed in Crespières. He could feel that hug she gave him.

"You're not a Nazi, William."

Wilhelm was suddenly aware of the length of time after "Aim" and before "Fire." It hurt. It hurt everywhere.

"You might've acted like a Nazi for a time, but you were never one in your heart."

Wilhelm wanted to hear another Apollinaire poem again. He wanted to see the sun again. He wanted to be in a warm bed again.

"Nazis don't care about people. Nazis don't try to save civilian lives."

He wanted to eat breakfast with Jacques again. He wanted to drink coffee with Nadine again. Reciting Rilke to her. Talking about his father. He wanted to hold Uncle Steffen once more. He just wanted one more chance to tell him goodbye.

"Nazis don't kill Nazi officers. Nazis don't get shot at by Nazis."

He wished he had a better goodbye with Nadine too. He wished he kissed her. Or even just to see her again.

"You stopped being a Nazi a long time ago."

He wished he had the nerve to tell her he loved her. Because he loved Nadine. He loved her so much. She was the best thing—

"FIRE!"

Gunshots.

Lots and lots of gunshots. They weren't synchronised.

And no pain at all.

And then silence.

Wilhelm muted his breath, tension releasing itself in small staccato bursts. He could still hear the crunch of grass. Footsteps approaching him. Fingers touching him. He flinched instantly.

"It's alright," a soft female voice was saying in English. "You're safe now."

Wilhelm exhaled a little more now, allowing those callused fingers to remove his blindfold. The light was abrasive. Wilhelm blinked his way through it.

The firing squad woman from before? And she was smiling at him. Why was she—?

Wilhelm gasped. "Nadine?!" he whimpered. He was grinning the hardest he had ever grinned. It really was Nadine. The whole time, she was Nadine. And he recognised the other three of the firing squad. Scragg. Durant. Émile.

Nadine walked around Wilhelm and started untying his wrists. Wilhelm finally got a good look at the scene around him. There were bodies everywhere. Bütz? Dead. Diehl? Dead. The warden? Dead. The other guards? Dead. The gravediggers? Dead. The Gestapo commander? Dead. No one left alive. Scragg and Émile were already dragging bodies into that open grave. Durant standing by on the side, his rifle at the ready, keeping watch for witnesses.

Nadine struggled to undo Wilhelm's wrist knot, huffing at herself.

"What are you doing here?" Wilhelm asked in a daze, still in shock.

Nadine chucked a bit as she finally slid the rope loose. The rest of the bind practically undid itself. "What do you think? We're breaking you out. You've got to get to New York."

Wilhelm rubbed his wrists. Looked over at Nadine. He was about to ask her if this was really happening, if this was real or just a vision. But then he was struck dumb by her eyes. Then by her confused expression.

"Are you alright?" Nadine asked gently. "What's wrong?"

Wilhelm just burst into tears. She was really there. He was really free. It was all really happening. And he hugged her as tight as he could. So much emotion. Crying tears of joy into her firing squad uniform.

"Oh!" Nadine exclaimed. She awkwardly stood there, feeling the weight of a grown man crying on her. She felt exposed, embarrassed in front of the guys. "William." She tried to peel him off but he wouldn't budge. She cleared her throat. "William? William." Nadine tried a bit harder, this time successfully, gently, separating herself from Wilhelm's grip. "We can do all that later. Let's get you out of here first, alright?"

Wilhelm sniffed. "Alright."

"Strip the commander and get into his uniform. You think you can do that?"

"Yeah."

"You can? Okay. Great."

Wilhelm waddled over to the Gestapo commander. Started removing his jacket. Nadine caught a glimpse of Durant snickering at her. She flashed back a silent scowl. Durant instantly dropped his smile. Kept looking out.

Wilhelm tried the Gestapo jacket on. It fit him well. But he felt eyes on him. He slowly looked to his left.

Scragg was glaring at him from his spot by the mass grave. He looked frightening.

Wilhelm awkwardly waved.

Scragg didn't budge.

Wilhelm looked down at the dead commander he was stripping. He finally realised the significance. "Oh. Yeah." He looked back at Scragg. "Sorry about taking your clothes before," he said in English, playfully but still sincere.

Nadine looked over Scragg. "He's apologising to you for before," she translated.

But Scragg kept staring at Wilhelm. He spat on the dirt, never breaking eye contact with him.

Wilhelm turned away, instantly uncomfortable. He crouched to de-trouser the commander. "What's his problem?" he whispered to Nadine as he pulled the pistol from the dead man's holster.

"I don't know," Nadine mumbled back. "He's been like that ever since we left France. I don't think he's a fan of the whole… you know… Nazi thing."

Wilhelm checked magazine of his new Luger. Three shots left. "Can't say I blame him." He reloaded the gun. Looked over at Scragg. He was still giving him that dirty look. "He knows I'm not anymore, right?"

"Don't worry, he's committed to the mission. I made him promise to follow my lead on this one."

Wilhelm slipped off his trousers. Quickly switched on the commander's. "Hey, how did you get everyone to go along with this anyway? Isn't this way out of your jurisdiction?"

"I told Roul the truth and he got them to go along with it."

Wilhelm stared at Nadine. "And what truth is that?"

Nadine hesitated. "That you were a German informant loyal to France with great firsthand Nazi intel who'd be invaluable to the Resistance if we extracted you and made you part of the team."

Wilhelm furrowed his brow. Looked off in disbelief. Returned to Nadine. "You sold me to the Resistance?"

"It's the only way they would've agreed to do it."

"Then who's going to save Jacques?"

Nadine smiled nervously. "Can we talk about this later?" she asked through gritted teeth. "*After* the prison break?"

Durant counted the bodies already in the grave. "We're missing one!" he called out in French.

Nadine's head whipped over. "What did he say?" Wilhelm asked her in English.

"He said there's a body missing," Nadine translated, confused. She hurried over to the grave. Counted the bodies herself. "I don't see the *Kommandant!*" she exclaimed angrily in French. "Where is he?! How'd he get away?!"

"I was moving bodies the whole time," Émile said. "What was Scragg doing?"

Scragg didn't say anything. He was still in his own little world.

Nadine stared at Durant. "What's your excuse?"

Durant swallowed. "I-I'm sorry. I don't have one."

Nadine grimaced. "Fuck!" She scanned the yard. All the trees. The ferns. "I can't see him. He must be inside." She faced her team. "Alright, until the alarm actually goes off, the plan stays the same. Agreed?"

"Agreed," everyone responded.

Nadine kicked the commander's body away from Wilhelm's feet. "Alright, we're done with him. Durant! Help Scragg move the commander."

Scragg and Durant beelined to the naked commander's body. Together they carried him to the grave. Tossed him onto the pile.

"Émile!" Nadine barked. "You've done enough body disposal. Keep your eyes on the main building."

"What about the burying?" Émile asked.

"We don't have time. Just add a layer of dirt. That'll be enough for now."

"Yes, sir!"

"Let's hurry, people! Sixty seconds!" Nadine noticed Wilhelm looking at her. She let out a self-conscious smile. "What is it?" she asked, switching to English.

Wilhelm grinned back. "Whatever it is you told them, you looked so…" He nodded. "It fits you. It really does."

Nadine beamed with pride. "I think I have you to thank for that."

Wilhelm approached the open grave, curious to see which man apparently got away. He scanned the faces just before Émile covered them with dirt. No scars over their right eyes. "Oh, God dammit," he muttered.

"What?" Nadine asked him in English, walking over.

"Bütz isn't dead." Wilhelm rolled his eyes. "*Again.*"

Nadine's face went blank. "Bütz? Bütz was here? At Plötzensee?"

"He was the *Kommandant*. Didn't you recognise him?"

Nadine cringed. "Bütz is a *KOMMANDANT* now?! Oh my God!"

"I know. He can't seem to die and he can't stop getting promoted. What an arsehole." Wilhelm looked at Nadine. "So what's the plan? How are we getting out of here?"

"The way we came in. They're expecting a Gestapo commander and four soldiers, they'll see a Gestapo commander and four soldiers."

"And if Bütz tells everyone we're not?"

Nadine reloaded her rifle. "Why do you think we picked the firing squad?" She threw in a smirk. Led the team back to the main building. Wilhelm put on the commander's cap, donned a serious face, and followed. Durant, Émile and Scragg marched in the rear, rifles kept to their sides.

As the team marched their way back into the main building, two things were most noticeable: the sounds of guards and prison staff mulling about, now wide awake and gabbing, and the lack of true commotion. Nadine looked behind her at Wilhelm. She was surprised but more suspicious. Wilhelm jutted his chin onward and the train continued.

Nadine led everyone around the corner. They all stopped where they were.

They were in the mess hall. The whole place was full of guards, wardens, SS officers, Gestapo, secretaries, and dog handlers, all sitting at tables eating their breakfast, gulping down their coffee, everyone still in that early morning tired smog. The conversation died down as eyes fell one by one on the suddenly *very conspicuous* firing squad standing there at the end of the room with guns in their hands. The crowded room went from active to silent in five seconds.

Nadine held up a casual hand. "*Heil Hitler.*"

"*Heil Hitler,*" everybody said back at different times, with varying levels of enthusiasm.

Wilhelm poked Nadine in the back. Nadine walked on, making sure not to look at anyone directly. Their caravan took their time across the mess hall, and they reached the end without any drama.

Wilhelm recognised the new hall they were in. The entrance was very close.

"Where is he?" Nadine whispered to Wilhelm. "Why hasn't he sounded the alarm?"

Wilhelm suddenly stopped walking. Looked off to the side. Durant, Émile and Scragg kept walking past him, each looking at him with confusion.

Nadine saw Wilhelm staring at a plain looking office door. She signalled the others to halt. "What is it?" she whispered, approaching him.

Wilhelm pointed at the office door's brass handle. "Does that look like blood to you?"

Nadine got closer. It was faint, but it was there, and it looked fresh. She looked up at Wilhelm.

Wilhelm looked back. Took a deep breath. "Wait out here."

"Try not to shoot," Nadine whispered. "There's a whole army back there getting caffeinated."

"They tune out more than you think. One shot won't raise any eyebrows." Wilhelm removed the safety on his pistol. "If I'm not back in five minutes, get yourself out. I mean it."

Nadine frowned a bit at the thought. "Alright."

Wilhelm nodded. He gently pushed the door open. Walked in alone.

The first room had just a secretary desk. No people in sight. Wilhelm held his pistol out in front of him, both eyes on wide alert. He stopped at the sound of hissed breathing coming in from the next room. He readjusted the grip on his Luger. Tiptoed around the corner. Crept into the adjoining office.

Sitting on the floor behind his desk was Adalwolf. Not Bütz. Not the *Kommandant* of Plötzensee Prison. *Adalwolf.* Blood was leaking out of the hole in his shoulder, dripping down his hands and onto his wrists. An emergency med kit open on the ground. He was desperately stuffing gauze into the wound. The spot he was shot in wasn't lethal, and it didn't look like he was in too bad of shape, but he was definitely scared. He flinched at the sight of Wilhelm holding that pistol. He held up both hands, the gauze still sticking to his shoulder wound.

Wilhelm stared back. Raised his gun at him.

Adalwolf trembled on his arse. He knew he lost. He couldn't speak. He couldn't even scream.

Wilhelm gripped the gun tighter. He aimed. What would hurt more?

What would be the most fitting? The other eye? To make him completely blind, the way he once promised? Just like he had been in front of that firing squad? Or the heart, where Wilhelm meant to shoot him back at Paris? Or perhaps the back? So he could die the way Corey did? Painful and slow? Or the cock, for all those girls he raped? Or the head? He executed all those civilians in the head. Those farmers. Those dreamers like Nadine.

Adalwolf stared back, fear taking over. Wilhelm was going to kill him. He was really going to die.

Wilhelm gritted his teeth. That man on the ground just wasn't a monster to him anymore. He was too complicated to be a monster. All he kept seeing was that man who used to be his friend. Playing chess with him at the *Westwall*. Laughing at his jokes. Listening to his stories. The first real friend he ever had. Before Belgium and France changed them. Back when the war wasn't even real to them yet. Just a sad little German boy traumatised by all those Great War horror stories his father and his sadistic friends raised him on. Too cowardly to ever stand and fight. Too insecure to stand by his own principles. To let his father know what he really wanted. Adalwolf's father was never going to forgive him for letting a famous traitor escape Plötzensee. Letting it all happen on his watch. Too scared for his own safety to even raise the alarm. He'll never be able to use his daddy's name to get anything ever again. He had nothing now. Just like Wilhelm once had nothing. That's it. That's what it was. That's what he kept seeing. He kept seeing himself standing on that beach at Dunkirk. Having hit rock bottom. Nowhere to go but up.

He kept seeing Adalwolf the way Nadine kept seeing him.

Adalwolf's face softened, realising Wilhelm hadn't shot yet. That he was actually struggling to. That surprised him.

Wilhelm frowned. Relaxed his arm. Lowered his gun.

Adalwolf let out a shocked exhale. Pain from his shoulder was finally returning.

Wilhelm released the clip of his Luger. It fell to the floor. He then ejected the bullet still in the chamber. Threw the rest of the gun aside. It bounced off the wall. Fell behind some filing cabinet.

Adalwolf looked up at Wilhelm. He was confused, disturbed… and wowed.

Wilhelm gave him a nod. Turned away.

"Thank you," Adalwolf murmured.

Wilhelm slowly turned back. "You don't deserve it," he murmured back. "Prove me wrong." Then he walked on. Left the office. Stepped back into the hall.

The others just where he left them. Nadine was shocked to see Wilhelm so soon. "What happened?" she asked in English. "Was Bütz not in there?"

"He was." Wilhelm jutted his chin at the entrance. "Let's get out of here."

"I didn't hear a shot. How did you kill him?"

Wilhelm hesitated.

Nadine's face turned sour. "What are you doing?"

"It's over."

"You're not letting him live!"

Wilhelm shushed, his eyes darting at the mess hall behind them. "Keep your voice down."

"Whose side are you on?!" Nadine hissed back. "He's a monster! He killed my family!"

"And I was there, remember? You forgave me."

"You didn't shoot anybody!"

"I shot plenty of people before then."

"But you're not like him! You actually feel bad about all that!"

"Not at first. Two years ago, he and I were the same person." Wilhelm sighed. "I know him, Nadine. He feels bad too, he just… He doesn't know how to show it. Maybe now he will."

Nadine glared at Wilhelm. "Get out of my way."

"Nadine."

"Get out of my way."

"Nadine, this is a rescue mission. We're in a prison full of Nazis. We need to get out of here, NOW."

"I agree, but first I need to kill the man that slaughtered my family!"

"Nadine!" Wilhelm stopped her with two hands on her shoulders. "Stop and *think* for a second."

"This is my fucking mission. I'm the one giving the fucking orders." Nadine pushed her way past Wilhelm. Turned the safety off her gun.

Wilhelm rushed after her into the office "Nadine, don't!"

Nadine stormed in. Shot Adalwolf in the head on sight. BANG! Blood shot out of his head. Nadine reloaded. Shot him in the good eye. BANG!

Reload. Shot him in the glass eye—BANG!—which shattered instantly. Reload. Shot him in the face. BANG! Reload. BANG! Reload. BANG! Reload. BANG! Reload. Click. Reload. Click. Reload. Click. She grunted. Smashed the butt of her rifle into his head. CRUNCH! CRUNCH! CRUNCH! CRUNCH! She threw the rifle down at his body. Grunted on her feet.

Wilhelm stood where he was at the threshold. Heartbroken. Nauseous.

Nadine finally saw him standing there. Found herself glaring at him and that stupid look of disappointment on his face.

Wilhelm heard footsteps behind him. Scragg, Durant and Émile with guns at the ready, all racing in. They stopped at the bloody scene before them. "*Merde*," Durant breathed with eyes wide.

"Is that him?" Scragg asked Nadine in French. He didn't mean the *Kommandant*.

Nadine nodded. She was suddenly feeling like herself again. All that anger and rage wafting away. Just as she had a chance to finally process what it was she'd done, a low siren rose from nothing, getting louder and louder until it filled the whole office. Wilhelm's whole body tightened. He shot his eyes up. Looked around. It was an alarm, alright. The prison break alarm. Durant and Émile were scared too. Even Scragg was scared. And then a new terror was heard: the colossal stampede of freshly caffeinated boots just a few rooms away, heading right towards them.

Nadine's eyes bugged and she screamed, "*RUUUNNN!*"

CHAPTER EIGHTEEN

A Dream Come True

Nadine's rifle was empty. Wilhelm's gun had been dismantled entirely. Scragg, Durant and Émile were the only ones with guns. They ran out first. Started shooting towards the mess hall, the onslaught already there. There was some return fire at first, but the stampede had no choice but to stay back just behind the threshold. Scragg and Émile kept up suppressing fire as Wilhelm, Nadine and Durant ran on ahead. They were only fifty metres from the entrance. Scragg and Émile ran backwards, firing their guns on the men just beyond their sights.

Nadine, Wilhelm and Durant made it outside, the blinding sun disorienting them momentarily. "On your LEFT!" Nadine screamed in French. She forced Wilhelm to the ground. Durant spun left and shot at a contingent of guards trying to cut them off. Wilhelm and Nadine crawled behind Durant. Scragg and Émile backed out of the main lobby of Plötzensee only to find a firefight. They spun around. Joined Durant in returning fire. Bodies were falling left and right. Durant picked Wilhelm up by his uniform's collar. He was suddenly back on his feet. Nadine crawled her way to the perimeter. Her eyes looked up at the open gate. The main road.

But just beyond the metal gate, a pair of guards emerged, their guns pointed right at her. Three more popped up. Unhooked the gates. They were about to close them. Cut them off.

"HOLD FIRE!" Nadine shouted in French, both of her hands up.

Wilhelm saw this. Raised his hands. "STOP!" he shouted to everyone in German. "We surrender!"

Nadine stood, her hands still up. "Scragg! Émile! Durant! Hold your fire!"

Scragg begrudgingly lowered his weapon. Threw it on the ground. Raised both hands. Émile and Durant did the same.

The guards slowly approached them at gunpoint. As they closed in, Wilhelm slowly approached Nadine, his hands still in the air. "What now?" he whispered in English.

Nadine shushed him.

"Did you just—?" Wilhelm scoffed. "Did you really just *shush* me?"

"Shut *up*!" Nadine growled. "I'm listening."

"Listening for what?"

Nadine held her breath. The soft hum of an engine approaching the gate. "Now."

Wilhelm blinked. "What?"

"NOW!" Nadine screamed in French. She dropped down. Scragg, Émile, and Durant instantly did the same, just like they rehearsed.

Wilhelm saw a van screech to a halt on the main road half a second later. Instantly dropped to the ground. Just as he did, a roar of machine gun fire erupted above him, two guns at least coming from the van. Bodies fell to his left. Bodies fell to his right. Bodies fell all over. Wilhelm squeezed his eyes tight. The sounds of skull and bullets tearing through muscle was too much for him. The first time he was ever in an actual war zone. A genuine battlefield. It was awful. It was so, so awful.

"GO! GO! GO! GO!" Nadine screamed, jumping on her feet. She grabbed Wilhelm. Ran with him towards the open van. They leapt inside, landing on some cushioning. Wilhelm lifted his head. Recognised Coste with a massive gun, Blaise on the other side with one of his own.

"Incoming!" Émile shouted in French, running full speed for the van.

"Out of the way!" Nadine yelled in English. She shoved Wilhelm away as hard as she could. Just as he did, Émile barrelled in, landing hard just where Wilhelm had been. Scragg and Durant hopped in right after him, rifles back in their hands. Coste and Blaise slammed the doors. Wilhelm heard the engine roar. The van suddenly shocked itself into motion. He turned his head. Recognised Roul in the driver's seat.

Suddenly everyone was cheering. Screaming. Hooting. Hollering. Hugging each other with big smiles. Triumphant relief everywhere. Wilhelm was so overwhelmed by it all, but even he couldn't help but smile. Nadine waddled over on her knees, her beautiful teeth shining in that barely lit van. "Are you okay?" she asked Wilhelm with a laugh. "I'm so sorry for pushing you like that."

"You kidding me? I'm so glad you did."

Nadine laughed. Hugged Wilhelm nice and tight. A real hug this time.

Wilhelm felt the hot warmth of her body, the sweat of her skin, and he squeezed her back.

Roul drove the van north out of Berlin. After twenty minutes, the air had finally settled. Everyone was calm again. All the French conversation had run its course, and Nadine was finally free to talk to Wilhelm again.

"I can't believe it actually worked," she told him, squeezing past Blaise and Émile. "I had a whole thing planned for the public execution and had to throw it all away last minute. But it's good that we did. This was so much easier."

"You knew about the execution?" Wilhelm asked, his back to Scragg and Coste.

"Of course we knew about the execution!" Nadine sat across from Wilhelm, swaying with every turn in the centre of the van. "After I dropped you off at Marseilles, I drove back to Orléans to deliver all those papers, right? Well, just as we suspected, they arrested me on arrival."

"Did they get the papers?"

Nadine chuckled. "Yes, of course. Just listen."

Wilhelm nodded apologetically.

"Roul came to pick me up," Nadine continued. "They had me in their jail of sorts, and the two of us talked about why I did it. Roul was very confused, as you can imagine, as to why I would do such a thing. So I told him everything. I told him about you, who you really were, that you were in Nancy, that Bütz was your CO, I told him about Jacques, Corey's death, Victor, Olive Branch, New York—"

"Wait-wait-wait-wait, you told him?!"

"Will you please just listen? Roul's okay. We can trust Roul." Nadine gestured around her. "And don't worry about these guys. They still can't speak English. I actually taught myself *German* in the last few months and they still can't speak any English!" She laughed. "So anyway, so, I told Roul everything and he's fine with it. I mean, he did think I was a bit loony about it, but he trusts my judgement. He knows I only make the right decisions, and everything I said checked out. Made a lot more sense than you being a Nazi courier, that's for sure. So he covered for me. I was allowed back in the Resistance and we returned to Crespières. Two weeks later, we get some radio chatter about your arrest in Marseilles. If it were up to me, I wanted to break you out *immediately*, but Roul wouldn't hear of it. He kept saying it was too risky, it wasn't our place, there was no point… whatever. He ruled it out as a lost cause. But I kept telling him to let me organise an op. That you needed to get to New York as soon as possible. It was more than just you at stake. It was Jacques as well, right? But he kept saying it was impossible. But I didn't care. I made you my mission."

Wilhelm grinned at that.

"I struggled with this plan for *months*," Nadine continued, her enthusiasm actually growing as she talked. "I never planned an extraction op before. I had never even *been* in an extraction op before. And during a public execution? How was that going to work? All those eyes on you? All those men with you from Plötzensee escorting you all the way into town? I always knew the firing squad was the way to go, but what if they had switched last minute to a guillotine? Or hanging? What was I going to do then? I had no idea. I had to go to Roul for advice, and he knew I wasn't letting this go, but he also knew I couldn't do it alone, so he said he was going to help, but only on one condition: that you drop the whole New York, Victor, Olive Branch thing to join the Resistance as an official German military informant. I'm sorry, I had to tell him yes. Believe me, I intend on reneging on that promise somehow. I just haven't figured out how yet. Now that you're here, I'm sure we can figure something out together." Nadine giggled again. "Anyway, so we briefed the guys about mostly everything, and we decided to enter Germany through Sweden, right? And we found out where the firing squad meant for you was stationed, so we intercepted their signals. They didn't get anything, but we got everything. When they were out for R&R one night, Scragg, Durant and I broke in and stole their uniforms, right? But we still had no idea what to do on the day of. We were there for your whole trial. Brainstorming. Looking over plaza layouts. Thinking up a plan, rethinking the plan. It was awful. Anyway, just last night, we intercepted a message from the Gestapo commander at Plötzensee. He said the new *Kommandant* didn't like you for some reason, some hotshot trying to make a name for himself by moving your execution up early and making it private. It was very discreet. Lots of secrecy. No one was allowed to know, not even on the day of, except for anyone who was going to be there. It was perfect! Bütz hated you so much, he practically handed over your escape to us on a silver platter!" Nadine sighed, finally out of steam.

Wilhelm kept smiling, his cheeks getting red. He felt all warm and fuzzy.

Nadine was smiling too. "Why are you looking at me like that?"

Wilhelm was just about to tell Nadine he loved her when Scragg pointed his rifle at the back of Wilhelm's head and pulled the trigger.

Everything that followed was pure chaos. The back of Wilhelm's head blasting open. The sound of the gunshot reverbing so loud in that tight van. The bullet ricocheting about. Everyone shouting as they dodged. Blood everywhere. All over Nadine. All over Scragg. All over Wilhelm. Wilhelm's body falling forward onto Nadine, dead as steak. Nadine screaming. Blaise, Émile, Coste and Durant all shouting, trying to understand what was happening. Roul losing control of the van from all the commotion, swerving all over the road. Roul slammed the breaks. Stopped on a grassy patch in the middle of the northern German countryside. Hopped out. Opened the van door. Saw the whole scene. Wilhelm's corpse. All that blood. Accusations being thrown left and right. Scragg was silent throughout, ignoring the angry chastisements from his brethren, how dangerous it was for him to fire a gun in such a confined space, all those harsh questions asking why he would do such a thing.

Nadine immediately hopped out of the van, her face in tears. Needing air. On the verge of a mental breakdown after what just happened. Blaise, Émile, Coste and Durant all tried to explain to Roul what Scragg did all at the same time.

"QUIET!" Roul shouted into the van.

Everyone went silent.

Roul glared at Durant. "Durant, sitrep."

"Scragg discharged his firearm in the van," Durant answered, his voice wavering from the shock and the motion sickness. "I think it was an accident."

Roul gave Scragg a knowing look. "Well? Was it an accident?"

Scragg met eye contact with Nadine standing just outside the van. He looked back up at Roul. "No."

Nadine saw red. She pushed past Roul. Pounced on Scragg. The two of them scrapped about the van. Roul and Émile tried to pull her off. Blaise and Coste struggled to subdue Scragg. Roul succeeded in pulling Nadine away, keeping her back with an extra shove to the chest. That hurt Nadine, making her uncomfortable. "Stay back!" Roul yelled at her, like a dog.

Nadine's lip trembled, raw tears pouring out. "HOW COULD YOU?!" she screamed at Scragg. "WE WERE SUPPOSED TO SAVE HIM! YOU PROMISED YOU WOULD!"

"HE SHOT MY FAMILY!" Scragg screamed back.

Nadine gasped. Her brain went all numb.

"I'm sorry," Scragg said. He looked at the others with a hint of remorse. "I didn't mean to. I wasn't going to. But how could I help it? How could I just stand by and watch him smile and breathe and be so close to me? *Knowing* he'd never be punished for it? *Knowing* you were all just going to move on? We were going to have dinners with him?! We were going to make him one of our own?! I held my tongue, alright? I took it. I did my job. I remembered the mission. I got that fucker out." Scragg looked at Roul. "I'm sorry. I know I could've got you all hurt, but I just couldn't take it anymore. I just kept thinking… if *she's* allowed to shoot the Nazi that killed *her* parents, I'm allowed to shoot mine. And I am so fucking glad I did. I'm not sorry about it AT ALL. I needed this." He looked at Nadine. "You know what I'm talking about. You felt it yourself. I saw how you were back there."

Nadine gaped, struggling to comprehend. Her lips moved, unable to form words at first. "B-b-b-b-but-but-but-but h-h-h-how do you know t-that he was the one that shot…" Her throat seized up.

"He shot my father's face off in Maubeuge. As soon as he saw it, he vomited everywhere. Doesn't that sound familiar?" Scragg's chin trembled at the very thought, that painful memory. "How could I forget something like that? It's the reason I got away. And Bütz was there too. I recognised him. He's the one my father tried to shoot. So who else could it have been?" Scragg paused. "Or does it not matter because he felt bad by the time he got to yours? Why does your family get to be avenged and not mine? Are they better because they all know English? Because your mother studied in London? I don't think so."

Nadine disassociated standing right there on her feet. Her gaze lowered involuntary. Down and to the left. Overshooting that awful sack of meat and fluid that was once a body. A man. A person with a soul…

Her eyes rolled back. She covered her mouth. Ran away from the van. Bent over. Vomited everything she had in her. All wet and loose. And it got everywhere. She suddenly felt dizzy and weak. She stepped a bit further. Fell to her knees. Frowned with tears in her eyes. And she stayed there, in that position.

Roul and Durant kept watch around the parked van. Scragg, Coste, Blaise and Émile dug a Wilhelm's grave with their bare hands, taking shifts when carpel tunnel took over. Occasionally they used the butts of their rifle as tools. But Nadine didn't help. She remained offsides, her back to the scene, and stared out at the countryside.

Wilhelm Gunter was buried on the side of that country road north of Berlin. No headstone. No marker. No clear identifiers nearby. No coffin. Just all the flesh and fluids they could throw scoop into the pit. No prayers were said. No final words were spoken. Everyone was too tired to talk and didn't want to piss Scragg off.

Coste, Blaise, Émile, Durant and Scragg took an extended smoke break inside the van to drown out the smell of all that blood and flesh. Roul looked out at that hunched girl still sitting on the side of the road. She hadn't moved for hours. He tenderly walked over. Sat beside Nadine. Looked out at that beautiful view. "I've never been here before," he said softly. "It really is pretty."

Nadine's lip was still in a scowl. She refused to look at him. "Did you know?"

"Did I know what?"

"Scragg. His father. Did he tell you?"

Roul bent a leg. Wrapped both arms around it. "It wasn't just his father. If Scragg's memory is to be believed, Wilhelm also killed his mother and older brother too."

"I didn't ask for the details," she growled. "I just asked if you knew."

"That it was Wilhelm?"

Nadine didn't answer.

Roul frowned. "Yes. I knew."

"When did he tell you?"

"Nadine, I really don't think that—"

"Was it before or after we left France?"

Roul hesitated. "Before. After your initial briefing."

Nadine stared at him. "And you still put him on this mission?"

"Stop."

"You knew the whole time that this could happen?"

"What was I supposed to do? Tell you?"

Nadine's lips struggled to form shape.

"You're not the only person who tells me their secrets," Roul said. "It's my job to know you all that way. To understand every part of each and every one of you."

Nadine scoffed softly. "Your job? Is that all this is? Just… part of your job?"

"Of course it is," Roul said, his brows together. "If we treat each other like we're family, then we're more likely to win this war."

"I'm so tired of hearing about the fucking war! That's not all there is! There's still people! We still have lives! We all have wounds! That doesn't change anything!"

Roul's expression turned to anger. "We're all tired of it, Nadine."

"Then why would you let this happen? He was the only person that ever really made me feel like me. The real me. Not *this*. You knew what getting him back meant to me, or at least I thought you did."

"I think you're very *stupid*…" Roul held his gaze on her. "…for thinking that. As smart as you are, you're still very, *very* stupid."

Nadine's lip trembled.

"What would you have had me do?" Roul asked her bitterly. "Tell Scragg he couldn't come because you had a crush on the man that killed his family?"

"I never said I had a—"

"I know that's not why you wanted to save him. Personal feelings aside, you knew his value to the Resistance. Scragg knew that too. He put his feelings aside. And he's one of the best shots we got. Without him, one of us, maybe even two of us would've died."

"But someone did die."

"Maybe even him too. Who knows?"

Nadine scoffed. "I didn't need you."

Roul widened his eyes. "Excuse me?"

"I could've got him out myself. It was fine. We could've made it, just William and I. We didn't need any of you."

"Oh, is that so?"

"He'd still be alive if he weren't in that van. If Scragg didn't come. If you just fucking told me like the father you were apparently just PRETENDING to be!"

Roul glowered. "*Grow up.*"

Nadine closed her eyes.

Roul stood. Brushed the dust off his trousers. "Get in the van."

Nadine didn't budge.

Roul huffed. Looked up at the sky. "Nadine, if we don't get out of Germany as soon as possible, it really would've been all for nothing."

"I'm not getting in there with him." Nadine shook her head. "He doesn't deserve a ride. Make him walk to back to Sweden."

"Nadine, get in the fucking van."

"Make him walk!"

"Why?!" Roul snapped. "Because he killed a Nazi?! Is that a crime now?!"

The breath left Nadine's lungs. She looked down, tears creeping their way back in. "He wasn't a Nazi," she whimpered. "His name was William Gunnison. He was a person. He had a home. He had dreams. He made mistakes." She kept thinking back on his smile. The way he was looking at her. "He was human."

"Not to Scragg he wasn't." Roul frowned. "Who are you to say otherwise?"

Nadine faced forward. Tried not to cry in front of him.

Roul turned towards the van. Hesitated. Spun back around. "Five minutes," he said, holding up five fingers. "If you're not in that van in five minutes, we're leaving you behind." He about-faced. Returned to the getaway van.

Nadine stayed right where she was, right there in the dirt. And she thought about William, just as he was.

And she cried.

And she cried.

And she cried.

PART FOUR

Brian

CHAPTER NINETEEN

Love Story (Celeste's Version)

"We're gonna slow it down a little with our next little lady. You know her, you love her… and now you're gonna meet her. Coming up next to the J. Roger's stage, please put your hands together for… *Celeste*."

A roar of randy hurrahs. Dirty fingers in boozy mouths blowing whistles. Lots of applause. A cacophony of cheers. The spotlight clicked on, a perfect circle of light on that dirty blue curtain. All the men in the room, regulars mixed in with the doe-eyed first-timers who'd only heard rumors about the place, only got more excited. The drunks were a tad louder than the others. Their feet stomped just a bit more. But it soon all faded away as the men, one by one, started holding their breath in anticipation.

And the silence lingered.

And then an accented contralto sang over the sound system, nice and slow: "*It haaad to be you…*"

Some more cheers, the regulars recognizing her. The newbies looked around, dying to catch a glimpse.

"*It haaad to be you…*" The curtain parted ever so slightly and a long fish-netted leg stuck itself out, foot wrapped in golden ballet fashion, stepping into the spotlight. "*I waaandered around…*"

The audience went crazy at the sight of flesh, the hootin' and hollerin' louder than ever.

"*And I fiiinally found… the sommmebody who…*" Celeste stepped the rest of her body into the spotlight. Bright red dress. Her face stoic. Porcelain. Her braided blonde hair pulled back. "*Could make me be truuue…*" she cooed with just her mouth.

All those men there in the dark cheered her on. And it smelled in that room. Stinking of beer and whiskey. Of sweat, hands and hormones. All for her. All for Celeste. And she felt those eyes running up and down her body. All along that dress of hers. What the regulars knew she had hidden underneath.

"*And could maaake me be bluuue…*" Celeste dragged her feet along the stage, one sultry step at a time. "*And even be glaaad… just to be saaad…*" She made eye contact with a table of sailor boys, all muscled in their pristine Navy whites, sitting closest to the stage. "*Thinking of… yooou.*"

The sailor boys grinned wide from the attention. They applauded and cheered her back.

Celeste winked at one of them, the blond one in the front. Then she walked the length of the stage in the opposite direction. "*Some others I've seen… might never be mean…*" She stopped at center stage. Bent herself back. Eyes closed. Going back as far as she could without falling over. "*Might never be cross… or try to be boss… but they wouldn't do.*" Celeste reached behind her. Simply touched her back neckline. Undid her rubber seam just a bit. "*For nobody else…*" she sang, pivoting, her back now to the audience. "*Gave me a thrill…*" The rubber trail she undid kept undoing itself, as if unzipped by an invisible hand, gravity opening her dress all the way down her spine. Celeste whipped her hands forward just as the rubber trailed reached its end, the sleeves falling off her shoulders, the dress splitting entirely in half. The crimson remains pooled on the stage floor, and what was left on Celeste was stunning.

The men practically screamed at the sight of it. A metal brazier held together by Arabesque chains. A long string of gold-colored crystals wrapped around her neck. A three-tiered necklace. Spiraled breastplates like whipped cream on an apple pie connected by more chains that draped down her midriff, low hanging dips. Matching cuffs on her wrists and biceps. Embroidered veneer gray skirt open at the front. A matching metal codpiece. Those men only dreamed of a woman like that.

"*With all your faults…*" Celeste kept singing in that low sultry contralto, the spotlight following her off the stage as she joined the crowd, her chains jingling with every step. "*I love you still…*" She made eye contact with the table directly to the right of the Sailor Boys. (They seemed a bit too randy for her taste.) "*It had to be you…*" She approached a middle-aged man in a suit, the one with the old fashioned in his hand. "*Wonderful you…*"

The Middle-Aged Man couldn't believe she was singing to him. His face went numb. He couldn't remember his name. His wife's name. How many kids he had.

Celeste moved her body close to his, close enough to touch but not quite. *"It had to be... you."*

All the men cheered on the lucky guy. Horny grins. Primal thoughts.

"For nobody else..." Celeste sang, her hazel eyes never leaving the Middle-Aged Man's, not even to blink. *"Gave me a thrill... with all your faults..."* She bent down. Brought her lips close to his. *"I love you still..."*

The Middle-Aged Man swallowed. He couldn't move. She might fly away.

But Celeste moved her face even closer to his. Her lips were almost upon him. *"It had to be you... Wonderful you..."* She closed her eyes. Stopped just before a kiss. *"It had... to be..."* Her voice fizzled out.

It was so silent in that room

"You." Celeste opened her eyes. Frozen in that position. Her lips practically on the Middle-Aged Man's. She could smell his warm breath. He could taste hers. He was practically trembling from it. Panting. Begging. Pleading.

Celeste leaned in just enough for her lipstick to leave a mark on his lips. Sharply backed away. *"Show me the way to go home..."*

The audience guffawed out their pent-up frustration. The Middle-Aged Man was finally able to exhale, grinning like a fool.

Celeste held a dramatic a hand up to her forehead. *"I'm tired and I want to go to bed."* She winked at the Middle-Aged Man. That got her some whistles. *"I had a little drink about an hour ago and it went right to my head."* She planted her tush on the Sailor Boys' table. Leaned back. In one smooth motion, she was flat on their table. *"Wherever I may roam..."* she sang into her microphone. Looked up at all those handsome Sailors. *"On land or sea or foam... you will always hear me singing this song... show me the way to go home."* She made eye contact with the blond one. "Welcome home, boys!" she ad-libbed.

Before they could catch her, she was back on her feet. The band picked up the pace as Celeste bounced her way back to the stage, her golden ballet shoes hardly made a sound. *"Show me the way to go home!"* she sang at a higher register, from the lungs. She stomped twice, cuing the drummer to pound the bass twice. The regulars knew to stomp along too. *"I'm tired and I want to go to bed!"* STOMP STOMP. *"I had a little drink about an hour ago and it went right to my head!"* She jumped off the stage. Landed on the STOMP STOMP. *"Wherever I may roam!"* Celeste sang with a growl, gliding between tables, letting herself have fun with it. STOMP STOMP. *"On land or sea or foam!"* STOMP STOMP. *"You will always hear me singing this song: show me the way to go home!* Everybody!"

"Show me the way to go home!" the men in the club sang back to her as one. STOMP. STOMP. *"I'm tired and I want to go to bed!"* STOMP STOMP. *"I had a little drink about an hour ago and it went right to my head!"* STOMP STOMP. *"Wherever I may roam!"* STOMP STOMP. *"On land or sea or foam!"* STOMP STOMP. *"You will always hear me singing this song: show me the way to go home!"*

"One more time!" Celeste ordered into the mic, running back up to center stage, the music faster than ever. *"Show me the way to go home!"*

STOMP STOMP.

"Let me hear it!"

"I'm tired and I want to go to bed!" the men sang back.

STOMP STOMP.

"What's the matter?!"

"I had a little drink about an hour ago and it went right to my head!"

STOMP STOMP.

"Wherever I may roam!"

"Where?!"

STOMP STOMP.

"On load or sea or foam!"

"Oh, of course!"

STOMP STOMP.

"You will always hear me singing this song!"

"What song?!"

"Show me the way to go home!"

"What song?!"

"Show me the way to go home!"

"One more time!"

"Show me the way to go home!"

The band suddenly cut out. Total silence in the theater. Just Celeste on the stage, staring up at the spotlight man, clutching the microphone with both hands. *"Show me... the way... to go... home."* She bent back as far as she could, arms spread out like wings, and the spotlight went out.

The crowd went nuts in the dark. Celeste rushed around the stage, her smile instantly gone. She scooped up what was left of her red dress. Rolled it into a crimson bunch. Dashed backstage, her metal chains jingling all the way. She wiped sweat from her brow. Ignored the stagehands' lecherous glances and lip licking. Rushed off before they could get a good look at her exposed backside. Passed Tina on her way to the stage.

Celeste beelined for her dressing room. Closed the door. Locked it. The emcee's sleazy voice mercifully muted. She then threw her red bundle on the ground. Unbraided her hair. Removed that awfully cold brazier and cod-piece. Slipped into a soft bathrobe. She sat before her boudoir with the homely yellow marquee bulbs. Hastily removed her makeup. Then she closed her eyes. Took a deep breath. Opened them. She was Nadine again. She felt like Nadine again.

J. Roger himself stopped by to thank Nadine as always. Gave her her week's pay. She checked the new week's schedule. Four shows this time, not three. Nadine then threw on her winter coat. Slipped on her gloves. Adjusted her hat in the mirror. Left the dressing room.

Tina was standing outside her own dressing room in nothing but a corset. Her big black curls falling all the way down past her shoulders. Smoking a cigarette between two long pink nails. "Great show tonight," she told Nadine in her native Italian accent.

"Thanks," Nadine said quickly. She kept on walking, her heels clicking on the floor.

"You're not walking home alone, are you?"

Nadine turned around. "Vicky's still sick. I don't really have a choice."

Tina threw her cigarette down. Stepped on it. "Just wait a moment. I'll call you a cab."

"I don't have the money."

"It'll be on me."

"No, it's fine." Nadine forced a friendly smile. "Thank you, Tina. I'm already in enough debt to Vicky as it is. I don't want to owe you too."

Tina frowned, unconvinced. "I just want you to get home safe."

"Don't worry about me. I will." Nadine tried again to leave.

"Oh, Nadine?" Tina called.

Nadine stopped again. Let out a soft sigh. Reluctantly turned. Walked back to Tina. "Yes, Tina?"

"I've been meaning to ask you. That thing you do with the dress..." Tina drew a line down the front of her body. "How'd you come up with that?"

Nadine adjusted the strap of her handbag. "I removed the zipper. Replaced it with rubber tubing. Then I sculpted the male end so it'd be secure enough to stay on but just weighted enough to undo itself with gravity."

"No, honey, I know how it works. I have eyes." Tina smirked. "My question was how you came up with it."

Nadine got a bit uncomfortable. She gripped her handbag tighter, her gloves squeaking from the friction.

Tina chuckled a bit. "I guess we're all perverts deep down, huh? Even the pretty ones."

Nadine looked away. Tucked some hair behind her ear. "Thank you." She abruptly turned and left the theater.

The January cold outside J. Roger's was fierce. The sound of traffic startled Nadine the second she stepped onto Christopher Street. She shivered in her coat. Rubbed her arms. Turned right. Walked fast uptown. Her heels clicked on the pavement. She didn't look at anyone. Just kept on walking. It was late. Dark out. Darker than she remembered. Maybe she should've taken Tina's offer after all. A free cab ride. But Tina might've wanted something in return… something that had nothing to do with sewing.

Nadine walked up 7th Avenue. Up ahead, mulling about the rest of New York's finest, was that blond Sailor Boy she had made eye contact with earlier. He was by himself. Drunk. Navy whites stained with some good old Manhattan grime. He made accidental eye contact with her.

Nadine flinched her glance away. Picked up the pace. Practically sprinted past him. She could sense his beady eyes on her. "Hey," Sailor Boy slurred, walking after her, pointing at her. "Hey, I know you."

Nadine kept on walking. Pretended not to hear him.

"Yeah! Celeste!" Sailor Boy clomped after her. "Where you going?"

Nadine felt a hand graze her elbow. She moved it away.

"*Hey*," Sailor Boy said, his tone shifting toward aggression. "Celeste, I'm talking to you."

Nadine wanted to run, but she knew it'd only make him angrier. So she slowed down a bit. Let him catch up.

"I knew it was you," Sailor Boy said with a wide smile. "I knew it." His throat made a weird sound. "Where you going? Wanna go somewhere?"

"I'm not Celeste." Nadine stepped aside to let a pair of pedestrians cross between them. "You're mistaking me for someone else."

"That was a great show you did. How bout you dance for me?"

"I told you, I'm not—"

"Sure you are." Sailor Boy moved closer to her.

Nadine tenderly stepped back into the alleyway. "I'm really not."

Sailor Boy kept creeping toward her. "Don't you know who I am? I saw how you looked at me. Don't pretend you wouldn't like it, baby."

"Please." Nadine suddenly changed course. Tried to leave the alleyway.

The Sailor Boy blocked her path with an arm on the brick wall. "You still got all those chains under there?"

"Please."

"You looked really good…"

"Please step aside."

"And what you did with that dress!"

"Step aside. Now."

Sailor Boy grabbed her coat. Pinned her against the alley wall. Forced open her buttons.

Nadine tried to wrestle herself away. "Help!"

"Shhh!" Sailor Boy's eyes were suddenly in a panic. He covered her mouth. It was dirty as hell. "Come on, baby, I'm not hurting you." Sailor Boy touched her breasts.

Nadine struggled. Screamed into his hand. Her eyes pleaded to the 7th Avenue passersby. Too many of them looked back at her, knowing exactly what was happening, clear as day, only to walk on anyway. Over and over it kept happening. Older men. Other women. Pretending not to look. Not wanting to start anything. Forcing themselves back onto their own business. Their own lives. Nadine felt so hurt by that. So cold. So scared she couldn't even scream anymore.

Then Sailor Boy reached further down her body.

And Nadine froze up.

Closed her eyes.

"HEY!"

PUNCH!

Nadine opened her eyes. Sailor Boy was on the ground with blood on his face. Standing over him was a young man with next to no muscle, flinging his right hand over and over in the air. "OW! *FUCK!*" he cried in pain.

Sailor Boy got up, dizzy from the sucker punch. He tried to return fire, but the young man easily dodged it with a step to the side. His racing breath looked like a cloud of cigarette smoke.

Sailor Boy tried again. Charged full speed. Sloppy right swing.

This time the young man punched the air at just the right time. Hit Sailor Boy in the nose. CRACK! Sailor Boy fell to the ground. Knocked out for the count.

The young man flung his hand even harder this time. "Holy *SHIT* that hurts! Damn!" He looked down at his knuckles. They were bleeding. He gently looked up at Nadine.

Nadine stared back. Scared. Thankful. In awe as well.

"Sorry about all the cursing," the young man rattled off. "I'm really not like that. I never even punched a man before. It always looks so romantic on the big screen. In reality, it hurts really *really* bad. God, I really wished someone told me how bad it was gonna hurt. Do you know how long it's gonna be like this? It won't take a week to heal, will it? Is bleeding bad? It never bleeds in the movies. I really don't… I really shouldn't be talking about myself right now. I should be talking about you. Hello. How are you? Are you alright?"

Nadine nodded, still in shock. "Yeah."

The young man looked down at Sailor Boy. "Wow. He's really out, isn't he? Did I kill him? Oh God, I hope I didn't kill him. That would really stink, wouldn't it? Never having thrown a punch, the first time I ever do I end up killing the guy? He would be a Sailor too, wouldn't he? If I killed a Sailor, that would *not* be good for me, would it?" The young man crouched down to Sailor Boy. Suddenly pointed at him. "Oh! There's a breath! I can see it. That's… That's good. Great. I don't feel so bad anymore. Not that I would feel bad because of the whole, you know, molestation thing. But I would feel a little bit bad having killed a person. Right? I mean come on, who wouldn't? I mean… I'm really not doing this right, am I? Figures. The most heroic I've ever actually been and I'm wasting it all acting like a fool. Again, I *really* need to stop talking about myself!" The young man chuckled boyishly. He shook Nadine's hand. "Brian Donahue. Nice to meet you. Don't touch the blood. Talking about myself again. Dammit. Oh! Sorry." He cleared his throat. "As you can see, adrenaline does not suit me well. Someone might get hurt." He laughed again.

Nadine picked up her handbag. "Thank you, Brian."

"Just thank you? Okay. That's fine. Whatever you want." Brian looked down at Sailor Boy. "Uh-huh." Back up at Nadine. "I think I should at least keep you company, you know, just until we get enough of a safe distance away. What do you think?"

Nadine smiled a bit. "Sure." She rebuttoned her coat.

"Sure?" Brian smiled. "Great. I'll calm down and be a lot normal. I promise." He stepped out of the alleyway first. Hesitated. Awkwardly held his arm out for her.

Nadine let out a chuckle. "My hero," she said, hooking onto his arm.

"Oh wow!" Brian exclaimed, starting his escort down 7th Avenue. "I did not… I didn't think it was going to feel that way."

"What way?"

"I don't know. So, uh… what's your name?"

"Celeste."

"Celeste? That's a beautiful name. Hey, what accent is that?"

"French."

"French! Wow. Cool. Were you from France originally, or…?"

Nadine simply smiled back at him.

"You're from France originally. I can tell." Brian nodded. "Sorry."

"You really don't have to apologize so much."

"Your English is great by the way."

"Thank you."

"Really great. Uh… Um…" Brian cleared his throat. "Not for me to tell you how to live your life or anything, but should you really have been walking so late by yourself? What if I hadn't come around?"

"No, I know. I normally don't do that. My roommate's sick. She usually walks me home from work."

"Oh, you two work together?"

"Yeah."

"What do you do?"

Nadine hesitated. "I'm a showgirl."

"Oh." Brian paused. "So Celeste isn't your real name, I assume?"

Nadine looked at him curiously. "What?"

"That's your dancer name, right? It sounds like a dancer name."

Nadine took a deep breath. "You're very, uh… Yeah. That's right."

"Oh. So what's your real name?"

"I don't think I want to tell you my real name."

"Okay, don't tell me your real name. I get it. I'm just the guy walking you down the block."

"Don't think I'm not grateful, of course. I'm still a bit shaken up."

"That's fine. My name's not actually Brian anyway."

"Oh really?"

"It's my dancer name."

Nadine laughed. "You're a dancer too?"

"Yeah, of course. Doesn't Brian Donahue sound like a dancer name?"

"Not at all."

"Maybe that's why I'm not a good dancer." Brian grinned widely.

Nadine laughed some more. "You are a good puncher though."

"Don't insult boxers like that. That was my first punch. I'm nowhere near as good as them."

"I never said you were."

"Thank God."

Nadine felt calmer already. A warm feeling filled her up. "There is something to say in you socking a war hero like that."

"A sailor boy in Navy whites does not a war hero make. I believe Shelly said that one."

"Percy Bysshe Shelley?"

Brian smirked. "Look who knows her poetry! No, of course the Shelley I'm referring to is actually Mary Shelley, writer of *Frankenstein*."

"As opposed to Mary Shelley the heavyweight boxer?"

"And we're back to boxing. Why is it every time I try to go literary with this conversation, you keep trying to bring it back to violence?"

Nadine laughed.

"Are you really a dancer or is that just a euphemism for boxing?" Brian teased.

"Seriously…" Nadine tightened her linked arm for extra emphasis. "Thank you."

Brian nodded cordially. "It's the least I could do."

Nadine discreetly looked Brian up and down. Very handsome. Lean. "Surprised you're not at the front right now. You wouldn't even need a gun with an arm like that."

Brian didn't say anything at first. His smile was faltering. "Draft hasn't gotten me yet, I suppose."

"You can always enlist."

Brian suddenly came to a complete halt. Dropped her arm. "Alright, I think we've walked far enough. Thank you, Celeste, whatever your name is. Have a very nice evening and a very good night." He spun around and walked back the way they came.

Nadine's brows drew together, her mouth gaping. "Wait! Where are you going?"

Brian switched to walking backwards. "Oh, and best wishes to your roommate. I don't know what she's got, but I'm sure she'll be alright. Unless it's consumption."

"Brian." Nadine strutted after him. "Wait. I'm sorry. I don't know what I said."

Brian stopped. Looked at her confused face. Started to frown.

Nadine stopped before him. Sighed. Tried an encouraging smile. "Come on." She held out an arm.

Brian reluctantly took her arm. She ended up leading *him* down 7th Avenue. He was too embarrassed to say anything.

As uneasy at that outburst made Nadine feel, she was even uneasier by Brian's silence. "We don't have to talk about it," she said.

"I know." Brian went quiet again.

"What other kinds of poetry do you like?"

"I think we're done talking about me. What kind of dancing do you do?"

Nadine hesitated. "Oh. Yeah. It's kinda…"

"Kinda what?"

"Dirty."

Brian looked at her. "How dirty? Like… striptease?"

Nadine bobbed her head. "Legally it can't be, but… yeah."

"What do you mean legally it can't be?"

"Stripteasing's been illegal for a few years now."

"I did not know that. When?"

"I don't know. I wasn't in the city then. I don't even know what it used to be, but right now it's pretty… it's not great." Nadine scoffed. "In fact, the reason Mayor La Guardia made it illegal in the first place was to protect the morals of young men." She thumbed behind her. "What just happened back there, legally speaking, was actually my fault. I was the one 'leading him on.' I can't even report it because of that. Can you believe it? I didn't turn him into that thing. He did it all by himself." Nadine shook her head. "If anyone had any idea how immoral our 'heroes' actually are…"

Brian bumped his brows. "You don't need to tell me that."

"What?" Just as Nadine turned her head, she caught a glimpse of a white blur in her peripheral vision. She gasped. "Oh God, he's back!"

Brian looked back. A bloody-faced Sailor Boy, struggling to walk a straight line, was after them with an angry look on his face. "Run!" Brian suddenly took the lead, pulling Nadine along as he dashed down 7th Avenue. Nadine screamed from the shock, followed swiftly by laughter.

The two of them easily outran their pursuer as they rounded the corner. Nadine looked in on a diner they were passing. Grinded to a halt. "In here!" She threw open the diner door. Brian ran in. Nadine slammed the door shut and they dropped to the floor behind a big leafy fern.

Sailor Boy rounded the corner. Stopped. No sign of Celeste or Mr. Suckerpunch. He looked both ways. Nothing. He ran on.

Nadine and Brian let out simultaneous exhales. They stood back up. "That was a close one," Nadine said, out of breath.

Brian looked around the diner they were in. How warm it was in there. Warm air. Warm light. "Would you like to get some coffee with me?" he asked her.

Nadine thought about it and smiled. "Sure. I'd love that."

Nadine and Brian sat across from each other in a booth. Before they had time to properly scope their menus, a waitress was on them. "We can't re-print new menus," she rattled off, bored and droll, like she had countless times before. "We've got no meat, no cheese no butter. The only milk we have, we cook with. If you want a glass, it comes out of a can. Only one cup of coffee per person. No exceptions. There's the door otherwise. What can I get for you?"

Brian chuckled a bit. "Coffee would be great."

"Make it two," Nadine said, tossing her menu aside.

The Waitress stuck her pencil behind her ear. She froze at the sight of Brian's bloody knuckles. "What happened to you?"

Brian self-consciously covered his cuts. "No, I'm alright."

"You should see the other guy," Nadine quipped.

Brian laughed nervously.

"You want some ice for that?" the Waitress asked. "We don't have much, but we have that."

"No, it's fine," Brian told her. "Just the coffee."

"No, you really should put ice on that," Nadine spoke up. "A cold compress will reduce swelling after fifteen or twenty minutes, as long as your bones aren't broken, which I don't think they are. But if you leave it untreated, bruised knuckles might limit your hand's mobility and increase the risk of you developing something more serious."

Brian and the Waitress stared at her.

Nadine looked up at the Waitress. "A good amount of ice in a towel, please? And wet it. Thank you."

The Waitress nodded suspiciously. "Two coffees and a cold compass, coming up." She wandered off.

Nadine bumped her brows. "Com*press*," she mumbled to herself. "Not compass." She noticed Brian staring at her. "What?"

Brian smirked. "You're just full of surprises, aren't you?"

"I don't know." Nadine picked her menu back up. Absentmindedly flipped through it. "So what do you do?"

"What do I do?"

"Yeah. What do you do?"

Brian blew some air out. "I go to NYU."

"Okay. What major?"

"Literature."

"Any specific kind?"

"Just Literature." Brian bobbed his head. "I also have a minor in Playwriting."

"Playwriting? Really?"

"Yeah. Matter of fact, I just got out of one now. *Garden Day* by Richie Hammond."

"Who?"

"Richie Hammond. You never heard of Richie Hammond?"

Nadine shook her head. "I really don't go to the theater very often. I know I should. I am here."

"Oh, absolutely. You really need to see *Garden Day*. Richie Hammond is the greatest playwright ever."

"I think Shakespeare would have to disagree with that."

"Shakespeare can do whatever he pleases. Richie Hammond *is* objectively better."

"Better than Shakespeare? Really?"

"I've seen every one of his plays at least five times. The man is a certified genius. He takes big, grand, morally complex issues—and I mean real epic ones: destiny, decay, societal rot, cursed cycles repeating themselves throughout time, the connection between all human beings—and he condenses all of that into simple domestic realism, specifically between fathers and sons. Oh my God, Richie must hate his dad." Brian laughed. "Oh, and he knows everything about men. Fatherhood. Masculinity. Our specific struggles, pressures, flaws. And his dialogue is so detailed, and yet it just flows out of these people's mouths. I actually gasp listening to his characters speak. It's like he…" Brian grins, trying to phrase it right. "He knows exactly what I'm thinking. It's like three hours of people saying exactly what I would've said."

Nadine disassociated a bit there. She used to be passionate about art once. All those nights reading Apollinaire to…

"Celeste?"

Nadine blinked. She forgot who she was with a minute there. "Oh, I'm sorry. I was miles away."

The Waitress came by with their coffee. She gave Brian a wet dish towel folded around ice cubes. "Thanks," Brian told her. The Waitress nodded and wandered off.

Nadine removed her gloves. Held her coffee cup. Smelled it. "I hate the coffee here," she mumbled.

"You haven't even tasted it yet." Brian winced as he placed the compress on his bleeding knuckles.

"In *America*. All American coffee tastes the same. The ones made in a cafetière, that's real coffee."

"What's a cafetière?"

Nadine forced down a little sip. "I believe you call it a 'French press' here. How reductive. Almost as reductive as this…" She frowned down at her cup. "I don't even think one can count it as a blend. It's just…"

"Coffee?" Brian laughed a bit.

Nadine smiled. "Yeah." She looked out the diner window. Pensive. Melancholy. "Nobody cares."

"Well, people care, they just…" Brian slid his coffee cup closer to him. "We're a bit busy at the moment."

"Exactly." Nadine looked at him. "I think that's the worst thing about the war. The whole world collectively agreeing to *stop*. If we're not out there, in all that, you and me, we're just an afterthought." She paused. "Imagine you're married and your wife just died. Or maybe you just came back from the doctor and he told you you've only got a few months left to live. It doesn't matter what you're going through. All eyes are supposed to be out there. On Germany. Japan. Italy. If you think about yourself even a little bit, you're deemed selfish, because there's so much more going on out there. You're supposed to be a good American. And good Americans think about those boys every second of every day, what duty they can do out here to help bring them all back home. Not their silly little lives." Nadine frowned. "For years now, we've just been… We don't know what to do. We can't plan. We can't cry. We can't smile. We don't know whether to dream or just sit around and be afraid all the time. That just brings a stillness over everything. A tense, paralyzing stillness. It's suffocating."

Brian simply smiled back in awe. "You might just be the smartest showgirl I've ever met."

"Oh, you meet a lot of showgirls?" Nadine teased, lifting her coffee.

"No." Brian studied her face. Her lips. Her eyes. "I still don't believe you actually are one."

Nadine swallowed her coffee. Put her cup down with a shrug. "But I am." She looked out the window, into the night. "This place has never seen war and it shows. You have no idea what it's like. What it does to people."

"I know I'm glad I'm not there now," Brian mumbled. "Believe me, everyone I know just has to see me, young fit me, walking out and about, and they're so quick to judge. I know what they're thinking. They're wondering why I'm still here and not off… I don't know, shooting people, starving in the snow, as if that's so great in the first place. No, I'm sorry, I'm prioritizing my education, my future. This war's not going to last forever. I need to be prepared for when it's all over. I refuse to feel guilty about it. Like you said, I'm still alive. I still have a life. Why should I pretend I don't?"

Nadine frowned. "But as to prove my point, you're… one of the…"

Brian raised his brows. "Excuse me?"

"Not everyone has that choice. I certainly didn't."

"You have the choice now, don't you?"

"What do you mean?"

"Go to night school. Study whatever you want. You don't have to worry about getting drafted and being sent off to the front lines. We do. That's always a risk for us."

"It's still a risk for you. Tomorrow you could get the notice saying you have to drop out of NYU and report for basic training. What's the plan then?

Brian tightened his jaw. Looked off. "I got deferred, alright?"

Nadine blinked. "What?"

"I don't want to talk about this right now." Brian sipped his coffee.

Nadine's eyes scanned Brian's body up and down, his perfect physique. "Why would they defer you?"

"I told you, I don't want to talk about it!" Brian snapped. "It's the one thing I specifically said I didn't want to talk about. I can talk about anything else."

Nadine hesitated. "There's a difference between not wanting to go to war and not caring about the war."

"You're one to talk."

"I never said I never cared about the war. I do." Nadine sat back. "I feel I'm still helping, in my own way."

Brian scoffed. "Oh really?"

"Yeah."

"Dancing for horny soldiers on leave?"

"It gives them joy, doesn't it? In this topsy-turvy world we're so unlucky to be born into, showing a little skin has the power to make everything better." Nadine hesitated. "And even if stripteasing is as immoral as everyone says, it's no more immoral than all the stuff going on out there. I have no shame about it. It's no different to me." She looked into Brian's eyes. "At least I'm doing *something*."

Brian lifted his cold compress. Checked the bruising on his fingers. "I don't want to die." He replaced the compress. "Better yet…" He looked back at her from across the booth. "I want to live."

"What's the difference?"

"Massive. I happen to know there are worse things than death." Brian sipped some more of his coffee. "Insanity. Loneliness. Grief. Pain."

Nadine withdrew into herself. She tried not to think about William. She couldn't bear to. But it was all coming up anyway like ancient bile.

"I can tell you're lonely."

Nadine looked up. "What?"

"It's alright. I'm lonely too." Brian placed the compress aside. "Do you want to tell me what happened?"

Nadine couldn't speak. It was starting to sting. It was becoming too real. Too sickening. "Let's do something!" she declared, forcing a wide grin. "Let's go out! Let's have some fun!"

Brian furrowed his brow. "Oh."

"I-I'm having such a great time," Nadine insisted with tears in her eyes. "I am. And I want to enjoy this." She swallowed. "What do you want to do? I'll do anything."

Brian blinked. "Celeste…"

"I-I…" Nadine shook her head. "I don't want to think about all that. I just… I just want a night off. Just one night. Where I don't have to feel like me. I can just be a girl, you know? Just another New York girl out with a New York boy somewhere, doing something." She smiled through her nerves. "You have no idea how long it's been since I've been just a girl."

Brian nodded, his eyes feeling a bit puffy themselves. "I haven't been just a boy for a while either."

"Great! So what do you want to do?"

Brian shrugged. "We can go see a movie?"

"Absolutely. What do you want to see?"

"I don't know." Brian thought about it. "There's this one my roommate saw the other day. He said it's really great."

"Great. Let's see that one."

"You don't want to know anything about it first?"

"What's it called?"

"*Ca… Ca…*" Brian huffed. "I can't remember. It's a weird name. But it's a love story, so—"

"Great." Nadine put her gloves back on. "Let's go before it starts."

Brian left two dimes on the table and walked Nadine out of the diner. They checked to make sure the coast was clear before walking off, headed for Times Square.

Nadine knew something was wrong the moment she heard the title of the movie. *Casablanca*. Instantly she thought of William, that backup refugee trail she told him to take if Fry couldn't get him out of Marseilles.

"Are you alright, Celeste?"

Nadine looked at Brian, not recognizing him for a second. She forced a grin. "Yes, of course. Can't wait to see it."

"I'm afraid you're going to have to settle for the movie."

Nadine forced out a laugh, assuming it to be another one of his jokes, not remembering what the setup was.

Brian bought the tickets. They got a good seat in the back of the theater. Nadine removed her gloves and stuffed them in the pocket of her coat. She felt the warm tingle of fingertips on hers, and to her surprise, she allowed it. She allowed this man to touch her like that. His warm, strong hand held hers, and she felt safe. She was on a date with a handsome boy. A sweet American boy. Smart like her. The war hadn't touched him in the slightest. And it never was going to touch him. She actually let herself go. She actually felt it. She was happy. And then the lights went down and the love story began.

But the voiceover instantly squashed whatever Nadine was feeling. A disembodied voice over a foggy globe, describing the fall of Paris and the refugee trail that had sprung up. Paris to Marseilles. Marseilles to Oran. Oran to Casablanca, where one could barter, steal or simply wait for an exit visa to Lisbon. That was the trail. That was the exact trail.

And it just wouldn't stop. All those Nazis goosestepping, Vichy French officers walking side by side with Nazis. And the café, Sam the piano player singing "Knock on Wood" with everyone stomping along, the band and audience as one. It was just like her J. Roger's set. And seeing Rick and Sam together, a white American and his colored companion, all those references to their time in Paris together, all she could think about was Corey Baxter and his butler Jacques. Corey was dead. Jacques was still waiting for rescue. Two years later and still waiting for rescue. No one left alive who knew how. She knew, didn't she? But she gave up. She gave up long ago. She couldn't even look at Rick and Sam anytime they were on screen together. It made her feel awful. Made her feel scared. But she couldn't show it. She refused to let Brian see her like that. She kept her pulse steady. She didn't move her hand. She felt Brian's eyes on her, the first time since the movie started, and she forced herself back down. She didn't move an inch.

But it just kept getting worse. The flashback of Ilsa and Rick's Paris tryst, that brief happy time they spent together. How free they were then. Free from the grief that would later befall them. Her and William. Her and William in Crespières. Reading poetry to each other. Sharing their true thoughts with each other. She had fixed him. She fixed his leg. She gave him a new life. She even saved his life, shooting down his noose. Even after knowing he was a Nazi. One of her Nazis. Even before learning the whole truth, that he was the one that saved her life in Nancy, she still shot him down. Why? Because he was still human. He was human and deserved to live. But not Bütz? William at that point was no different than Bütz at the end. She didn't even know William didn't directly kill her family, and yet she saved his life. Why couldn't she do the same for Bütz? William tried to tell her too. He tried to warn her. But she shot him anyway. She didn't think. She just shot Bütz and got William killed. Why did she do that? Why?

And seeing Rick and Ilsa's tense reunion in Paris, his bitter heart torn out, Rick spitting vitriol at Ilsa for running away without a proper explanation. She just ran off like he meant nothing to her at all. All Nadine could think about was Roul. Would he say those things to her if they ever crossed paths again? How bad she had hurt him? Ilsa at least had the decency to leave a note for Rick at the station. Nadine didn't even do that. How he must hate her so.

And then Yvonne, that French floozy, coming back to the café on the arm of a Nazi. Her spat with that French refugee insulting her. (Nadine could understand the French they were saying.) That hurt her most of all. How could she care for a Nazi? Wilhelm Gunter was one of the four men that attacked her farm. He just stood by and did nothing while her mother, father and three brothers were all shot one by one! Why did she help him escape Crespières?! Because he was handsome?! Because he made her feel special?! Because he saved her life once?! He killed Scragg's family! He blew his father's face off! He was a killer! And she cared for him! She actually… Could she even say she…?

And then the singing! Oh God, why did they have to sing?! And of all the songs to sing, "La Marseillaise?!" To use it to drown out the Nazis no less?! All those refugees and their cracking voices! And Yvonne the Nazi lover, realizing her mistake, singing her heart out with eyes full of tears. And she was staring right at her! Why was she there?! Why was she happy?! Why was she with some American boy?! She left them behind! She ran away and left her country behind! They needed her and *she left them all behind to die!*

"What's wrong?" Brian whispered to her.

Nadine helplessly looked back at him. "Can we go?"

Brian hesitated. "Yeah. Of course."

"I need to get out of here." Nadine immediately grabbed her coat. Glared up at Yvonne's face.

"That's fine." Brian stood.

Nadine rushed after him, too dazed to apologize to the people she was stepping over.

As soon as they got to the lobby, Nadine raced past Brian. "I'm sorry," she whimpered, throwing her coat on in a hurry.

"It's alright," Brian told her, trying to be supportive. "I'm sure the ending's not that good anyway."

Nadine pulled a glove out of her pocket. Desperately put it on. She couldn't even look at him. "I just want to go home."

"I'll get you a cab."

"No!" Nadine snapped. Twice in one night now. She fished deep into her coat pocket. Empty. "Oh, where is it?!"

"It's freezing out there. Let me get you a cab."

"I can't find it! I just want to *GO!*" Nadine patted her jacket down one last time. Huffed. Stormed away. Pushed through the theater doors.

In a daze, she wandered. Her ungloved hand blistering in the wind. Floating aimlessly. And she felt sick. Her mind filled with faces. Awful faces. Angry faces. Dead faces. And she felt her world spinning. Concaving. And she just wanted to get home. Anything to go home. And she heard an awful voice in her head singing that awful song. All those men in the crowd. All of them wanting her, just like that Sailor Boy. All of them singing up at her.

Show me the way to go home...

People collided into her on the street. They sneered at the madwoman who couldn't watch where she was going.

STOMP STOMP.

I'm tired and I want to go to bed...

She could see her mother's disappointing glare. All that handed down *haute couture* knowledge and she used it to customize a dress into undoing itself in front of a crowd of perverts.

STOMP STOMP.
I had a little drink about an hour ago and it went right to my head…
She nearly tripped on a curb.
STOMP STOMP.
Wherever…
She always said she hated being a honeypot.
STOMP.
I…
STOMP.
But that's all she was now.
MAY…
STOMP.
ROAM…
And she chose it too.
STOMP.
Even though she hated it.
STOMP.
STOMP.
ON LAND…
And now she can't get out.
STOMP.
OR SEA…
She can't get out!
STOMP STOMP.
Everything was dizzy.
ORRRR
STOMP.
She felt like she was going to throw up.
FOOOAAAMMM…
STOMP. STOMP.
You will always hear me singing this song…
She finally reached her building. She felt familiar warmth again. It even smelled familiar. She was home. She was back home.
Show me…
Second floor.
The way…

Third floor.

To go…

Fourth floor. At the sight of that door, the last one of the left, she smiled. She was back to herself again. She was back to Nadine again.

Home.

Nadine unlocked the door. Turned on the light. Plopped on a chair. Closed her eyes. Groaned. Let it all out.

Then she heard coughing.

Nadine opened her eyes. Vicky in a bathrobe grabbing a fresh handkerchief from the laundry pile. "You took your time getting home," Vicky grumbled, sounding worse than she did that morning.

"I'm sorry. Did I wake you?"

"Yeah." Vicky petted Nadine's head affectionately. Kept walked into the kitchen. "What did you get up to?"

Nadine sighed. "I went to the movies."

"That's nice." Vicky grabbed a glass. Waddled to the sink. "What did you see?"

"*Casablanca.*"

"I think I heard of that one." Vicky filled her glass with water. "Supposed to be good."

Nadine simply bumped her brows.

Vicky took a drink. Waddled past Nadine. Looked down at her. "Where's your other glove?"

Nadine looked down at her ungloved hand, all red and tingly from the sudden warmth. "I think I—"

KNOCK-KNOCK-KNOCK.

Vicky and Nadine whipped their heads to the door. "Who the hell could that be at this hour?" Vicky asked.

Nadine's mouth fell open. She grabbed Vicky's hand. "Answer it! Please!"

"No way. I'm still asleep."

"Vicky, what if it's immigration? Or the police?"

"This late? Even they wouldn't dare."

"They could've followed me from the club! Just answer it!"

Vicky saw the panic in Nadine's eyes. She could tell she was scared. Something must've happened on the walk home. "Alright. Just relax. I'll get rid of them." Vicky headed for the door.

Nadine rushed into the bathroom. Sat on the toilet lid. Left the door open just enough to eavesdrop. She could hear a man's voice talking softly to Vicky. It was probably some salesman, or maybe another person in the building, someone that wasn't supposed to know Nadine was living there, not paying rent. When she first heard the knock, she instantly thought it was Sailor Boy, the one with the hands. Maybe he spotted her somewhere during her mad dash from Times Square. She wasn't being careful. She wasn't thinking ahead. Maybe he did find her. Maybe it was him.

She heard Vicky slam the door. "*Cel-este!*" Vicky sang. "A man was asking for you!"

Nadine couldn't believe it. Her heart was racing. She was practically in tears.

Vicky opened the bathroom door. Saw Nadine like that. Her teasing smile vanished. "Hey, what happened?"

Nadine was about to tell her all about Sailor Boy, that attack she endured, when she recognized the glove in Vicky's hand. "That's my glove." She snatched it out of Vicky's hand.

"Yeah. A really cute boy was asking for Celeste." Vicky leaned against the doorframe. "He certainly didn't look like a regular."

Nadine felt the warmth of the glove. Brian. He followed her home. He skipped the movie and followed her home. Just to make sure Sailor Boy didn't come after her. Just to make sure she got home safe. And to return her glove, of course. He did all that for her. He cared enough about her to do all that for her. *Her.* And what did she do for him?

Nadine looked up at Vicky desperately. "Did he say anything else?"

Vicky furrowed her brow. "What?"

"What, did he just… give you the glove and leave?"

Vicky scoffed. "What else would he have said? 'Olive Branch?'"

Nadine's face went numb at those words.

Vicky rolled her eyes and walked away. "I'm going to *bed!*" she whined.

Nadine frowned. "Good night." She tentatively stood. Returned to the living room. Stood at the window. Looked down at the street. To her surprise, there he was. Brian. Standing in the middle of street. And he was looking back up at her. But after a moment, he just walked away. Nadine watched him go the whole length of the street, a grateful yet remorseful smile on her face, until he was just out of sight.

CHAPTER TWENTY

A Couple of Cowards

Nadine walked across Washington Square Park and sat on the fountain, just like she had the past three days. Lit up a cigarette. Scanned the faces of all those NYU students mulling about. None of them the one she was looking for.

At that time, Brian was walking past the Garibaldi Memorial with Leonard, Hector and Nevil, his three closest NYU friends. "No, I'm telling you," Brian was telling them, "the city of Troy never actually existed."

Leonard shook his head. "No way. Too many works referenced the war."

"But all their sources trace back to Homer, and we all know how accurate he was."

"So wait," Nevil said, "you're saying the *city* wasn't real or the war wasn't real?"

"Both."

"Yeah, I'm with Leonard on this. That can't be true."

"Why not?"

"Because why are we studying the *Iliad* if it's all fake?"

"Because it's a mythology class! It's not about the history. It's the storytelling."

"But Greece was real! Athens was real! Sparta was real!"

"This the academic version of there not being a Santa Claus," Hector quipped.

"Wait till you find out about the Library of Alexandria," Brian said.

Nevil put a hand to his heart. "Ugh… Too soon." He bugged his eyes. "Wait. No. Don't you dare! Don't you take that away from me!"

"Hey, sorry to break it to you, Nevil, but…" Brian stopped walking. His face went blank. Eyes fixed on the fountain ahead.

Leonard, Hector and Nevil stopped walking. Leonard waved a hand in front of Brian's face. They all looked to see what Brian was gawking at and their mouths simultaneously dropped.

Standing just before the fountain, squashing her cigarette, was a tall blonde beauty in a fur coat staring back at Brian. She was wearing the same look he was.

Brian swallowed. "I'll catch up with you guys later," he told his friends.

"No way," Nevil murmured, his horny eyes fixed on Celeste. "We're not going anywhere. You kidding me?"

Brian pursed his lips. Walked away from the guys.

"The war might not be real," Leonard murmured to the guys, "but Helen of Troy sure is."

"I'd go to war for her in a heartbeat," Hector said.

"I'd *start* a war over her in a heartbeat," Nevil added.

"He's not going with her, is he?" Leonard asked.

Hector blew his lips. "No way. She's got to be a whore. Look at her."

"Don't worry, I am." Nevil licked his lips.

As Brian approached Celeste, he certainly had mixed emotions. He was happy to see her, of course. Surprised to see her. Even a bit moved. But she had wounded him. Neglected him. He lost so much sleep that night. Why now? Why not before?

Nadine sensed a tense atmosphere in Brian's approach. She had anticipated that, sure, but not this strong.

Brian stopped before Celeste, both hands in his pockets. "Good afternoon," he said coldly.

Nadine simply nodded back. "I've been trying to find you a few days now."

"Really?"

"Yeah."

Brian nodded skeptically. "Well, you found me. What's so important?"

Nadine hesitated, building up the courage. "How's your hand?"

Brian showed her his knuckles. Refused to emote.

Nadine smiled. "They look better."

"I know." Brian frowned. Waited for her to make her next move.

Nadine held up her own right hand. "Thanks for the glove."

"Celeste, I have friends waiting."

"No, please, just…" Nadine put her gloved hands together. Frowned. "I want to explain what happened that night. I think I can now." She hesitated again. "I need to, at least. You deserve it."

Brian tightened his lips. Memories of their diner conversation crept in. Her smart points. Her gorgeous smile… but he squashed them flat, before they had a chance to linger in his mind, before they could achieve color. Focused on the silhouette in the window instead. The one that refused to answer the door. The one that chose to shun him after everything. He couldn't sleep at all that night. "I have class," he told Celeste.

"We can talk later then. Is there some place—?"

"I have to study." Brian looked at her sternly. "Don't you have something to do too?"

Nadine was admittedly hurt by that. "Please. Just let me explain."

"I have friends waiting. I'm sorry." Brian stepped back. Turned away.

Nadine's heart raced. She blurted out, "Nadine!"

Brian stopped. Turned around. "What?"

"My name's Nadine. Nadine Sauvageot."

Brian's face softened at that. "Nadine."

Nadine nodded, resolute in her decision.

Brian hesitated. The cold January air suddenly didn't seem so cold. "That is a beautiful name."

Nadine smiled. "I know. That's why I wanted you to know it."

"Hey Loverboy!" Leonard shouted from afar, hands cupped around his mouth. "Who's your friend?!" Hector and Nevil chuckled foolishly behind him.

Brian winced, refusing to look back and acknowledge those numbskulls.

Nadine wasn't bothered by it. She only had eyes for Brian. Nothing left to give. It was all up to him now.

Brian took a deep breath. Scratched his head. Pointed in the general direction of 3rd Street. "There's a jazz bar over there. The Blue Note. I go there sometimes for a drink after class." He hesitated. "If you're there around 7, you might find me."

Nadine tried not to show too much relief. Inside, she was jumping for joy. "Alright."

Brian nodded cautiously. "I really should go now."

"Good luck. With your class, I mean."

"The Blue Note at 7. Don't forget."

"I won't." Nadine waved tenderly. "Bye."

"Bye." Brian turned and left. Took his time walking back to his friends.

"Who the hell *are* you?" Leonard teased.

Nevil's eyes were still on Celeste. "Who the hell is *she*?"

"She's just a friend," Brian grumbled, not stopping as he passed them.

Hector scoffed. Looked at Leonard. "Told you."

"Stop."

Leonard, Hector and Nevil followed in a pack, making obscene comments about "the French chick" the whole way to class. But Brian didn't care. He didn't listen. He was too giddy. He never let it show, but his heart was aflame.

Brian returned to his apartment around 5:30. He showered thoroughly. Combed his hair. Sprayed on some cologne, that bottle his uncle got him. He even brushed his teeth, twice to be safe. He had to sit down to calm his nerves. Then 6:30 came around and his nerves switched tracks. It turned into anticipation. Then as he left his apartment, it became good ol' fashioned *excitement*. He was going to see her again. Nadine. Beautiful Nadine.

Brian walked into the Blue Note at 6:45 and sat at the counter. His back to the front door. Perfect location. Close enough to hear a new arrival but angled just right to seem casual about looking for her. He ordered an old fashioned and waited for 7:00 to arrive. The band always started at 7. He didn't even have to keep looking at the clock. He'd know as soon as the music started. How convenient. How cool he looked, meeting a girl in a bar. A beautiful girl. One who had been waiting days for him to pass through Washington Square Park. A girl that actually liked him. The one he saved from that monster of a Sailor. That good for nothing Sailor rapist coward. Drunk no less. Oh, what a hero Brian was that night, huh? Such a masculine guy. And sensitive too. He listened to her. Picked her brain. He was a shoulder for her to cry on. But he was stern too. He stood by his principles when he snubbed her. And yet humble and forgiving, like Solomon. She could have any guy she wanted. She's gorgeous, of course, but also smart. She's smart to want him. That's right. She has great taste, and great wit, and great— Oh, the band started! It's 7:00! Where is she?

Brian casually looked toward the door. But she wasn't standing right there like some sort of fairy queen, the way Ingrid Bergman did walking into Rick's Café Américain in *Casablanca*, all that suspenseful music coming in to really emphasize the shock of her doing so. Brian casually faced forward again. Sipped his drink. Waited for her.

Ten minutes later, he was still waiting.

Thirty minutes later, he was still waiting. That's when the anger started, on the :30.

Then forty-five minutes. Brian debated what to do. Should he order another drink? Another three? Should he just leave out of spite? How could he be so stupid? How could he take her back like that? She hasn't changed! This is exactly how she was that night! What a fool he was! What a stupid, naïve, good-for-nothing piece of—Oh, there she is.

Nadine gave Brian an apologetic smile as she approached the counter. "I'm sorry I'm late," she shouted over the music.

"It's alright. I wasn't worried."

"I almost didn't bother, to be honest."

"That would've been bad."

Nadine looked around the Blue Note. "Is there somewhere we can talk? I can't hear myself think up here."

"We can't have that." Brian picked up his third old fashioned. Led her across the club to the corner-most booth, as far from the band as they could possibly be.

A waiter approached them as soon as they sat down. "Something to drink, miss?"

"A glass of Sauvignon Blanc, please," Nadine said.

"And put it on my tab," Brian added. "Brian Donahue."

"Of course, Mister Donahue." The Waiter walked off.

Nadine smiled at Brian with surprise. "How sweet of you."

"It's nothing." Brian sipped his drink, feeling like Carey Grant for the first time in his life. "So you wanted to talk about that night?"

Nadine nodded. "Yes."

Just then the Waiter returned with Nadine's glass of wine. "Sauvignon Blanc?"

Nadine took the glass. "Wait a moment." She put it to her lips. Gulped the Sauvignon Blanc down. Big yellow bubbles popping up.

Brian's mouth slowly went agape. The Waiter couldn't believe it either.

Nadine finished the last of the glass. Forced it all down. Burped. Instantly covered her mouth, a girly act of modesty. "Another please," she said sweetly, handing the glass back. "Thank you."

The Waiter nodded cordially. "Of course." He walked away with bugged eyes.

Nadine daintily dabbed her lips with her handkerchief. "I think I needed that," she said a bit too masculinely. She cleared her throat. Looked at Brian. "You alright?"

Brian couldn't breathe. The boy was in love. "Of course. Please continue."

Nadine took a deep breath, enjoying that Bordeaux fog she made for herself. "Yes." She looked Brian straight in the eye. "My entire family was killed by Nazis when they first invaded France—"

Brian coughed on his drink. "Oh, we're going right into it then."

"Yes. Finally." Nadine paused. "I only survived because one of them spared me. One of the Nazis, I mean. Even though he saw me, he let me go. I ran away. For weeks I hid in plough sheds until the French Resistance found me. They needed a nurse so they turned me into the nurse they needed."

The waiter returned with Nadine's second glass. "Sauvignon Blanc?"

Nadine took the glass off the tray. "Bring another while you're at it." She waited for the waiter to walk away. Drank a third of her new glass in one go. "Seven months after I joined the Resistance, a man stepped on a landmine not too far from our camp. I fixed him like I fixed hundreds of other soldiers. But when he woke up, we realized he could only speak English. He didn't know a word of French. Believe me, we tested him, but he didn't."

"I don't understand. I thought they were on our side."

"An Englishman still in France so soon after Dunkirk? That was suspicious. We needed to find out if he was a spy or a deserter, so my CO Roul ordered me to seduce him a bit. Get whatever I could out of him while he was bedridden." Nadine paused, her heart getting heavy. "His name was William Gunnison. He told me he was a Private in the British Army. He was a very good person. Very smart. We talked every day those two weeks he was there. About everything. Things I couldn't talk to the others about. I felt like I actually found a friend in all that. Someone who actually understood me. And I felt for him. What he had been through. He had been forced to fight in a war he despised. Follow orders without question. No matter how hard he wanted to disobey." Nadine tightened her mouth. Shook her head.

"You sound like you loved him."

Nadine froze. "Why would you say that?" she asked, panic in her voice.

That threw Brian off. He shrugged. "You just do."

"But I couldn't have loved him."

"Why not?"

Nadine hesitated. "Because he was a Nazi."

"Sauvignon Blanc?" the Waiter said, dipping his tray down.

"On the table, thank you." Nadine drank more from the glass in her hand. The Waiter placed the third glass on the table.

Brian raised a petrified finger. "I'd like a Scotch please."

"Of course, sir," the Waiter said. "What would you like?"

"I don't care. Whatever you have."

"Domergue?"

"Whatever. On the rocks."

"Of course, sir." The Waiter walked away again.

Nadine stared at Brian, anxious for his reaction.

Brian struggled to process it. He held a hand to his mouth, eyes down. He looked up at her. "I thought you said William was British."

"I didn't say that," Nadine murmured. "I said that's what he told me. His real name was Wilhelm Gunter. He was a deserter, all right, but for the opposite side. He turned on his CO. Killed seventeen Nazi officers, one for every civilian they forced him to kill in Belgium and France. And for that, the Third Reich tried him for treason and sentenced him to death."

Brian stared at her. "That doesn't mean you didn't love him."

Nadine frowned back. "His platoon was the one that killed my parents."

"Your Domergue, sir," the Waiter returned, holding out a tray.

Brian plucked up the Scotch. "No more please."

"Would you like to close—?"

"I'd like some *privacy*," Brian snapped. "That's what I'd like. Thank you very much."

The Waiter hesitated. "Of course, sir. Pardon me." He awkwardly left.

Brian drank his Scotch. "Alright, so you fell in love the Nazi that killed your parents. Then what?"

"He didn't kill my parents," Nadine corrected. "He's the one that saved me. Remember?"

"Of course he is!" Brian slammed his glass down. "Why didn't you just open with that?"

"I don't know. I'm not a storyteller. I'm just…" Nadine paused. Sipped some more wine. "I never told anyone about William before."

"I thought you said his name was Wilhelm."

"Can you just…?" Nadine huffed. Rubbed the bridge of her nose with closed eyes. "I don't know."

Brian softened. He could see that pain on her face.

Nadine shook her head. "I don't know who he was. I don't know how much of what he said was the truth. I don't know how much of it makes sense, if any of it makes sense. I only know how I felt at the time. I know he didn't remember how he knew me when he first woke up. He didn't figure it out until I mentioned how my family died. And even then, he didn't tell me he was the one that saved me. That part I remembered on my own. That makes me think he really was a good person."

"How does that make him a good person?"

"Because that information would instantly exonerate him. Someone who'd withhold that information would have to be a good person, right? I don't know. I don't know anymore." Nadine finished her glass of wine. Swapped it out with the full one. "I seem to be the only one that thought of him like that."

Brian sat in silence.

Nadine zoned out. Traced the rim of her glass. "One of the guys at the camp with us, Scragg… I always thought of them as my brothers. Scragg was no different. He was a bit quiet, perhaps. And he might've fancied me. Maybe he did. Maybe that had something to do with it."

"To do with what?"

Nadine drank some more wine. "After Germany sentenced William to death, I wanted to break him out of prison. They all knew who William was at that point. I had to lie to get them to go along with it. I told them he was willing to be an informant for us, a promise I had all intentions of reneging when the time came, but we never got that far." Nadine's heart raced. "What I didn't know… Roul knew, but I didn't… was that the Nazi that killed Scragg's family was William. Wilhelm. Whatever."

Brian went cold. "Jesus."

"I guess my lie must've put him on edge, the man that killed his family joining the team and all. But even then, he promised to go along with it anyway. He said he was going to follow my lead. So what did I do? I found out that the *Kommandant* of William's prison was his old CO. He's the reason William did everything he did. Turns out *he* was the man that killed my family. So as soon as I saw him, I didn't think. I just shot him in his office, the way he shot my family. That set the alarm off. I almost got everyone killed. But we got out. We got William out." Nadine looked at Brian with tears in her eyes. "But Scragg decided to follow my lead and do the same thing to William."

Brian moved his drink aside. He didn't feel alright. "He killed William?"

"Right in front of me!" Nadine's lip trembled. She closed her eyes. Turned away.

Brian wasn't even sure what to say to something like that. None of it seemed real. It seemed too perfect to be real. But clearly it was.

"If I just thought about it, if I-I wasn't so quick to…" Nadine opened her eyes. Even in the dim lighting, Brian could see how red they were. "It's all my fault. I was supposed to save him, but I got him killed. I got William killed. And of course Scragg got away with it. What did he do? All he did was shoot a Nazi. Just like I did." Nadine took a deep breath. Put aside her glass of wine. It wasn't helping at all. "I hated them for that. William was a person torn apart by the war, just like I was. He was my friend. He was a really really good friend. That was it for me. I snuck away as soon as we got back to France. Didn't tell anyone. I didn't leave a note. I just ran. Drove myself to Marseilles, caught a boat to Lisbon, bought myself a visa and I've been here ever since." Nadine frowned. "So the movie… That movie you took me to, it brought it all up again. That's it. That's my explanation."

Brian took her hand. Held it tight.

Nadine looked down at it. That sweet hand holding hers. She couldn't believe it. "I left them all behind," she said, glaring up at him. "France was dying, Brian. She needed me more than ever and I just *left!*" She pulled her hand out of Brian's grasp. "Who knows how many people need me to fix them now that I'm not there? And Roul, he was like a father to me. How does he feel about me now? How do any of them feel about me now? I just threw them aside, and for what? For some… compulsive liar I foolishly believed? A murderer? A coward?" Her lip trembled, her teeth clicking. She covered her mouth. "I'm sorry."

"It's alright," Brian whispered, hurt by the sight of a woman in pain. "Under the circumstances, I probably would've done the same thing."

"But would you have? Would you really?"

"Maybe."

"How could you possibly know what you would've done? You weren't there. That's what I mean about you Americans. You all think you would've been heroes, but you have no reason to think that way!"

Brian hesitated. "I'm just saying… Maybe the reason this all hurts you so much is because you're the only one that saw the real him. If you turn on William too, the good him would be gone forever. It'd be like you were killing him all over again."

Nadine looked away. "That's not…"

"I think it is. Whether you're punishing yourself for doubting him or punishing yourself for believing him so much you ran away in his name. Either way, it's just guilt. It's all in your head. You can heal from that."

Nadine slowly shook her head. "I really wish it was all just in my head."

"What do you mean?"

"When William hit that landmine, he was in the middle of something. A rescue mission. If he hadn't been killed, it would've worked. It would've really have… Maybe it would've."

Brian furrowed his brow.

Nadine took a deep breath. "He was in Paris a few days before chasing a Nazi, that old CO of his. Doesn't matter. He shot an American by accident. His name was Corey Baxter. William tried to save his life, but it wasn't enough. He died. And his butler, Corey's butler, Jacques, he never found out it was William. As far as he knew, William was just some bystander, a Good Samaritan. I really do think he wanted Corey to live. I felt… I just know that part is true. But Corey didn't want to go to hospital. Turns out him and Jacques were hiding something, and Corey was protecting Jacques… somehow. I can't remember why. But with Corey gone, Jacques was suddenly in danger. They had all these boxes in his house, boxes they were protecting, and Jacques needed them out of Paris as soon as possible. And so he asked William, Good Samaritan that he was, to deliver a letter of his to a man named Victor here in Manhattan. That's all he told him. Victor. And when he did, he'd have to say the words 'Olive Branch' or else Victor wouldn't accept the letter. The address was on the letter, apparently, but it got destroyed when William stepped on the landmine. But he wanted to keep going. He spent his whole life doing what other people wanted. Forced to obey orders he disagreed with. Doing nothing. Watching others suffer. This was a chance for him to do everything he could to save Jacques, to fix the mess he single-handedly put him in. It's the reason I drove him all the way to Marseilles. It's the reason I went all the way to Berlin to save him. It's the reason…" Her voiced finally fizzled.

"It's the reason you loved him."

"No!" Nadine said with a grimace. "It's the reason I went to New York! That's what I was going to say!"

"I don't believe you."

"Well, you don't really know me, do you?!"

Brian simply stared back. "As of this moment, I think I know you better than anyone else on Earth."

Nadine could feel her body hollow out. Those were some powerful words he just said. "And?"

Brian shrugged. "I think it makes sense."

"No, it doesn't."

"I think it does."

"No, it doesn't! I never found Victor! I have no idea where he is! It's been two years, Brian! Two years since Corey died! There's no way. It's too late. Jacques's dead. I know he is."

"But what if he isn't?"

"They're air-raiding Paris as we speak! If the Nazis didn't get him by now, I'm sure the Allies already did!" Nadine got dizzy. She closed her eyes. Put her head on the table.

Brian merely frowned down at her head. "But what if he isn't?"

"What are you doing to me?" Nadine whined, lifting her head. "I've been through all this already. It's better I accept what I am."

Brian drank some more Scotch. Put the glass down. Thought a bit. "My uncle has a friend in the government. He's the one that pulled some strings. Got me deferred."

Nadine furrowed her brow at the sudden topic change. "Did you want him to do that?"

"What do you think?"

Nadine hesitated. "Did you ask him to do that?"

Brian didn't speak at first. "What do you think?" he repeated, slower this time.

Nadine stared at him. "Why?"

Brian half-frowned. Fought through it. "Because my father came back *wrong*." He shook his head. "He fought in the Great War. He was… Something must've happened because he…" He let out a bitter laugh. "Why am I telling you this?"

"Just tell me."

"He came back homosexual, alright?" Brian's throat closed. Nadine could hear it squeak.

Nadine cringed a bit. "Oh."

"And the reason I know that is because…" Brian stopped talking. "He…" He stopped again. "With me, he…"

Nadine felt chills down her spine. "Are you saying he…?"

Brian exhaled hard. "Yes! Thank God. I didn't have to say it. Yes. Thank you. He did. Which is why I lived with my uncle most of my life. My father's in an asylum now. So there. Now you know me too." He finished his Scotch.

Nadine put her hand on Brian's. "It's not your fault."

"I know it's not." Brian uncomfortably moved his hand away. "It was the war. I know it was. The war turned him homosexual and he took it out on me. But that's not my point. My point is… When I told you I had no intentions to enlist, you probably thought that was me being a coward. But in reality, it's the bravest thing I could do. I don't want the war to turn me homosexual. I don't want to hurt anyone the way he hurt me. But it hurts because I can't tell anyone about it. They'd understand why I'm still here if I only explained myself, but I can't. I've never told anyone what I just told you. I can't put myself through all that. Only the ones who understand would… So what I'm trying to say is that I might not understand war, but I understand this. I understand you in this. You can't talk about William just like I can't talk about my dad. And you think being here instead of France makes you a coward too, but you're not. It's a brave thing you're doing. You're finishing what William Gunnison started. You're trying to save a Frenchman's life."

Nadine let out a heavy sigh. "That's what I was trying to do, yes."

"I know you still can."

"But how? How could you possibly know that?"

"I know I'm not a hero. I'm too smart for all that. I'm too bookish. I watch other people have adventures." Brian smiled. "But not the night I met you."

"I know. That was quite a punch."

"That's not what I'm talking about. I meant meeting you."

Nadine blinked. "I don't follow."

"I'm going to help you find Victor."

Nadine scoffed. "Brian. It's over. I tried everything already. I did everything I could."

"There's no way you could've. You're just one person. I can help you."

"You've done enough for me, really."

"But what about Jacques?"

"Why do you even care? It's not your mission. It's not even mine!"

Brian grinned. "Nadine… Don't you understand? This isn't a mission. It's a *quest*! An actual bona fide quest in this day and age! Can you believe it?!"

Nadine stared at Brian, her face going numb. "Oh my God."

"You're not just saving Jacques here! You're saving William's eternal soul! You actually have a chance to redeem a man from beyond the grave!"

"Are you…?" Nadine shook her head. "Are you actually a child?"

"What? No! I know what this is! This is what I do! This is what I can do! This is how I can actually be a hero to somebody! And it would fix everything, wouldn't it? It would fix you. It would save Jacques. Who knows what it would do to Victor. And William! Him too!"

"This is not a tale from Greek mythology, Brian. This is not some Arthurian legend. This is real life. These were real people. I'm a real person. This is not a story."

"But you believed it, didn't you? You understood once. You came all the way out here, didn't you? To finish what William started—"

"AND LOOK WHAT HAPPENED!" Nadine snapped.

Brian instantly deflated.

Nadine grimaced. Looked away. "I'm sorry. I just don't think of it the same way you do."

Brian desperately frowned at her like a lost little puppy. "But you did once… didn't you?"

"Of course I did." Nadine wiped her eyes. Stared into space. "I spent everything I had to get here. It was the only thing I believed in. It was the only morally right thing. The only thing that made sense. But I never realized how big this place was. How little I had to go off of. I thought I could just look

'Victor' up in the phone book. Do you know how many people have 'Victor' somewhere in their name in New York? Hundreds. I knocked on hundreds of apartment doors. I must've said 'Olive Branch' more than anyone else in the history of the world. I've had cops called on me. I've been arrested so many times. The last time I was, they threatened to deport me. I ran out of money. I had no food for weeks. I slept in the park. Even after sixteen months dancing at that awful club, I barely have that money back. I can't leave even if I wanted to. If someone catches me outside J. Roger's, or if the place gets raided again, they'll arrest me and deport me. If someone finds out I've over-stayed my visa, they'll arrest me and deport me. And I've got nothing out there. No home. No family." Nadine shook her head. "I'm sorry. I know you find it so romantic, but in reality it's the worst thing that's ever happened to me. The same emotional bullshit that got William killed…" Nadine frowned. Sighed. Looked at Brian. "It pretty much killed me too."

The two of them sat in silence, as silent as a jazz club could be with a big band in the next room.

After a heavy beat, Brian spoke up. "Jacques needed Victor's help to get him and all those boxes out of Paris."

Nadine furrowed her brow. "What?"

"Jacques needed William's help to get his message to Victor. William needed your help to fix his leg. He still needs your help, to find Victor when he couldn't." Brian paused. "What if the only reason you haven't found Victor yet was because you didn't have my help?"

"What could you possibly contribute that I couldn't?"

"I'll tell you one thing. I know why you're supposed to say 'Olive Branch.'"

"Sure you do."

"When God told Noah to build the ark and put two of every animal inside, he and his family rode that flood for forty days and forty nights. When the rains finally stopped, Noah sent a dove to go out and find land to prove it was safe again out there. When the dove came back, what did it have in its mouth?"

Nadine's eyes widened. "An olive branch."

Brian nodded proudly. "'Olive Branch' is Jacques's question to Victor: 'Is my ark of goodies safe to land?'"

Nadine gaped. "Oh my God. Brian!"

Brian opened his arms wide. "SEE? What did I tell you?! *This is my thing!*" He put his arms back down. That cocky look stayed on his face. "You still think I won't be able to help?"

Nadine's heart raced. She could taste the very thing she never thought she'd be able to taste again. Suddenly it all seemed so simple. It all seemed so possible.

And it would fix *everything*.

CHAPTER TWENTY-ONE

Some Speculation

Nadine pushed the plunger down on her French press and carried it into the living room. "I had been here five weeks at least," she told Brian, joining him on the floor. "I'd already went through all the Christian name Victors. At least it felt like I did. And I was starting to lose track of what surname Victor I was on. Safe to say, I was getting antsy. And as I was going through yet another payphone phonebook, I suddenly had a new thought. What if Victor was actually 'Victoria?' What if that was the reason I hadn't found her yet?"

"That doesn't make sense."

"I know, believe me." Nadine poured Brian's coffee into an empty cup. "I was losing my mind." She poured herself a cup. "Cheers."

"Cheers." Brian blew the top of his coffee.

"I felt the chances of Victoria A or Victoria Z being the one was statistically low, so I decided to switch it up. I ran my finger down a random page until I landed on a Victoria. Sure enough: Victoria Heatherwood, 343 W 21st Street, Apartment 4C. I came out here. Knocked on the door. Vicky answered. And I thought I was making sense at the time, but she said I was acting like a madwoman. Obviously starving to death. Disheveled. I kept saying 'Olive Branch' over and over like it meant something."

"No wonder they all called the cops."

"Exactly. So she let me inside. Calmed me down. I explained everything as best I could. Turns out she didn't even have a phone anymore. She hadn't had a phone in *seven years*!"

"Seven years?!"

"Which meant every Victor Christian Name I'd already crossed off my list wasn't even every Victor in New York anymore. Believe me, I hated hearing that. It made me cry, actually."

Brian half-frowned sympathetically. "Aww…"

"It's okay." Nadine smiled. "And so, what started off as a simple 'Hey, let me make you some lunch' turned into me shacking here until I found my footing. No rent. No utilities. I just buy my own food." Nadine drank her coffee. "She's the one that got me the job at J. Roger's, actually."

"Really?"

"Come on. Drink your coffee. Tell me how you like it."

"Alright." Brian took a sip. "Oh wow, you weren't kidding."

"I know."

"Holy cow." Brian drank some more, trying not to burn his tongue. "Where's Vicky now?"

"At her other job. She's a secretary at Burkes & Carter, some law firm."

"They have no idea she dances?"

"Obviously not. Though I'm sure being an unmarried woman in a place like that is no different than fighting off the regulars at J. Roger's."

"Which came first, I wonder?"

"I don't know. She really doesn't talk about herself." Nadine sipped some of her coffee. "Damn, that's good."

Brian placed his cup aside. Grabbed his legal pad and pen. "Alright. You ready to start?"

"I think so."

"I'm just going to ask whatever comes to my mind."

"Fine by me."

"But try to be simple with your answers. The more you overexplain, the harder it'll be for me to gauge from my notes what you actually know and how much you're just speculating."

Nadine smirked. "You're taking this very seriously."

"I have to, Nadine. A man's life is at stake."

"Allegedly."

Brian raised his brows. "I'll mark that down as speculation."

Nadine rolled her eyes. "Don't mark it down. I was just a joking."

"Try not to joke either." Brian jotted the date at the top of the pad. "Everything William told you about Olive Branch he told you over one two-week period, correct?"

"It wasn't the entire two weeks. I only got little bits and pieces at first."

"So when would you say you had your first serious conversation about it?"

Nadine had to think about it. "Probably after the first week. It had to have been after he gave us his dog tag number. I remember that was early on."

"You don't remember the date?"

"The exact date?"

"It would help."

"Oh." Nadine blew her lips. "Well, I know he stepped on the landmine on the 17th, so… It might've been the 23rd?"

"Of January?"

"Yes."

Brian jotted the date next to William's name. "January… twenty-third… 1941?"

"That's right."

"1941. And everything he knew about it, he learned from Jacques directly, right?"

"Yes."

"So when would that have been?"

"Two days before the landmine, so… the 15th."

"Good." Brian jotted all that down. "That's very good."

"How is that good?"

"It was all relatively fresh in William's mind by the time he relayed it to you." Brian thought about his next question. "When did Corey get shot? Was it the same day? January 15th?"

"Yes."

"In Paris?"

"Correct."

Brian added that next to Jacques's name. "So to summarize… William shot Corey Baxter on the 15th of January, 1941. Later that day, his butler Jacques told William about Victor, Olive Branch, all that. The letter got destroyed two days later… and William told you everything Jacques told *him* on or around 23rd. Am I correct about that so far?"

Nadine drank more coffee. "Yeah."

Brian chewed on the end of his pen. "Just to clarify, you do not know Jacques's last name?"

"I don't. But I do know he's French and black."

"Alright." Brian added that detail. "You said Corey Baxter was American?"

"Yes."

"Any clue how old he was?"

Nadine hesitated. "How old?"

"Was he a young man? Very old? Middle aged?"

"I-I don't remember. Probably on the older side."

Brian wrote that down. "Is Victor American?"

Nadine stared. "What?"

"Is Victor American like Corey or is he French like Jacques?"

Nadine gaped. "I don't know."

Brian wrote that down. "What about Jacques. Was he from Paris?"

"I don't know."

"Do you know where in France Jacques was from?"

"No."

Brian added that. "What about Corey? Do you know what part of America—?"

"I don't know anything about birthplaces. I'm sorry."

"It's alright." Brian wrote that down as a notation. "Did the two of them travel anywhere together?"

"Who?"

"Corey and Jacques. Did William mention any other places they might've visited?"

Nadine looked off, suddenly feeling very uncomfortable. "No. I don't know."

"Is that a 'No' or an 'I don't know.'"

"'I don't know.'"

Brian hesitated. Wrote it down anyway. "Okay, did…?" He sighed. Looked around the apartment. "Oh! Did they have a phone?"

"A phone?"

"Would either of them be in a Paris phone book?"

Nadine went quiet, trying to remember. "I don't know."

"Did they live in Paris before the occupation?"

"They must have. He said that they…" Nadine closed her eyes. "Oh God. William… He said he wanted to take Corey to a hospital… Corey said no… so he took him to his home instead. But I know he also said a doctor tried to save him and that he lost too much blood."

"So they must've called Corey's physician. That means he had a phone."

Nadine nodded. "You're right. He must've had a phone."

"Great." Brian wrote that down. "You said he was losing blood. Where was he shot?"

"I don't know. I wasn't there."

"Where on his body, I mean."

"Oh. His back. William said it took hours for him to die." Nadine hesitated. "No wait, *I* said it would've taken him hours. But he didn't deny that, so…"

"I'll write it down." Brian added a speculation asterisk. "How did William know where Corey lived? Did he tell him?"

Nadine stared. "What do you mean?"

"Did Corey actually tell William his address or did William have to check his papers for it?"

"What difference would that make?"

"If Corey had documentation with his name and address on it, that would be something we could look up."

Nadine stayed silent a long time. "He didn't say." She paused while Brian wrote that down. "But speaking as a nurse, um… I doubt Corey would've been able to say very much."

"That sure sounds like speculation."

Nadine pursed her lips. "Maybe it is."

"I'll note it anyway." Brian jotted a little asterisk. "Try not to add anything. Just stick to what you remember William telling you directly."

"Okay."

"Did Jacques live with Corey or did he have his own separate residence?"

Nadine hesitated. "Given his occupation, he must've lived there." After a pause, she added, "Oh he definitely is. He's got all those crates to protect."

"So if we found out where William took Corey or wherever the doctor was called to, Jacques might still be there?"

"If he's still alive, yes."

Brian added that. "Do you know what was in the crates?"

"William speculated it was evidence of the German Republic. That would explain why the Nazis would want to destroy it."

"So that's *his* speculation? Not something Jacques told him?"

"Yes."

"Did he actually use the word 'evidence?'"

Nadine had to think about that. "No, he said… 'Proof that world even existed.'"

"What world?"

"What?"

"What world did it prove existed?"

"The German Republic."

"But everyone knows Germany used to be a republic. Was there something specific about it that the evidence would've proved?"

"That I don't know." Nadine paused. "He did say there was a box of letters, and photos…" She gasped. "Oh my God! The photo! That's right! I can't believe I forgot about the photo!"

"What photo?"

"William specifically mentioned a photo." Nadine excitedly sat up. "Taken in Berlin. Jacques was in it."

"Jacques was in Berlin?"

"Corey too, I think. No, he was definitely in it. But the reason I even remember William mentioning the photo is because he said there was a Nazi in there too."

Brian wrote all that down. "A Nazi with Jacques?"

"Yes. Though it might've been with Corey because…" Nadine gasped again. "That's right! Roul did a check on William's alibi and found out the Baxters were a family of Nazi sympathizers! That must've been why they were in the same photo together! It must've been some German coal industry function! Jacques would've only have been there because Corey was there!"

Brian wrote that all down, adding a speculation asterisk. "Who was the Nazi in the photo?"

"I don't know his name, but William called him a controversial Nazi."

"Aren't they all controversial?"

"That's what I said." Nadine pondered some more. "And that's when William said Hitler had him killed!"

"The Nazi?"

"Yes!"

"So he knew the Nazi?"

Nadine hesitated. "Hitler?"

"No, William. He was a Nazi too, right? Did he recognize the Nazi from personal experience or did Jacques have to tell him he was a Nazi?"

Nadine felt a cold chill down her arms. "I… I-I-I don't know. He didn't say."

Brian wrote a notation. "Did he say when the photo was taken?"

Nadine instantly opened her mouth. Stopped. "Oh my God, he did, but…" She huffed. Closed her eyes. Strained. "Come on! I know it, I know it, I know it…"

"Was it from the Weimar days too?"

"Yes, but…" Nadine bumped the sides of her head. "I know the year. I know it. I just…"

"It's okay. We can come back to that."

Nadine opened her eyes with a sigh. "Fine."

"Who else was in the photo? Was it just Corey, Jacques and the Nazi, or were there others too?"

Nadine scrunched her face. "Yessss?" she strained out. "Yes. Yes. He said there was a whole bunch of other people, but I don't know how many."

Brian jotted that. "Was Victor in the photo?"

Nadine stared, her eyes unmoving. "I don't remember."

Brian wrote that down. "Was it just Jacques and Corey's association with the Nazi that made them a target? Or was there more of an ideological reason for Jacques to be in the danger he's in?"

"What do you mean?"

"Were they communists? Jews? Gypsies? Polacks? Anything the Third Reich targeted specifically?"

"William never said, so… I suppose they weren't. He certainly made a point to identify Jacques as black, so I think that would've come up."

Brian wrote some more. "What was his rank?"

Nadine furrowed her brow. "Jacques's?"

"William's. Sorry."

"Oh." Nadine blinked. "Why? What does that have to do with anything?"

"Was he high ranking or was he near the bottom?" Brian paused. "Everything you know about Jacques got filtered through him first. I need to know more about William himself."

Nadine hesitated. "I don't know what his real rank was, only that he pretended to be a British Private."

"So he must've been a *Soldat*."

"A *Soldat*?"

"That's the German equivalent of a Private. If he was a *Hauptmann* or something higher, he most likely would not have pretended to be a British Private."

"That sounds like speculation."

Brian chuckled. "It's just a theory I have. I think people like to pretend they're better or equal to what they actually are." He wrote all that down, adding an asterisk to his own point. "Do you know where in Germany William was from?"

Nadine hesitated. "I don't remember."

"What about his family?"

"His mother got sent to a sanatorium when he was a child and his father was killed in a pub fight when he was twelve."

"A pub fight?"

"Yes. With Nazis, as a matter of fact."

Brian suddenly furrowed his brow. "How old did you say William was when you met him?"

"I didn't."

"How old was he?"

"He said he was twenty."

"So his father would've died in…" Brian did quick mental math. "1933?"

Nadine did the same mental math in her head. "If he was born in '21, yeah."

"You just said he was twenty."

"He might've been born in 1920 and hadn't turned twenty-one yet. Why?"

"1933 was a big year for Hitler. He did a lot of major assassinations leading up to his rise as Chancellor."

Nadine stared. "What are you saying? His father was the Nazi in the photograph?"

"It's possible, isn't it?"

"No, because…" Nadine thought back, an uneasy feeling in her stomach.

Brian waited some more. "Did he say why the Nazis killed his father?"

"I don't know. Not really."

"Hadn't he already revealed he was a Nazi when he told you about it?"

Nadine's stomach pit stung some more. "No. As a matter of fact, he didn't."

"So that could've been…?"

"Part of the lie? Yes. I suppose he could've made it all up." Nadine frowned deeply, angry eyes staring into space. "His father might be alive for all I know."

Brian suddenly realized the calamity he had just unearthed. He put the pad and pen down. "Let's take a break."

Thirty minutes later, Nadine was still sitting on the floor, still in that negative zone, her cup of cafetière coffee ice cold beside her. Brian had relocated to the kitchen table to reread his notes. He looked up. Saw that crestfallen look still on her face. She was obviously still thinking about it. And who could blame her? He shouldn't have asked so many questions. He had to think of something. Anything to stop Nadine thinking like that.

Brian crouched next to her. "I'll be honest, there's not much here to help us find Victor."

Nadine sighed. Rubbed her eyes. "I know."

"But I think we have enough to find Jacques." Brian turned the legal pad toward her. "We know Corey Baxter's full name. We know his butler's name. We know who shot him. We know where he had been shot. We know he died the day he was shot. We know he died at his home address and we know that address has a phone."

Nadine looked up at Brian, a spark reignited behind her eyes. "And we know they were in Paris before the war, which means—"

"Which means they'd be in an old Paris phone book." Brian grinned. "Is there anyone you know in Paris who could find that out for us? Someone we could trust?"

"I don't know."

"What about the Resistance?"

"They were in Crespières, but—"

"Where's Crespières?"

"About twenty miles or so outside Paris."

"That's good enough, isn't it?"

Nadine shook her head. "Even if they're still in Crespières, which isn't likely, I…" She paused. "I can't."

Brian took a deep breath. "That's alright. We can find someone else."

"There is no one else."

"No one else at all? No one you knew as a nurse?"

Nadine blinked. "Wait, there is." She looked at Brian. "Doctor Garnier. The surgeon that trained me. He's in Neuilly-sur-Seine. That's practically Paris. And he's a part of the American Hospital of Paris, which means *we can call him!*"

"Call him? What, long distance?"

"Yeah."

"To *Paris?*"

"We'll just reverse the charges. It's a hospital. They can afford it. The best part is they'll have access to all the Parisian death records!"

"Will he actually do that for us?"

"For me he will. Absolutely." Nadine jumped to her feet. "C'mon. Let's go."

Brian checked his watch. It was almost noon. "What? Right now?"

"Why not? C'mon, before it gets too late over there." Nadine grabbed her coat. Threw it on. Brian reluctantly grabbed his and followed her out.

Nadine led Brian to the payphone on 9th and W 21st, the closest one to Vicky's apartment. She lifted the receiver and spoke to the Operator. "Hello, I need to make a long-distance call to the American Hospital of Paris. Reverse the charges please."

"Just a moment," the Operator droned. Silence on the line.

Nadine looked uneasily at Brian. Brian nodded back with encouragement.

The Operator came back on. "Who may I say is calling?"

"Nadine Sauvageot."

"Nadina *whaaat?*"

"Sau-va-geot."

"Savage-it?"

"Sauvageot."

"Suffragette?"

Nadine groaned. "Yes. Fine. Just make the call."

"Hold on." The Operator put Nadine back on hold. Dialed the number for the American Hospital of Paris using the list they had received from the Department of War. The dial tone rang twice.

An AHS Secretary picked up the phone. Started rattling off a French spiel.

The Operator talked over her. "Hello, this is a collect call from Nadina Suffragette in the United States for the American Hospital of Paris. Do you accept the charges?"

The Secretary hesitated. Slowly hung up the phone.

The Operator huffed. Switched back to Nadine. "They hung up."

Nadine furrowed her brow. "What?"

"What happened?" Brian asked her.

Nadine covered the receiver. "They didn't accept the charges."

Brian stopped to think. "Is there a way you can call Garnier directly?"

"Yes, but it's only for emergencies."

"This is an emergency."

"A *medical* emergency."

"In a way it is. Do it."

Nadine frowned. Put the phone back to her ear. "Operator, try a different number." She then rattled off a Parisian number, the one Roul told her to memorize, the one she used to report William's calf injury. "And reverse the charges again."

"Of course." The Operator dialed the number. The tone rang. Twice. Three times. Four.

3,600 miles away, Doctor Renart Garnier was eating a humble sandwich when the phone rang. Not just any phone. The special phone. The Resistance line. He immediately stopped chewing. Threw down the sandwich. Wheeled his chair over. Picked up the phone. "Doctor Garnier speaking," he said in French.

"This is a collect call from Nadina Suffragette in the United States for Doctor Renart Garnier at the American Hospital of Paris. Do you accept the charges?"

Doctor Garnier hesitated. "Don't you mean Nadine Sauvageot?" he asked in English.

The Operator rolled her eyes. "Yes, that one. Say yes to accept the charges."

Doctor Garnier closed his eyes. A long-distance call from the United States. Even if it was Nadine, even if it is an emergency, he couldn't afford to take it. Paris needed the AHP now more than ever. "Tell her I'm sorry, but I can't accept."

The Operator instantly dropped the call out of annoyance. Switched back to Nadine. "He refused the charges, lady."

Nadine frowned. "I don't understand."

"If you can't afford the call, just hang up and write a letter, alright? Let someone else use the line."

Nadine slowly hung up the receiver. "What a rude woman."

"What happened?" Brian asked. "Did he refuse the charges?"

Nadine wordlessly stepped out of the phone booth. Adjusted her coat. Crossed her arms. Thought up a plan.

Brian watched her anxiously. "What do we do now?"

"I don't know." Nadine turned to him. She almost didn't want to ask. "How much money do you got?"

"Not enough to call Paris long distance."

A gust of wind blew past. Nadine tightened her coat. "How about this? We send a telegram to Garnier. We give him all the questions we have. Then we call that same number next week. If he knows nothing, he'll tell us and we'll hang up. If he knows something, it wouldn't take long for him to tell us, right? A couple minutes at most? We can split that between the two of us, surely."

Brian hesitated. "I'm serious. I really don't have much outside what I've already put aside for my tuition."

Nadine sighed. "We can't use a payphone anyway. It'll take us a whole minute just to reload the damn thing." She tongued the inside of her cheek. "I might have a better idea. Follow me."

CHAPTER TWENTY-TWO

Quite the Toll

Nadine led Brian to the Epiphany Branch of the New York Public Library on E 23rd Street. She stopped at the desk of the first male librarian she saw. His nametag said "Johnnie."

"Yes?" Johnnie asked her, smiling politely. "Can I help you?"

Nadine donned a flirtatious smile, a Celeste classic. "Yes. My grandmother's in Paris right now. She's having surgery at the American Hospital of Paris next week. I told them I'd call them afterwards just so I'd know she's safe."

Johnnie blinked. "Okay?"

"But the problem is I don't have a phone. Is it alright if I call them from here?"

Johnnie scrunched his face. "I'm sorry, miss. I'm afraid we can't afford a call like that."

Nadine made herself look like she was about to cry. "You can't? What am I going to do?"

Johnnie was ready to double down on a refusal… but for such a pretty woman—a French woman, in wartime no less—who simply wanted to know her grandmother was alright… "We'll have to send you the bill," Johnnie blurted, shocked to hear himself say it. "If you're alright with paying for the call, we'll provide the phone."

"Great!" Nadine cried, letting out a girly giggle.

Johnnie reluctantly grabbed a piece of paper and a pencil. His manager was going to kill him. "May I see some identification?"

Nadine hesitated. "Actually I don't have my identification on me. But you can call my employer. They'll verify everything about me."

"And who's your employer?"

"Burkes & Carter."

Brian furrowed his brow at that.

Johnnie wrote that down. "Alright, we'll call them Monday morning, Miss…"

"Heatherwood," Nadine told him. "Victoria Heatherwood."

Brian was taken aback by that, but he kept his stone face.

Johnnie saw nothing but honesty on Nadine's face. "And what is your address, Miss Heatherwood? For the bill."

"343 W 21st Street, Apartment 4C."

"And you know exactly when your grandmother is coming out of surgery?"

"The doctor told me to call at 7 in the morning Eastern time next Friday the 29th."

Johnnie folded up the paper. "I'll give this to my manager. After he checks in with your employer, we'll get it all set up for you this Friday." He handed her the note.

Nadine grinned widely as she took the paper. "Thank you so much, monsieur. God bless you."

Johnnie bashfully smiled back. "Of course. And best wishes to your grandmother."

"Thank you." Nadine turned. Led Brian outside. "How's that, huh?" she whispered slyly, finally out of character.

Brian chuckled. "You're amazing."

Nadine and Brian spent the rest of the day laying out their plan. They needed Garnier to contact embassies, look up directories, even dig out old phone books, the ultimate goal being Corey Baxter's telephone number. If they could reach his old house directly, no matter what happened, they'd have a guaranteed answer. If Jacques answered the phone, they'll know he's still alive and whether or not he still needed their help. If he didn't answer, that would mean he found some other way to get out of France. If the telephone had been disconnected, the house might've been destroyed in an air raid. If someone besides Jacques answered the phone, especially someone speaking German, they'd have to assume Jacques had been captured, Corey's house given away to some German officer and his family.

Nadine and Brian proofread their telegram together. In it they gave Corey Baxter's first and last name, his nationality, the fact that he had a butler named Jacques, a colored Frenchman, and the circumstances of Corey's death. They added the possibility that Corey Baxter might've had dual American citizenship. They ended their telegram with the date and time of their intended call, next Friday at 7 AM Eastern Time. Brian stopped by Western Union on his way back to his apartment and sent it off.

Nadine and Brian met up again the next morning to calculate how much phone time with Garnier Nadine could afford. They took into account the price per minute, all the long-distance charges and fees, and realized Nadine could only realistically afford forty-five seconds of call time. Anything more than a minute would cost more than Nadine was willing to spend. Even if Garnier was in the middle of a sentence, they both agreed to hang up at exactly forty-five seconds.

Nadine woke up early on Monday to tell Vicky about the call she was about to receive as secretary at Burkes & Carter. To avoid getting her in trouble with her own managers, Vicky would have to pretend to be someone else to verify her own identity. Vicky was startled by Nadine's trick involving her workplace, but she chose to trust her roommate on this one. Sure enough, later that day she received a call from Johnnie's manager at the Epiphany Branch of the New York Public Library and pretended to be her boss's secretary, confirming the employment of Victoria Heatherwood of 343 W 21st Street, Apartment 4C at Burkes & Carter.

The days leading up to the Garnier call were nerve-wracking for both Brian and Nadine. Nadine had to call out sick from J. Roger's for the week, claiming to have caught the same nasty cold Vicky had had. Brian couldn't focus in class, too excited by his own real-life adventure to care about any mythological ones. Every night, they met up for dinner or drinks. They talked out their anxieties about Olive Branch whilst also taking the time to get to know more about each other. Nadine truly felt seen for the first time in years, feeling her New York life finally had a purpose. And Brian, well… the boy was in love for the very first time. What else is there to say?

Then Friday morning came. Nadine and Brian walked into the Epiphany Branch. Met up with Johnnie and his manager. Followed them into the manager's personal office. They asked if they needed anything to drink, water, coffee, something, but they refused. Then they let them be, Johnnie sitting outside the office, checking the call's start and stop time for their own records.

Nadine told the Operator the long-distance number using the manager's phone. As it rang, she looked at Brian.

Brian held up his stopwatch, ready to click at her cue. Their hearts were pounding.

The call got picked up. "Nadine?" It was Doctor Garnier.

Nadine instantly nodded to Brian.

Brian clicked the stopwatch. ClickClickClickClickClickClickClickClick-ClickClick... Nadine and Garnier were speaking to each other exclusively in French. Brian couldn't understand a word. He just kept staring at that second hand. ClickClickClickClickClickClickClickClickClickClick... His eyes darted from the watch-face up to Nadine. He didn't like the look on Nadine's face. It was clear she didn't like what Garnier was telling her. Click-ClickClickClickClickClickClickClickClickClick... Then she started asking what seemed to be like follow-up questions. Brian spun his finger, urging her to hurry up, but she mostly ignored him. ClickClickClickClickClickClick-ClickClickClickClick... Forty seconds. Brian held up five fingers and counted down to zero. ClickClickClickClickClick... "Alright! Now!"

But Nadine didn't move.

Brian reached over to hang up the phone himself. Nadine slapped his hand away. Kept on talking to Garnier, much faster this time.

Brian stared in shock, ice in his veins. "Nadine? Nadine, what are you doing?"

Nadine lowered the receiver a tad. "It's not good."

"I know it's not good. You're still on the line!" Brian reached over again to hang up.

"Stop!" Nadine swatted Brian away again.

"What are you doing?!"

"Just wait!"

"It's been an entire minute!"

"WAIT!" Nadine snapped back.

"You need to get off the phone."

"I know I do! Just listen!"

"You're still on the phone!"

"*I'm* the one paying the bill here!" Nadine hissed at him. "Please, just listen!"

Brian gritted his teeth. How dare she throw that at him.

Nadine tried to calm herself down. She had been feeling the time pressure ten times worse than Brian had. "Garnier checked both embassies. Neither

France nor the United States have any records of a Corey Baxter having ever lived in Paris."

Brian stared. "Neither of them?"

"Neither."

"So it wasn't his real name?"

"Probably not."

"Then how'd he have an ID?"

"He must've told the Nazis his name was Corey Baxter to have that printed on all his occupation papers, but Garnier wouldn't have access to all that."

"Or they could've just faked the documents."

"Yes, that too."

Brian's heart skipped a beat. "So what are you saying? Jacques might not even be his real name either?"

Nadine didn't say anything. She didn't think of that.

Brian stared in horror at the receiver in her hand. "Why are you still on the phone?!"

"I'm on hold."

"GET OFF THE PHONE!"

"Will you keep your voice down?!" Nadine whipped her head toward the office door, Johnnie sitting just outside. "We'll never be able to make this arrangement again. I need to get more out of Garnier."

"How?! It took him an entire week to get all that already!"

Nadine put her ear back on the receiver. Nope, still on hold. "During my training, I befriended Garnier's mortician Boutierre. We had a conversation about John Smiths and how nations abroad would be able to identify them throughout the occupation. Boutierre told me he was going to compile a list of every American killed in Paris during the occupation along with all the circumstantial details necessary for a reverse lookup. I asked Garnier if he ever made that list. He said did but only up to August 1941." Nadine stopped to catch her breath. "So even if we don't know Corey Baxter's real name, we know William shot someone on January 15th, 1941 with a shot to the back and that that someone was at least an American citizen. Garnier's going downstairs now to Boutierre to check his list. If we can get Corey Baxter's real name, we can find out who Jacques is that way. It won't all be for nothing."

Brian shook his head. "You don't have the money to spend on that information."

"But we're so close!"

"Stop and think about what you're doing here! This is exactly the kind of shit you did that got William killed!"

Nadine glared at him.

Brian's face muscles released instantly. "Wait. I didn't mean that."

Nadine pointed at the door. "Get out."

"No, please, you need to—"

"Out!"

"Just get off the phone and I will."

"Now!"

"Please get off the phone."

Nadine could suddenly hear Garnier's voice again. She put the phone back to her ear and spoke some French. Turned away from Brian. Ceased acknowledging his presence.

As much as Brian wanted to leave, he forced himself to stay. He checked the stopwatch. Two minutes now. He just sat there and watched the time go by. He wanted it to go on longer. He wanted it to cost Nadine a fortune. The only reason she was at this point was because of him. She had given up already. How dare she hurt him like that regarding his finances. How dare she ignore all his careful planning. His intelligence. His instincts.

When Nadine finally lowered the receiver, she was too spent to even hang it up. She simply let the receiver fall to the floor. Brian instantly reached over and pressed the hang-up button himself. He finally turned off the stopwatch. "Five minutes. Oh yes, very wise. I hope you're proud of yourself."

Nadine closed her eyes. "It's already bad enough—"

"No, please, tell me. What was the *ludicrously* expensive information you just ascertained from Doctor Garnier? Please! I'm dying to hear it!"

Nadine tried her hardest not to cry.

"Stop that!" Brian found himself yelling. "Own up to it, will ya? What did you get?!"

Nadine glared back at him. "There's been nothing reported about *any* American dying on 15th January from a gunshot wound."

Brian grimaced. "What does that even mean?"

"I DON'T KNOW!" Nadine cried, her eyes filling with tears. "I have no clue what any of it means! I'm more confused now than I ever was at the start. Why'd you even make me do all this?! Why couldn't you just leave me alone?!"

Brian gaped angrily. "Why did—?! This was all YOUR idea!"

"I was fine! I had a life! I had money! I had moved on FROM ALL OF THIS!"

Brian laughed hard. "Oh really? You moved on?"

"And then you had to come along and drag me back into it! Because it's a QUEST! You stupid, stupid man-child! Don't you realize I've lost every penny I have now? Every goddamn dollar I've earned letting pig after pig drool over me three to four nights a week for *sixteen months of my life*, is GONE! All GONE! And it was all for nothing! I'll never be able to leave there now, Brian! I'll never be able to pay these people back!"

"I told you to get off the phone!" Brian yelled back at her. "You didn't listen to me! You did this to yourself!"

Nadine gasped, the fire of fury returning. "Well, maybe if you were as smart as you said you were, we wouldn't have to make a damn phone call to Paris in the first place!"

"I hate to break it to you, *Celeste*, but I am just as smart as I said I was! You're the stupid one! YOU'RE the one that fell in love with a fucking Nazi! YOU'RE the one that believed every goddamn word he said!"

Nadine slapped Brian hard across the face.

Brian nursed his cheek. Glared back at her.

Nadine covered her mouth with both hands. "I'm sorry! Oh God, I'm so sorry!" She reached out for him.

Brian flinched away. Stood up. Stormed out of the office.

"Brian!" Nadine put the phone back on the hook. Gathered her things. "Brian, wait!" She left the office. Raced past Johnnie. "Brian!"

"Excuse me, miss?" Johnnie called after her, walking with a clipboard in his hand. "Miss Heatherwood?"

Nadine whipped around, all flustered and out of breath. "Oh, I'm sorry."

Johnnie saw the tears in her eyes. "Oh my God… Was it bad news?"

Nadine nodded, wiping her face. "Yes. Yes, I'm sorry. I just have to—"

"My manager needs you to sign this before you go." Johnnie held out the form, holding the pen up for her to take. "For liability reasons, as well as to confirm your address for the invoice."

Nadine recognized Vicky's name and address all over the form. "I'm sorry, I'm very upset right now, as you can imagine." She sniffed, not entirely faking it. "I'll just come back later to sign it."

Johnnie's face hardened. "I need you to sign this right now."

"I promise I'll come back, I just have to…" Nadine pointed behind her. "Please. I just need to—"

"Miss Heatherwood, I cannot allow you leave until you sign this." Johnnie held it out some more. "We know your name, we know where you live, we know where you work… Do you really want us to get the police involved?"

Nadine's chin trembled. "Alright." With weak fingers, she signed the form and handed back the pen.

Johnnie nodded heartlessly. "You should be receiving our invoice in about two weeks. Have a good day." He turned around and walked away. "Sorry for your loss."

Nadine felt cold. She wandered out of the library. Snow was drifting down, soft and fluffy clumps under overcast sky. She looked around for Brian, where he could've gone. To her surprise, he wasn't far at all, sitting on the curb, curled up, his hard face staring into space.

Nadine wrapped her arms around her chest. Slowly approached Brian. Sat on the stone curb next to him. They wallowed in silence for a few minutes.

Brian looked over at Nadine. "It doesn't mean he lied to you," he whispered. "Corey was Jacques's protection, right? Of course they'd lie about their names. That's why he couldn't go to a hospital. The doctor they called must've been in on whatever they were hiding. He'd able to cover up Corey's death, surely."

Nadine wiped snow off her pant leg. "You don't know that."

"And the fact that Corey's death still hasn't been reported must mean Jacques hasn't been captured yet."

"Or it means Boutierre simply missed a name on a list. He's not a government agency. He's just one man."

"'Just one man' isn't nothing."

"It is nowadays."

Brian shook his head. "You're wrong."

"I know what I'm talking about. I've seen it firsthand." Nadine stood back up. Looked down at Brian. "There are committees going on right now, entire conferences of men in a room discussing the logistics of how to kill hundreds of people a day as efficiently as possible. There are buildings being bombed, pinnacles of architecture, priceless works of art, all crumbling to dust this very second. History books being burned. Advancements in science, philosophy, literature being destroyed. There are babies getting conceived right now from war rape. There are nurses killing invalids with cyanide to spare them the pain of Nazi capture. There are doctors, actual doctors, experimenting on POWs and Jews for their own twisted amusement. Children are getting killed. Old men and women are getting killed just for being old. Young men from every corner of the world are having their innocence blown out of them with every mortar, every bullet to a friend's head right in front of them. Limbs are being blown off that can never be reattached. Japanese pilots are crashing their planes on purpose. Submarines are getting blasted open underwater, killing everyone inside in a microsecond. People are starving to death in occupied territories. In Paris right now, there are Frenchmen turning on their own, collaborating with the enemy government so they can have better food and be exempt from forced labor. The world is on fire right now, Brian. We're the unluckiest generation in the history of the world. We're the ones born in Hell." Nadine had to stop talking like that. She was making herself sick. "And we're losing our minds because we can't connect a shady Frenchman and his American pen pal? Wake up, Brian. In the grand scheme of things, it really doesn't matter."

"That's like saying we don't matter." Brian grimaced at her.

Nadine let out a soft helpless sigh. "Well, maybe we don't." She walked away from Brian.

"I'm not giving up," Brian spoke up, turning toward her, his butt still on the curb. "If you're not going to help me find Victor, I'll do it in my own."

Nadine scoffed. "Don't you realize if Victor's even real, his name's probably not even 'Victor?!' That means we've got NOTHING to work with, Brian! Nothing!"

"But why would William lie about Victor? It doesn't make any sense."

"Because he would've said anything to get me to help him flee France! He was a Nazi that got himself caught by the French Resistance! He saw how vulnerable I was and played on my emotions! I was nothing but a free cab ride to him!" Nadine frowned. "That's all I was. Just a cab."

Brian shook his head. "I don't believe that."

"Well, I do." Nadine wiped her eyes. Swallowed hard. "Who are you to say otherwise?" She turned back around and walked away. Down the street. Faded from his sight.

Brian stayed right where he was, right there on the curb. And he thought about Nadine, just as she was.

And he cried.

And he cried.

And he cried.

CHAPTER TWENTY-THREE

Second Chances

Nadine tuned off the boos as she raced off the stage, still in her red dress. Ignored the perplexed stagehands. Made it back to her dressing room. Closed the door. And then she properly realized what she had just done was *bad*. Really bad. J. Rog was about to have a fit on her. She was about to lose her job. And with all that money she still owed, only days away from its due date, interest ready to compound itself... What would she do then? She had nothing.

And why? Because she saw Sailor Boy sitting in the front row again? Just one guy among many? What if it wasn't him? What if it was just another blond clean-shaven boy in Navy whites? They all looked alike, didn't they? He didn't act like he recognized her. He looked happy.

Unless it was Sailor Boy. Then his happiness was far more sinister, wasn't it?

Tina burst into Nadine's dressing room, all dolled up for her set. "What did you just do?"

Nadine gaped at her. "I don't know. I just... I just couldn't do it tonight."

"J. Rog is looking for you." Tina desperately looked behind her. "Oh God, here he comes. He's pissed."

"Isn't he always pissed?"

"No, pissed as in *angry*!"

J. Roger shoved past Tina. The little Italian gnome was in rare form tonight. "What the fuck do I pay yer fer?" J. Roger yelled at Nadine. "What the fuck was that? You can't just walk off the stage!"

"I must be still sick," Nadine mumbled, turning away.

"Bullshit." J. Roger spun Nadine back around. "Look at me when I'm talking to you, bitch!"

"Rog!" Tina started.

J. Roger held up a silencing finger to Tina, his eyes never leaving Nadine's. "What are you on, huh? Downers? Dope? What?"

Nadine shrugged. "Nothing. I'm not on anything."

"Well you better be on fucking something! What happened to you? You used to be something, kid. You really did."

"I still am. Please."

"Oh, you are?"

"It's just tonight, I promise. My head's just not in it tonight."

"Yeah, well, maybe you should go take that head to some other club, cause I'm through trying to figure it out."

Tina gasped. "Roger, no."

"Is your name Celeste?" J. Roger snapped at Tina. "No? Then this doesn't concern you."

"Please, J. Rog," Nadine begged. "I'm sorry. It won't happen again."

"I can get another hot act like you in a heartbeat. One that'll put out too. I'm through doing you favors."

"No, please! I need this job! Give me another chance!"

"It's her time of the month," Tina interjected. "That's why she ran off the stage, Roger. She started bleeding."

Nadine hesitated. "Yes. That's right. That's all it is."

J. Roger looked down at Nadine's crotch. "You've never had a problem with that before. What, red doesn't go with red no more?"

"What do you mean red?" Tina asked with deep brow furrowing. "Roger, it's February!"

J. Roger looked back at her. "So?"

"So it's blue. Show him, Nadine."

Nadine opened her mouth. "You want me to show him my…?"

"Wait-wait-wait!" J. Roger waved both hands. "Hold on. *Blue?!*"

Tina glared at him. "Yeah."

"And blue *hurts*," Nadine concurred.

J. Roger cringed. "What, do you bitches have TB or something?"

"All girls have blue Februarys, *Rog*!" Tina exclaimed.

"You seriously didn't know that?" Nadine chimed in.

"Of course I knew that!" J. Roger swallowed hard. "I know everything about women."

Tina and Nadine gave each other knowing looks. Tina had known Roger longer than any of them. She knew how to confuse and control him. This was her way of saving her.

Vicky walked into the dressing room, coming down from her own set. She had sensitive eyes on Nadine. "Hey. You okay?"

"Vicky!" J. Roger snapped his fingers at her. "Settle something for us. What color are you bleeding right now?"

Vicky furrowed her brow. "Uh… blue? It's February? Hello?"

J. Roger shook his head. "Fine. Whatever." He looked Nadine up and down. "One more show. Knock 'em dead tomorrow or yer dead. Capeesh?"

Nadine nodded. "Thank you, J. Rog. You won't regret this."

"And try not to get any blue on the…" J. Roger waved a circle at Nadine's codpiece. "It's a rental." He marched past Tina and Vicky.

Tina waited until J. Roger was far enough away. "God, men are so stupid!"

They all laughed in unison. Nadine smiled. "Thanks for covering for me."

"No problem, toots." Tina took one step out. "If he gives you any more grief, wave me over, alright?"

Nadine nodded.

Tina left, closing the door behind her.

Nadine sat before her boudoir. Vicky watched Nadine's reflection, building up the courage to say what she came here to say.

Nadine started removing her makeup. "God. If the me from the two years ago saw me begging like that to stay here, she wouldn't have believed it."

Vicky solemnly sat beside Nadine. "You need to get out of here."

"Believe me, I wish I had the option."

"What if you did?"

Nadine looked at her. "It'll take a year at least for me to pay off that invoice with interest. I just got to suffer a little bit more."

"I sent a check to the library this morning. Your debt is paid."

Nadine froze. "Vicky."

"Don't." Vicky shook her head. "I don't want any vows of repayment or any wishy-washy maudlin whatever. Just take it and get out of here."

Nadine kept staring. "But how?"

"I had a rainy day fund, just in case I ever wanted to get out of New York in a hurry. Go somewhere simpler instead. A place where no one knows me. But it's been ten years since I started adding to it and I haven't done shit." Vicky frowned at Nadine. "I guess I like being stuck too much."

Nadine nodded, understanding what she meant in a small way. "I'm not going to balk at free money, believe me."

"Good."

"But why me?"

Vicky didn't talk for what felt like a long time. She could feel her mouth drying up. "You know how you blame yourself for what happened to that William guy?"

Nadine nodded.

"That's how I feel about you. Some people are born for this business, like Tina. For other people, it's only temporary. Just until they get where they need to be. But you never chose to do this. You had other things, far more important things to worry about." Vicky paused. "You're only here because I forced that role on you."

"No. Vicky—"

"I could've gotten you into Burkes & Carter instead. I chose not to. I thought to myself, 'Here's a pretty girl. Smart. Younger than me. What if they like her better? What would I do then?'" Vicky paused. "I was only thinking of myself. My security. That was selfish of me. Unbecoming." She frowned. "Once I saw you grow into it, though, I didn't feel so bad. You were making your own costumes. Planning your set. You made it your own after all. So then I thought… 'Maybe I was wrong about her. Maybe she'll be alright.'" She paused. "But then you came home late that one night. The night I was sick."

Nadine's heart raced. She refused to let on. "What night?"

"You know what night. You couldn't even answer the door. I recognized that look you had on you. I had it a few times myself." Vicky looked off. "More than a few, actually."

Nadine's mouth opened slightly.

Vicky forced a smile at her. "Ever since that night, I knew… No one should *ever* have that look. I had to make sure you never had that look again."

Nadine frowned back. Brought Vicky in for a hug.

Vicky hugged back a bit before pulling herself away. "I'm glad it was something simple like that invoice. Believe me, I'm better off without the dough. It's been my crutch for years. My instability buffer. A way to justify my excuses. Keep myself down. But it seems this war ain't ending anytime soon. Maybe I should take advantage of all those good factory jobs out there.

Earn me some real man money. Maybe some benefits too while I'm at it." Vicky shrugged. "It'd be a rainy day fund for me too then, wouldn't it?"

Nadine stared off.

"Nothing wrong with that, huh?" Vicky asked, shoving Nadine a bit.

Nadine smiled a bit, but let it go. "I don't know. This is all so sudden."

"You don't have to quit tonight. Just think about it. What would you do with a second chance?"

Nadine exhaled. "Honestly, the first thing I can think of is calling Garnier back and getting him to check the post offices."

"Oh God!" Vicky groaned, rolling her eyes.

"If Corey and Jacques… whoever they are, if that wasn't just them calling themselves that, if that was their actual occupation aliases, there would be a record there."

"You're debt-free again. Don't be stupid."

"I know. I learned my lesson, believe me." Nadine went quiet again. "It's just strange not having to worry about it anymore."

Vicky touched Nadine's shoulder with a smile. "Just think it over. It costs you nothing to consider." She got up and left the dressing room, closing the door behind her.

The February cold outside J. Roger's was fiercer than it had been the month before, but Nadine couldn't feel it. The traffic noise, usually so startling the first step out, meant nothing to her. She just stared off, her mind a blank. Blissfully blank. She really had no pressing concern on her mind. The mystery of Olive Branch had been replaced by the invoice debt, but now that had been replaced by… nothing?

I can actually hear myself think.

Nadine strolled down Christopher Street in the dead of night, hands in her pockets, just meandering her way uptown. She got to 7th Avenue and slowed to a crawl at that alleyway entrance, the one the Sailor Boy assaulted her in. But thinking about it didn't bother her this time. All she could think about was Brian. Her hero. Her savior.

How long has it been? Three weeks? A month? Has he given up too? Or is he still driving himself mad?

Nadine frowned. Walked on, her mind still standing at that alleyway entrance. *Maybe I should get back with him. He is handsome. Gentle. Chivalrous. But he's such a boy, isn't he? Naïve. How annoying he can be.* Nadine visualized Brian walking beside her, escorting her down 7th Avenue. *He's just like me. Not me now. What I should have been. What I would have been in a different life, had the war not come. Maybe my annoyance is actually jealousy.*

But is that the life I want? The wife of Brian Donahue? I'll never be that girl again, no matter who I marry. I'm not that girl anymore. That girl died in Nancy with the rest of them.

Nadine sat in that corner diner, the one she sat in with Brian that night. She stared into her cup, the lousy American coffee throwing steam back at her. *Maybe I should just go back to France. Rejoin the war effort. Go back to saving lives. I'd feel useful again. Do I have the money for that? Perhaps. Another one way ticket, though... That's not very wise. Maybe I can get some sympathy from everyone. I am a Resistance Fighter. I am a nurse. They're so patriotic here. Maybe I can get a free ticket out of it.*

But do I dare return to Roul? To Scragg? Durant? Any of them? Going back would only confirm what Roul told me, wouldn't it? That I was stupid. It'd be a coward's retreat. It's been almost two years. He's already lost a daughter. He had to lose me too. Did I ruin him? Did I do nothing to him? Nothing at all? I don't want to know. I can't know the answer to that.

Nadine wandered through Time's Square. A hundred bundled theatergoers waited in line for the next showing of *Casablanca*. Nadine looked at all their faces. *But did I actually love Brian? If I had to ask, was that really love? I could've been stopping myself. Once or twice I felt it, the restraint. Then it's love, right? I have no one I can ask. Shouldn't it be more obvious? More of a no-brainer?*

Nadine turned around. Took the long way back to Vicky's apartment. *I did love William, didn't I? But why? Because he saved my life? Was that all it was? Did I let it blind me? It was who he was. He was trapped, just like me. I had to help him. I was compelled to be with him, to save him. I never felt that way about Brian. No, I did. I'm just tired. Don't want to get hurt again. I don't know.*

Nadine felt her stomach harden. *Did William know he was telling me bullshit? Had he also been deceived? He couldn't have been a deceiver. I would've felt it... would I have?*

No, I don't think I would have. I turned on the Resistance because I fell in love with my patient, a Nazi no less. I found so many ways to justify it. It was the right thing for William. It was the right thing for Jacques. And then I blamed Roul for what happened to William. I threw him away. And it was easy too. Justice for William. Justice for Jacques. I went halfway around the world to finish what he started, and what did I do? I gave up. I wasted two years of my life being the one thing I never wanted to be, just a female body, a vessel, a mindless tease. But I justified that too. I needed money. It was easy. It was there. Then Brian stirred it all up again. I wanted it to end. I put myself into debt all because I wanted it to end. I got sloppy. If not for Vicky, I'd been a lifer at J. Roger's, the new Tina. Maybe Roul was right. I am stupid. I always have been stupid.

Nadine slowed down. Stared at the building across the street.

The lights were on under an awning. On the glass: GREENWICH SCHOOL.

Nadine wandered across the street. Opened the door. Stepped inside. It was warm in there. Bright. The soft voices in the classrooms. Teachers lecturing. Chalk on boards. Ingénues flipping their pages simultaneously.

Nadine tenderly approached the announcement board. Scanned the list of summer classes. It brought back memories of her younger days, when life was still warm, the world full of possibilities.

And I believed it. I wasn't wrong to. It was true back that. It's not true now. Not anymore. Everything can change just like that. Even being in a place like this. I don't belong here anymore. Brian belongs here. I belong at J. Roger's. I don't care what Vicky says. It's a world I understand. A world where I'm still appreciated. Where I'm one of the best. I get enough love every night. Isn't it wiser for me to stay? Isn't it smarter?

Nadine frowned. Said one last goodbye to that wonderful place. Turned to leave.

"Excuse me?" a young woman asked, approaching Nadine with a smile. "Are you lost?"

Nadine stared back. "That's a loaded question."

"That sounds like a yes." The young woman held her hand out toward a nearby bench. "Sit."

"I don't want to keep you."

"It's no problem, really." The young woman sat herself down, leaving enough space for Nadine to join her. "What's on your mind?"

Nadine instantly felt suspicious. She had to force it away. Remind herself she wasn't in France. She wasn't at war. So she sat down. "Do you work here?"

The young woman instantly cackled. "Oh no. No. I'm just early."

"You're a student?"

The young woman nodded. "Economics."

"That's impressive."

"Thank you." The young woman looked curiously at Nadine. "What accent is that?"

"French."

The young woman nodded. "I figured you were. I was an immigrant in distress once. I can spot one a mile away."

Nadine relaxed. "You too?"

The young woman nodded. "I'm Elżbieta."

"Nadine."

"Pleasure to meet you, Nadine."

"Your English is superb."

"Thank you. That was the first class I took."

"How long have you been in States?"

"It'll be two years next week."

"Wow. Congratulations. I'm almost at two years myself."

"And how's it been for you?"

Nadine hesitated. "I'll be fine."

Elżbieta smiled gently. "You don't have to pretend with me."

Nadine softened. She looked up at that list of classes. "I used to love places like this. Everyone always said I was exceptional. Despite that, I actually think I was."

Elżbieta nodded. "But now?"

"Now... I don't know what happened. I used to have all this potential and now I'm miles behind."

"You think too much has damaged you. And now you feel like you have nothing but walls."

Nadine stared at Elżbieta. "How did you know?"

"I was the same way when I first came here. Everything was so different. I felt so lost. But then I realized I had to allow myself to become American."

"I have no interest in being an American."

"Why not?"

Nadine frowned. "Nothing's happened to these people. There is no war here. No fascism. No Resistance. No destruction. No death."

"Isn't that a blessed relief?"

"No." Nadine shook her head. "They don't know. They can't possibly know. But I do."

"Maybe it's different for me. The country I was born into no longer exists. I needed this place to be a sanctuary." Elżbieta paused. "What is it for you?"

Nadine hesitated. "I don't think I know anymore."

"You're still torn between two lands?"

Nadine looked away.

Elżbieta took a deep breath. "I want to tell you something. Something I wish someone had told me."

Nadine looked back at Elżbieta.

"Two years ago, I had nothing. I knew nothing. I was alone. But now I have so much. I met a wonderful man who only wanted me to be exactly as I was. I love him so much. He's in the Air Force now, avenging my family, my homeland. Fighting the fight I could never on my own. And not a second goes by when I don't think about him, what he's doing for me." Elżbieta nodded, daydreaming in her seat. "He said he's going to marry me when the war's over. I'll be Mrs. Darrin Andrezj. We'll have a house in Pennsylvania and a family of our own. Surrounded by green. And I'll know how to manage our money. I've never had money before. And we'll live happily ever after. All that horror that came before will be nothing more to me than a bad dream."

Nadine frowned. "I used to have someone."

Elżbieta's smile fell, morphing into the saddest of frowns. "I am so sorry."

"It's alright." Nadine wiped her eyes. Sniffed. "He saved my life. That's how we met. Then he was in danger, and I tried to save him, but… it only made things worse."

Elżbieta stared at Nadine, her blood getting cold.

Nadine shook her head, oblivious to Elżbieta's existential shock. "It wasn't my fault directly, but… I still blame myself. Believe me, I want to be here. It's what I've always wanted. My whole life I wanted to get out of France. Off of that farm. Off to some foreign land where women could learn, like my mother did. I was going to be the smartest woman there. And I'd meet a smart boy who saw only my brain, not my body." Nadine looked at Elżbieta. "But how could I now? I let the man I loved down. He had his whole life ahead of him, and now it's all gone because of me. Should I be allowed to get everything I always wanted when he can't? That's not fair. I should be living the life he was supposed to live. Finish the business he easily would have if I hadn't…" She stopped talking. "I used to have this drive, this fight in me, but it's gone now. It was all I knew. Now I… I don't know. Am I supposed to just move on from that? Marry a rich man? Allow myself to become some other man's life extension? A submissive housewife guaranteed to a bland domestic life? I can't be a housewife. It's just not me. It was never me." Nadine frowned. "But maybe it's what I deserve. Because he can't be him. And he can't be him because of me."

Elżbieta lowered her head. "When I was on the refugee boat to Oran, we got boarded by a U-Boat wanting to strip us for parts. And one of the Nazis boarding us, he wanted to…" She bobbed her head. "I tried to fight him. I hit him. He would've killed me right there if another refugee hadn't saved me. A complete stranger saved my life. They were about to shoot him right then too, but I said something, the first thing I could think of that would spare his life."

"What did you say?"

Elżbieta shook her head softly. "It doesn't matter. It didn't work. When I got to Lisbon, I looked him up. Turns out they arrested him anyway for killing that Nazi. He's probably dead now."

Nadine simply stared at Elżbieta, in awe.

"Of course I blamed myself," Elżbieta whispered grimly. "I could've come up with something better. Something that would've worked. But one night I was laying in Darrin's arms in Central Park. All those stars above us. And I realized it was the happiest I had ever been in my life. If that man hadn't saved my life, my body would've been at the bottom of the Mediterranean. I could've let my guilt define me, but what good would that do? It would only have wasted the life he gave back to me. To repay his sacrifice, I needed to live a life worth sacrificing for."

Nadine felt tears in her eyes.

Elżbieta smiled back with encouragement. "What you deserve… is to be free, Nadine. So be free. Be the freest you can possibly be."

Nadine allowed herself to smile back. She brought Elżbieta in for a tight hug.

The two immigrants went their separate ways after that. They never crossed paths again. They never learned of their mutual connection. But they never forgot that conversation. Elżbieta had finally saved someone, a fellow lost soul in a foreign land. And Nadine, who had spent so many years saving others, thinking of others, worrying about others, finally allowed herself to be saved in return.

CHAPTER TWENTY-FOUR

The Silver Lining

Brian Donahue buried his grief of losing Nadine by focusing all his days on that quest to save Jacques. In a way, it worked as a willing act of denial. He knew he'd win Nadine back if he managed to save Jacques, so they weren't *really* separated.

The mystery was harder to crack by himself than he thought it would be. At least Nadine had met William. Brian was so far removed from the Corey Baxter shooting. It made him dizzy just thinking about the trajectory from France to Berlin to New York, Olive Branch being the baton in some world-spanning relay race. Now that it was his turn, what would he do with it? What will be his contribution? Will he finish the race? Or will he fail, costing the team the gold?

Brian's strategy was to identify the Nazi in the picture. The Nazi was the reason Jacques was in danger. He had been in the presence of both Corey and Jacques at one point. His identity had to be important. After Brian found it, the plan was to then find out who Corey Baxter really was. Even if his name wasn't Corey, he had to have been a member of the Baxter family. They were all Nazi sympathizers. It would make the most sense. Plus, their movements would be very well-documented. If Brian could pinpoint exactly when an assassinated high-ranking Nazi and a prominent member of the Baxter family were in Weimar-era Berlin at the same time, he'd be able to establish a timeline. Then he'd be able to learn who Jacques really was and how to contact him directly.

Brian started with the NYU library system. It was horde of knowledge Nadine never would've been able to access. But to his surprise, the librarian on duty revealed NYU had no books on the history of the Third Reich. No rise of Hitler chronicles. No pre-war examinations of the German Republic. Nothing published after 1918. To the students of NYU, Germany simply didn't exist after the Great War.

Brian asked to speak with the head librarian and the two met in his office.

There Brian received an unusual lecture, the head librarian doubting his patriotism, questioning his motives. Brian initially claimed to be writing a paper for class, but he couldn't name the class or his professor. When he changed his alibi to him researching a play he was writing, the head librarian ended the conversation with a simple order: "Just make it up then."

Brian tried again at the New York Public Library, specifically the Main Branch in Midtown across from Bryant Park. There were plenty of books there on Nazi Germany. Adolf Hitler. The Third Reich. Its high command. But nothing written from the German's point of view. Not enough names beyond the main four (Hitler, Goebbels, Göring, Bormann). Only the major events that made American newspapers, the majority of which occurring after September 1, 1939, the Invasion of Poland. Somehow their American and British authors managed to take the entire history of another country and make it all about themselves. Did they really think no one on the Allies' side wanted to know the whole story of the great enemy they had been fighting for the past five years?

March arrived and Brian was no closer to finding the Nazi in the photo. He barely slept anymore. His grades were plummeting. He was drinking more than was good for him, which only made it harder for him to read late at night. And then the pressure crept in. The realization that Nadine was right. She had tried to spare him from this. She had already been through it all.

Brian's friends even noticed a change in him. They also noticed the French babe with the great breasts wasn't around anymore. He hated the things they said about her. They only saw her body. They couldn't believe their relationship was so much more than physical. Sexually motivated. Carnal. Base.

By April, the late-night doubts were taking over, Brian's grip on his own life slipping away. Every survival instinct in his body was trying to get him to stop, to realign back to the way it was, that zone he always thrived in. But Brian resisted. He knew this was what he was meant to do. If Sailor Boy had threatened her with a knife, Brian wouldn't have naturally stepped in to save her. If he stole her purse, same thing. It wouldn't have been instinctual. He never would've put himself in such danger. But for her to have been *molested* of all things… That made him the perfect hero for her in that moment. The trauma he had endured at the hands of his father was merely the foundation for that hero's act. It was all fate. Even the wartime trauma that turned his father homosexual had to happen. His father's abuse was the reason he had his uncle pull those strings to get him deferred. It was the reason he was still in the country at the time of Nadine's attack. He needed to save Nadine so he could save Jacques. That way Brian could fight the Nazis without ever having to step onto a battlefield. It all made sense. Everything bad that happened to him all had a higher purpose. He finally had an answer why. Why did it happen to him? Why, Dad? Why?

Brian visited a small library of historical nonfiction on the Upper East Side and hit the jackpot: an old copy of *Hitler's Enemies* by Max Feierabend, a German-born Jew who emigrated to the United States in '35. It gave Brian a shortlist of candidates that might've been in that photo. By Easter Weekend, he was able to move on to phase two: finding Corey Baxter.

Brian found many footnotes across multiple textbooks that, only when combined, told a brief story of the Baxter Family. They had been in America since the Gilded Age, starting with Chicago's infamous coal tycoon Darryl Baxter. Since he never had a son and heir, the bulk of Darryl's fortune was divided between his three living brothers and their children. Together, they were able to spread the Baxter empire across the Atlantic, taking advantage of Germany's crippled economy in the wake of the Great War. They became Nazi sympathizers after the Depression and became Nazi Germany's top coal supplier. But that was all Brian could find. There were no books anywhere on the Baxter family after they relocated to Europe.

Brian didn't need a lecture to figure out why that was: the Baxters were Americans turned traitor. They might as well not exist. And anyone that wanted to know about them… well, they shouldn't. So why should they encourage such an unpatriotic line of questioning by allowing entire books on the subject? Don't they know there's a war on?

Before Brian knew it, it was June. Six months since he first saved Nadine. Two *and a half* years since Jacques first needed William's help. It made Brian sick to his stomach. He couldn't do it anymore. He had nothing left in him. And now he had a crippled GPA. What a mess he made of his potential.

Every inch of Brian's eating space was covered in Nazi books. Nazi charts. Nazi military diagrams. Nazi names, Nazi iconography. Brian hunched over the mound. Hair disheveled. Eyes tired yet frozen open with despair. And he was eating a handful of oats—that handful of oats being a bottle of Jack—

when he heard the door knock. He didn't bother to get up. He just ate some more oats.

Leonard opened the door, shocked and yet not shocked to see Brian still in that state. He let himself in. "It's such a beautiful day. You really need to get outside."

"I can't," Brian mumbled.

Leonard looked over the menagerie of Hitler books. "They're not going anywhere, believe me."

"That's not the point."

"Are you anywhere closer to anything?"

"Yes." Brian pulled a book from the pile. Held it up for Leonard. "That's the Nazi in the photograph."

Leonard took the book. Stared at the short mustachioed Nazi on the cover. "Are you sure?"

"He better be." Brian took another swig. "He's the most documented of the bunch."

Leonard tossed the book on top of the pile. "Come on. Get dressed. We got to get you moving."

"Why?"

"Because you're decaying in here! Look at yourself, Brian. You haven't slept. You haven't bathed. You stink of booze."

"I'm focused."

"You're losing your mind!" Leonard cringed at all those books. "And you really shouldn't have all these books in your apartment."

"Who's going to know?"

"Whoever sold them to you. Plus you're asking all those questions at the library. You're probably already on a list somewhere."

Brian's eyes widened. He sat up.

"Come on." Leonard tried to pull Brian by the arm.

"Wait." Brian looked up at Leonard. "What did you just say?"

Leonard blinked. "'Come on?'"

"No, before that."

"'Having all those books might've put you on some list?'"

"What kind of a list? What do you mean?"

"I don't know. A subversive literature list? It's very suspicious during wartime. You could get into trouble, seriously."

"THAT'S IT!" Brian jumped up. Raced to the phone.

Leonard watched Brian dial, panicking himself. "What?! What's it?"

Brian grinned up at Leonard. "I think you just helped me find him." He held the phone to his ear. The dial tone rang two times before it was picked up. "Uncle Bill? It's Brian. I have a question for Wilbur. Can you give me his number?"

Three days later, Nadine and Vicky were strolling down W 21st Street arm in arm, smiling ear to ear, basking in the warm summer sunshine. They were both free from that sleaze J. Roger, Vicky working nights at a munitions factory, Nadine as a waitress in that diner off 7th Avenue, and they were about to start their weekend summer courses at the Greenwich School, Vicky for Bookkeeping, Nadine for Business Management. They had just bought some new clothes and all the supplies they needed. Life was good. Life was actually really good.

Nadine and Vicky climbed the stairs of their building. "You'll be able to do all three?" Nadine asked her.

"The hours aren't so bad at the factory," Vicky replied in between breaths. "There're so many girls, so much demand for work. Everyone's working part time. Plus Burkes closes at five. I can do it."

"But what if your grades start suffering in the course?"

"You can do my homework too, can't you?"

Nadine chuckled. "That would ruin the point of the course."

"I'll be alright." Vicky led the way out of the staircase onto their floor. "How's waitressing? As bad as it looks?"

"No, actually it—" Nadine stopped in her tracks. Brian was sitting outside their apartment door.

Brian saw them there and stood. He had cleaned himself up as best he could, but he still looked quite unkempt.

"Brian?" Nadine asked, trying not to be too overzealous. "What are you doing here?"

Brian took a deep breath. "I found him."

Nadine's heart skipped. "What?"

"The Nazi in the photograph." Brian stepped forward. "His name was Ernst Röhm. He was the head of the *Sturmabteilung*, the SA."

"What's the SA?"

"Hitler's private army in the early days. They were in charge of instigating street fights against their political enemies, protecting party leaders during rallies and assemblies. A goon squad of sorts." Brian finally noticed Vicky standing there. "Oh, I'm sorry."

"No, it's fine." Vicky looked around them. "Did you want to do this out here?"

"You can go in, Vicky," Nadine told her. "We won't be a long."

"No way," Vicky said with a smile. "This involves me too. I'm dying to know myself."

Vicky unlocked the apartment door and the three relocated to the living room. Nadine put a kettle on the stove.

"So who was this Ernst Röhm guy?" Vicky asked, sitting on the floor.

Brian sat in the chair. "He and Hitler were really good friends in the beginning. They both joined the German Workers' Party at the same time in 1919."

"How do you know all this?" Nadine asked from the kitchen.

"I found his biography in a bookstore downtown. And when I mean they were friends, I mean they were *friends*. Röhm was Hitler's first real friend. He was the only one allowed to call him 'Adi' instead of '*Mein Führer*.' Hitler trusted him more than anyone. They planned the Munich Beer Hall Putsch together."

"I'm sorry, the what?" Vicky asked.

"Hitler's failed coup in 1923. He was tried for treason the following winter and sentenced for five years in prison. He only served nine months though. Röhm was found guilty too. Sentenced to fifteen months. Then his sentence was suspended and they placed him on probation. Nadine, can you get me some water?"

Nadine poured Brian a glass. Walked it over. Joined Vicky on the floor.

Brian drank half the glass. Placed it aside. "When Hitler got out, the SA was outlawed. Röhm was forced to make a legal alternative, the *Frontbann*, but he wanted to revive the SA and integrate the *Frontbann* into it. The *Frontbann* at that point had 30,000 men in it. But Hitler wanted to keep a low profile so he could overtake the government legally the second time around. This proved a spot of contention between Hitler and Röhm. After a few years of Röhm getting tired of constantly getting out-vetoed by Hitler and the Nazi Party going legal all of a sudden, he resigned from his post in 1925. Three years later, he was recruited by the Bolivian military attaché to the Netherlands to serve as the military adviser for the Bolivian Army. He was there for two years. Then in 1930, Röhm received a personal telephone call from Hitler himself asking him to return to Germany and lead the SA again."

The kettle blew. Nadine jumped up. Moved the kettle off the stove. Poured the hot water into three cups and added teabags. She returned with the three cups of tea and handed them out.

"Go on," Vicky told Brian eagerly.

"At this point, the SA had over a million members, but they were just in charge of the roughing and toughing this time. Main Party security was being handled by a new faction, the *Schutzstaffel*."

"The SS," Nadine explained to Vicky.

"Thanks to Röhm's SA, they were able to intimidate all the Nazi's rival parties. The communists. The Jews. That's why the Nazis ended up number one. Hitler never would've been made Chancellor if not for his buddy Röhm." Brian paused to sip some tea. "And that's when all the rumors started."

"What rumors?" Vicky asked.

"Turns out, Ernst Röhm was a homosexual." Brian put his cup back down. "Hitler knew the whole time and didn't care. It didn't matter. But when the Party's enemies found Röhm's love letters, it was a huge scandal. Hitler was forced to make a choice. And what do you think he chose?"

Vicky and Nadine shook their heads.

"Hitler defended his friend," Brian told them. "He actually defended Röhm. Kept him in charge of the SA. Even after the rest of the Nazis called for his removal. Röhm was grateful, of course, but now he was entirely dependent on Hitler. But Röhm still wanted the SA to be the radical army it used to be. His dream was a new German Army with his SA at the core. By '34, Hitler had plans to consolidate his power and expand the *Reichswehr*— the German Army—but he wanted social stability this time, refocused economy, so the German people would be comfortable suddenly going to war. Hitler was thinking about the future but Röhm was still stuck in the past, still obsessed with the very thing that got them both arrested back in '23. And the other commanders didn't trust Röhm. They couldn't control him." Brian paused. "And so, faced with yet another choice between his oldest friend and his continued rise to power, Hitler ordered the death of Ernst Röhm and the rest of SA's high command. The Nazi propaganda machine claimed they were planning a coup. Röhm and his friends were rounded up. Sequestered. Hitler even allowed Röhm the dignity of shooting himself to avoid the shame of a firing squad. But Röhm refused. He told the guards, 'If I am to be killed, let Adolf do it himself.'"

"Wow," Vicky said.

Nadine frowned. "Did he?"

"Kill Röhm himself? No. When the guards came back, they found Röhm still alive in his cell. His chest all puffed out in defiance. And so they shot him where he stood."

Vicky sighed. "Monsters."

"After his death, Hitler told Germany that Röhm was killed because of his homosexuality. As so to cover their tracks, the Nazis added homosexuals to their list of persecuted targets." Brian stood up. Relocated to the table. Rummaged around his pockets. Pulled out many crumbled pieces of paper.

Vicky and Nadine joined him at the table. "So where does the photo tie into all this?" Nadine asked.

Brian smoothed out one of the pieces of paper. "The man in the photo had to have been Röhm. A simple Private like William would absolutely have heard of him. And it would explain why Jacques is in danger. Any history of fraternization with Röhm would be seen as suspicious to the current Nazi regime. If anyone went public with the real Röhm, the one that didn't match the propaganda, that would threaten the Führer's image, wouldn't it?" Brian showed them the list of dates he had on the paper. "1923, the Beer Hall Putsch. 1924, Hitler and Röhm arrested and tried for treason. Late '24, Hitler out of prison. 1925, Röhm resigns from the SA. 1928, he leaves for Bolivia. 1930, Hitler calls him back. The only time he was outside Hitler's circle was in 1924 when Hitler was still in prison and between 1925 and 1928. Röhm was on probation in '24, so I ruled that out, which means the photo could only have been taken between 1925 and 1928." Brian grabbed another crumbled piece of paper. "Based on his movements around Germany in those years, I've narrowed his time in Berlin to three possible weeks."

"Three weeks?!" Nadine exclaimed.

"Yes." Brian pointed to the three timespans he had written down. "The third week of July 1927, the second week of August 1928, and the first week of January 1929." He looked at Nadine. "I've been trying for months now to cross-reference those dates with the members of the Baxter family traveling to Berlin the same time Ernst Röhm was."

Nadine huffed. "Brian…"

"I don't care what you think. I don't believe it."

"Did you find anything?" Vicky asked.

Brian hesitated. "It's very difficult to find any information on the Baxters in America because of them being Nazi sympathizers."

Nadine bumped her brows. "Figures."

"But then I remembered my uncle's friend Wilbur, the one that got me deferred."

"You got deferred?" Vicky asked.

"He has access to classified government intelligence." Brian grabbed a third piece of paper from his pocket. "I called him up a few days ago. Asked him if any member of the Baxter family traveled from the United States to and from Berlin during any of these weeks. He just got back to me this morning."

Nadine's eyes widened. "That-that's written down somewhere?!"

"Any suspicious travel to and from now-enemy territory is written down somewhere. That way the U.S. government can monitor and deter all espionage efforts happening stateside now that we're at war with Germany."

Vicky gaped. Looked at Nadine.

Nadine's heart pounded in her chest. "He found him. He actually found him."

Brian softly shook his head. "No. He couldn't find anyone named Baxter."

Nadine frowned. "Oh."

"But he did find something of note." Brian flipped the same piece of paper over. "During the third week of July 1927, an associate professor of mathematics at Columbia University traveled to Germany and returned seven days later. He wasn't a sympathizer or anything. They just put him on the list because he was working at an Ivy League institution. If he had been turned out there and sent back as a spy to subvert American college students, they'd at least have a record of him traveling to Berlin. But Wilbur said he's also of note because he wasn't born in America. He looked up his immigration records. He said he came to America from England more than fifty years ago."

Vicky raised her brows. "*Fifty?*"

"That would put him around the same age as Jacques and Corey," Nadine said, her eyes widening.

"I thought that as well." Brian looked at Nadine. Finally let out a victorious smile. Turned the paper toward her. "Guess what his name was."

PART FIVE

Victor

CHAPTER TWENTY-FIVE

Very Close

Vicky, Nadine and Brian took the subway up to Morningside Heights and got off at 116th Street. Entered the Low Memorial Library of Columbia University.

As Nadine and Brian approached the desk, Vicky strolling behind them, they were certain deep in their hearts that Nigel Victor was the Victor they had been looking for. The mystery was finally over. Now was the time for answers. The time for action. They were terrified, more terrified than they were excited. They've reached the end of the quest. They'll finally know if it was too late to save Jacques. They'll finally know if their individual failures cost a man his life. They'll finally know the truth behind that ominous codeword: Olive Branch. They'll finally know what was in those boxes Jacques wanted to protect, what happened to them. Maybe it was a Nazi treasure worth millions. Maybe it was worthless junk not worth the sacrifices they've made. They'll finally know. Good news or bad, they'll finally know.

"Hi there," Nadine said to the Librarian, a persnickety man name Fred. "I'm trying to locate a member of faculty here. Would you be able to help me?"

"I don't see why not." Fred put down the book he had been cataloging. "I used to be a student here back in the day. God, it's been ten years already."

"That's nice," Brian said with a smile.

"An Ivy-League educated librarian," Vicky grumbled. "Good to know higher education's worth it."

Fred furrowed his brow. "I was a Classics major. This is my dream job."

"Ignore my roommate," Nadine said gently. "She's on her way to her factory job. She's not staying long."

Fred half-frowned, letting out a dismissive groan. "Who did you want to speak to?"

Nadine was so nervous. She couldn't just come out with it. "Sir… can you tell us… is Nigel Victor still a professor here?"

Fred blinked. "Nigel Victor?"

"He would've been in the Mathematics Department," Brian added. "We know he was an associate professor fifteen years ago. He might've been promoted since then."

Fred nodded. "Absolutely. Of course. He was my statistics professor freshman year." He studied their excited faces. "I guess you're unaware that he passed."

Nadine turned to stone, right then and there. Brian couldn't move either. "He's dead?" Vicky asked for them.

Fred nodded with solemn grace. "I'm sorry. I'm afraid so."

Even Vicky was despaired. She took Nadine's hand.

Nadine tried not to cry. "When?" she rasped.

"I'm sorry?"

"When did it happen?" Brian asked. "Did he pass recently?"

"Oh no. It had to have been at least…" Fred paused to think. "1936 or so. Sometime around there."

Nadine nodded in a daze. "Thank you." She turned. Wandered over to a nearby bench. Sat down.

Vicky and Brian approached her, just as crestfallen. "It's alright," Vicky murmured, sitting down. "There's nothing you could've done."

"Jacques must not have known either," Nadine whispered. She looked up at Brian. "There's no way he knew."

Brian took a deep lonesome breath. "It proves he's real. Which means it was all real."

"But we still don't know if Jacques's okay." Nadine paused. "Now we'll never know."

Vicky discreetly checked her watch. "Oh dear. I'm sorry. I have to go."

"It's alright." Nadine kissed Vicky's cheek. "Don't be late."

Vicky stood. Waved at Brian. Hurried off.

Brian plopped beside Nadine on the bench. "Now what do we do?"

"I can't not know anymore." Nadine looked at Brian. "I won't be able to live like I've been until I know for sure he was the Victor we were looking for. That there's not another one out there waiting for us."

Brian frowned. "What about Jacques?"

"I've lost men on the table. I've gotten over it. Because in the end, I knew I did all I could do." Nadine swallowed. "If I've done all I could do here, I can live with it. I just need to know it was him. That Nigel was our man."

Brian nodded. Took her hand. Guided her to her feet. They returned to the Fred's desk.

"Excuse me again," Nadine said, smiling with gratitude. "You said you knew Professor Victor?"

"Yes, of course," Fred told her.

"*Nigel* Victor?"

"Yes."

"Was he British?"

"Absolutely." Fred chuckled a bit. "He put a lot of students to sleep, I'll tell you that. But I loved him. Probably because I was so good at statistics."

Nadine smiled. "Was he a mentor of yours?"

"Not especially, but…" Fred thought back. "He did have a nice tradition I was a part of. A black-tie dinner at the end of the semester for the best students in the class. I never had a suit before. I had to go out and rent one. A few of his former students would show up too. He remembered all their names. It's amazing how smart he was." Fred grinned. "Professor Victor really was such a great guy. So sociable. He could talk to anybody. It really hurt me when he went. It's amazing how fast you forget about someone when you've been apart from them for so many years."

Nadine nodded, instantly thinking of William. She hoped she wouldn't do the same to him. "Did he have any family? Anyone we could talk to? To pay our respects?"

"Did you know him?"

Nadine hesitated. She looked at Brian. "In a way."

"A mutual friend of ours wanted us to deliver a message to him," Brian said. "He must not have known about his passing."

Fred nodded. "I'm sure. Unfortunately most of his colleagues back then aren't here anymore, so…" He furrowed his brow slightly. "Actually I do remember his brother. Yes, his brother was there too, at the party."

"Was he faculty?"

"No, he was a writer, I think. A poet, maybe. I remember he was quite a bit nervous around us. He stayed by Professor Victor's side the whole night. They were very close, you see."

Brian and Nadine looked at each other. "Do you know how we can get in touch with him?" Brian asked.

"I can find out. My supervisor might be able to help you. Give me a second." Fred stepped out from behind the desk. Wandered over to his supervisor's office.

Brian and Nadine didn't speak to each other in his absence. They didn't look at each other. They just waited, paralyzed with anticipation. They knew there was no point. But what else were they to do?

Ten minutes later, Fred returned. "I spoke with my supervisor. Turns out she remembers Professor Victor as well. He used a read here a lot in between classes. She said the Library Department sent a bouquet of flowers to Professor Victor's brother after his death. They always do that with the next of kin. I made some inquiries and it seems we still have the address they sent it to." Fred held out a business card. "He might still be there."

Brian and Nadine took the card. Looked at it together. It was Fred's supervisor's business card. On the back, written in pen, was a name and a Manhattan address:

Elliot Victor
195 W 10th Street
Apartment 4B

CHAPTER TWENTY-SIX

Victor's Brother

Nadine and Brian took the subway all the way back down to Greenwich Village. They found the building easily enough. Nadine got into character on the walk up to the fourth floor, ready to go by the time they got to apartment 4B. She took a quick breath. Looked to Brian for strength. Knocked on the door.

After a few moments, the doorknob slowly turned and an old man peaked out with almost petrified unease. He had just a whisp of white hair on his head, the skin on his face jigging with every movement, and there were liver spots abound, but his blue eyes were noticeably sharp. "Who are you?" the old man asked in a wavering British accent.

"I'm sorry to bother you, sir," Nadine said gently. "Are you Elliot Victor?"

Elliot hesitated. Looked suspiciously at the young man standing silently behind her. "What do you want?"

"My name's Nadine. This is my friend Brian. Is it okay if we talk to you for a moment? It's regarding your brother."

Elliot hesitated. "What about Nigel?"

"I'm sorry to hear that he passed. I only just found out."

"Did you know him?"

"Yes," Nadine lied. "My mother used to work at the Columbia library. Monique Sauvageot? She knew your brother well. They used to talk all the time when he took his reading breaks there. He must've mentioned her?"

Elliot's lips wavered. "Alright. Go on."

"I used to read in there too. I sat at the same table as Mister Victor… that's what I called him. I didn't know what a professor was back then. I was only six. But I always remembered how nice he was. He was my favorite part of that place. I looked forward to seeing him every time my mom took me with her to work."

Elliot smiled at that. "Nigel really was the best person. Always so openly and friendly to everyone. Nothing like me at all."

"I only just came back from school and I was hoping to see him again. I just wanted to give you my condolences."

Elliot nodded. "Thank you, my dear. It means a lot. But I'm sorry, I don't typically—"

"He told me about you too."

Elliot opened the door a bit wider. "He did?"

"He told me you wrote. I even read a few."

Elliot blinked. "You read my novels?"

"Oh yes. I very much enjoyed them."

"I read some too," Brian chimed in.

Elliot smiled a tad. "Really? Well…" He looked down at his clothes. "I suppose I could… Would you like some tea?"

"Absolutely." Nadine looked at Brian. "Tea sound good?"

Brian nodded. "Absolutely."

Elliot let them in. The apartment smelled old, and it was noticeably quiet. No pets. No servants. No other people. Elliot headed into the kitchen. "I only have Darjeeling."

"Darjeeling's fine." Nadine sat in the living room.

Brian noticed there were only two chairs. "Why don't I make the tea?" he suggested to Elliot. "That way you two can talk."

Elliot looked curiously at Brian. "You know how to make tea?"

"Of course I know how to make tea."

"The leaves are in the cabinet." Elliot waddled past Brian. Sat in the chair closest to the window.

Brian opened the kitchen cabinet. Found the jar of Darjeeling and a kettle. He could hear Nadine and Elliot talking low in the next room. "He always told me he wanted to go back to Europe," Nadine was saying. "I always wondered, did he ever do it?"

"He had so many friends at that campus," Elliot told her, ignoring her question. "Tell me, did you ever meet Professor Watkins? He talked about Professor Watkins a lot. They were very good friends."

Brian pulled out two teacups. There wasn't a third one available. He furrowed his brow.

"No, I never met Professor—"

"He's gone now, of course," Elliot interrupted. "Everyone's gone now. I never even hear from them anymore."

Out of curiosity, Brian opened the next cabinet over. Two plates. Two bowls. Two goblets. He pulled open a drawer. Two forks. Two knives. Two spoons. Only two of everything.

"Yes, well…" Nadine was saying, looking behind her, wondering what was taking Brian so long. "As I was saying, did Nigel ever—?"

"I was at one of his black-tie parties once," Elliot rambled on.

"Yes, I've heard."

"He always made a show of his best students. What nice boys they were."

Brian filled the kettle with water. Couldn't hear anything during that time. Shut off the water.

"Nigel was very smart, you see," Elliot was saying. "Always good with numbers. Ever since we were young together. Far better than I, I'm afraid. I was never the brains between the two of us."

Brian put the kettle on the stove. Turned it on. Returned to the main room. Nowhere for him to sit.

"No, I'm sure you were," Nadine said encouragingly. "But please, Mister Victor—"

"Call me Elliot, please."

"Elliot. Did Nigel make that trip?"

Elliot blinked. "What trip?"

Nadine huffed. "The trip to Europe. The only he always wanted to take. Remember?"

Brian ambled about the apartment. There was a photograph on the wall, Elliot and his brother Nigel many decades before. They were smiling on a park bench together. Very handsome, they were. Another picture next to it, just of Elliot sitting in the same chair he was then, by the window. And then another picture of Nigel, just him that time. No pictures of the rest of their family. No pictures of wives or children. Just Elliot and Nigel. Brian thought that was odd. But then again, he had no pictures of his parents either. His mom died while Dad was away in France. He didn't even have one of his uncle and he was the one that practically raised him.

"Which books of mine did you read?" Elliot asked, interrupting Nadine again.

Nadine massaged the bridge of her nose. "It's been such a long time."

The kettle went off in the kitchen. Brian went in to retrieve it. Poured out two cups. Threw in some tea leaves. Carried them into the next room.

"Thank you," Nadine said, taking her cup with two hands. She returned her attention to Elliot. "I think it was your first one."

Elliot stared at Nadine. Ignored Brian holding out his steaming cup of tea. "My first one?" he asked suspiciously.

"I forgot the name, but… I really did enjoy it."

"What do you mean you read my first one?"

Brian cleared his throat. The teacup was getting heavy. "Sir?"

"Who are you people?" Elliot glared up at Brian.

Brian's heart stopped. "What?"

"You never knew my brother." Elliot shot a fearful look at Nadine. "He never would've recommended my first book to anyone. Who are you really?"

"Maybe it was your second one," Nadine blurted, controlling her panic. "Like I said, it was a long time ago."

"Really? What was it called?"

Nadine hesitated. "Like I said, I don't remember—"

Elliot stood sharply, almost knocking into Brian. Brian moved the boiling cup away just in time. "Leave me at once!" Elliot said loudly. "Never come here again!"

Nadine put her teacup down. "No, Elliot, please—!"

"Get out now or I'm calling the police!"

"Alright." Nadine stood slowly. "You're right. I never met Nigel."

"I thought not!"

"We just need to know if Nigel traveled to Berlin in the summer of 1927."

Elliot stared at her. The old man was actually trembling. "How do you know about that?"

"Please. Just tell us. Did he make that trip?"

"WHO THE HELL ARE YOU PEOPLE?!" Elliot screamed. "I told you to get out! LEAVE!"

"A friend of his is in trouble!"

"OUT!" Elliot shouted, pointing.

"He's in Paris," Brian said. "His name is Jacques."

"He said your brother would know how to help him," Nadine pleaded.

"Get out!" Elliot shoved Brian away with two hands, enough to make him stumble. "NOW!"

"He's a strong one," Brian quipped to Nadine, nursing his shoulder with one hand.

"Please," Nadine urged Elliot, standing her ground. "He's someone your brother would've met out there. Do you know why he was out there?"

"OUT! NOW!" Elliot smacked Brian some more, this time in the back.

"Ow!" Brian cried. "Alright! We're going! We're going!" He looked at Nadine. "We're going."

Nadine frowned back. She and Brian marched out of the apartment.

Elliot followed them closely and slammed the door behind them. They could hear the lock turn. Elliot even added the chain.

Nadine and Brian hunched over in the hallway. "Well, that was a mistake," she whispered.

"I don't think it was." Brian looked at Elliot's apartment door. "He only had two of everything in the cabinets."

"So?"

"The man lives alone, right? No photos of a wife or kids. So why would he have two of everything?"

Nadine shrugged. "I don't know. In case someone came over?"

"But only two? Did he not have any other friends besides his brother?"

Nadine slowly turned her head toward the door as well. "Fred said they always sent flowers to the next of kin. Nigel must've been a bachelor as well."

"What are you saying?"

Nadine looked at Brian. "What if Nigel lived here too? What if *this* was the address Jacques wrote on that envelope?"

Brian frowned at the apartment number. "I didn't see a phone in there. Did you see a phone in there?"

"No." Nadine sighed. "He was never in the phonebook. I was never going to find him."

Brian nodded. "Now we know we tried. Let's get out of here."

But Nadine kept staring at Elliot's door.

"I can't understand it either," William had said. *"Jacques said Victor wouldn't accept it otherwise. Bit of a hermit, apparently."*

"Nadine?" Brian asked.

Nadine kept staring at the door, the gears in her head turning.

"Professor Victor really was such a great guy," Fred had said. *"So sociable. He could talk to anybody."*

Brian tapped Nadine on the shoulder. "Nadine."

Nadine moved her shoulder away, her heart racing, eyes frozen on that door.

"Nigel really was the best person," Elliot just told them. *"Always so open and friendly to everyone. Nothing like me at all."*

Nadine ran up to the door and knocked over and over, lightning fast.

"What are you doing?" Brian hissed.

"Elliot!" Nadine kept knocking. "Elliot!"

"Nadine!" Brian looked around for angry neighbors. "Leave the man alone! Let's go!"

"Elliot!" Nadine shouted through the door. "Please! Open the door!"

"Go away," a weak voice spoke through the door.

"Please open the door, Elliot."

They could hear it unlock. Elliot opened the door with the chain still on it. They could only see his eyes, red and tear-stained, through the gap. "I just want to be alone, alright? Please just let me be alone!" He moved to slam the door again.

"Olive Branch!" Nadine blurted.

Elliot stopped the door from closing. Slowly opened it back up. "What did you say?"

"Olive Branch," Nadine repeated. "We were told to come to this address and deliver a letter and say those words. It wasn't your brother Jacques wanted us to find. It was you, wasn't it?"

Brian raised his brows. Shot a look at Elliot, seeing him in a new way.

Elliot stared back at Nadine. Unable to speak. Unable to move.

"You went to Berlin with Nigel that summer, didn't you?" Nadine asked him. "You did everything together. One of your friends is in trouble, Elliot. You're the only one that can help him get out of Paris.

Elliot's brows moved together slightly. "François sent you?" His voice sounded different that time.

Nadine gaped a little. Looked back at Brian. "He said his name was Jacques, but… we know it's not his real name now.

Elliot looked at the two of them. "Is he black?"

Nadine's face lit up. "Yes!"

"French?"

"Yes!"

"An American with him?"

"Yes! Corey Baxter!"

Elliot hesitated. "Who the hell is Corey Baxter?"

Nadine's excitement petered off. "We were hoping you'd tell us."

"I don't know a Corey Baxter. I knew an *Andrew* Baxter."

"Andrew?" Brian asked.

"We always called him Andy, but…" Elliot looked Nadine in the eye. "You said François is in danger?"

Nadine nodded.

Elliot slammed the door. Before Nadine could react, she heard the chain unlock. Elliot whipped the door open. "Come in." He stepped aside. "Come on. Quickly now."

Nadine and Brian stepped back in. Elliot's voice was definitely different. She couldn't quite place how.

Elliot closed the door and locked it. "The letter. Where is it?"

"It got destroyed," Nadine told him. "I don't know what was in it."

"What do you mean?"

Nadine hesitated. "I never actually met François or Andy. I was told about them though a friend of mine. His name was William."

"Where is he now?"

Nadine frowned. "He died."

Elliot frowned too. "I'm sorry."

Nadine nodded. She made difficult eye contact with Elliot. "You should know… Andy's dead too."

Elliot stared. "Oh wow…" He had to sit down.

"Don't forget the boxes," Brian spoke up. "He needs your help getting them out."

Elliot shook his head. "I don't understand. What boxes?"

"The boxes in the house," Nadine said.

"I don't know what you're talking about."

"He's got boxes! That's…" Nadine huffed. Looked at Brian. "Isn't that what you said—?"

"We assumed that's what 'Olive Branch' meant," Brian explained. "Noah's Ark. The dove with the olive branch."

Elliot shook his head. "I'm sorry, I don't know anything about any boxes. I haven't heard from François in… Oh God, sixteen years."

Nadine blinked. "Sixteen years?"

"Believe me, I'm as shocked as you are." Elliot stared off. "I thought all this time… I thought he hated me."

Nadine tenderly approached Elliot. "What's going on, Elliot? Please."

"My name's not Elliot."

Nadine furrowed her brow. "It's not?"

Elliot shook his head. He looked her in the eyes. Smiled with blessed relief. "My name… is *Jack Branson*."

Brian and Nadine stared back with puzzled, unimpressed expressions.

Jack's eyes bounced between them. "Nothing? Nothing at all?"

"Were you famous or something?" Nadine murmured.

"Was I *famous?!*" Jack scoffed. "You never heard of the Montgomery Street Scandal?"

Nadine and Brian shook their heads.

"Oh." Jack half-frowned. "Well, you must've heard of the Collins Affair at least. That one almost ruined me."

Nadine and Brian shook their heads again.

"And the cruel irony of life continues." Jack smacked his lips. "Give me a moment." He stood. Waddled to a dresser. Opened it. Rummaged through the drawers.

Brian sidled up to Nadine. "His voice is different, right?"

"I thought so too," Nadine whispered back. "What is it, Irish?"

"I think so."

"Here it is." Jack pulled out a perfectly folded newspaper. Waddled it back over to them. "Gander on this with your young eyes."

Nadine held up the newspaper for Brian to see too. It was a copy of *The Times* dated April 18, 1889. The paper was old and brown.

Jack crossed his arms. "Believe me now?"

"'The Sins of Jack Branson,'" Nadine read. "'By Dr Haywood Goldsborough, Reader in English Legal His—'"

"Skip all that." Jack rolled a finger impatiently. "Get to the main part."

"'I do not believe in fate,'" Nadine read aloud. "'The world is too large and chaotic, and human beings are burdened with too much weakness to achieve anything resembling a destiny. But every so often, by complete accident, the stage is set for something magnificent. The once-in-two-hundred-years kind of magnificent. The perfect moment. History being made. Legends being born.'"

Jack beamed. Turned toward the window.

"'Such a moment occurred at Old Bailey on Friday when Jack Branson, a male…'" Nadine raised her eyebrows.

Brian froze. His eyes darted up at Jack. That old man with the twisted grin on his face.

Nadine took a breath. "'…when Jack Branson, a male *prostitute* from Dublin, took the stand for the Defence and delivered a testimony so infamous, so sensational, that the transcriber stopped recording from pure shock.'"

Brian's face hardened. He stepped away from Nadine. Away from the paper.

"'Such a moment deserves to be louder than words,'" Nadine continued reading, her excitement growing with interest. "'No description could properly recapture how Mr Branson affected the courtroom. His brazen effrontery reduced the gallery to utter silence, and several elderly women fainted at his words.'"

As Jack heard Nadine read the article in that soft, silky French accent of hers, he couldn't help but think back on that day. Before the verdict came and stole all the joy from it. When it was just him in that courtroom. His found family in the gallery. His Oliver. And his heart grew heavy. His smile faded. It started to hurt.

Nadine kept reading, oblivious to Jack and Brian's reactions. "'However, his power was not as simple as his use of explicit language. Mr Branson was also sharp and witty. His defiance, already highlighted in his bestseller *The Sins of an Irishman in London* (his secret authorship just one of many surprises that morning), was one of strength and pride, with no fear towards the society that sought to oppress him.'"

Brian leaned against the wall, sick to his stomach. He gathered up to courage to look at Jack again. To his surprise Jack was visibly melancholic. Good.

Nadine kept on reading. "'His commentary on truth, in which he deconstructed the hypocritical nature of our justice system and the wishful thinking of our laws, was nothing less than a revelation. At the risk of sounding maudlin, I predict that Jack Branson's testimony will one day be studied in every major school of law in the world.'"

There was no joy on Jack's face. No lightness throughout his body. Just sadness. Cruel, unending disappointment.

"'Just as significant as his words is the man himself. Without exaggeration, "Dublin Jack" just made himself the most famous male prostitute in history, a distinction both well-earned and incredibly disgusting. It's also the truth.'" Nadine lowered the paper. "Wow, so you're…!" She stopped herself. Recognized the pain Jack was in.

Jack's eyes were on the windowsill. "I was born in Dunderrow, by the way. Not Dublin." He turned around. Returned to his chair.

Nadine gently re-folded the paper. Noticed Brian standing against the wall. "What's with you?"

Brian only glared back at her.

"I'm alright, dear," Jack answered. "Just the cruel irony of life twisting the knife once more."

Nadine placed the paper aside. Knelt before Jack. Took his hand. "What's going on? I've been wondering for so long. I need to know."

Jack stared at her, his sadness slowly replaced by panic. "What do you mean? How long have you been looking for me?"

Nadine rolled her lips. "Two and a half years."

Jack's face sunk even further. "That long?" he whispered. He shook his head. "Oh, that poor, poor man."

"Tell us," Nadine whispered. "Please. What does 'Olive Branch' mean?"

Jack looked down at Nadine. Those eager hazel eyes of hers. Oliver looked at him like that once. The night they met. How they green were. Like the Cliffs of Moher. They seduced him. Took hold of him. Made him whole for the first time ever. He smiled back at Nadine. "Alright." He sat up. Glanced over at that second chair. Oliver's chair. He could still see him there, reading the morning paper like he always did. He was looking up at him. Smiled. Gave him an eager nod, as if to say *Go on. Don't keep the poor girl waiting.*

Jack found himself nodding back. He stood once more. Returned the paper to the dresser drawer. Rummaged some more. Came back to his chair with a photo, the one he received in the mail all those years ago. He gave it to Nadine.

Nadine gasped at the sight of it. "Oh my God, Brian! Brian! That's him! There's Ernst! This is the photo! The photo William was talking about!"

Jack furrowed his brow. "Who's Ernst?"

"The Nazi on the side there. That's Ernst Röhm. He's how we were able to find you."

"That guy? Really?"

Nadine stood. Showed Brian the photo.

Brian took the photograph. Stared at it. All those 'people' smiling back at him. How close he was to ripping it to shreds, right there in front of Jack. "That's Röhm alright." He practically threw it back at Nadine. It floated down to the floor.

Nadine was appalled by his behavior. Gently picked the photo back up. "Sorry about him," she mumbled to Jack.

Jack watched Brian with an uneasily feeling. He'd seen that face before. He knew what was going on inside that handsome head of his.

Nadine returned to Jack. Pointed to the black man in the photo. "So that's Jacques—*François.* Sorry." She blinked, suddenly realizing. "Wait. Jacques. Jack. That's why he called himself that, wasn't it?"

Jack shrugged. "I don't know. He never used to before."

Nadine pointed to the white man closest to François. "Is that Andy?"

"Yes. Darryl Baxter's only son."

"I thought Darryl Baxter didn't have a son," Brian said coldly.

Jack hesitated, having felt the sting of Brian's tone. "Well, he would say that, wouldn't he? Considering what Andy was."

Brian clenched his jaw. Looked away.

Nadine raised her brows. Tried to be gentle. "You mean… a homosexual?"

Jack nodded. "Yes."

Brian closed his eyes.

"François too?" Nadine asked.

"Yes, of course. They were lovers. Well, to be more poetic about it, life partners." Jack looked down at the photo. "This here was the fortieth anniversary reunion of the infamous whores of the Montgomery Street Brothel, London's first homosexual brothel. It might've been the first in the world." He took the photo from Nadine. Held it only by the edges. Pointed to a man in the back. "That is Charlie Smith. He was the mastermind behind the operation. A famous publisher in his day. Very famous. Prestigious. But in secret, he was homosexual just like us, and he used his family fortune to buy protection from the police. It kept us afloat. We were very successful for a time. The whole idea was to start a movement that would ultimately lead to the decriminalization of homosexuality in England. A world where we could walk the streets without fear of arrest, with no secrets or shame at all." Jack smiled. "One of my clients was Edgar Withers. He was running for Parliament at the time. His opponent put it in the press and Edgar countered by suing him libel. And he won, even though I told the truth, the whole truth and nothing but."

"How?" Nadine asked.

"I don't know. People are stupid." Jack pointed to the man next to Charlie. "That is Denny Evans, one of my closest friends. After the Brothel got shut down, he moved to Rome and became a famous artist. A piece or two of his is hanging in the Louvre right now. He's also the greatest bartender ever." Jack paused to admire Denny's perpetually happy grin. "And he only had one leg, so that made him easily accessible, if you know what I mean."

Nadine looked at him awkwardly. "Alright."

"That was a sex joke, woman. Keep up." Jack pointed to the handsome devil sitting close to Charlie and Denny, "That is me."

"Wow." Nadine moved closer for a good look. "How old were you here?"

"I had just turned seventy."

"You still looked good."

Jack let out a bumpy noise, not happy or sad, just… bumpy. "You never realize how much you depend on your looks until they're ripped away from you." He smiled at the even handsomer devil sitting next to him. His body got warm just looking at him. "And that… is Oliver."

Nadine noticed the longing on Jack's face. "Who's Oliver?"

"The man you claimed to know so well." Jack threw a snarky look at her. "The man legally known in this country as 'Nigel Victor.'"

"That's your brother?"

"He was never my brother." Jack sighed wistfully. "He was the best thing that ever happened to me."

Nadine nodded, instantly understanding. "What about the women?" she asked, pointing to the gorgeous dolls arm-and-arm with each other.

Jack chuckled. "Ah, but you see… those aren't women. They're Liverpudlian cross-dressers."

Nadine gaped. "They're men?!"

"'Mary and Louise' we called them. Their real names were Georgie Belcher and Corey Kehoe."

"Corey?" Nadine looked up at Brian. "Is that why Andy chose the name Corey?"

"I don't know. Maybe." Jack moved his mouth to one side. "Why him is the question. They were never particularly close."

Nadine pointed to the two older men standing on the side. "Who are these two?"

"Them? They weren't part of our group. On the left is Dr. Magnus Hirschfeld. On the right is his life partner Karl. They were our hosts, as it were. We were their honored guests for the weekend."

Nadine nodded. "Why Berlin? What was out there?"

Jack frowned slightly. "Oliver and I first came to this country in 1889. The Brothel had just shut down. All of us scattered to the winds. Andy and François had moved to Paris to start a brothel of their own. Mary and Louise chose to go to Amsterdam to join De Wallen, the red-light district there. Charlie went back to his family in Scotland to retool. Denny went to Rome, like I said. But we never really felt apart from each other. Charlie had developed a correspondence network. We gave him our addresses. Sent him our letters. He made copies and sent them out to all of us. Keeping the family together was his next venture, it seemed." Jack stood. Returned the photo to its home. Sat back in his chair. "As Oliver and I approached Ellis Island, we knew what had to be done. Before the Montgomery Street Scandal, I had been roped into a nastier business, the Collins Affair. I had to flee to Ireland to wait it out. I started a whole new life as a footman, but my name found its way over there and ruined everything. I learned my lesson this time. I wanted a fresh start in America. It's what he and I deserved. So we decided to change our names at immigration. Pretended we were brothers. That way we'd be able to live together with no one batting an eye. My English accent was always better than Oliver's Irish accent, so I agreed to play the Englishman for the rest of our lives."

Nadine gestured to the empty chair. "May I?"

"Of course."

Nadine sat down properly. Leaned in to listen. "Why 'Victor?'"

"Oliver asked me to pick out his new name. He was never born 'Oliver Hawkett,' you see. He forged it himself as a little boy in a London orphanage, to take the power away from the evil nuns running the place. So for him to allow me, *me* of all people, to choose the name for him?" Jack smiled, his cheeks turning red. "I was beyond honored."

Nadine's heart melted at that.

Jack ran a finger along the length of his armrest. "I chose Victor to be his surname because I felt Oliver was the greatest Englishman that ever lived, just like how Queen Victoria was greatest Englishwoman that ever lived, so… 'Victor.' And I thought he looked like a Nigel, so… 'Nigel Victor.'"

"Did he choose 'Elliot' for you?"

Jack nodded. "It was only fair." He looked at Brian, still standing there with that awful look to him. "Turns out it was better I pretend to be English, considering how poorly this country treats its Irishmen."

Brian kept staring at the other side of the room. No comment.

Jack bumped his brows. "Anyway." He looked at Nadine. "Oliver was always superb at forging his qualifications. He actually managed to convince an Ivy League institution that he was a prestigious mathematician. I, however, continued my previous passion of novel writing." Jack went quiet. "Let's just say I wasn't nearly as successful as he was in that regard."

"But your first book was a bestseller, wasn't it?" Nadine asked.

"Under the name 'Jack Branson,' yes." Jack scowled. "Actually, it was never officially under *any* name. I had it anonymously published. Worst decision of my life. If it was something I could take credit for out here, I'm sure my masterpieces would've sold in droves, but no. To answer your question, no, I never had a bestseller." Jack stifled his annoyance. "It seems I'm incapable of repeating that first blip of notoriety."

Nadine chose to stay silent on that point.

"But I was happy nonetheless," Jack told her. "Oliver and I were the happiest of men. Because of our lie, we were safe. And even though we had to lie out there, in here we were practically in the Garden. Everything was perfect. We got a letter every week from someone, one of our brothers, updating us on their lives. And that's how it was for a while. Even during the Great War, Charlie kept the letters flowing. We never felt alone." Jack went cold. Stared off. Lowered his head.

"I don't think you answered my question," Nadine said softly.

Jack lifted his head with a start. "I'm sorry. What was the question?"

"Berlin."

"Oh yes." Jack sat up. Smoothed out his pants. "After the war ended, around 1925 or so, we received a letter from Mary and Louise. They had nearly got imprisoned for cross-dressing and had to fuck their way out of Amsterdam."

Nadine blinked. "I'm sorry, they—?"

"They had heard rumors about Berlin, what it'd become after the Great War. If the stories were to be believed, cross-dressing wasn't criminalized there. That sounded too good to be true, but what did they have to lose?" Jack paused. "They told us it wasn't just tolerated there. It was *celebrated*. 'A cross-dressing Mecca,' they called it. And not just cross-dressing either. Homosexuality. I didn't believe it. 'Impossible,' I said. But then a year later, Charlie wrote to us himself. He and Denny had just opened a bar there together. Not just any bar, a bar for homosexuals. They weren't the first ones to do it either. They claimed there were over a hundred homosexual bars in Berlin. A hundred! Can you imagine?" Jack shook his head. "And so we planned to have a reunion there every year. All of us could be together again. Andy. François. Mary. Louise. Denny. Charlie." Jack frowned. Looked out the window. All that light shining in. "I was so nervous," he told them, his mind traveling back sixteen years, to that very room, that very chair…

CHAPTER TWENTY-SEVEN

Reunion, 1927

Jack threw himself down on his favourite chair, an absolute wreck. "That's it. I'm not going!"

Oliver rolled his eyes as he carried a pile of clothes into their bedroom. "We've already bought boat tickets."

"No! Don't you understand? They're going to bring up Edgar and the book, I know they will."

"Don't be ridiculous," Oliver called from the next room.

"I'm not being ridiculous!" Jack snapped. "If not that book, they'll definitely ask about the others."

"Why would they bring it up? They know it upsets you."

Jack jumped to his feet. Stormed into the bedroom. Oliver was sorting his clothes into a trunk. "You know François's going to bring up the money," Jack told him. "There's no filter on that one, even in written form."

"So what if he does?" Oliver asked. "What's he going to do?"

"I don't know, but he'll do something. I know he will."

"You're exaggerating."

"I am not exaggerating!" Jack snapped. "It really upset him. It upset me!"

Oliver rolled his eyes again. "I know it did."

"He's not touching that money."

"It's your money."

"It is my money!"

"Then what's the problem?"

Jack struggled to think of one. "I'm going to have to turn him down again."

Oliver shrugged, unfazed. "That's fine."

"No, it's not! It was bad enough the first time. Now I got to do it again to his face?" Jack instinctively looked at the mirror behind him. "Oh wow."

Oliver looked up briefly. "What now?" he asked calmly.

"How did I get so old?" Jack rubbed his cheeks, all that loose skin starting to hang. "I can't believe I'm seventy. This is awful."

"I'm no young man either, you know. Sixty-seven's not far off."

"It's miles apart!" Jack let out a dramatic sigh. "I don't like this. It's going to be weird seeing them all again."

"It's *not* going to be weird."

"Of course it'll be weird! It's been almost forty years! How's it NOT going to be weird? They'll all look different and sound different! It won't be fun at all. It'll just make us feel like crap for coming out here."

Oliver gave him a smile. Walked around the bed. Got really close to Jack. Tenderly held both sides of his face. "Breathe."

"I'm sorry."

"*Breathe.*"

Jack took a deep breath in. Let it out. He looked into Oliver's eyes, those beautiful green pools. "I love you," he whimpered. "Oh God, I so love you so so so much."

"I love you too." Oliver kissed him sweetly, tenderly, their lips smacking a little. Oliver smiled. Caressed Jack's cheeks. "Where are you?" he whispered.

Jack closed his eyes. Nodded. "I know."

"Say it out loud." Oliver petted Jack's hair. "You'll feel better. You know you will."

Jack swallowed. Opened his eyes.

"Where are you?" Oliver asked again.

Jack inhaled, his breath whistling. "Here."

"Where's here?"

"With you."

"That's right." Oliver placed his forehead against Jack's. They closed their eyes together. Their warm breath intermingled. "I'm not going anywhere."

Jack squeezed his face, trying not to cry. He kissed Oliver again. And again. Over and over and over and over until they laughed it all out.

The next morning, Jack and Oliver stepped out of Apartment 4B. Trunks in their hands. Back to Nigel and Elliot. Back to the Victor Brothers. They still felt the difference, even after all these years. Jack greeted his neighbours with that British accent he hated using. He let Oliver do most of the talking, as usual. And as Oliver delivered their alibi, where they were going for a week, Jack simply admired how beautiful Oliver still was. He was all his. Somehow that made everything alright. Everything. The failure of his novels. The loneliness he felt at home, waiting for Oliver to return from all those dry lectures at Columbia. No friends in America. No family except in written form. But it was worth every minute. What they had was the greatest treasure on the earth. Jack wouldn't change a thing at all.

Jack and Oliver boarded the ship and set off for London, where they transferred to a boat headed for Hamburg. Jack was panicking the whole way, convinced they were going to miss their connection, the morning train to Berlin, thus missing the entire reunion. But Oliver's levelheadedness calmed him down. They made the train in time and were finally able to relax all the way to Berlin.

Jack and Oliver lugged their trunks through Lehrter Bahnhof. Oliver held Mary's letter of directions. "What do we do?" Jack asked anxiously. "Are we supposed to wait here?"

"He says we're supposed to go to…" Oliver blew his lips. "I can't read that."

Jack spotted two men walking towards them, a seven-year-old boy in tow. "Excuse me?" Jack asked them. "*Sprechen sie Englisch?*"

"Yes, we speak English," the first man said with a smile.

"Oh, thank God! We're trying to find…" Jack looked at Oliver.

Oliver handed the Germans Mary's letter. Pointed to the words at the bottom. "How do we get *there?*"

The two men held the letter closer. "Oh, *Motzstraße!*" the second man exclaimed. "What a coincidence. We just came back from there."

Oliver grinned. "Wow! What are the odds?"

"So what you're going to do…" The first man pointed to their left. "Take that exit. Turn left. Go all the way down until you cross the river Spree. Keep going until you get to the Siegessäule, the…" He snapped his fingers. "It's a… a very tall statue with an angel on top."

"It's very big," the seven-year-old boy added.

Jack and Oliver chuckled.

The first man proudly petted the little boy's head. "Once you're there, go around the circle and take the south road. Keep going until you see a sign for Motzstraße. It's a big road. Very long."

"Thank you so much!" Jack shook the first man's hand. "You have no idea how lost we were…"

"Kiefer."

Oliver shook Kiefer's hand as well. "Thank you, Kiefer."

The second man shook Jack's hand. "Steffen."

"Kiefer and Steffen, thank you very much," Jack said. He looked down at the little boy. Gave him a tiny wave. "*Au wiedersehen.*"

The little boy waved back. "Goodbye."

Jack and Oliver laughed. "Thanks again," Oliver added, and they carried their trunks to the exit Kiefer told them to take.

Kiefer watched them leave, a strange feeling in his heart. He looked to Steffen, asking in German, "Do you think they're…?"

"Oh, they definitely are," Steffen said with a smile.

Kiefer nodded. Looked down at his son. "Let's go, Wilhelm. We don't want to miss our train."

Wilhelm immediately sprinted down the platform. Kiefer and Steffen laughed. Kiefer put an arm around Steffen's shoulders as they strolled together, taking their time after little Wilhelm, never once losing sight of the boy.

Jack and Oliver crossed the Lutherbrücke, the bridge over the river Spree. They could see that tall golden statue, the Siegessäule, in the distance. Jack had to stop walking from sheer wonder. It was so hot there in Berlin. Blue sky. Golden sun. It was really happening. They were all in the same city again. It was just a matter of finding each other.

"What's wrong?" Oliver asked him.

Jack smiled back at his beloved. "Nothing. Nothing at all."

Oliver kissed his fingers. Tapped them on Jack's lips. That made Jack blush. They kept on walking.

Thanks to Kiefer's directions, they were able to find Motzstraße. They stood at the crossroads of Motzstraße and Martin-Luther-Straße as Oliver struggled to read the last of Mary's instructions.

"Well I'll be!" a dainty English voice exclaimed. Mary herself was crossing the street towards them, looking gorgeous as always in a red curly wig and a flowing day dress. He needed more makeup than usual to cover his age lines, ultimately netting zero with how he looked the last they saw him.

Jack instantly burst into tears at the sight of him. He loudly sobbed as he ran into the street. Clapped both arms around Mary. Spun him around in a triumphant hug.

Mary laughed, the spin making him dizzy. "It's nice to see you too, Jack." He noticed all the tears on Jack's face. "Hush up, will you? You're making a scene."

"Sorry." Jack wiped away his tears. Snot clung to the back of his hand.

"You better not shake my hand with that one," Louise quipped, revealing himself. His face was pale and powdered into linelessness, Ghost Chic as usual, and he wore the same blond wig, but his muscle definition had noticeably faded since the last time they saw each other. "I know where it's been: *on Mary.*"

Jack burst into wild happy sobs again. He hugged Louise tighter than he did Mary, knowing he could take it, crying just as loud.

Louise couldn't help but smile as he hugged back. "Aww, I missed you too, Guinness."

Oliver found himself getting emotional too. He hugged Mary and Louise in turn. Slipped Jack a handkerchief.

"Why are you guys dressed up?" Jack whimpered, dabbing his eyes. "Isn't that a bit risky?"

"Not anymore! Look!" Mary pulled a folded document out of his padded bosom. "Official walking papers of the Institut für Sexualwissenschaft. Louise, show them yours."

Louise pulled his out of his chest. "That one's too easy." He handed his walking papers to Oliver. "They can't arrest us. It's not illegal if it's a scientific experiment."

"A scientific experiment?" Oliver asked. "Are you guys…?"

"Nope," Mary answered. "Just Magnus working his miracles." He stuffed his papers back where they came from. "He knows what he's doing."

"He's one of us," Louise added.

"C'mon." Mary held his arm out for Jack to take. "He's dying to meet you."

Jack reluctantly took Mary's arm. Oliver took Louise's and the four of them strolled down Motzstraße.

"Magnus is your boss, right?" Jack asked Mary. "The one who founded the Institut?"

"Yes sir," Mary said. "He didn't just find the Institut. Back in '97 he founded the… What was it called again? Louise?"

"The WhK," Louise answered. "It's short for something German. In English, it translates to 'the Scientific-Humanitarian Committee.'"

"Yes, that. It was his campaign to repeal Paragraph 175."

"What's Paragraph 175?" Oliver asked Mary.

"Repealing it would've decriminalised homosexuality in Germany," Louise answered.

"Sound familiar?" Mary asked Jack.

Jack gave a shocked look back at Oliver. "That was in '97?"

"Yup."

"1897?"

"As opposed to what? *1997*?"

"Isn't homosexual still illegal here?" Oliver asked.

"Technically yes," Louise said. "But since the war ended, they haven't been enforcing it."

"No one seems to care anymore," Mary declared proudly.

"What do you mean no one cares?" Jack asked. "Someone must care. It's still illegal."

"There are no arrests. No raids. No scandals. No censorship. Nothing. Ever since the Kaiser abdicated, Berlin's become a very different place." Mary pointed up ahead. "Look there. See for yourself."

Jack's mouth fell open. He unhooked from Mary. Walked on ahead. Stopped in the middle of the road.

They had reached the main district of Motzstraße. Men were holding hands on both sides of the road. Cross-dressers and transvestites were out and about as well. In broad daylight. On the left side of the street was a bar, a *gay* bar, filled with men just like the ones on the street. Some were looking back at Jack, openly flirty with their eyes. Across the street was another bar just like it. In fact, Jack could see six similar establishments from his vantage point alone.

Oliver walked up next to Jack, his eyes just as wide, just as gobsmacked as he was.

"Darling?" Jack asked him.

"Uh-huh?"

"Remember that night in Dubeau Frères? When you asked me if I believed we'd be able to live like normal people one day?"

"Uh-huh."

"And I said not in our lifetime?"

"Uh-huh."

Jack looked at Oliver. His lip started trembling. "Guess, I was wrong, huh?"

Oliver looked at Jack. He was crying too.

Jack took Oliver's hand. "I was so wrong!"

Oliver pulled Jack in and kissed him on the lips. Right there in the middle of the street. In broad daylight. In front of all those people. It didn't seem real. It had to have been a dream. But it wasn't a dream. It was real. It was all so terribly, wonderfully real.

Mary and Louise took Jack and Oliver to the Institut für Sexualwissenschaft, the first sexology research centre of its kind. Mary introduced them to their boss, Doctor Magnus Hirschfeld, and Magnus's life partner Karl Giese. Jack, Oliver, Magnus and Karl sat in the Institut's private garden for some afternoon tea. Mary and Louise had to leave to pick up François and Andy at the train station.

Magnus poured them all cups of Darjeeling, knowing it was Jack's favourite, as he recounted what inspired him to pursue gay rights activism. "Of course I was greatly affected by the trial of Oscar Wilde," he said in a deliberately prominent Jewish-German accent. "Much like everyone else. 'The Ballad of Reading Gaol' left me *markerschütternd*." He looked to Karl. "'*Markerschütternd?*'"

"'Shaken to his core,'" Karl translated.

Jack and Oliver nodded.

"Yes, unbelievingly so," Magnus continued. "But in fact it was one of my patients, not Mister Wilde, that inspired me to form the WhK, the Wissenschaftlich-humanitäres Komitee. I had been treating a young army officer for depression at my naturopathic practice in Magdeburg for many years. Sadly, he took his own life in 1896. In his suicide note he revealed to me that, despite his best efforts, he could not end his desires for other men."

Jack couldn't say anything to that. "That's awful," Oliver murmured.

"He wanted to tell his parents too," Magnus added, looking especially at Jack. "But claimed he lacked the strength to do so. He couldn't even write out the word 'homosexual.' He just called it '*that.*'" Magnus shook his head. "I'll never forget that last sentence he wrote: 'The thought that you could contribute a future when the German fatherland will think of us in more just terms sweetens the hour of my death.'"

Jack let out a heavy breath. "That's… I don't know what that is."

"You would not believe how many homosexual patients he's lost to suicide," Karl said.

"And the ones that attempt even, the…" Magnus gestured along the inside of his wrist. "In German, we call them '*suizidalnarben.*' The scars that get left behind. They never truly heal."

Jack hesitated. "I met someone once who had those."

"Yes, I know," Magnus said with a nod. "Tucker from the Collins Affair. I read your book."

Jack's face lit up. "You did?"

"A first edition, no less. That's very hard to come by nowadays, from what I hear."

"How did that happen by the way?" Karl asked Jack. "The censoring. Charlie didn't want to tell us for some reason."

Jack's enthusiasm faded. "Yeah, probably because he knew how much it upsets me."

"Oh, I'm sorry," Magnus said. "We didn't know."

"No, it's fine. It won't change anything." Jack took a deep breath. "Edgar used the damages he got from Charlie and Geoffrey Grant to buy the publishing rights to my book. Then before he died, he sold the rights to a Christian Fundamentalist publishing company. They took out the addendum, removed all references to sexuality, homosexuality, corruption, violence, anything they considered indecent."

Magnus shrugged. "That's the whole book."

"I know. They intentionally drove it out of print. They also bought up all the old copies and grinded them down. Even if I wanted the rights back, they would never sell them to me. It was anonymously authored, after all. I have no claim to it."

"You can always sue them," Karl suggested.

"We all know how well you do in court," Magnus added with a smile.

Jack frowned. Looked away.

Oliver noticed Jack's discomfort. "It's been quite a while since then," he told them. "Jack feels it's better if he moves on from it all."

"But think of the good it can do," Magnus insisted. "How well it would sell here in Berlin. Perhaps other districts will sprout up in its wake."

"I don't want to be rude, Dr Hirschfeld," Jack told him, looking him in the eye. "But I've already made my decision on the matter."

Magnus nodded. "Of course. My apologies."

Jack sat back. Disassociated. Pretended he wasn't there.

Magnus gave a discreet look at Karl. "Jack, have you ever heard of the Eulenburg Affair?"

"No," Jack replied.

"It was the most widely publicised sex scandal in Imperial Germany. In 1907, General Kuno Graf von Molke was caught having a homosexual relationship with Prince Philipp von Eulenburg."

"The Kaiser's best friend," Karl added.

"Despite their best efforts to keep it quiet, a journalist by the name of Maximilian Harden found out about the affair and published his accusations in an imperialist periodical called *Die Zukunft*. Molke responded by suing Harden for criminal libel."

Jack gave a surprised look to Oliver.

"I testified for the Defence in that case," Magnus said, a hand on his heart. "I told them plainly as an experienced sexologist that the relationship between Molke and Eulenburg was absolutely a romantic one, even without evidence of sodomy. And of course I couldn't help but throw in how, in my professional opinion, homosexuality was part of the plan of nature and creation, just like normal love."

"Germany was appalled to say the least," Karl said proudly.

"I was called a freak in the *Vossische Zeitung*—The German equivalent of the *Times*—and my work 'pseudoscientific.'"

"And who won the trial?" Oliver asked.

Magnus grinned at Jack. "We did."

Jack stared back.

Magnus nodded. "Thanks to me, the jury sided with Harden."

"The first time," Karl mumbled.

"Yes, well…" Magnus shrugged. "The Prussian government threatened to take away my licence and imprison me under Paragraph 175 if I didn't retract my statement, but even still…" Magnus looked at Jack. "The first trial was the real one. Do you know why I did that? Why I said all that in front of all those people?"

Jack stared back, his heart racing.

Magnus nodded. "You're an inspiration to us all, Jack Branson. Berlin as it is now would not have been possible had it not been for you. The Institut would not have been possible. Even the WhK. I thought of your book throughout all that. This…" Magnus gestured around him. "This is all yours too, Jack. All of it. So if you want the bones of your memoir to rot under the church's boot heels, fine. That is your prerogative. But don't think you've done nothing. You have not done nothing. You have done so much. You have saved lives. You have set an example not many even thought possible. You've changed the world."

Jack couldn't breathe.

Oliver smiled. Took Jack's hand.

Magnus noticed new arrivals stepping out into the garden. "And now the collection is complete."

Jack and Oliver turned around to see François Brion and Andy Baxter walking into the sunlight. François looked almost exactly the same, just as thin and catty as he always was. But Andy had aged *bad*. He was no longer the cock-hungry young bucko getting railed every night. He was only fifty-eight and aged worse than Jack did!

Oliver hugged François and Andy first, Jack awkwardly taking his time to greet them. François caught him looking. The awkward atmosphere was already brewing.

"Hey," Jack mumbled.

François nodded emotionlessly. "Hey yourself."

Jack hesitated. His lip tightened. "Listen. About that letter…"

"It doesn't matter." François shook his head. "Really. It's in the past. Don't worry about it."

But Jack didn't believe him. He knew he shouldn't have written it. He knew he should've had Oliver look it over. But he was drunk. He was angry. He sent it anyway.

François was thinking the same thing. But he brought Jack in for a hug anyway.

"Hey Jack!" Andy exclaimed, his American energy still the same. "Come on, baby. I want to hug him now."

François sighed. Undid himself from Jack.

Andy's eyes bounced between the two of them. "Oh boy!" he declared with a grin. "You two are still mad about the money thing, aren't you?"

François and Jack instantly cringed.

"Yeah," Andy teased, nodding. "Yeah, you are. I can tell. There's that European silence you guys love so much. God, I've missed you guys. You really haven't changed a bit." He looked at Magnus. "Well, except for Jack's money, *but we're not allowed to talk about that!*" Andy laughed.

François looked up at the sky, struggling to contain his anger. "Andy…"

But Andy kept going. "Our brothel really hasn't been doing so well since the war, and now Jack and Oliver have more money than they know what to do with, but they don't want to open a brothel of their own in Manhattan or give any of it to us—"

"ANDY!" François yelled.

Andy instantly shut up. Nothing on his face but shame. "Sorry," he mumbled, uncharacteristically grim.

François, Jack and Oliver avoided looking at each other. They just stood there in awkward, shameful silence.

Mary popped his head out of the Institut. "Who wants to go see the armoury of dildos they got upstairs?"

"ME!" Andy cried. He immediately dashed away from those sourpusses and ran inside, chasing Mary and Louise up the stairs.

Magnus and Karl gave François, Jack and Oliver an official tour of the Institut für Sexualwissenschaft, founded in 1919. "Over there is our library," Magnus told them, pointing. "You'd find books there on gender, homosexuality, transvestites, eroticism, intersex persons. We treat alcoholism here. We provide gynaecological examinations, martial and sex counselling, contraceptives. We also spend a great deal of time and money treating and researching venereal disease."

François hummed with raised brows. "Venereal disease! You don't say."

Jack tightened his face. He wouldn't dare…

"I'm sure you boys know quite a lot about that." Magnus laughed.

"Oh, we do," François said coyly. "When we started our brothel in Paris, we made sure to have a doctor to check our boys for that sort of thing. I believe you actually know our man, Dr Hirschfeld. Edwin Gateau?"

Magnus nodded with delight. "Oh, of course. I'm quite familiar with Dr

Gateau's work on venereal disease. We actually have a few books of his in our collection."

"I'll tell him you say hello then." François threw a nasty smile at Jack. "You okay there, Jack? No need to be squeamish. We're only talking about syphilis."

Jack didn't say anything. Oliver couldn't either.

That wasn't good enough for François. He elbowed Jack in the arm. "You know all about syphilis, don't you, Jack?"

Magnus looked at Jack, his obvious discomfort. "What is he talking about?"

"Oh, he didn't tell you?"

Jack bugged his eyes at François. "François, I really don't think you should be talking about this."

"About what?" François asked sarcastically. "It's no big deal. You just gave us all syphilis, that's all."

Oliver closed his eyes.

Magnus furrowed his brow. "Jack, is that true?"

"No, it's not!" Jack snapped.

"No need to be so modest," François teased. "We are among friends, after all." He looked at Magnus. "One of his clients liked women too. A female whore gave him syphilis. He had sex with Jack, gave him syphilis. Jack had sex with *everyone*, knowingly giving all his clients syphilis. And they all had sex with us. Now we all got syphilis. Thanks for that, Jack. Thanks for the syphilis."

Jack grimaced. Looked away.

François scoffed. "He's still embarrassed about it, as you can see. He didn't even put it in the book. And he put *everything* in that book!"

Jack stormed off. Pushed through the front door of the Institut. BANG! BANG! BANG! BANG!

Oliver's heart raced at that awful sound. "I'm sorry. He'll just be a moment." He raced outside.

Jack was kicking a garbage bin over and over. BANG! BANG! BANG! BANG!

Oliver pushed Jack aside. "Stop that!" he cried. "What's wrong with you?"

"He's the worst!" Jack yelled at the top of his lungs, his face getting red, the veins on his neck popping out. "That's what he is! The bloody WORST!"

He kicked the bin again. BANG!

"Come on. He was just teasing you."

Jack angrily pointed inside. "That was no tease! That was blatant, cruel, nasty slander right there!"

"Look at yourself. This is supposed to be a happy time. You're getting yourself all worked up."

"He's the one! He started it!"

"Lower your voice. Breathe."

Jack forced himself to breathe slow breaths. "You can see it, right? He still wants the money."

"He doesn't want the money."

"Of course he wants the money! Why wouldn't he? Why else do you think he got Andy to crawl back to his father, huh? I don't care what he says. That whole inheritance trial thing, it was all François's idea. Not Andy's. François's."

"You know how horrible it feels to lose all your money. Hell, I was practically born in that orphanage. I get it too."

"Desperation I understand," Jack countered. "What I don't understand is why he keeps painting me as some evil gay Judas for not throwing my life savings at him. I'm not Charlie. I'm not prepared to just throw my savings away on some foolhardy cause."

"It's not foolhardy."

"It is with François at the helm! He knows what he did wrong. He's only got himself to blame for his brothel going sour."

Oliver hesitated. "It's not *your* life savings, you know."

Jack glared at Oliver. "Don't you dare."

"I'm not saying anything, I'm just…" Oliver shrugged. "I understand why he'd be upset. It's not really your money."

"He didn't know them!" Jack shouted. "*I* knew them. They left everything to me specifically. Not him. Me. That makes it my money. I earned it. The only other person who gets to have any of it is you. He doesn't get to shame me for that!"

Oliver cautiously approached Jack. Held him close.

Jack felt his blood pressure level off. He held Oliver back. "I'm sorry."

"I know." Oliver rubbed Jack's back. "I've already forgiven you."

Jack sniffed. Closed his eyes. Savoured Oliver's warmth. "I just want to see Denny."

"I know."

"I miss him so much."

"We'll be there soon. He's not going anywhere. Don't worry."

Jack swallowed. "God, I'm ruining this whole thing, aren't I?"

"You haven't ruined anything."

Jack sniffed again. "I haven't?"

"You haven't."

"You sure?"

"Absolutely. Everything's exactly the way it was."

Jack nodded. "Thank you."

"Of course." Oliver kissed Jack. Smiled. "I love you."

"I love you," Jack whimpered. He kissed Oliver again.

They walked back inside hand-in-hand and resumed the tour. François said nothing else to them. He knew he went too far bringing up the syphilis like that. But he never admitted it. He never apologised.

After the tour, Jack and Oliver carried their cases to the hotel next door and checked in. Andy and François had the room next to theirs, Mary and Louise the one across the hall. After everyone showered and dressed, they all met up in the lobby so they could head out together.

"What room are Charlie and Denny in?" Jack asked Mary on the walk over.

"Oh, they're not staying here," Mary said. "They practically sleep at that bar these days. You know them. Practically a factory, those two. I'm surprised they haven't dropped dead from exhaustion already."

The six of them left the hotel and made their way across Berlin to the Cosy Corner, Charlie and Denny's cellar bar. The plan was to stay there for dinner and a few drinks before going down to Nollendorfkiez to see something called a "drag show" at a nightclub called Eldorado. Mary and Louise refused to elaborate what a drag show was, but they insisted Magnus and Karl would be there to explain it all with the most up-to-date scientific lingo.

Mary and Louise descended the steps of the Cosy Corner first. The lighting was dim, the air was filled with cigarette smoke. All the boys in the bar had their eyes on the newcomers. Jack felt a familiarity to it, realizing how long it had been since he was last ogled by so many horny men at once. He was so distracted by all that lustful attention that he didn't see Denny standing right in front of him.

"There he is!" Denny cried over the crowd noise with a wide smile. Jack held him tight as Denny kissed both his cheeks. "Oh, I've missed you terribly! You have no idea!"

Jack was ready to cry again. "I missed you too."

"You're sitting next to me." Denny waddled his crutch towards the long eight-man table in the back of the bar adorned with candles. "I want to hear everything."

"We already put everything in the letters."

"I don't care. I want to hear it. It's so much better when I can hear you say it all to me." Denny sat himself down, moving his crutch behind his chair.

"Jack Branson," Charlie Smith said, stepping up to the table. He clapped Jack's hand. Gripped it hard. Pulled him in for a tight, tender hug. "How are you?" he whispered.

"So happy," Jack whispered back.

"I'm happy you're happy." Charlie put both hands on Jack's shoulders. "I've never been happier myself."

"Even with me here?"

"Especially with you here."

"Oh look, the oldest men at the table," François quipped to Mary.

"Seventy's the new twenty, François," Charlie countered, making his way around the table to say hi to everyone. He saved Oliver for last. They stepped away from the table and had a tender conversation, talking quietly, deeply to each other.

Jack admired the two of them from afar. He could only imagine how hard it must've for the two of them to be away from each other for so long. They were all family, of course, but Oliver and Charlie? They were brothers. Real brothers. In every way except literally.

"Alright everyone," Charlie announced, taking his place at the end of the table. "Before the food comes out, I want to say a few words to everyone. I know it's a bit loud in here, but it is a Friday and money is money."

Everyone at the table laughed.

Charlie looked at them all one-by-one, their faces glowing in the candlelight. "Forty years ago today, we started something amazing. We thought we had failed, but now… Look around you."

Jack, Oliver and the others turned their heads. Looked at all those homosexuals around them. Chatting on couches. Ordering drinks at the bar. Making out against the wall.

"It worked," Charlie said simply. "So let's celebrate. We're in the Promised Land, gentlemen. These are the fruits of our labours."

Jack grinned. He held Oliver's hand under the table. Oliver squeezed back.

Charlie's smile faded, donning instead a look of reverence. "Sadly, we're unable to have a perfect reunion today. We've lost a couple of brave men since last we met who deserve to sit at the table with us."

"Here here!" Louise cried.

"And so, to honour them, I've had Denny pour us out a couple shots." Charlie passed rocks glasses to Jack and Denny, the two sitting closest to him, and they passed them down until everyone had two glasses each, one filled with gin and the other with Scotch.

Denny lifted his gin glass. "I think Jack should lead us off with this one."

Jack nodded solemnly. He stood. Picked up his glass of Beefeater. Raised it high. "To Stockley Munce."

"WHO?!" Mary blurted.

"Mr Munce, you moron!" Louise chided.

"His name was *Stockley*?!" Mary cringed. "No wonder he drank this shit."

Jack found himself getting misty-eyed. "He was a really great man. A brave man. And we all loved him."

Oliver smiled. Squeezed Jack's hand for support.

Jack powered through it. "A fantastic postman… And the greatest bloody father anyone could ever ask for."

Everyone nodded at that.

Jack closed his eyes. Said a little prayer. "I really do miss him."

"As do we all." Charlie raised his Beefeater. "To Mr Munce."

Everyone raised their gin. "*To Mr Munce.*" They each downed their shot. Jack felt nothing, having sipped from Munce's bottle many a time, and Denny didn't really mind the taste. Everyone else, however, was absolutely losing their minds.

"What the FUCK was that?!" Mary screeched.

"Tastes like car fluid!" Andy tossed his glass away.

François hacked like a cat. "More like rotten fish."

Louise flat-out yelped at the ceiling.

"That explains *so much*," Charlie grumbled, trying not to vomit.

"It hurts!" Andy screamed, his face still cringing. "Why does it hurt?!"

Louise yelped at the ceiling again.

"It's really not that bad, you guys," Jack said.

"Yeah, it actually is," Oliver mumbled, moving his glass far, far away.

Charlie cleared his throat. "Alright everyone, time to wash it down with the good stuff."

"Thank God," François grumbled.

Charlie stood. Held up his Scotch glass. "Besides Jack, I think it's safe to say I knew Morty Blasmyth the best. What an amazing man he was. A tender man. True man of the cause."

Jack nodded. "Absolutely."

"With the best moustache on the planet," Andy added.

"No one can deny that," Denny said with a laugh.

"And he was the best bloody Commissioner Scotland Yard ever saw," Oliver said.

"Here here!" Louise chimed.

"Absolutely," Charlie said. "During his three-year tenure as Commissioner of Police of the Metropolis, there wasn't a single raid on his watch. Not one arrest. Not one enactment of Labouchere Amendment."

"A true homosexual," Mary added. "One of us, through and through."

"To Morty Blasmyth," Jack declared, raising his Scotch.

"*To Morty Blasmyth.*" They all drank their Scotch. Sat in silence. Savoured every drop.

Jack looked around. There was a sad air at that table. A mournful feeling. Everyone's eyes stared off. Glum frowns. All minds deep in thought.

"May they rest in peace," Charlie said softly.

After dinner, the entourage moved to the Eldorado, where Magnus and Karl were waiting for them. Everyone took their seats and the show, the "drag show," began. A German blonde in men's clothes strutted out on stage. She sang. She danced. She threw out bawdy jokes. Everyone loved her.

"So this is a drag show, huh?" Jack asked Magnus. "A woman wearing a suit?"

"That is not just some woman in a suit." Magnus pointed up at her. "That, Mr Branson, is Marlene Dietrich. Mark my words. Five years from now, every man on Earth will know her name. She is a star in the making!"

Jack nodded, not entirely convinced. "Do men dress up as women here too?"

"Oh yes."

"You think that will catch on in five years too?"

Magnus smirked at Jack. "Don't worry about the future, Mr Branson." He jutted his chin at the stage. "Just enjoy the show while it's playing before you."

"I already do, Doctor. I absolutely do."

The show ended, the entire club cheering like mad for Frau Dietrich. All except Mary. Mary just sat there, shaking his head, unimpressed.

"Why aren't you clapping?" Louise asked him over the applause.

"I don't think women should be wearing men's clothes," Mary shouted back.

Louise stopped clapping. "What?"

"I don't think woman should be allowed to wear men's clothes," Mary said louder. He shrugged. Crossed his arms. "I'm sorry. I don't think it's right."

Louise stared at Mary. "*BITCH?!*"

Charlie looked around the club. "Oh no," he groaned.

Denny looked over. "What?"

"Don't look," Charlie mumbled, facing forward. "Ernst is right behind me."

Denny scoffed. "Oh God. Again? Is he drunk?"

"When's he not drunk?"

François discreetly looked behind Charlie at the small moustachioed German in a brown military uniform. He did look quite brutish. "You know that guy?" he asked Denny.

"Do not look at him," Denny hissed slowly. "Worst night of my life, I'll tell you that."

François cringed. "You and him? Really?"

Denny flapped a hand. "Canteen in the desert. That's not the point. The point is he's insane. I mean actually insane. He tried to overthrow the government a few years ago."

"What?"

"Yeah. And he almost succeeded too." Denny shook his head with a cringe. "Him and his precious 'Adi.' God, he wouldn't shut up about him the whole night."

"Is he a soldier?" François asked, discreetly looking behind him.

"No, he's just a Brownshirt."

"What's a Brownshirt?"

"A conspiracy theorist with muscle." Denny shrugged. "Don't worry. No takes them seriously anymore."

François hesitated. "Anymore?"

"Yeah. After the Kaiser abdicated, men like him tried to take advantage of the unrest. But the economy's fine now. No one has anything to be angry about anymore."

Magnus waved a photographer over. "I hired a photographer," he told Jack and Oliver. "In honour of your first Berlin reunion."

"Oh wow!" Oliver sat up. "Thank you, Magnus."

"You have to be in it with us," Jack told him. "Karl, you too. C'mon."

Magnus shook his head. "No, don't be ridiculous. It's your reunion."

"You're the one that finished what we started." Jack grabbed Magnus's arm. "You're the reason we can even have reunions like this. Please. We'd be honoured."

Magnus nodded. Took Karl's hand. "Alright."

"Everyone!" the photographer shouted over the crowd. "Get into positions."

Charlie, Denny, François, Andy, Mary, Louise, Jack, Oliver, Magnus and Karl all stood and got close to each other. Arms around shoulders. Lovers especially tight with each other. As the photographer stepped back to get everyone in the shot, Denny absentmindedly looked around and made accidental eye contact with Ernst. "Oh, why did I look?!" he hissed at Charlie.

"Denny!" Ernst Röhm slurred in broken English, stumbling towards him. "Beautiful one-leg man."

Charlie stepped away from the group. Stopped Ernst before he could get too close. "Not now, Ernst. He's taking a photo with some friends."

"Let me be in photo."

"It's for friends only." Charlie gently pushed Ernst away. "Come on. You're in our shot."

Ernst grimaced at Charlie. "You know who I am? You know who I'm friends with?"

"Take a photo with him then."

"I want to talk to Denny."

"No!" Charlie said sternly. "He doesn't want to talk to you, alright?"

Jack poked his head out. "Charlie, what's going on?"

"Don't worry. He's nobody." Charlie looked Ernst in the eye. "You're in our shot."

Ernst frowned at him. "How dare you call me nobody. I'm no different from you."

"I know what you are."

"I don't care. I don't care about Negro. I don't care about one-leg man. We all like men. We all same."

"No. Don't pretend you're just that. You're not."

"What I am have nothing to do with this." Ernst grabbed his brown shirt. "I can be both."

Charlie shook his head with pursed lips. "You and I are not the same. Please get out of our shot."

Ernst frowned over at Denny.

Denny wasn't looking back. Intentionally ignoring him.

Ernst look back at Charlie. "Fine. I go. I go." He stepped away.

Charlie sighed. Turned around. Rejoined the gang. Smiled for the camera.

Ernst turned to leave, hurt by the rejection. He stopped. Stared at the camera. Checked to see if Charlie was looking. He wasn't. Ernst slowly crept his way back into frame.

"Alright, everyone!" the photographer announced. He held up three fingers. "*Drei. Zwei. Eins.*"

FLASH!

CHAPTER TWENTY-EIGHT

Olive Branch

Jack was hungover the next day. He was too old to drink like that. His whole body refused to function. As sick as he was, he couldn't vomit. Oliver kissed him in bed and left him to rest.

Jack finally emerged from his stupor hours later. He got dressed and retraced his steps back to the Cosy Corner. It hadn't officially opened yet, the bartenders and the rest of the wait staff being the only men in there, but Jack dropped Charlie's name and was allowed entry.

Jack knocked on Charlie's office door. The man himself was sitting at his desk, reading what looked like vendor invoices, the late afternoon sun pouring in. "Jack!" Charlie stood with a smile. "What are you doing here?"

"Oliver and the others are off exploring the city," Jack said, stepping in.

"You stayed behind?"

"I needed the rest, believe me." Jack sat across from Charlie. Noticed an empty space on Charlie's wall. "You're missing a painting."

"I'm having them blow up that photo we took last night." Charlie sat back down. "I'm really going to miss you guys."

"We'll be back next year."

"I know, but..." Charlie shrugged. "It's just not the same. Even you right now, sitting across from me..." He smiled. "What brings you in?"

"Nothing particular." Jack folded his hands on his abdomen. "Can you believe it's been almost forty years since I last sat in your office like this?"

"God, I know." Charlie sat back, his smiled fading. "I'm sorry I couldn't have been more help with the books."

"You helped plenty. It's not your fault they didn't sell."

"You really are an excellent writer. It's a shame you're not catching on over there."

Jack tried not to react. Played nonchalant. "Never say never. The next one could be it."

"Is there a next one?"

"There will be." Jack took a deep breath in. "I just have to figure out what went so wrong with the others."

"Nothing was wrong with them. It's the industry. American publishing is so different than it is out here. Maybe my advice isn't suited for that market."

Jack shrugged. "Don't blame yourself. That's all I'm saying."

Charlie nodded. "How's Oliver?"

"You saw him last night."

"I mean in general. In America."

"Didn't he tell you already?"

"I know what he told me." Charlie looked Jack in the eye. "You know as well as I do how much that boy likes to downplay things, especially to me. I've always known I can trust you to give it to me straight." He smirked. "I still can, can't I?"

Jack gave a flattered smile. "Of course."

"Then tell me."

Jack looked off, the smile still on his face. "I've never seen him happier. He loves what he does. He's a natural teacher. He still reads. He reads for hours in that library. He loves the other teachers."

"The subject isn't too much?"

"No way. He told me once that history, philosophy, literature, they're easy to teach. It's just names, dates and definitions. But maths is different. The brain has to work to generate the answers. The students have to figure it out all by themselves. And that exercise makes their brains stronger, their minds more absorbent. He's so proud of his boys." Jack paused. "He said it was like you back at that orphanage. He's breaking them out. Giving them a new life."

Charlie nodded. "What about you?"

"We still love each other. He holds me every night, just the way I like it. We go out to dinner a lot. We go to plays. The cinema. He's gotten into base-ball too. He loves the Giants. Huge fan. We'd go to every game if we only had the time. Otherwise, we go on walks. Coney Island. And there's snow there too. It's beautiful. Magical." Jack paused. "It's wonderful. Every day is wonderful.

Charlie looked at him enigmatically. "I didn't mean you and him. I meant you."

Jack hesitated. "What do you mean?"

"Are you happy?"

"Don't I sound happy?"

"Are you?" Charlie's expression turned serious. Genuine. "Are you happy?"

Jack's face went blank. "I'm happy Oliver's happy."

"That's all?"

Jack shrugged. "I'm pretending to be his brother. I'm pretending to be English. I'm pretending to be someone named 'Elliot.'"

"That was your idea, I thought?"

"It is. It was." Jack looked off. "It's justified masochism, is what it is."

Charlie smirked. "It's what?"

"You heard me." Jack smiled too. "Doesn't mean it doesn't hurt."

"What could make it better?"

"Being Jack Branson again with no consequences."

Charlie nodded. "And Oliver knows you want this?"

"Yeah." Jack looked Charlie in the eye. "Of course he does. But what could I do? Use Morty and Munce's money to start a brothel? Take that publisher to court? Win my memoir back? What good would that do? Oliver would get roped in too, wouldn't he? If Columbia finds out he's a homosexual, that's it for him. I can't be the reason he loses his happiness."

"I'm sure he wants you to be happy, Jack."

"He does. He disagrees with me 100%, but, uh…" Jack chuckled a little. "He doesn't deny what it is I'm doing for him. It's a sacrifice. And I do it all for him. I'd do it again in a heartbeat."

Charlie frowned at that.

"Why are you frowning?" Jack asked, forcing a smile. "I'm used to it. I'm used to… settling for less. I've done it my whole life. Any step I take in any direction always seems to cost me something. If I have to do this in order to keep my life exactly the way it is now, so be it. I don't need to sell books with my real name on 'em. Oliver loves my books. That's fine with me. I give Oliver hope. That's fine with me. I don't need friends. I don't need to see you guys every day. I have Oliver. I'm fine with that. I'm happy."

Charlie sighed. "As long as you're happy."

"I AM happy!" Jack scoffed. "Jeez."

Charlie half-frowned. "Now that you're here, I might as well tell you something."

Jack calmed himself down. "Yeah? What?"

Charlie took a deep breath. "You're not going to like what I'm about to say."

"Just say it."

Charlie scratched his head. "I wish I never..." He swallowed. Looked up at Jack. "You were right. I should've kept my name in your book."

Jack groaned. "Not this again. I told you all already! I'm not fighting for it!"

"It's not just you who'd be affected. It's all of us. We're all in that book. Morty too. He deserves to be known as the man that gave us the immunity."

"I don't have any claim to it. You know that."

Charlie opened the bottom door of his desk. Pulled out a manuscript. "You would with this." He plopped the stack on his desk.

Jack stared at it. "What the hell is that?"

"You know what it is." Charlie crossed his arms. Sat back. "One day, no one's going to remember your day in court. Sure, to you it might just be words on a page, but to the margins of history, it's the Holy Grail."

"The book didn't make this happen," Jack said, gesturing around him. "The world doesn't need it anymore."

"You don't know that. What if it's the one thing that turns other cities worldwide into other Berlins? It will outlive you, Jack. It'll outlive me. I don't want to be forgotten. I want people to know who I was, who I really was. You understand that yourself. You have Oliver. I have no one, Jack. No one. No one the way you do. If I died today, I would've died not having held anyone. Never having anyone kiss me the way I'd want them to. You're the only one I can even bear to say these things to. Everyone else needs me to be some activist ideal."

"You don't think Magnus feels the same way?"

"He has Karl! And no, I'm sure Magnus doesn't feel this way because he never made a special point to hide it! He put his name on everything. He did exactly what I tried to do with the Brothel with the WhK, except I beat him to it by an entire decade! Who's going to know that, huh? It's not fair." Charlie shook his head. "It just isn't fair."

Jack frowned. "I guess I didn't think of it like that."

Charlie shook his head. "It would be so much easier if you two just moved out here. You'd sell a million copies overnight. I'd be able to see Oliver. I could feel like myself again with you, and…"

Jack hesitated. "It's not like we haven't been writing each other weekly for the past forty years."

"Yeah, well, that's what I thought too." Charlie huffed. Looked out the window. "I thought it'd be enough. Turns out you're…" He looked into Jack's eyes and said nothing. He just admired his face. His features. His warmth. "It's not the same," Charlie murmured. "You being here is so much better. It made me realise how much I'd been depriving myself."

Jack nodded sadly. "I guess I'm just more used to long distance relationships than the lot of you."

"Guess so." Charlie went quiet again.

Jack looked down at his knees. "Should I not have come?"

"No, I'm glad you did." Charlie smiled. "I won't be able to see you off tomorrow, so I'm glad we had this last chance to—"

"That's not what I meant," Jack whispered. He tenderly looked up.

Charlie's smile went away. He swallowed, haunted eyes staring back.

Jack's blue eyes never left Charlie's.

Charlie lowered his gaze first. "I don't know," he mumbled. And just like that, he returned to those vendor invoices, the manager of the Cosy Corner back on the job.

Jack's heart broke. He cleared his throat. Stood. "See you next year, huh?"

Charlie flipped a page. Didn't look up. "See you next year."

Jack frowned. Looked down at the manuscript. *The Sins of an Irishman in London.* The original unpublished version. He slid the manuscript off the desk. No reaction from Charlie. Jack slowly turned around. Left the office. Left the bar. Walked all the way back to the hotel.

It was near dark when Jack got back to his room. Still empty. Dark. Quiet. What a familiar sensation. Made him homesick. He hadn't felt homesick in years.

Jack lay on the bed. Flipped through that old manuscript of *The Sins of an Irishman in London.* Relived a bit of the good old days. After a bit, he closed it with sigh. Put it down next to him. Stared out his balcony window.

A little red dot glowed out there in the dark. Faded away.

Jack smirked a bit with recognition. He slid off the bed. Stepped out onto the balcony. Stared out at the Berlin skyline at dusk. He looked to his left.

François peered back at him, hunched over his own room's balcony, smoking a fag. "Abandoned by your lover too, huh?"

"They'll be back soon." Jack leaned against the railing. "I've been avoiding you."

"Oh, I know." François took another drag. "Can't say I blame you. I don't seem to know how to shut up."

"No, it's fine." Jack smiled at him. "I just remembered that you and I are in the same situation."

"Is that so?"

"We're both happy exactly where we are. Happy with fine."

"I wish I wasn't fine." François flicked ash over the railing. "But let's not talk about it. I don't want another fight."

"Thank you." Jack paused. "This reunion's a giant sales pitch, isn't it?"

"Absolutely."

"Of course this place is important. It's beautiful. It's remarkable."

"It's reinvigorating," François chimed in. "I think I can do it again this time."

"As you should." Jack took a deep breath. "When I first got to America…" He smirked. Looked at François. "I never told anyone this. Try not to spread it around."

"Oh, now I'm *definitely* listening."

Jack nodded. "When I realised how different New York was, I realised I made a big mistake. All I ever wanted was a simple life. A simple, Irish farmland life. No changes. No tricks. Guaranteed safety. I thought America would give me the opportunity to have that again." Jack shook his head. "There is no place quite the opposite of 'simple, Irish farmland life' than New York fucking City."

François snorted. "I'm sure."

"Everything I hated about life was happening to me all over again. Rebuilding my life? Not only did I have to do it again, I had to come up English. Another fake name. Another lie of an existence." Jack smiled slightly. "But then I realised it *was* going to be different this time. Oliver. He was the missing piece. And oh, what a missing piece he was. Those first few years, what a massive difference it was having him around. Every time I got upset, whenever I panicked about some new thing, some unfamiliar change on the horizon, he knew just what to say."

François nodded, thinking lovingly of Andy.

"He came up with the perfect solution." Jack looked over at François. "Whenever we were out of the apartment together. In public. On the subway. In the park. Whenever I felt a bit too much like Elliot Victor, or Nigel Victor's brother, whatever… He'd look at me. Tell me to breathe. And he'd ask me who he was. And I'd have to tell him."

François furrowed his brow. "'Who he was?'"

Jack nodded.

"Who was he?"

"My Olive Branch," Jack said.

"'Olive Branch?'" François took another drag. "What does that mean?"

Jack looked at François with an almost painfully warm smile on his face. "Oliver Branson."

François was moved by just the way he said it.

Jack nodded proudly. "That's what did it. That was his secret message. That even with all the lies, all the deception, that part was never going to change." He looked back out at the Berlin skyline. His Olive Branch was out there somewhere, having a gay old time. But he'd be back. "He knows me so well, François. He knows how to calm me down. How to keep me level. Just what to say to make me alright again." Jack looked at François. "It's not enough to be the man you're always meant to be. That man has to be witnessed. Complemented. You know exactly what I mean, don't you?"

François took one last drag. "I do," he said uncomfortably, flicking the fag over the edge. Watched it fall, all the way down. "It's why the brothel's so important to me."

Jack uneasily looked away. "I'm sure it is."

"It'd be a place for men like us to be witnessed, Jack. For them to find Olive Branches of their own."

"Don't turn this on me."

"No, I get it. You and Oliver. Andy and I are the same way. Except you and I differ in one regard."

Jack looked behind him. "I really should go back inside…"

"You know the risks and you use them as an excuse to do nothing. I know the risks and I power through them anyway."

Jack tightened his mouth shut.

"You know I'm right," François whispered.

"You don't what it's like to lose someone!" Jack snapped, against his better judgement. "I lost Oliver for four years, remember?"

"I love Andy just as much as you love Oliver. What you have is no bigger or better than mine."

"Don't take him for granted. That's all I'm saying." Jack shook his head. "I know how bad we must look from a distance, sitting in an ivory tower and all, but if you were in my shoes, you'd understand."

"I understand security. I understand guaranteed happiness. I even understand you, Jack. I do. You want to know something else I understand? What it's like to have no money."

"And we're back."

"How difficult it is to hit the bullseye with the first arrow. It takes years to course-correct even the simplest mistakes. You have no idea what that's like, do you?" François tilted his head. "Oh wait. That's right. *You do.*"

Jack glared at him. "Stop."

"Don't you realise I asked *you* for the money and not Charlie because I thought you'd at least understand?"

"Prove to me you deserve the investment!" Jack spat. "Because from where I'm standing, you don't. Alright? You're no Charlie Smith, François. You're no Oliver Hawkett. If I gave you Morty and Munce's money, you'd piss it away in an instant!"

"How am I supposed to prove it to you that I can handle it if you don't give me the chance?!" François snapped back, his voice raised. "Jesus! You FUCKING hypocrite!"

"Face it! You will NEVER be able to recreate Montgomery Street! Those days are never coming back, no matter how hard you try! No matter how much money you throw at the problem!"

"Don't pretend you're better than that! The only reason you're so high and mighty right now is because it all fell into your lap. You never fought for it. You didn't do shit!"

"Says the man asking me for a handout!"

"Believe me, I hate this more than you do." François grimaced. "I wanted to be able to say I did it all by myself. I *need* to be able to do it all by myself."

"Is that so?" Jack looked at François. "You made Andy crawl back to his father for that inheritance."

"That was his idea."

"Don't pretend you didn't encourage him."

"No! As a matter of fact, YOU did!"

"Please."

"He wanted to be just like you. He wanted to wow the jury the way you did. He chose to put himself in that position because he wanted to do all he could to make my dream come true."

"And look what happened. You both got nothing and he got himself disinherited."

"The old bastard bought the courts! The police! The newspapers! At least we tried! If we would've won, we would've won MILLIONS!"

"But you didn't, did you?" Jack shook his head. "Not a shock there."

François was fuming. "You didn't work a single day for Munce's money."

"No! No! No! I DID earn it!"

"No, you didn't."

"I was the only real son he ever had!"

"You stopped being his son the moment you left London. Did you ever come back to visit him? Did you ever write to him? Did he even know you changed your name?"

Jack said nothing to that.

François scoffed. "Though I'll give you one thing. You did work hard to get Morty's... On your knees."

"Shut up."

"Stringing the poor guy along for years. Pretending you loved him."

"Shut your bloody mouth."

"No wonder he left you everything! You let him hit it anytime he wanted to!"

"Shut up!"

"And you loved it, didn't you? You loved being everything that poor man could ever think about all those years later!"

"SHUT UP!"

"You fucking *whore!*"

"SHUT THE *FUCK* UP!" Jack screeched.

François laughed bitterly. "'Shut up,' he says. Believe me, when everyone stops to thinks about it, they will. They'll shut the fuck up about you. Really, Jack. What is it you actually did? You're no writer. Clearly. No wonder your books aren't selling."

Jack grimaced at him. His lip trembled.

François leaned in closer. "Face it. The only thing you ever did was have one lucky day. You sure have been riding it. All those stars aligning like that. Just for a day though. You've never had one since. That's why you don't even want to try for a part two. You know it won't be the same. It'll never hit as hard. It'll never succeed. It'll never be worth it. Plus, you might lose something along with it. Maybe even Oliver. If you didn't know you peaked, it's like you didn't peak, huh? But you did. You know you did. Because on that very, *very* lucky day, you lost. People like to forget that part, but you did. You lost. Because even at your best, you're still not enough. And every day you've only gotten worse." François shrugged casually. "Don't worry. There's a whole new generation of homosexuals who've never had to pretend the way we did. They'll find new heroes to worship. And one day you'll stop screaming 'shut up' at them and start begging for someone to even look at you. Because you are selfish little attention whore that's done nothing to earn that messiah complex you're so addicted to. And yet you downplay it so publicly, for no other reason than how good doing so makes you look. 'Oh he's so humble!' 'Such a martyr!' But you're just telling them what to think, Jack. One day, they'll actually listen to you. They'll start seeing you as I do, as you really are, and they'll stop caring. Because you're exhausting. People love to forget things that exhaust them."

Jack felt sick to his stomach. "You don't know me anymore."

François frowned. Looked down. "Maybe I don't." He looked back up. Faced Jack. "Or maybe I know you so well that I know just what to say to hurt you."

✳ ✳ ✳

Jack took in a slow, deep breath. "That was the last thing he ever said to me." He looked over at Nadine. "When I found out François was going to be at the reunion in '28, I backed out at the last minute. Told Oliver he couldn't go either. So he didn't."

"Did you ever go back?" Nadine asked.

Jack shook his head. "I never saw them again."

Nadine held a hand to her chest, moved. Brian refused to react, still standing against the wall.

Jack sniffed. Hung his head. "The letters stopped a few years after that," he whispered. "From all of them. Denny. Mary. Louise. Andy. Even Charlie. Not one. They just stopped one day." His lip trembled. "What none-none-none of them, what they couldn't understand, I *knew* I didn't have a support system. A real support system. I never did. Not from my family. Not from… from them. Letters. Just letters for years. That was fine with me. For them, maybe not. But I was used to it. It was just a fact of life. I was on my own. I didn't want to burden them with my problems. I had Oliver for that. It really didn't matter. I was supposed to be a farmboy in Ireland. That was supposed to be my life. Just a simple…" He shook his head. "I was forced into a dangerous world. I didn't ask for it. I didn't want it. I knew it didn't suit me. I just read books and did my work. I wasn't an activist. I wasn't a warrior. That wasn't the role I was meant to play. I never thrived in chaos."

Brian's eyes drooped at Jack's words.

"Then I had the ability to choose what I wanted again," Jack continued. "I knew a simple life was better for me. I wasn't naïve. I knew my limitations. I knew skills. I had no shame in insisting on it because I knew it was for the right reasons."

Nadine looked at Brian. Brian sensed her looking, the reason she was looking at him, but he still refused to look back.

"I just naturally assumed that…" Jack cleared his throat. "That a simple world would only generate simple problems. But I didn't realize until they stopped writing how much I took *them* from granted. How much of my soul I'd already given them. Not just them, my community. The fight. How much it all really meant to me. How much they needed me… They're the ones that really knew me. They understood me. I thought I could do it alone, but I was wrong. Because I wasn't really alone back then. I never knew what it was like to be alone, truly alone… until I lost them."

Nadine felt chills. Her eyes drooped, thinking of home, of Roul, of all of them.

"Why was I so ashamed?" Jack asked aloud. "Why was I so proud? So selfish and elitist? Charlie must've been so hurt when I skipped out on the second reunion. Denny too. I can't imagine the web François must've weaved in my absence." He shook his head. "Oliver insisted I was wrong, that there must've been a logical reason for their silence. He kept telling me to hold onto hope. An answer will come one day. But I was there on that balcony. I was there in Charlie's office. I said what I said. I knew what I said. He didn't. Of course I was the reason. Of course it was all my fault." Jack paused. "And even if I didn't believe him, I still depended on Oliver telling me that over and over again because…" His lip bounced across his face, tears in his eyes. He squeezed them shut. Openly wept, sad old man wails, sharp and wheezy.

Nadine moved closer to Jack. Petted his back. Shushed gently. "It's okay," she whispered. "Shh. It's alright."

"And it was so sudden!" Jack cried with a shaky voice. "A heart attack! He just collapsed and… and I-I didn't even get a chance to say how much I…" He sobbed himself into speechlessness. Cried into Nadine's shoulder.

"I'm sure he knew."

Jack shook his head.

"Yes," Nadine said, nodding. "He knew. Of course he knew."

Jack swallowed. Took deep breaths. "Yes. Of course he knew."

Nadine guided Jack's head away. Looked into his eyes. "You know something? Believe it or not, I was just like you once."

Jack furrowed his brow, his face wet with tears and snot. "You were a whore too?"

Nadine smirked. "No. A farmgirl."

"You were?"

Nadine nodded proudly. "But I didn't want to stay there. I wanted to move on to bigger and better things. And then I got my wish. The war came, my family was killed, and I was no longer a farmgirl."

"I'm so sorry."

"It's alright." Nadine took a deep breath. "I found a new family, just like you did. French Resistance fighters. They made me a nurse, far from what I wanted to be, but… It's what they needed from me. And I was actually ashamed of it, even though I was actually good at it. I hated it because it wasn't my idea. I wanted to go back to the plan I had before." Nadine frowned. "First chance I could, I ran. I know I hurt them. I justified it as the right thing at the time, but in truth I abandoned them. I abandoned the fight. I lost my way. For so long, I thought a part of my soul had been destroyed. That it was never coming back." She smiled at Jack. "But now I know what I had with them was real. It wasn't temporary. It wasn't transactional. It was real. It was love. Because they knew me better than I knew myself. We don't like what they see when that happens, do we?"

Jack smirked. "No."

"No. Exactly." Nadine paused. "I know now there's nothing I could've done that would've broken the bond we had before."

Jack shook his head. "But how? How could you know that?"

Nadine hesitated. "Because I still love them. Even after all those horrible things we said to each other, I still need them. And François… François needs you too. Even after all these years, he still needs you."

"But why? Why now? Why only him?"

"I don't know." Nadine wiped Jack's tears away with a gentle thumb. "You'll have to ask him when he gets here. But I'm sure he'll have a perfect explanation."

Jack smiled widely. "You're so perfect, you know that?"

"She really is," Brian finally spoke up.

Nadine looked behind her. Brian was already smiling back at her. His eyes tender and loving. And she realized at that moment was it was like to be loved, just as she was, warts and all. And she realized she loved him back.

Jack gripped Nadine's hand with both hands. "François is at 23 Rue Boissière. That's where his brothel was, at least. He might still be there. Please, find him."

Nadine nodded. "We will."

"Hurry!"

"Of course." Nadine gently stood. Looked at Brian. Led the way. Brian reluctantly followed.

Jack sat in that now-silent apartment and cried. He wasn't alone after all. For so long he thought he was so alone.

CHAPTER TWENTY-NINE

"Heroes"

"The letters stopped coming a few years later and then Oliver died of a heart attack," Nadine concluded, her mouth dry from all the talking.

"And *that's* the Victor Fred knew?" Vicky asked, enraptured by the wild tale. "The one that died in '36?"

"Yes."

Vicky exhaled. "Jeez Louise, what a story."

"We sent the address to Garnier as soon as we could. We should be hearing back in a few days." Nadine looked over at Brian. He was still in that bitter little world of his. "What's with you?" she asked, annoyed.

Brian simply looked up. "What do you mean?"

"You've been like this all day."

"I'm just sick of hearing about him, that's all."

"Sick of hearing about him?" Vicky snorted. "You're the one that came to us! You found him!"

"Yeah, thanks for reminding me," Brian sniped. "It's already bad enough it happened. You have to go ahead and twist the knife too?!"

Nadine's heart skipped a beat at his tone. "Brian, what's wrong with you?"

"What's wrong with me?" Brian parroted, his voice getting louder. "What's wrong with me? I'll tell you what's wrong with me. I've just spent the last six months of my life researching, tracking down names, spending money on books, harassing librarians, losing sleep, my GPA's in the toilet, all because I thought I was saving somebody! I thought I was making a difference! Turns out all I've been doing is reuniting a couple of FAGGOTS!" Brian shoved the table. Vicky's coffee spilled. All the dishes clanged loudly, making Nadine and Vicky flinch. Before they had a chance to react, Brian was on his feet and out the door.

"Brian!" Nadine jumped to her feet. Ran out of the apartment. She could see Brian's head for only a second before it disappeared down the stairs. "Where are you going?!"

In his apartment, Jack read letter after letter in his favorite chair by the lamplight. He could finally see the big picture, that beautiful display of humanity in Nadine and Brian (and William) fighting so hard to reunite him and François. Just then, he heard a knock at the door. That sound used to scare him. Now it only made him giddy.

Jack threw down the letters. Raced to the door. It was that handsome lad from early, Nadine's friend Brian. "Did you find him? François? Did you hear anything?"

Brian glared back at him. Breath steady. Muscles tight. Heart racing. Bile dancing around his throat. "Not yet," he said slowly.

Jack nodded, admittedly disappointed. "I suppose it would be too soon for that."

Brian said nothing. He just stood there in the hallway.

Jack narrowed his eyes slightly. "Do you want to come in?"

"Are you really a homosexual?"

Jack was taken aback by Brian's tone. "I think you should come inside."

"Answer the question."

"Yes. Please come inside. Before someone hears…" Jack swallowed.

Brian tilted his head a bit. "What's the matter?"

"I don't know." Jack's heart was pounding. He let out a sociable chuckle. "You're scaring me a little."

Brian stepped inside. Jack reached over to gently touch his shoulder. Brian instantly dodged away. "Don't touch me!"

Jack let the door close, his eyes on Brian, realizing something was very *very* wrong. "How about I make you some tea?"

Brian stuck a threatening finger in Jack's face. "How about you don't fucking move?" He took a step closer, backing Jack against the wall.

"Please," Jack wheezed. "I don't understand."

Brian watched the fear on the old man's face. He thought it'd feel good, but everything about it felt wrong. Sour. He felt gross. But he forced himself through it. Just being there, with a thing like that, brought back bad memories. All those nights when his father called him over to his beside… when he…

"You…?" Brian stopped talking. His mouth shut tight. His nose breathing loudly.

Jack's eyes studied Brian. He couldn't understand. He so desperately wanted to understand.

"Have you ever…?" Brian stopped himself again.

"Have I ever what?"

"Tell me the truth."

"I will."

"Swear to me."

"I will."

"I SAID SWEAR!"

"I swear!" Jack held up both hands. "I swear I'll tell the truth! I swear."

Brian nodded, hate flowing through him freely. "Have you ever done anything to a kid?"

Jack furrowed his brow ever so slightly. "A kid? No."

Brian saw nothing but honesty in his eyes. "Have you ever wanted to?"

"No, of course not. Why would you think that?"

"Because you're a homosexual."

"I am a homosexual." Jack shook his head. "I don't understand. What does that have to do with kids?"

Brian turned away. Grabbed his hair. Gripped it tight. Pulled it as he paced back and forth. "I don't understand!" he cried, his tough guy act crumbling fast. "That's what… That's what you do. That's what you people do."

"And who told you that?"

Brian hesitated. "My uncle."

"Your uncle?"

"That's what he said. He said homosexuals prey on kids."

Jack hesitated. "And you believed him?"

"Of course I believe him!" Brian cried. "He saved me! He did everything for me!"

"Okay. Good for your uncle." Jack shrugged. "But he's wrong. We don't do that. Pedophiles do that, not homosexuals."

Brian's eyes darted all over Jack's face. Again, no dishonesty in sight. "No, he said homosexuals. I know he did."

"I'm sorry, is your uncle a homosexual?"

Brian grimaced. "What?"

"It's a joke, kid. Is he a homosexual?"

"No, my uncle's not a homosexual!"

"I know he's not. I am. I'm telling you, we don't do that." Jack took a step closer. "Who hurt you, Brian?" he asked gently.

"Who says…?"

"Did someone hurt you?"

Brian swallowed. "Yes."

"Who hurt you?"

Brian closed his eyes. His breath wavered. "My f-father."

Jack's heart broke. "Bloody hell."

"My uncle said it was because of the w-war. It made him homosexual."

"Which is exactly what a man would say if he found out his brother was a pedophile." Jack shook his head. "Nothing can *make* someone homosexual. We're all born that way."

Brian stared blankly. "I don't understand."

Jack sighed, groaning a tad. "Alright. You like girls, don't you, kid?"

"Of course I like girls."

"That girl that was here…"

"Nadine."

"Nadine. You like her, don't you?"

Brian hesitated. "Yes."

"You want to do things to her?"

"Respectful things."

"I'm talking after the respectful things. Nasty things. You want to do nasty things to her too, right? Come on, Brian! You're a young hot man. Decent shoulders. Face of a movie star. Of course you do, don't you?"

"Yes, alright, yes."

"There you go." Jack paused for effect. "Now… Did someone make you feel that way about girls?"

Brian didn't answer.

Jack pursed his lips. "Well, don't think too hard about it. Did someone have to teach you or not?"

"No, I-I guess they didn't."

Jack nodded. "Alright. Now imagine this: what if someone told you're not allowed have sex with girls? Ever?"

Brian swallowed. "Why would they?"

"They find a way. What would you do?"

Brian looked away. Thought it over. "Go through my studies… I guess?"

Jack huffed. "No. Stop. You *want* to have sex with girls, right?"

"Yes."

"You *want* to have sex with Nadine, yes?"

"If she wanted me to."

"I've seen her this afternoon, Brian. Believe me. She wants to."

"She does?"

"Stay with me here."

"Okay."

Jack pointed two fingers toward his eyes. "Look at me."

"I'm looking at you."

"You're looking at me?"

"I'm looking at you."

"Alright." Jack paused again. "If you wanted to have sex… with a girl… with *Nadine*… but you weren't allowed to… for no reason… how would you feel?"

Brian hesitated. Looked off. Scrunched his face a bit.

Jack scoffed. "Oh please."

"Um…" Brian scratched his head.

"Don't hurt yourself now."

"No, it's just…" Brian made reluctant eye contact. "I've never actually *had* sex."

Jack stared. "Oh my God."

Brian looked off again. "I think."

Jack furrowed his brow hard. "*Oh my God.*"

"So isn't it just… exactly the way I am now?"

Jack put his face in his hands.

Brian widened his eyes. "Am *I* the homosexual?!"

"No."

"Was it me all along?!"

"Brian, no. Come here." Jack guided Brian to his favorite chair. Pushed him down into it. "Wait here." Jack waddled to his bedroom. Brian could hear drawers being opened. Papers thrown about. After a few moments, Jack reemerged with a thick stack of papers held together with studs. "This is my memoir: *The Sins of an Irishman in London.*"

"The one Charlie gave you in Berlin?"

"The one and only." Jack looked down at it. Held it out for Brian to take. "Try not to spill coffee on it."

Brian held it with wonder. Like it was a newborn babe. "You want me to read this now?"

"No, you're in my chair." Jack thumbed behind him. Brian jumped up. They traded places. "Go take it to the park or something. Go to bed with it. Take it to the beach. Whatever. Just read it, kid. It'll tell you everything you need to know about people like me. What we are. What we aren't. Might even tell you a thing or two about life. The real world. The world outside of books. You know who also had a problem with that?"

"No."

"Oliver. Oh yeah. Big fiction freak. Couldn't tell the difference." Jack smiled. "And I loved him more than life itself."

Brian flipped a bit through the manuscript. "Are you…? You're not giving this to me, are you?"

Jack didn't react at first. "I admit, I don't know you very well. But I do know a wounded son when I see one. I would know. I was one myself." He looked down at the manuscript with mixed emotions. "I can't seem to make up my mind about that stack of paper. When I wrote it, I thought it would solve all the world's problems. Then I disowned it. Then I regretted it because no one was praising me for how good it was. I put myself in the papers just to get the credit back. Five seconds later, it was taken away again. But this time I hated it. I thought it was prettier than me. More successful than me." Jack paused. "It was when life was a lot more fun. Every day an adventure. Every risk easy to take. You tend to lose that spirit as the years go on. You really shouldn't. You always need that, that risk-taking." Jack paused again. "But if there's one thing that hasn't changed about that stupid book is how badly *other* people seem to need it. Maybe it'll give you closure. Or maybe it won't." He smiled. "I saw a play once with Oliver. Years ago. Back when we first got here. I still remember the opening line: 'The world can be so unbearably cruel, so predictably banal—'"

"'—to the point when a good life seems to hold no purpose!'" Brian had on the widest grin Jack had ever seen. "That's *The Earth Turns Without Us!*"

Jack grinned. "Ah. You're a Hammond fan as well, I see."

"A fan?" Brian scoffed. "Richie Hammond is my favorite playwright of all time!"

"Mine too."

"Really?"

"Of course. He puts Shakespeare to shame."

Brian slapped his knee. "That's what I've been saying!"

"You see *Garden Day* yet?"

"Of course."

"What did you think of it?"

"I loved it. I love everything he does."

"I was actually just thinking about *Garden Day* just before you came in." Jack sat up. "After everything that happened today, I was reminded of the monologue Virgil gave Deirdre at the end of Act II."

"Of course."

"Not a lot of people talk about that scene."

"I agree."

"Let's see if I can remember…" Jack stood. Licked his lips. Held both hands out. Performed: "'What affects our small human lives so are the works of others. Simply others. Simple others. When we hurt, when we do wrong to our brother, we put bad out in the world, and that bad latches itself onto another poor soul and does its worst. But when we heal, when we save, when we love, somehow it finds its way back to us. In those moments, it's clear to some that the best parts of life come from others. Simply others. Simple others. The hearts of others. The same others that have the power to hurt us.'" Jack smirked at the sight of Brian's enthused grin. He placed a comforting hand on his shoulder. "'We are not the heroes of our stories, Deirdre, but the heroes of others'. Merely players in a single solitary tale in scenes unseen by time. Without direction, without notes, without lines, except for the ones we write for ourselves.'"

Brian applauded as Jack gave melodramatic bow gestures. "I believe that last line is supposed to be 'the ones we write ourselves,' not *for* ourselves.'"

"Alright, smartypants, you get the picture." Jack walked into the kitchen. "I'm getting some water. Would you like some?"

"No thank you." Brian hesitated. "Hey, what year did you say you and Oliver saw *The Earth Turns Without Us*?"

"I remember it was right after Munce died, so… '97 or so? Sometime around there?"

"Really? That long ago?"

"Definitely."

Brian blinked, confused. "Richie Hammond's that old?"

"Mmm-hmm."

"That's odd. I could've sworn he was only a few years older than me."

"Back then, he was. We met him once after the show. You could really do that in those days. Handsome fellow. Gay too."

Brian's face went numb. "Wait, really?"

"Yup. Gay as a Christmas goose." Jack poked his head out of the kitchen. Flashed Brian a cheeky grin. "Good thing you didn't put any money on that one. You would've lost." He winked. Returned to the sink.

Brian half-frowned. Looked down at that manuscript in his hands. "Yeah," he murmured. "I guess I would have."

Three days later, Nadine sat uncomfortably in her kitchen. She hadn't heard from Brian since he stormed out. She felt helpless. She had a feeling Jack's homosexuality made him uncomfortable, but she didn't know how to help.

A knock on the door made Nadine jump up, full alert. Sure didn't sound like Vicky. She ran to the door. Opened it. It was Brian. He had a big stack of papers in his hand. "Good afternoon," Brian said, much calmer and demurer this time.

Nadine had to process the change. "What is that?" she asked, pointing to the manuscript.

"Jack's memoir." Brian stepped into the apartment. "I went to see him the other day when I stormed out of here."

"You did?"

"Yeah. We had a good talk." Brian gently placed the manuscript on the table. "That Jack is an amazing man. I can't believe it."

Nadine blinked. "Okay, what happened? What changed?"

Brian shrugged. "I read it."

Nadine looked down at the manuscript. "You read it?"

"It didn't explain why my dad did what he did, but… Now I know he wasn't a homosexual. It's probably just how he fizzed."

Nadine furrowed her brow. "What?"

"Something in the book. You should read it. No rush, of course." Brian petted the title page with a single finger. "Remember when we first met? That first conversation we had? You were saying something how… because of the war, there's this stillness over everything? The world's just stopped? Something like that?"

Nadine nodded.

"Well, I realize now what was going on inside myself." Brian nodded shamefully. "In a way, I was holding myself down the way you were. Until I had answers. Why it happened to me. My uncle just gave me an answer. It wasn't a good answer, of course. He was just downright incorrect, and it almost got someone hurt."

"What do you mean?"

"Ignore that," Brian said quickly. "I simply needed to free myself. And all this time, I thought my job was to free you. That's why I needed to find Jack for you. Because doing so would free you. Free you from all that guilt you were carrying inside you. So you could resume your life again." Brian paused. "What I did for you, Jack just did for me. And when they find François, he's going to do the same to Jack. All these wars in us, these wars we thought nobody else cared about, they're all resolving themselves. We weren't alone after all, it seems. But none of that, *none of it*, would've happened if I hadn't met you. If you hadn't carried it within you for so long." Brian moved a hand to Nadine's cheek. Caressed it with his thumb. "I wasn't meant to save you, Nadine. You're the one that ended up saving me."

Nadine smiled warmly.

Brian smiled back. "You're my hero." He moved in to kiss her.

Vicky burst open the apartment door. "Nadine! Brian!"

Brian and Nadine snapped back to reality. Stepped away from each other. Deflated hard with disappointment.

Vicky stayed in the hall, a teasing grin on her face. "Didn't realize I was interrupting *Gone with the Wind*."

"What is it, Vicky?" Nadine asked, out of breath.

Vicky whipped up an open telegram. "Garnier found him! He's alive!"

"What?!"

"François's alive! He's still in that old house! He's safe!"

Nadine put both hands to her mouth and squealed. "Oh, thank God!" she cried, grinning like mad.

Brian didn't react at all. "Vicky, we were in the middle of something. Can you please give us a moment?"

Vicky raised a brow. "Excuse me?"

"Thank you." Brian nudged the door closed.

Vicky gaped at them. "But this is my apartment—?!" The door slammed shut.

Nadine laughed. Brian put his eyes back on her, his debonair charm resumed. "Where were we?" he whispered.

"Here." Nadine closed her eyes as he planted one on her. He pulled her in and she kissed him back. He had one arm around her shoulders, another on her waist. Her leg even popped. It was that good.

CHAPTER THIRTY

The Ark that Jacques Built

Jack, Nadine and Brian waited beside a runway at Floyd Bennett Field. Nadine's sundress fluttered in the wind. She had to hold her hat down. Brian checked his watch, squinting in the sun. Jack sat on the hood of a nearby Jeep, his mind far away with an uneasy look on his face.

Nadine suddenly looked up and pointed. "There it is!"

Brian whipped his head up at the sky. Jack saw it too. The old man slid gently off the hood, his mouth open with wonder.

An all-black Lysander overshot their position, its engine roaring as it passed. It made a left turn, lined itself with the runway, and began its descent. It landed gently as the military men of New York's Naval Air Station guided it to the designated point, the spot Jack, Nadine and Brian were waiting at. They stood in a line as the Lysander got closer and closer. Nadine and Jack were especially nervous. Brian, despite having no emotional stakes in what was to come, was nonetheless in awe. He just knew history was about to play out before him.

The Lysander came to a complete stop. Its engine turned off. Its door opened and two men stepped out, the pilot helping the feeble passenger down the plane steps. When they got to the ground, they removed their helmets.

Nadine put on her bravest face for the very tired but otherwise healthy Roul Lesauvage. Roul almost didn't recognize her at first. The woman standing before him looked so cosmopolitan, so confident, so… American. But he knew it was her and was filled with a deep pride that cut through his shame and sorrow. He gave her a humble nod that doubled as a salute.

At the same time, Jack watched François Brion slip off his helmet, frazzled from such a terrifying experience. His black face was noticeably gaunt from years of malnutrition. His wrinkled eyes squinted in the cloudless summer sky. He didn't recognize any of the people standing before him, especially the younger ones.

"Monsieur Brion," Nadine said in French, stepping forward. "Welcome to New York. How was your journey?"

François looked at Brian. His clothes. His face. For a second he thought it might've been him.

"Monsieur Brion?" Nadine asked again.

"Where's William?" François asked her in French.

Nadine didn't answer. She looked at Roul.

Roul knew what she was thinking. He half-shrugged.

Nadine frowned. "Monsieur Brion, my name is Nadine Sauvageot. I'm sorry to be the one to tell you this but… William Gunnison was killed about two years ago."

François stared at her. His face laxed. His eyes slightly widened. He exhaled shakily, not too different from that wind buffeting around him. "I was wondering why…" He frowned.

"I was a very good friend of his. I know he wanted to help you. If you had any idea what he went through to try and…" Nadine paused. "He was a great man. You would've been proud of him."

François closed his eyes. "How? How did it happen?"

Nadine hesitated. "He got captured by Nazis and was executed."

François nodded. "Nazis are killing everyone these days, huh?"

Nadine didn't say anything.

François finally noticed the old man standing beside Brian. He froze. Jack. And he was alone.

Jack frowned back.

François tenderly waddled over, his shoes scraping the asphalt. Even Brian could sense the pain between them. The regret. The shame. The sorrow. François stopped before Jack. Said nothing. Neither did Jack. They just stood there, staring at each other.

"I'm sorry about Andy," Jack whispered.

François nodded. "I'm sorry about Oliver."

Jack put his old arms around François. François put his old arms around Jack. And they hugged, not as tight as they used to, and yet no army would be able to tear them apart.

Nadine looked away out of respect. Faced Roul instead. He was on the verge of tears himself. "Thank you for this," Nadine told him. "I know you didn't have to."

"I wanted to," Roul insisted. "I needed to. To make up for William."

Nadine had to look at the ground to stop from crying. "I'm sorry I said all those things."

Roul gave her a big hug. "I'm sorry too."

Nadine lost himself in his embrace. She closed her eyes.

"Not a day's gone by when I haven't missed you silly," Roul whispered to her. "I'm so glad you're okay."

Brian watched Nadine and Roul's tearful embrace. Looked over at Jack and François, their tearful embrace. And he felt the strangest sense of jealousy. He wished he had someone in his life, someone just his own, that he could tearfully embrace like that. But at the same time, he reminded himself that these reunions, these long overdue recouplings, all came at a painful price. Wasted years. Wasted time. Awful pain caused by thoughtless words. These relationships, though healed now, at long last, had once been fractured. And so he considered himself one of the lucky ones, and he swore never to damage a relationship to the point where a tearful reunion was the only way back.

The five of them relocated inside the airbase itself. While Jack and François spoke to each other in private, Nadine, Brian and Roul had a conversation at the opposite side of the lounge.

"This is Brian," Nadine told Roul in French.

Roul gripped Brian's hand. "Captain Lesauvage."

Brian winced. Tried to break free. "Nice to meet you."

Roul pulled Brian in. Threw on an intimidating scowl. "What are your intentions with my daughter?" he asked in French.

"Roul!" Nadine playfully smacked Roul in the shoulder.

"What did he say?" Brian asked.

Roul chuckled. Let Brian go. "Can't blame me for trying."

"What is he saying?"

Nadine laughed. "Are you alright?" she asked Brian in English.

Brian nursed his soft hand. "It's fine, it's just…" He looked at Nadine. "His calluses have calluses."

"What's all this I hear about a letter?" Jack asked François on the other side of the room.

François's brows moved together slightly. "You never got the letter?"

"It got destroyed, apparently. William stepped on a landmine two days after you gave it to him. They say it was a letter of instructions?"

"No. I only told William that so he'd make sure it got to you safely."

"Great job."

François rolled his eyes.

"What was in it then?" Jack asked.

François hesitated. "We can talk about it later." He looked over at Nadine and Brian. "If the address got destroyed, how did they find you?"

"Nadine was William's nurse after the landmine. He told her some things about you, apparently. She used what he told her to get as far as New York. Then she met Brian and told him everything William told her, and Brian figured the rest out from there. You know what did it? The Nazi in our reunion photo."

"That guy?"

"Yeah. Ernst something? Turns out he's more famous than the lot of us combined. Oliver's name was on some list somewhere out here and they cross-referenced that with Ernst's movements. But how did he know about the photo?"

"William must've told Nadine about it."

"You showed him the photo?"

"The big one Charlie used to have in his office." François hesitated. "After about a year of not hearing from you, I started getting worried something had happened to William. He had told me it was a bad idea keeping a photo of Ernst in the house, so I burned it."

"That's alright. I still have mine."

"Good.

Jack suddenly got uncomfortable. "Why was Charlie's big copy in your house?"

François didn't answer.

Jack inhaled sharply. His whole body started to ache. "You're right. We should talk about this later."

"Do you make her happy?" Roul asked Brian in French.

Brian blinked at Nadine's translation. "Why are you asking me?" he asked back.

"Answer the question, boy. Do you make her happy?"

Brian gaped a bit at Nadine.

Nadine raised her brows back. "Well?" she asked in English. "Do you?"

"Don't I?" Brian asked nervously.

Nadine smiled. "Yes." She beamed at Roul. "Yes, he does," she said in French.

Roul nodded. "Then of course I approve."

Jack and François joined the others. "I need food and coffee," François announced.

"Don't worry, we know just the place," Brian told him.

"Can you stay for some coffee?" Nadine asked Roul in French. "Or food? You must be starving."

"I cannot, I'm afraid," Roul told her. "I have a long journey ahead of me." He looked at François. "I can assure you, Monsieur Brion, as long as there's a French Resistance, your house and its contents will be protected."

François looked uneasily at Nadine. "You were William's friend. Can I trust him?"

Nadine looked Roul right in the eye. "Entirely."

Roul's heart leapt at that. He gave one last salute to Nadine and ran out onto the runway. Nadine and Brian watched Roul hop back into his plane, lock his helmet on, and take off. The black Lysander soared through the skies over them back the way it came.

Brian and Nadine took Jack and François to that corner diner near 7th Avenue, the one Nadine worked at. There they filled up on good food and coffee, the most their ration cards would allow. Jack and François did most of the talking. Anecdotes of the old days. Stories of that old curmudgeon Mr. Munce. The rocky start to Jack and François's friendship. What it was like being a brothel whore. Their bawdiest, raunchiest nights in that old house on Montgomery Street.

Nadine accidentally let slip that she used to have a bawdy profession herself. The conversation pivoted on a dime, Jack and François asking plenty of questions about her former career as a stripteaser. At first she was uncomfortable bragging about such a thing, but Jack and François's eager questions and excitement at the dirty details allowed her to see the humor in it, all that hard work she put in. That gave her a semblance of closure to the whole ghastly chapter of her life.

The last of their plates were taken away, the conversation dwindling on embers. As they finished their watered-down coffee refills, a solemn silence fell over the foursome. It was time at last. Time to breach the topic they had been trying to avoid all night.

No one wanted to be the one to ask François outright, so they just stared in space. Uncomfortable frowns on their faces. François looked at Jack. Jack looked back. He didn't want to hear. He didn't want to know anymore. He wanted to stay in ignorance. Lost in that wonderful world of their memories. For a moment, François wanted to give him that. Or maybe even lie. Say they all ended up okay. A happy ending after all. But alas, he simply didn't have it in him to fib. He only had to give the truth once, but give it he must.

François took Jack by the hand. Held it for strength. Looked across the booth at those gentle souls staring back at them. They'd already come this far. And so François began that woeful tale of his, the tale he wrote out on paper the night Andy died. No one follow-up questions. The waitress never came by with their bill. François simply told his dour tale in one uninterrupted burst.

"I wanted to apologize to you sooner. The next reunion. The sooner the better. Safe to say, you and Oliver not being there put a pall over everything. It was all we could talk about. I didn't say anything about our fight, but I was very unhappy you weren't there. I didn't go to any more reunions after that one. Honestly, I don't even know how many more there were after that. I was too busy with Paris. I asked Charlie for a loan at the '28 reunion and that allowed the brothel to have a bit of a revival, you see. Just like it was in the old days.

"Of course Berlin was still miles ahead of us. By '29 they even had a gay rights organization, the League for Human Rights or something like that. Denny and Charlie were part of it. Even that Nazi in the photo, Ernst Röhm, was a part of it. But everything changed after the Depression. Hitler rose to power. I stopped hearing from all of them the same time you did. It had nothing to do with you, Jack. No one blamed you. No one knew the reason you didn't come back in '28. They just assumed Oliver couldn't make the trip because of work, or maybe you missed your connection like you almost did the last time, or you were simply unable to get boat tickets. Something else. They never would have known it was because of a fight between us. But it was strange to me how sudden their silence was. One letter a week, maybe two, then nothing? Something had gone wrong. It took me years to find out what happened.

"The trouble started when a group of Nazi university students stormed the Institut back in '33. Magnus was out of the country on a speaking tour. Mary and Louise got beaten up pretty bad. Rooms were smashed in. All his books removed. Then the police came and shut the whole thing down. Forever, they said. Four days later, they burned all the books from Magnus's library. All that research on homosexuality, transvestism, gender theory, sexology, everything. And they shut down all the bars too. Eldorado. The Cosy Corner. After Hitler took power, it seems, they started enforcing Paragraph 175 again. The lucky ones got out as soon as they could. Mary and Louise fled to Austria. They thought they'd be safe there. But Denny and Charlie chose to stay in Berlin. They wanted to wait it out. Thought the Nazis were just some temporary fad. Sooner or later it was all going back to the way it was before, and they'd be there when it happened, ready to reopen again. But there was something else keeping them there. Denny had heard rumors of 'pink lists,' names of gay bar proprietors and regulars, taken during the German Republic days. Denny and Charlie ran the Cosy Corner, so chances were good they were on a list somewhere. Andy and I might've been too. Maybe even you and Oliver. I don't know. They might not even be real. Either way, they were real enough for Denny and Charlie. They couldn't risk our letters to each other tracing their way back to Charlie. Nazis opened all the letters going across Germany, you see. Charlie had no choice but to stop our forwarding. No letters no more, to no one. That's why it stopped. It stopped for all of us.

"The last I heard from Denny was in 1938, just after the *Anschluss*. Charlie's death notice. It was old age, thankfully. It's that letter that gave me the answers I needed about the post stoppage, the Institut, what happened to Mary and Louise, all that. Charlie left us all a lot of money, you see. Denny knew how dangerous it was for him to break the radio silence, but he wanted to at least let me know about the money. He knew how much I needed it.

"He ended the letter by saying was going to notify Mary and Louise next about Charlie's death and the money, followed by you and Oliver. Only then would we be able to get our share of Charlie's estate. Andy and I waited desperately for the follow-up. Months went by. Nothing. Then we got a letter from Mary of all people, hiding out in the Austrian countryside. They got Louise, he said. They were supposed to get Mary, but Louise had taken his place somehow. It was a very erratic letter. I couldn't understand what he meant. But he needed us to drive to his hideaway and smuggle him out of Austria as soon as possible.

"I wanted to go, but Andy told me to stay. He was right. If I had crossed the border, they would've marked me suspicious the moment they saw my skin. Even though Andy was American, he was still a Baxter, even if his family refused to acknowledge it. They had all become Nazi sympathizers at that point. A Baxter son roaming around German circles would not have been seen as strange. And so he kissed me goodbye, got in the car, and drove himself all the way to Austria.

"Andy was gone for almost a year. I was so scared, convinced something had happened to him. I was practically losing my mind in that old house. Bouncing off the walls. But then one day, I saw that old car drive down the road and it was Andy. Andy was back. He was fine. He was safe. I was so happy, Jack, I nearly cried. I realized what you meant, what you said during our fight, how I never really almost lost Andy. I had tasted what that world would've been like, and I vowed never to take him for granted again.

"But Andy was alone when he returned. Mary wasn't with him. I asked what kept him so long, and he told me the delay was due to him having to be especially careful out there. Strategic. His name got him into deep places, Nazi strongholds. He was able to get the whole story. What happened to the others.

"It was that death notice to Mary and Louise that did it. The moment it crossed into Austria, the Nazis had it in their possession. Denny's name was on a pink list after all. They found his hideout in Germany. Arrested him on sight. Andy never learned what they did to him to make him give up Mary's real name, George Belcher. But even then, it wasn't enough. They shot him. Andy told me they typically didn't kill homosexuals on the spot. Most times they sent them to the concentration camps or the German front lines. That's not why they killed Denny. Not because he was gay. They killed him because he was a cripple.

"They came for Mary next. Somehow—and I still don't know how—Louise found out their plans and managed to take Mary's place. Passed himself off as Georgie Belcher. Mary never would've allowed it, but that's apparently what happened. They sent Louise to a concentration camp. I think he thought he might've thought he had a better shot in a place like that, being a bigger guy and all, but he didn't make it long where he ended up. It might've been starvation or the harsh working conditions or the disease… It didn't matter. Louise didn't last six months.

"When Andy got to Mary's hiding spot, all he found was an empty cabin with a few boxes, half the stuff they used to have in their flat at Saltzburg. Why only half, Andy didn't know. Mary was nowhere to be found. Maybe he ran. Maybe he got caught traveling back and forth. Maybe he changed his mind and tried to go after Louise alone. I don't know.

"Andy waited around for days. Mary never came back. That's when Andy decided to stay out there a bit longer, to find out everything he could. But he knew he might've been on a pink list somewhere as Andrew Baxter, and any Nazi checking in with another prominent Baxter about their cousin would know he had been disinherited for homosexuality. So Andy had to pretend to be another Baxter, a distant relative no one had heard of. He looked like a Baxter. He knew secrets only Baxters would know. So he took Louise's Austrian citizenship papers from Mary's things and took them to a forger. Changed 'Corey Kehoe' to 'Corey Baxter.' Suddenly he was a proper Baxter again.

"As Corey Baxter, Andy traveled all over German occupied lands. He went to Berlin first. Emptied Denny's flat. Got most of Charlie's things. He inquired to the police. Got a tour of Louise's concentration camp. He found Mary's flat in Saltzburg. He was so brave, my Andy. A true Baxter if ever I saw one. I couldn't have been prouder. Throughout all his travels he looked for Mary, but still… nowhere to be found. No trace in sight.

"Andy spent his last months gathering all of their things. Denny's. Charlie's. Mary's. They had destroyed most of Louise's possessions when they arrested him, so there wasn't much of his left to get. His wigs. His dresses. All photos of the two of them. Gone. Anything that survived was just Mary's. Andy took his time. Filled that cabin in Austria with the lot of them. As much as he could fit. The rest he had stored in Berlin. They were going to give Denny and Charlie's flat away to some Nazi commander, but Andy managed to get it for himself.

"When he got everything he could get, when it was all safe somewhere, he drove back to Paris and told me everything. He needed my help getting all those boxes back to the brothel. We had all those empty bedrooms we weren't using. It would be safe in Paris, just until the end of the war. But I had to pretend to be his butler in order to travel with him, which meant I needed an alias of my own. I chose your name, Jack. I realized in those dark days of my isolation how much I loved you. How little I had respected you before. Why? Because you had more money than I did? What was money when men like us—right after the most accepting and tolerant era for homosexuals—were being rounded up like dogs? I needed your strength. I needed your courage. And so I became Jacques. I took my lover's hand and we drove headfirst into the Beast.

"It took weeks to get what we could into Paris. Multiple trips. That last time we drove into Paris, a swastika was hanging from the Eiffel Tower. The Nazis had taken Paris. The occupation had begun. Andy wanted us to keep going, but I couldn't. There was no safety anymore. I realized then firsthand what you meant before, why you were so insistent on not opening a brothel of your own in New York. You were right. How easy it was for me to judge you from the outside. I knew then what I would've done in the same situation. Living in a city that hated men like me. Under a fake name no less. I chose to do nothing, just like you did. We holed ourselves up in our own little world. Lived our happiest lives in private. How happy I was in those last few months, just like you were. I couldn't do anything to risk losing him again. I just thought if I stayed in there, Andy leaving only to go to the market, that we'd be safe. But then I heard William knocking on the door, standing with Andy in his arms, the love of my life bleeding out, and I realized how wrong I was. Andy had told William not to take him to the hospital, just in case they found out his occupation ID had been forged. They would've taken me too. He knew that. So I called Doctor Gateau, that sexologist we used in our brothel's early days. He knew our secret. I knew we could trust him. But he wasn't a proper surgeon. I should've thought of that.

"In our last hour together, Andy thanked me for everything. He said it was such an adventure being my partner, my lover. He got to see the world. Feel like a man. Like a real Baxter. He said he regretted nothing. That he loved me eternally. He told me not to be afraid. That I could handle it. Because I was François fucking Brion, the greatest man he ever knew. And the last thing he ever said to me… he made me promise to make up with you, Jack. However I could. Because you knew me just as well as Andy did. And you loved me, faults and all, just like he did. That I needed to put aside my gripes and make peace with you while we still had time.

"And so I asked William to deliver my letter of apology. I couldn't send it out blindly and risk the Nazis coming for me. I might've been on a pink list myself somewhere, or maybe Denny gave me up in that same interrogation, or they knew about me from Charlie's mailing records, or they got my name from Louise, Mary, either of them. I couldn't risk it. I knew I could trust William after what he tried to do for my Andy." François smiled at Nadine and Brian. "I told him not to tell anyone a thing, especially the French. But I'm so very glad he did."

Nadine and Brian smiled back, their hearts wrecked by the story.

Jack was devastated in his own way, but more than anything he was relieved. He had born such guilt out of his family's silence. Now he knew Oliver was right. It wasn't his fault. They really did love him all this time.

François took a deep breath. Looked at Jack. "It's all still at the house. Charlie's things. Denny's. Mary's. What little I have of Louise's. Andy's. All our letters. Photos. Documents. Mary and Louise hid a lot of stuff from the Institut among their junk. Proof it existed. Proof Berlin was once a homosexual's metropolis. That such a thing actually happened in our lifetime. The Cosy Corner. Eldorado. It was all real, not just a daydream. And our Brothel as well, the one on Montgomery Street. Charlie had so much. We all thought it was junk when we had our freedom. We used it to line our drawers. To pad our boxes. Now it's the most valuable treasure in the world. More valuable than even our memories of them."

Jack frowned back. He thought of what Charlie said about his book.

François tried to hold back tears. "And so I've come here to ask you to forgive me." He swallowed. "And to ask if you could be *my* Olive Branch."

Jack nodded. "Absolutely."

François smiled back.

Nadine and Brian held hands. Looked into each other's eyes, both thinking the same thing: never to take each other for granted.

François sniffed, his cheerful demeanor finally allowed back in. "You know the reason we needed Doctor Gateau in the first place was because Jack gave us all syphilis back at Montgomery Street."

Nadine and Brian's mouths dropped. "WHAT?"

Jack grimaced. "Goddamn it."

"You never told them either, huh?" François asked with a smirk. "He left it out of the book too."

Jack rubbed his eyes. "Listen…"

"He told us you fought at the Institut about something," Nadine said. "I did think it was weird that he glossed over that part after telling us so much."

"He's always been embarrassed about it," François said.

"*For the record*," Jack said sternly, "I never gave it to any of them directly."

"No, but you did get it from one of your clients and knowingly gave it to the rest of them."

"I didn't knowingly give anyone anything. I didn't know what syphilis was. *And*, mind you, since the reunion in Berlin, penicillin has been invented. Everyone's been inoculated as far as I know, so it's no longer an issue."

François scoffed. "Doesn't change the fact that you were careless."

Jack sat back. Smiled at Nadine and Brian. "Maybe you didn't get it from my clients."

François whipped his head at Jack, his white eyes wide with fury. "You shut your mouth."

Nadine grinned. "What?"

"Nothing. Ignore him."

"No," Jack teased François. "No need to be so modest. We are among friends, after all."

Brian bounced a finger between the two of them. "What, you mean you two—?"

"Never happened!" François snapped.

Jack gestured a calm hand. "Granted… we were drunk."

"Shut up," François scolded.

"And I hadn't gotten back with Oliver yet—"

"SHUT UP!"

Jack got really close to François's face and hissed, "*And I wanted a taste of THE DARK MEAT!*"

Nadine and Brian laughed.

François glared back at Jack. Shook his head. "You insufferable slut."

"Well?" Nadine eagerly asked.

Jack looked back casually. "Well what?"

Nadine shrugged, trying not to be so vulgar. "What did it taste like?"

"What do you *think* it tasted like?"

Nadine covered her mouth, trying not to cackle.

"Chocolate?" Brian asked. Nadine snorted behind her hand.

Jack gave François a disappointed frown, trying his hardest not to break. "I wish!" He snorted too. His face tightened. His head twitched. His lungs unable to breath. His entire body shaking from the biggest laughing fit he's ever had. "*LICORICE!*"

Nadine, Brian, and Jack broke out into the most vulgar display. The loudest snorts. Laughs. Cackles. Guffaws. Going on and on for far too long. Loud enough for the whole diner to hear, with no shame whatsoever. François only sat there, judging them all with blank eyes and a default frown. As Jack came back down to Earth, François was staring at him, but once Jack was stable enough to finally open his eyes, François let slip the subtlest of smiles. Just a simple message between old friends: *I've missed this.* And Jack smiled back, only for a second, an equally simple response: *Me too.*

Jack unlocked the door to his apartment. François cautiously stepped in. "It's not bad," he murmured, turning his head around the corner. "Smaller than my last place. But I suppose it's enough for two."

"That was the idea." Jack turned. Nadine and Brian were still standing in the hallway. "Would you like some tea?" he asked them.

"No, it's alright," Nadine said cordially. "We'll let you be. It's been a long day for all of us."

"Just wait one moment then." Jack retreated into his bedroom.

François wandered over to Nadine and Brian. "I suppose I have to share a bed with him."

Nadine smirked. "I'm glad you're finally here."

"I can't believe I actually am." François allowed himself some real vulnerability for a second. "It hurts my heart to think of that brave young man... I never got a chance to thank him for everything he did for me."

Nadine's face turned serious too. She looked at Brian.

Brian nudged his brows up, a silent act of encouragement.

Nadine swallowed. "François, there's something you need to know about William. Something he should've told you at the time."

"What is it?"

Nadine hesitated. "William was the one that shot Andy. It was an accident."

François stared back with cold eyes. His face was unreadable.

"He was chasing a Nazi and shot first around a corner and..." Nadine paused. "Andy was just in the wrong place at the wrong time."

Pain crept into François's eyes. He lowered his head. Let out a single hard sniff. "Thank God," he mumbled. "I thought he acted out when he shouldn't have. That wouldn't have made any sense. My Andy never would've been so careless." He nodded with a smile of relief. "Now I know he didn't do anything wrong after all. A Nazi didn't shoot him. Thank God."

Brian awkwardly looked at Nadine.

"See, that's the thing…" Nadine fiddled with her fingers, trying to get it out. "He *was* a Nazi."

François shook his head. "No, he wasn't."

"He was," Brian said.

"His real name was Wilhelm Gunter," Nadine added. "I assure you, he was."

François kept staring at Nadine. "No," he said softly, sweetly. "He wasn't."

Nadine's shoulders relaxed. A toothless smile crept across her face. "I suppose he wasn't."

François nodded gently, as graceful as a bow.

Jack returned to door with an old cigar box held together by many thick rubber bands. "I wanted to give you something," he told Nadine and Brian. "As a token of my appreciation."

"It's alright," Brian said. "It was nothing, really."

"I wouldn't be so quick to say no if I were you." Jack held the cigar box under his arm. "François and I were talking, and…"

"When Charlie died, he left everything to the rest of us, to be evenly split seven ways," François interrupted. "We're probably not going to be able to get anything until the war ends, but because the other five died before they got theirs, Charlie's will dictates their portions are to fold into ours."

Jack nodded. "But we both agreed we don't need any more than our initial share, so… we think you two should have the rest."

Nadine didn't know what to say. She only looked at Brian.

"H-how much are we talking here?" Brian asked, trying to downplay his excitement.

"Oh, uh…" Jack looked at François. "His family was old money…"

"But then the Depression took a chunk out of it," François said. "And with all the taxes, death duties, debts, *et cetera*, there can't be more than…"

He bobbed his head, trying to give an honest ballpark. "A couple million or so left?"

Nadine and Brian almost fainted. "A couple million?" Nadine asked.

"That doesn't include the castle in the Highlands," François said, "the flats in London, Venice, Vienna, the painting collection of his grandmother, all his family's stock in war bonds, munitions, communications, aviation… that would all have to be calculated and appraised, so… Who knows until then."

Nadine couldn't breathe. She tried not to smile too big. "That's, uh… very generous."

"You've done so much for us these past two years. All those sacrifices you must've made. It's only fair."

"But until then, I think you should have this." Jack removed the cigar box from under his arm. Handed it to Brian. It was heavier than it looked. "I've never been able to trust other people with my money. Force of habit, it seems. I've always said there's nothing more secure than an old cigar box under your mattress to keep your savings. It's even Depression-proof."

Brian unwrapped one of the rubber bands. Peeked inside. Lots of chaotic dollars. Hundred dollar bills. Too much to all fit in there.

"That's every penny Mr. Munce and Morty Blasmyth left me after they passed," Jack told them. "It might not be as much as Charlie's estate, mind you, but it'll still give you the freedom you deserve. Go wherever you please. Be whoever you want. Live life while you can. May your hearts never grow old."

Nadine's lip trembled. She looked at François. "Don't you…?"

François shook his head. "It's yours. I already got my prize."

Nadine hugged François. "Thank you." Then she hugged Jack, who smiled and caressed her back. Brian took turns hugging them as well.

"I hope this means you'll drop in every once in a while," Jack told them. "If you want more stories about the Brothel days, the trial, or just want to talk some Richie Hammond, our door will always be open to you two."

"I will take you up on that," Brian insisted. "I'd love that."

Jack nodded. "Goodnight, you two."

"Goodnight."

Jack gently closed the door, François behind him taking a long-awaited rest in Oliver's chair.

EPILOGUE

Marchons, Marchons!

Nadine sat on the edge of her roof, Jack's memoir open on her lap. She could hear the door opening behind her.

"There you are. Vicky said you were up here."

"I just wanted someplace quiet." Nadine smiled at the sight of her Brian, handsome Brian, sitting beside her, ready to soak up the same nighttime Manhattan view.

"The lighting isn't great," Brian said.

"It's enough." Nadine closed the memoir. Held it against her chest. "I wasn't really reading anyway. I was mostly thinking about William."

"How so?"

"He must've known François and Andy were gay, right? He recognized Ernst Röhm by sight. He would've known the reason Hitler killed him. The official reason anyway."

Brian shrugged. "Perhaps."

"He never had a problem with it. He never said, 'I don't need to save him. He's on his own.'"

"Like I did?" Brian asked, unenthused.

"You didn't know what gay was. That's alright." Nadine thought of something. "Maybe that's why no one wants to just let them be. Because they don't know how wrong they are."

"But what good would educating them do? Everything Jack and his friends did to make Gay Berlin was undone only a few years later."

"But it happened. A normal homosexual like Jack was able to make it happen. Gay Berlin was real. Those people need to know it at least happened. Who knows what that would do for their lives? It might help them feel less alone. It'll give them a sense of purpose."

Brian suspiciously looked at her. "Why are you so excited about this?"

"How lucky am I to be one of the few dancers in New York to be granted enough money to get out of the business overnight. Save myself from a life they arrest you for. Gay men don't have that option. Why should I get to be free when the world still says they can't be? Look." Nadine flipped open the first page of Jack's memoir. "'Nothing is more powerful than the written word,'" she read. "'Here's the proof: you have absolutely no idea who I am.'" She looked up at Brian. "Jack wrote that fifty-five years ago. Don't you think it's about time someone changed that?"

Brian stared at her. "You're finally free of Olive Branch for the first time in years and now you want to start up another one?"

"If we don't make the first step on this one, who would? Who else would have a personal investment the way we do? Who else has all the facts? The time? The expertise? The experience?"

"But what about all that stress? The despair? All those hard, awful days in between all the good ones?"

"We have each other this time. That'll make a difference, won't it?"

"I don't know." Brian pursed his lips. "I like the idea of us going back to normal, honestly."

Nadine softened at that. "I was never going to be a housewife, Brian. I have no intention to be. And now that I've found something that allows me to use my brain, I'm not giving it up now."

"I'm not saying—"

"I have a real purpose now." Nadine gave him those doting eyes she knew he loved so much. "I know I can do this one, Brian. I just need your help."

Brian thought about it. That fire in her was blazing, alright. He smiled. "Your brain is what made you most precious to me. I wouldn't ask for anything else."

Nadine nearly melted right there. She kissed him under the stars and the second quest was born.

Brian came up with the concept: a one-man show adaptation of Jack's memoir. Brian would help adapt it, Nadine would direct the production, and Jack himself would perform it every night for the gay community of Greenwich Village. He'd be able to use that platform to tell his story, the story Edgar Withers spent the rest of his life and beyond trying to silence. Doing so would immortalize Charlie, Denny, Mary, Louise, Oliver, Andy, all the men they've lost, as well as crediting Mr. Munce and Morty for their contributions. He could even recreate the trial, how the biased jury cost them the Brothel. He could tell them about Berlin, how Dr. Magnus Hirschfeld made it happen before it was taken away. He could talk about Ernst Röhm and how a simple PR maneuver cost the gays their utopia, their safety, their rights, their dignity, how fragile their history had become. And he could tell the world about William, how his selfless heroism made their reunion possible.

When they pitched the idea to Jack and François, Jack expressed his doubts about returning to the limelight after so many years. Nadine convinced him by explaining how fitting it would for them to use Charlie's money, the money originally meant belong to the seven of them, to give something back to the gay community. And so Jack took François's encouraging hand and agreed to do the one-man show.

Nadine and Brian bought out J. Roger's, sacking the man himself and rehiring the dancers to be their stagehands, costumers and lighting crew, a way for Nadine to give legitimate jobs to those poor women, freeing them from a doomed life of dancing like monkeys. Vicky, fresh off her bookkeeping course, joined the team and helped keep their budgets in line. Tina, who was actually not a woman but in fact a transvestite, used her connections in the Village's homosexual scene to spread the word.

As their show grew in complexity, Jack, François, Nadine and Brian saw an awful lot of each other, and they grew closer in ways they had never anticipated. The young couple saw Jack and François as the parent figures they never had, a source of wisdom, of judgment-free advice. The old men saw Brian and Nadine as trusted companions, good friends, developing humans they could guide toward a better life, free of the same mistakes they had the first time.

My Sins opened off-Broadway the following Spring to a surprisingly generous turnout. Jack took the stage, nervous at the start, and recited his lines. He started with his life in Dunderrow on Branson Farm, recounting his days as a closeted gay boy. The Incident—that is, his affair with Danny O'Brien. The tumultuous fallout between his parents and neighbors. His banishment. His hard journey to London. Writing all those letters back home and receiving none back. Meeting Mr. Munce. Working as his telegram delivery boy. Concocting a secret prostitution business. Becoming the sexual darling of England's closeted aristocrats. Oliver's romantic attempts to recruit him to an all-male brothel, London's first, as a way of ushering in a world free of persecution. Vic and Pete, the evil bobbies. Jack cautiously refusing Oliver's offer. The Collins Affair. That greedy Tucker turning them all in. Pete stealing all his money. Mr. Munce refusing to help. Jack fleeing to Ireland to work as a footman for Lord Harrington. Chester the Second Footman screwing him out of the job. Jack returning to London after two years to finally take Oliver's offer. The hard negotiation between the two of them for him to stay. How he met François, Denny, Mary and Louise. How rough it was being around so many homosexuals, fighting the "self-serving" reputation he had made for him. How he learned to forgive Mr. Munce. Meeting Charlie Smith, the cause's true mastermind. How Jack managed to save the Brothel on its first night. How he changed the operational structure in time to something more erotic. How he got Morty Blasmyth the Superintendent to grant them police immunity. Jack and Oliver falling back in love. The arrival of Andy Baxter, inspiring Jack to write a book. All the stories he got from the others, forging their bond. Jack sleeping with that piggish Tory Edgar Withers, the future MP. Jack and Charlie making the hard decision to censor parts of the book and Jack's true authorship. *The Sins of an Irishman in London* becoming a massive bestseller. The death of Jack's mother. Geoffrey Grant using Jack's book to out Edgar, thus sparking the infamous Montgomery Street Scandal. Jack's initial refusal to testify. What made him change his mind. *Withers v Grant* and Jack's brave testimony. That shocking verdict. Charlie being forced to shut down the Brothel. Jack's found family separating, keeping in touch only through letters. How Edgar butchered Jack's memoir. Jack's utopian American life with Oliver as Elliot and Nigel Victor. The Reunion of 1927 in Gay Berlin. Everything Dr. Magnus Hirschfeld did, inspired by Charlie and Jack. How the death of Ernst Röhm started Nazi persecution of homosexuals. What happened to all his friends. And finally, the brave efforts of Wilhelm Gunter, a Nazi who deserted the German Army and gave his life to reunite François and Jack.

Jack's performance was stunning. Tears were coming out of everyone's eyes by the end. The authenticity in his voice, in his emotions, in his words. The buzz kept the show open consistently enough to make it financially feasible. Nadine and Brian moved into an apartment together on Christopher Street, just a few doors down from the theater, and they focused next on how to improve the show.

The war ended the following summer, and Charlie's bountiful inheritance finally made its way across the Atlantic. Nadine and Brian received their generous shares as promised. They sold the castle in the Highlands and most of the apartments but chose to keep the flat in London. Roul kept his promise and shipped all of François's boxes across the sea. Nadine and Brian stored them all in the theater itself.

Now in possession of all the items François and Andy had accumulated (including the last surviving Berlin photograph, Mary's old wigs, most of Denny's artwork, Charlie's letters, the original manuscript of Jack's memoir), Nadine and Brian decided to incorporate them all as props for the show, adding a crucial layer of authenticity to *My Sins* that launched it into a new stratosphere of popularity. Notable attendees among the budding artists of Greenwich Village were a young Truman Capote and an up-and-coming author by the name of Gore Vidal. Vidal was so moved by Jack's show, in fact, that it inspired his first novel, the unashamedly gay and quite controversial *The City and the Pillar.*

A few months after V-J Day, Nadine and Brian, now done with their studies, finally got married. Jack and François were in attendance, and Roul himself walked Nadine down the aisle. Nadine Donahue gave birth to their son the following year, and she named him William. François and Jack were able to hold little William in the hospital.

Two weeks after William Donahue's birth, François Brion passed away in his sleep. No one had any idea how old he was, not even Jack. But they all knew he was happy and at peace in the end. He left everything he had to Nadine and Brian.

Performances of *My Sins* continued every day until October 3, 1947 when Jack Donald Branson suddenly passed away at the age of 90. His funeral was held in a church. Like his show, the turnout was startling, longtime fans of *My Sins*, hundreds of people that knew his entire story, who were just as heartbroken as Nadine and Brian were. "Elliot" was buried at Trinity Church beside "Nigel Victor." As per Jack's last wishes (requiring some theatrical trickery from Nadine and Brian), they were able to change the headstone to "Jack and Oliver Branson." And like François, Jack had left everything to the young Donahues.

Memories of *My Sins* lived on throughout the Village, many New Yorkers still talking about that unforgettable show a year after Jack's death. Given once more the chance to return a normal life, Nadine and Brian chose yet again to fight to preserve Jack's legacy. They planned on capitalizing on

Jack's lingering reputation by opening a Jack Branson Society right there on Christopher Street, in the same theater he used to perform in.

The Jack Branson Society finally opened to the public in 1950. Any visitor would be able to get close to all the artifacts François and Andy had stored in those crates during the French occupation. One of the Society's first attendees proved to be one of its most significant: Harry Hay. Harry had seen *My Sins* back in '46, and he had been mesmerized by Jack and his story. At the end of his tour, Harry offered Nadine and Brian a partnership with his new homophile organization: the Mattachine Society. Nadine and Brian said yes.

The first Mattachine meeting was tense to say the least. Nadine and Brian did not feel welcome, but Harry fought hard to convince the others of their loyalty to the cause, despite their blatant heterosexuality. Thanks to Harry's vouching, Nadine and Brian were allowed to continue working with the Mattachine Society as the Jack Branson Society was able to grow.

William Donahue's childhood was particularly cold from his perspective. Nadine and Brian worked so many hours, often handing their son off to babysitters and good ol' Aunt Vicky, but William also felt a lack of direct affection from his parents. Nadine was never the maternal type, and Brian intentionally chose never to touch, kiss, or even hug his son in any way whatsoever.

As the Mattachine Society grew in its own popularity, its radical political aims diluted themselves. A disillusioned Harry Hay left his own organization in 1953, leaving Nadine and Brian a bit in the lurch, but they were able to ride Mattachine's growing popularity throughout the fifties. The national version of the Mattachine Society eventually split up due to infighting, and the Mattachine Society of New York was established in 1961.

The following year, the Jack Branson Society and MSNY became founding members of a new network, the East Coast Homophile Organizations. The Jack Branson Society reached a new peak of popularity, with visitors crossing states lines just to see their collection.

Throughout all this growth, Nadine and Brian traveled to London every so often to acquire more evidence of the Montgomery Street Brothel. On one such visit in 1964, 18-year-old William Donahue snuck away from his parents and had a London adventure of his own. He got caught up in the free love mod scene and had unprotected sex with a complete stranger, 19-year-old London local Laura Kenney. William returned to America with his parents a week later, having no idea that Laura was pregnant.

The non-confrontational Mattachine Society of New York officially condemned the Stonewall Riots the moment they happened. When history started favoring the latter, the MSNY started to appear out of touch to a new generation of radical gays. The Jack Branson Society drastically lost popularity in favor of the loud and proud homosexuals marching in the streets, arguing more for policy change instead of old victories that bore no relevance anymore.

In 1970, Nadine and Brian, now in their fifties, made the tough decision to shut down New York's Jack Branson Society and move everything to London to start over there. William at this time was establishing himself in New York's business district, but Nadine and Brian refused to leave their son behind. They even threatened to cut him off financially if he did not join them in London. This would cause an irreparable rift between William and his parents. To Nadine and Brian, William had no idea how lucky he had it, having had no idea how hard life could be, how crucial it was for their family to stay together. But to William, his parents were forcing him to live his life on their terms, with no care for what he really wanted to be. But because he was still financially dependent on his parents, he agreed to the move, but he did vow to hate the Jack Branson Society for the rest of his life. It was the reason his dream was being taken away from him. But deeper than anything, he resented the fact that his parents cared more about some dead Victorian guy than their own son.

In 1971, the Jack Branson Society reopened to decent success on Montgomery Street itself, not far from the site of the original Brothel. A few months later, Laura Kenney knocked on the Donahues' door holding her seven-year-old Terrance, revealing to Nadine and Brian that she had slept with William out of wedlock back in '64 and had been raising his baby without him. Nadine and Brian were furious with William, even though she never told him she was pregnant, and they forced him to marry Laura so they wouldn't have any bad press that would jeopardize the Society. William again had no say, and he married Laura quietly and swiftly. But he did have a say when it came to being a father to little Terrance, and so he chose to put in only the minimum effort.

In 1972, a movie came out called *Cabaret* that Nadine and Brian realized seemed very familiar. They did some research into the story's genesis and realized *Cabaret* was based on the stage show of the same name from 1966, which in turn was based on a 1951 play called *I am a Camera*, which itself was an adaptation of Christopher Isherwood's 1939 novel *Goodbye to Berlin*. Christopher Isherwood wrote the novel based on his days in Weimar-era Berlin, where he had been a frequent visitor at a gay bar called the Cosy Corner, the one Charlie and Denny founded. Nadine in particular was profoundly affected by that revelation. She never forgot the night she saw *Casablanca*, the power it had on her. Seeing *Cabaret* single-handedly revive the conversation on pre-Hitler Berlin only confirmed to her that a motion picture would be the ultimate legacy for Jack. And so the priorities of the Jack Branson Society changed, its ultimate goal now being a feature film of Jack's life story.

Terrance Donahue grew very close to his grandparents, and it especially broke his heart when Nadine died in 1976 from Stage IV lung cancer that had metastasized to her brain. She was only 57.

Brian was distraught, drinking heavier than ever. Unable to function without his inspiration, he begged William to take over as President of the Jack Branson Society. William repeatedly refused to take the mantle. He had finally come around to being a proper husband to Laura and a good father to Terrance, and he was adamant against throwing his dreams away *again*. They had a nasty row, Terrance overhearing it all. In it, Brian revealed that he and Nadine wanted more kids to prevent forcing this decision on William, only for Nadine to endure multiple miscarriages. William felt especially unloved from that revelation, that his parents had been "stuck" with just him. Wanting to hurt his father more than ever, William agreed to become the second President of the Jack Branson Society… and did absolutely nothing with it. He didn't care enough to take advantage of the budding gay scene in London. He never searched for new artifacts. He never advertised the Society. He just didn't care. He prioritized his own life instead.

Brian, seeing Nadine's dream of a Jack Branson movie crumbling further and further away, and having nothing else in his life except for her, descended deeper and deeper into alcoholism. He died of liver failure in 1980. He was only 56.

William Donahue changed after the death of his father. He realized how much hated himself for his selfish behavior. How much he loved his parents after all. How important it was to have a legacy. That their dreams were just as valuable to them as his was to him. And he was having suspicions that Terrance was gay, just like Jack was. Realizing he had to change, William came to his senses about the Jack Branson Society and decided to become the best President it ever had, the one that made the Jack Branson movie happen.

William started by relocating the family back to New York City, to the very theater they were at the first time. He then decided to use his heterosexuality to his advantage, rebranding the Society as a preservation of priceless Victorian artifacts, not just some gay history museum. This legitimized the Society in the eyes of New York's academic elite, which allowed William to network freely among them.

Terrance had always been fascinated by the family business. He had so many questions. Why did Nadine and Brian form the Society in the first place? What ever happened to Jack and Oliver after they left London? But William never told him those answers. He never told him about Olive Branch or William Gunnison. He never revealed his parents had known Jack and François for many years before their deaths. He never told him about the one-man show they helped Jack make. He never cared to know himself, having hated the Society his whole life. Because William never cared, Terrance never knew, and there was no History of the Jack Branson Society for Terrance to turn to.

In 1985, at the age of 21, Terrance Donahue met an older man at one of his dad's Society networking functions. His name was Liam Abernathy, a 50-year-old Classics professor at Columbia University. Terrance gave Liam a personal tour of the Society's collection, and Liam was very impressed by Terrance's intelligence and passion for history. Despite Liam being eleven years older than his father, Terrance found himself falling in love with the older gentleman, and the two dated each other in secret. Turns out they had a lot in common. Traditional backgrounds. Passion for the plays of Richie Hammond. Complicated relationships with their aloof fathers. Liam had realized that Terrance was the man he had been searching for his whole life, and Terrance loved Liam's devoted care, his unashamed expressions of love, all the things his father had always been too closed-off to give him.

One night, Terrance surprised his parents with a visit from Liam, who he introduced as his boyfriend. Laura accepted their love blindly, but William was livid. William and Terrance had the nastiest fight of their lives that night. William was adamant that Terrance never see Liam again, the only reason being his age. He even said Brian would've been against the relationship too, having been molested by his own father. Terrance was hurt by that information, revealing a side to his grandfather he never knew and wished he didn't hear, but more so that William would use it as a reason for him to stay unhappy.

William then gave his son another reason to breakup with Liam: how bad their relationship would look to the gay community. The Society was already suffering due to their permanent historical connection to Harry Hay, who at that time was causing controversy by frequently attending North American Man/Boy Love Association meetings and loudly arguing for the inclusion of pedophiles in Pride parades. If that wasn't already bad enough for the Society, it would be even worse if word got out that the President's son was sleeping with a man nearly thirty years his senior. It would jeopardize all their recent strides among New York's historical elite. It might even be the reason the world doesn't get a Jack Branson movie, which is the one thing Terrance's grandmother wanted more than anything.

Terrance countered by calling William a hypocrite for even *pretending* to respect his parents, blaming William for Brian's death, calling it a death from a broken heart. That hurt William, since it was something he'd already suspected himself, and he lashed out at his son in a blind fit of rage, how easy Terrance always had it, how real life was full of pain, sacrifice, being forced to do things you don't want to do. William tried to stop himself here, but he couldn't. It kept flying out after decades of captivity. He went on to list all the things he never wanted. He never wanted to be burdened with the Society. He never wanted to move to London. He never wanted to marry Laura. And (worst of all) he never wanted to be a father. But that's life. William had to be a man and suck it up, and it's about time Terrance did the same thing.

That one outburst ended up ruining William's life. Terrance left his parents in tears, more bonded to Liam than ever, and vowed never to speak to his father again. And Laura, who had not known the truth behind her marriage, realized she had made a big mistake. She filed for divorce, moved back to London, and started a whole new life without him.

William, now alone for the first time in his life, tried to apologize to Terrance for the things he said that night. Terrance found it nearly impossible to forgive his father, but thanks to Liam's gentle insistence, he reluctantly accepted a truce. He agreed to work for William as the Society's resident tour guide, which allowed the father and son to spend a lot of quality time together.

The Jack Branson Society finally reached New York City mainstream in 1991, just in time for the rise of New Queer Cinema. William Donahue received a phone call one day from a prime Hollywood producer by the name of René Scragg, known professionally as "The Professor." The Professor's father had known Nadine Donahue personally, as a matter of fact, back when she was Nadine Sauvageot. They fought in the French Resistance together. To honor the connection between their parents, The Professor wanted nothing more than to work with William on an official Jack Branson movie.

The Professor himself made a special trip out to New York City to take a tour of the Jack Branson Society. Terrance showed him around, after which William joined them in his office to talk shop. That was when The Professor revealed the key changes that needed to be made for the picture to happen, the biggest one being Jack's character had to be a woman. All the prostitutes had to be women, in fact. Except Oliver. Oliver's character would be merged with Charlie's, and that composite would be the primary love interest for "Jacqueline." (*Pretty Woman* had just come out and made a lot of money, so The Professor was trying to capitalize on the trend of charming sex workers falling in love with their rich clients.)

All that sounded perfectly fine to William. He had been aching to finally hand over the keys and be rid of the Society forever. But Terrance interrupted him, passionately vetoing against the decision, urging his father to fight for the most accurate screen depiction of Jack, one that acknowledged his homosexuality as well as his role as a male prostitute, arguing it would be what he deserved, let alone what Nadine Donahue would've wanted. William was stunned by how much Terrance cared about Jack Branson's legacy. It was a passion he never truly had himself. And it convinced him to ultimately refuse The Professor's offer.

As Terrance entered his thirties, he found himself wanting a deeper role in the Jack Branson Society. He was not only a Donahue, but also a homosexual Donahue, the first and presumably last of its kind. With William's permission, Terrance and Liam worked on a side project digitizing the Society. They officially launched the website in 1994. They photographed all the items, cataloged them, and posted it all online. Then they moved onto their next project: an official republishing of *The Sins of an Irishman in London*. They spent a year transcribing and editing the crown jewel of the Society's archives, the original unabridged, uncensored manuscript Jack originally gave Charlie back in 1888.

Their hard work paid off in 2006 when William Donahue received a phone call from famous Hollywood director Roland Emmerich (*Independence Day, Godzilla, The Day After Tomorrow*). Roland had discovered Jack Branson's story through the Society's website, and he wanted to honor his own homosexuality by dramatizing a prominent episode of his community's early history.

Roland Emmerich himself made a special trip out to New York City to take a tour of the Jack Branson Society. Terrance showed him around, after which William joined them in the office to talk shop. That was when Roland revealed the key changes that needed to be made for the picture to happen, the biggest one being the removal of all references to sex work. That would've been too much for mainstream America to handle. And Mary and Louise needed to be removed from the narrative as their over-the-top femininity was now considered offensively stereotypical. (*Brokeback Mountain* had just come out and made a lot of money, so Roland Emmerich was trying to capitalize on the trend of brooding passing-for-straight working-class heroes suffering in an oppressively homophobic world.) Roland also didn't care if 60s-esque homosexual activism, complete with picketing and passionate speeches on courthouse steps, was complete anachronistic for the 1880s. It made for a better story and more of what modern straight audiences expected to see.

William didn't need Terrance's help to making that decision. He turned Roland down. Mr. Emmerich would eventually reroute and direct an incredibly anachronistic dramatization of the Stonewall riots instead, which bombed on release.

In 2007, William Donahue, now at the age of 60, finally retired as President of the Jack Branson Society, knowing how much Terrance wanted it more. Terrance's first act as President was to fight for the republication of *The Sins of an Irishman in London*, officially credited to Jack Branson for the first time in its history. Much to his disappointment, however, major New York publishers were unimpressed by the Victorian memoir, written by a gay man no one already knew about. To them, it simply wasn't worth the risk. In the hopes of that changing one day, Liam and Terrance put everything they could into Jack Branson's Wikipedia page, all the verifiable data they could gather, in the hopes that it would inspire some other Hollywood hopeful down the road.

In 2015, Liam Abernathy passed away at the age of 80. Terrance was heartbroken, but he had his renewed relationship with his father to keep him going, all thanks to Liam.

A new disease started popping up in New York in the early months of 2020. The Society had to be shut down, and William Donahue never recovered after he contracted COVID-19. He died in April at the age of 74. Terrance couldn't even hold a funeral for him.

After lockdown ended, the Jack Branson Society never returned to its pre-COVID attendance levels. To make matters worse, a water pipe burst in 2022, flooding a good 25% of the Society. Priceless artifacts were destroyed, the worst of them being the last surviving photo of the 1927 Berlin Reunion.

Terrance spent the next six years in court suing the City of New York for its failure to prevent the water damage caused by urban mismanagement. He spent thousands of dollars to win back the same thousands of dollars in damages, leaving him with nothing but cynical interpretation of American justice.

In late 2035, 71-year-old Terrance Donahue looked around that old building of his, all those artifacts he had been preserving for so long, and realized no one cared anymore. Their regulars were simply a mailing list, one that hadn't grown in quite a long time. There was nothing more to do, and he had no energy left to try and forge a new path. Terrance started to dance around the idea of shutting down the Society for good.

Just then, his office phone rang. Assuming it to be more creditors or a scam call, Terrance took his time answering it. "Terrance Donahue, Jack Branson Society."

A younger man's voice spoke over the phone. "Hi, Mr. Donahue? My name is Drew Lawrence. I'm CEO and Head of Production of Ephemeral Pictures. How are you doing this afternoon?"

Terrance scratched his old face. "It's evening."

"Is it? My apologies. I'm just calling to see if you were available to give myself and my Head of Development Kev Foster a private tour of your Society this Friday. I'm willing to compensate for the inconvenience, of course."

"Sadly, Mr. Lawrence, all the tours we do these days are private tours."

"Oh. Well, I'm willing to compensate nonetheless."

Terrance hesitated. "What is this regarding?"

"Well… We've actually already started production on a Jack Branson biopic. I was only made aware of your Society today. We saw that drawing of Jack on your website, the one with the blue eye?"

"Yes."

"You have that on display there, I'm assuming?"

"Of course."

"Oh, good. I'd really like to see it."

"You want to fly all the way out here to see a sketch?"

"No, actually. Um… Oh how do I say this…? We're willing to make allowances to our production to get your Society's stamp of approval. That would mean a lot to us and our marketing team."

"It's already written?"

"Yes."

"And if I don't like it, you'd stop production on it?"

Silence on the phone. "I'm afraid I can't do that, Mr. Donahue. It's already a force in motion. But it is early enough for us to make some tweaks. That being said, I have a feeling you'll approve. I'm a great admirer of Jack Branson. In fact, I've been wanting to make this movie for quite some time. I found his Wikipedia page all the way back in 2019, as a matter of fact."

Terrance furrowed his brow. "2019?"

"Yeah, that long ago. I was listening to 'Rent' by the Pet Shop Boys on my greatest hits CD of theirs… I had listened to that song about a thousand times at that point, mind you, but that one time I was listening to it was the time I got curious about the history of male prostitution, so I did some digging and… Well, I've always thought Jack Branson's life story would make a phenomenal movie. Sadly, I was outvetoed by my partner at the time, but we've had a falling out since then, and I'm in charge somewhere else now, so… Yeah. This is the only project I wanted for Ephemeral. I really hope you approve it, Mr. Donahue, because I really *really* want this to work."

Terrance was unsure. He felt exhausted, just like his father had been at one time. He was ready to be rid of it. But was he betraying his grandmother's dream? Was he letting the Society down? Was he letting Jack's memory down? The only thing that stood out about this one was what Drew said at the end there. He had carried Jack's story with him for nearly twenty years, never once letting it leave his sight. Maybe that was enough. Maybe Terrance could work with that. Drew easily could've gone around him. It was in the public domain, after all. He didn't need to ask for Terrance's blessing. So what was the harm in another tour? One last tour for old times' sake?

Drew Lawrence and Kev Foster were twenty minutes late for their tour, and their concept was to turn Jack's story into an animated Pet Shop Boys musical they'd call *Branson!* Terrance was appalled by such sacrilege, but somehow Drew managed to convince him. Throughout Drew's rambling passion pitch, Terrance saw a bit of himself in him. The same perfectionist attitude. The same addiction to unnecessarily hard work. Drew certainly had the skills. He had the money. He had the ambition. Maybe Terrance just needed to give him some guidance and trust him to do the rest.

Terrance agreed to view the final cut before making his decision. Before Drew and Kev left, Terrance gave them a transcript of the original *Sins of an Irishman in London* manuscript, the one he and Liam had worked all those tender hours on.

Sixteen months later, Terrance received word from Ephemeral Pictures that the final cut was ready for viewing. To his surprise, *Branson!* had been retitled.

Drew and Kev flew Terrance out to Los Angeles and showed them what they had made: *The Sins of Jack Branson*. Terrance was overwhelmed. Drew had used Jack's manuscript to transform their original batshit idea into something larger, a true reconstruction of Jack's world, just as Terrance always imagined it to be. Drew even added the right personal touches from his own life, episodes that coincidentally aligned with Jack's in ways that should never have been possible. It seems Drew Lawrence was meant to restore Jack's fractured narrative, but he only could've gotten there thanks to Terrance's help and trust.

When the lights came back on, Terrance could only stare up at the empty screen. Drew made his way to Terrance's row. Saw those red eyes of his and his tear-drenched face. Drew gently sat beside him. "Terrance?"

"I wish my grandparents could have seen this," Terrance whispered, closing his eyes, sobbing into his hand. Drew placed a comforting hand on his shoulder, prompting Terrance to pull Drew in and hug the shit out of him, crying into his expensive jacket. "Thank you, Mr. Lawrence. Thank you."

The Sins of Jack Branson would go on to become a gargantuan critical and commercial success. The number one movie of 2037's box office. The recipient of thirteen Academy Award nominations. *The Sins of an Irishman in London* was officially republished, credited solely to Jack, its original text and names restored, addendum and all. It went on to become a #1 *New York Times* Bestseller, selling more copies in a single month than it ever did the first time.

In the years that followed, tributes started popping up worldwide, statues and plaques of Jack Branson, Oliver Hawkett, François Brion, Andrew Baxter, Georgie "Mary" Belcher, Corey "Louise" Kehoe, Denny Evans, Charlie Smith, Morty Blasmyth and Stockley Munce erected in London, Glasgow, Paris, Liverpool, Berlin, Cardiff, Rome, Chicago and New York. Their role in Weimar Berlin, as well as their numerous other contributions to gay rights, were never forgotten again.

Nadine Donahue's dream had finally come true, all thanks to her grandson Terrance and an autistic gay man from Pennsylvania named Drew Lawrence, born Jacob Andrezj, who never would've been born had his grandmother Elżbieta not been saved by a German deserter by the name of William Gunnison.

FROM THE PUBLISHER

Thank you so much for reading *Olive Branch*. This was a different kind of book for me, with a lot of problems that arose last minute like my hard drive crashing, but I'm especially proud of it now. My husband even said it's the best thing I've written yet. I'll leave that for you to decide.

I believe the most interesting stories are those with personality, intelligence, and just a bit of strange. That can only be possible with a singular creative voice. I chose to self-publish my novels through David Schulze Books so I could tell my stories without compromising my final cut privileges.

All I ask in return is an **honest** review on Amazon, Goodreads, B&N.com, or the social media platform of your choice. Doing so not only provides feedback I can use on future projects, it also directly supports my growth as a career author.

If you want to mention this book on Facebook, Twitter, or Instagram, don't forget to add #OliveBranch or #DavidSchulze.

Thanks again, and I hope you read more of my work.

— David Schulze

COMING SOON

Brian was right, by the way. Richie Hammond *was* only a few years older than him in 1943.

But Jack was right too. Richie was in his mid-twenties back in 1897.

In fact, Richie Hammond has been twenty-five for the last nine hundred years…

…and boy does he HATE his dad.

My God Father
The Fourth Novel by David Schulze

ABOUT THE AUTHOR

David Schulze (né Stehman) was born and raised in Phoenixville, Pennsylvania. A lifelong admirer of movies, mythology, and classic literature, David loves stories across all mediums.

In 2017, David graduated from Emerson College with a BA in Writing for Film and Television and a Minor in Literature. He has written nine feature screenplays and four shorts, many of them placing in screenwriting competitions. Falling back on his love of prose, David adapted his ninth feature, *The Sins of Jack Branson* (2018 Final Draft Big Break Contest Quarterfinalist) as his debut novel in 2021. His critically acclaimed second novel *Andrezj of Hollywood* won the 2024 IPPY Bronze Medal for West Pacific Fiction, and his novella *unplugged* was selected as one of the 100 Best Indie Books of 2024 by *Kirkus Reviews*.

David lives in Marlton, New Jersey with his husband Howie.

For exclusive stories, in-depth analyses, and updates on future projects, go to davidschulzebooks.com